'What's happened?' she gasped. It would appear a miracle had occurred overnight.

'We sailed through the Straits of Gibraltar while you were asleep,' Theo said gleefully. 'We're in the Mediterranean. Oh, Queenie!' He took her in his arms. 'I know you've hated every minute so far, even though you didn't say a word. Next time we come, we'll fly halfway and you'll never have to make that terrible journey again. Now, do you feel like a hearty breakfast?'

'Yes!' she breathed. Afterwards, she'd put on her shorts and sunbathe.

That night in the lounge, she and Theo drank champagne and danced to Frank Sinatra records. It was turning out to be the holiday of a lifetime, after all.

D1357474

Maureen Lee was born in Bootle and now lives in Colchester, Essex. She has had numerous short stories published and a play staged. *Queen of the Mersey* is her eleventh novel. *Stepping Stones*, *Liverpool Annie*, *Dancing in the Dark*, *The Girl from Barefoot House*, *Laceys of Liverpool*, *The House by Princes Park* and *Lime Street Blues*, and the three novels in the Pearl Street series, *Lights Out Liverpool*, *Put out the Fires* and *Through the Storm* are all available in Orion paperback. Her novel *Dancing in the Dark* won the Parker Romantic Novel of the Year Award. *September Girls* is her latest novel in Orion paperback. Visit her website at *www.maureenlee.co.uk*.

BY MAUREEN LEE

The Pearl Street Series

Lights Out Liverpool

Put Out the Fires

Through the Storm

Stepping Stones

Liverpool Annie

Dancing in the Dark

The Girl from Barefoot

Laceys of Liverpool

The House by Princes Park

Lime Street Blues

Queen of the Mersey

The Old House on the Corner

The September Girls

Queen of the Mersey

Maureen Lee

An Orion paperback

First published in Great Britain in 2003
by Orion
This paperback edition published in 2004
by Orion Books Ltd,
Orion House, 5 Upper St Martin's Lane,
London WC2H 9EA

9 10 8

Copyright © Maureen Lee 2003

The right of Maureen Lee to be identified as the author of this work has been asserted by her in accordance with the Copyright, Designs and Patents Act 1988.

All rights reserved. No part of this publication may be reproduced, stored in a retrieval system, or transmitted, in any form or by any means, electronic, mechanical, photocopying, recording or otherwise, without the prior permission of the copyright owner.

All the characters in this book are fictitious, and any resemblance to actual persons, living or dead, is purely coincidental.

A CIP catalogue record for this book is available from the British Library.

ISBN-13 978-0-7528-5891-3

Typeset by Deltatype Ltd, Birkenhead, Merseyside

Printed and bound in Great Britain by
Clays Ltd, St Ives plc

The Orion Publishing Group's policy is to use papers that are natural, renewable and recyclable products and made from wood grown in sustainable forests. The logging and manufacturing processes are expected to conform to the environmental regulations of the country of origin.

www.orionbooks.co.uk

For my agent, Juliet Burton, with love.

June, 1939

Chapter 1

'What are you doing here?' Vera Monaghan enquired.

'I live here, Mam,' Mary replied, grinning. It was a game they sometimes played.

'Well, I've never seen you before. When did you arrive?'

'Five years ago last week,' Mary said promptly.

'Ah, I remember now! You're me little girl. What's your name? I can't rightly recall.'

'Mary.'

'So it is. You know, Mary, sometimes I can't believe you're real.'

Mary pinched herself. It hurt. 'I am, Mam. Honest.'

'Come and give your mam a hug so she'll know you're really real.' Vera threw her fat body into a chair and held out her arms.

Mary scrambled from under the table where she'd been tying knots in the fringe of the chenille cloth, sat on her mother's knee, and showered the beloved red face with kisses. 'D'you believe I'm real now, Mam?'

'I do, I truly do. You're me little angel, the best surprise a woman could ever have had.'

'And a man,' Mary reminded her, thinking of her dad.

'And a man,' Vera agreed.

Mary had arrived, quite unexpectedly, when her mother was forty-seven and already had eight children, all of them boys, the youngest seven and the eldest almost twenty-one. She had thought her childbearing days were long over and Mary had taken her and Albert entirely by surprise. The lads had considered the whole thing hilarious. They hadn't realised people as ancient as their mam and dad still indulged in a bit of nooky, and if ever a boy woke in the dead of night when the old folk were in bed, he would listen hard, just in case they were at it again.

When Mary was brought home from the maternity hospital, the entire family stood around the cot, staring down at the tiny baby. They had a *girl*!

'Girls don't have willies,' remarked Tommy, nine. 'How will she wee, Mam, without a willy?'

'She'll find a way,' his mother assured him.

'She's pretty,' said Caradoc, the youngest.

'You were all pretty when you were babies.' Vera looked at her eight big lads whom she loved with all her heart and found this hard to believe. Dick, the eldest, was six feet two and excessively hairy.

'*I* wasn't pretty,' growled Victor, aged twelve.

'Oh, all right, so you weren't.' Anything for a quiet life, she thought, although Victor, with his long dark lashes and rosy cheeks, had been the prettiest of the lot.

'We've got a sister,' Dick said in awe.

'I've got a daughter,' Albert Monaghan said in much the same tone.

Mary became their pet, better any day than a kitten or a puppy. The younger boys brought their paintings home from school to show their sister and were hurt when she tore them to pieces with a delighted shriek.

'She doesn't understand great art,' their mother told them. 'Not yet.'

The four older boys were working. On Friday, pay day, they would buy Mary sweets or chocolate, sometimes a toy. Once, Mrs Monaghan found her two-year-old daughter's mouth stuffed with bubble gum that took a good ten minutes to remove.

'She's getting spoilt rotten, Vera,' Albert would say fondly, though he was the worst of the lot. Mary had more dolls than she had brothers.

'Too much love never hurt anyone,' his wife would reply.

They were a contented couple, the Monaghans, happy with each other, loving their children, and Mary had been the icing on the cake. Vera had once been pretty herself, but bearing nine children had created havoc with the body that had once been described as a figure eight and now resembled a great big nought.

'Everything's collapsed,' she would tell people dramatically. 'Me breasts, me tubes, me womb. Everything.'

Her shape hadn't been helped by her diet during the early years of marriage, long before any of the boys had gone to work, and money had been short. Albert didn't earn much as a tram conductor and there were a lot of mouths to feed. Often, the family would sit down to a plate of scouse, sometimes blind, if meat couldn't be afforded, while Vera sat down to nothing at all.

'I had mine earlier,' she would explain when her husband wanted to know why she wasn't eating. All she'd had was a couple of slices of bread dipped in the scouse pan.

Albert believed her because she was putting on weight, not losing it. Vera ate bread like there was no tomorrow. She particularly enjoyed it fried. It reminded her of what a proper meal would taste like.

Then Dick had started working, followed shortly afterwards by George, then Frank, Billy, Victor, Charlie and Tommy until, by the time Mary was five, there was only Caradoc still at school. Money wasn't exactly rolling in, but they were flush compared to the old days. Yet still

Vera couldn't keep off the bread. She'd grown used to it. Anyroad, people said it was the staff of life. Her excess flesh was soft and doughy and Mary liked to poke it with her finger and watch it slowly rise back up.

She did so now, sitting on her mother's knee, then examined the red, shrivelled elbows that always fascinated her.

'Why aren't mine like that?' she wanted to know.

'I've told you before. 'Cos you're not fifty-two, that's why. Now that we've established who you are and what you're doing here, are you going to stay on me knee all day?'

'If you like.'

'What I'd like,' Vera said, trying to sound stern, 'is for you to untie the knots you've made in the fringe of me bezzie tablecloth. I've only just noticed and it looks dead peculiar. That cloth was a wedding present off your Auntie Dolly.'

'All right, Mam,' Mary said equably. She slipped off the soft, cushiony knee, and was under the table, undoing her morning's work, when there was a knock on the door.

'Who on earth can that be!' her mother exclaimed when she went to answer it. It must be a stranger, because the front door was wide open. Everyone they knew would have walked straight in.

Mary heard a voice babbling hysterically and a few minutes later, her mother returned with a girl about her own age.

'This is Hester,' she said. 'She only lives across the street. Her poor dad's had an accident at work and her mam's had to rush off to Bootle hospital, so we're looking after her for a while.'

'Hello,' Mary said brightly as she continued to undo knots.

To her and her mother's consternation, Hester burst into tears. She reminded Mary of one of her dolls, the one with the bouncy cascade of golden ringlets and frilly frock that she'd christened Shirley after Shirley Temple. Hester's frock was pink with puffed sleeves and lace edging around the collar and hem. Like the Shirley doll, she had bright blue eyes and a mouth like a petal. Mary had seen her before, but they'd never spoken. She lived almost opposite, had no brothers or sisters, and never played in the street with the other children. Afternoons, she went for walks with her mam. On Sundays, her dad went with them. They both looked younger than some of Mary's brothers and 'kept themselves to themselves', according to her own mam.

'I want my mummy,' Hester sobbed.

'Sorry, luv, but you can't have her. You'll have to make do with me for the time being.' Vera picked up the girl, threw herself back into the chair she'd not long got out of, and gave her an extravagant cuddle. After a while, Hester stopped crying and complained her frock was getting creased.

Mary and her mother exchanged covert winks. It wasn't the sort of house where people worried about creases. Hester was set down and told to amuse herself with Mary, while Vera got on with the dinner. Half the boys came in at one o'clock for a meal, including Dick, now twenty-five and living in rooms in Shelley Street, having been married for two years to a rather odd young woman called Iris who was out at work all day. There was mince ready to be served up on a thick slice of dry bread. On the assumption Hester would eat her share, Vera would have to make do with just the bread. She didn't mind.

Glover Street was a narrow cul-de-sac of flat-fronted,

three-storey houses less than a hundred yards from Gladstone Dock, Bootle. When their growing family could no longer be squeezed into their nice house in Southey Street where Vera had dozens of friends, the Monaghans had been forced to move to a property with more space. They were one of the few families in Glover Street to have a house to themselves, the rest mainly having been split into flats or lodgings. There were fewer children than in her old street, and people came and went by the minute. She hadn't made many new friends.

Vera wasn't one to complain, she was a lucky woman and she knew it, but she'd never felt entirely settled in the new house. The properties were stoutly built, the rooms spacious, and they even had an inside lavatory, but as the years crept by, the cul-de-sac had become surrounded by factories and warehouses, until by the time the Monaghans moved in, industry held Glover Street in its tight, forbidding grip.

The most dominating feature was the rear wall of the grain silo at the end, almost twice as high as the houses, blocking out the sun from midday on. During working hours, a nearby foundry emitted a never-ending thudding, hissing noise and a terrible, choking smell. Vera's favourite time had once been early morning, when she would wake, Albert sleeping peacefully at her side, to the harsh cry of the seagulls soaring overhead and the mournful hoot of the boats on the river. She would listen to the busy Dock Road as it came to life; the rumble of the overhead railway, the crisp clip-clop of a horse and cart on the cobbles, the clatter of lorries. She would look at the sun through the bedroom window if it was shining, savour it, knowing that, unless she managed to get out of the house, she might not see it again that day.

Lately, Vera Monaghan had wished she didn't wake quite so early. She'd sooner not have her thoughts to herself. During those dawn hours, she'd imagined the boys leaving home, getting married, happily settling down and providing her with grandchildren whom she would love to bits. When that happened, she would move back to Southey Street with Albert and Mary. But now the only thing that preoccupied her was the war that was likely to start any minute. There were signs of it everywhere; air raid shelters had appeared at the end of every other street and gas masks had been delivered – Vera had hidden theirs in the cellar so she wouldn't be reminded of the horror that might face them. Worst of all, she had four strong lads over eighteen who would make fine soldiers; Dick had left home when he got married, the others might be leaving much sooner than expected, and Vera wasn't sure if she could stand it.

Laura Oliver hurried down loathsome Glover Street, also worried about the war, about her husband, about her daughter, about every damn thing. How long would Roddy be off work with a sprained ankle? She supposed she should thank God it hadn't been broken when he'd fallen off that stupid ladder. On the other hand, a broken ankle might have delayed his call-up, even put it off for ever. She'd known a chap who'd broken his leg falling off a horse and he'd walked with a limp ever after. Roddy wouldn't be allowed in the Services with a limp. On the other hand, would he still be able to climb a ladder?

She knocked on the open door of number seventeen, the house where she'd left Hester, and prayed she hadn't been too distressed without her mummy. The woman in the house was obscenely overweight, but looked quite kind. Her husband went out in a uniform of some sort, so clearly had a respectable job, and she had a whole tribe of very presentable sons as well as an impish little daughter, always laughing, unlike Hester who hardly laughed at all.

The fat woman came into the hall and gave her a warm smile. 'Oh, there you are, luv! I've been thinking about you all afternoon. How's your husband? Hester's in the yard with our Mary playing bat and ball. Come in, girl. I've just put the kettle on for a cuppa.'

'I should be getting back . . . oh, but I'd love a cup of tea. Thank you.' Laura was drawn to the caring, sympathetic face, the warm smile. She was badly in need of sympathy at the moment. 'I'd better introduce myself,' she said courteously. 'I'm Laura Oliver.'

'And I'm Vera Monaghan. Laura's a pretty name. I've never come across it before.'

She followed Vera Monaghan along the narrow hall into a comfortable room overlooking the tiny backyard. It had too much furniture, most of it chairs. A mother-of-pearl crucifix stood in the centre of the mantelpiece, accompanied by holy statues and photographs of the Monaghans' numerous children at various stages of their lives.

'How's your husband?' Vera asked again.

'It turns out it was only a sprained ankle. He fell off a ladder.'

'That's good, luv. Still, a sprain can be very painful.'

'Yes, but he thought he'd broken it, so he's quite pleased. They're sending him home in an ambulance later this afternoon. Has Hester been all right?' she asked anxiously.

'She was a bit upset at first, but she soon settled down. She ate a good dinner, and she's been with Mary in the yard ever since. I'm afraid her frock's got a bit dirty.'

'That doesn't matter.'

'What was your husband doing up the ladder?' Vera enquired.

'Putting in a window.' Laura grimaced. 'He works for a builder.' It hurt to say it. Roddy's ambition had been to become an architect, design grand buildings. He had intended to take a degree in the subject at university. Instead, he hadn't even completed his final year at St Jude's, missing his matriculation.

'Our George is a builder's mate. He sawed the tip of his finger off on his first day. Fortunately, it was on his left hand, so it didn't inconvenience him too much.' Vera had gone into the kitchen while imparting this piece of information. She returned with tea in two severely cracked cups that didn't match the saucers. 'You don't come from Liverpool, do you, luv? At least, you haven't got the accent.'

'No, I'm from Sussex, a little village not far from Eastbourne.' She didn't add, 'Where my father is the vicar,' and wondered, as she often did, if he was sorry he'd sworn never to speak to her again. He'd probably thought she'd return home with her tail between her legs, meekly beg his forgiveness, profess sorrow for the sin that he would never cease to remind her of for the remainder of his days. It hadn't entered his head that she and Roddy loved each other so much they were prepared to run away. They'd never regretted it, even though they'd ended up in Bootle, in Glover Street, so different to anything they'd known when growing up that it could have been in China.

Hester came running in. 'Mummy!' she cried, as if Laura had been there all the time. 'I've got a bump on my head. Mary hit me with the bat.'

'It was only an accident.' Mary followed behind, a pretty girl, with short, dark, curly hair and a mischievous face. 'Anyroad, she knocked the ball right into me belly. I bet I've got a bump there too.'

'I didn't mean to,' exclaimed Hester.

'Neither did I.' The two girls glared at each other, until Mary said, 'Would you like to come upstairs and play with me dolls?'

'Yes, *please!*'

'Come on, then.' They rushed out of the room and their light footsteps could be heard scrambling up the stairs. Laura felt a tiny bit hurt that she hadn't been missed, but then supposed it was a good thing. Hester was starting school in September. Mother and daughter would be separated for the first time. It would help if she got used to other people in the meantime.

'She's not a bit like you – Hester,' Vera remarked.

'No, she's got thinner features, like Roddy, but the person she's most like is my mother.'

'I bet she's pleased about that, your mam.'

'I'm afraid she's dead. She died when I was eleven.' Her father had immediately packed his only child off to boarding school. He'd always been disappointed that she wasn't a boy. Laura had often wondered what her mother's reaction would have been when she'd had to confess she was pregnant.

'I've seen your husband on his way to work. He's very handsome, lovely and tall.'

'Isn't he!' Laura glowed. She was neither tall nor short and her own face had been described as 'wholesome'. It had character, she'd been told. Her eyes were a quite ordinary brown, her mouth far too wide, and her nose was merely a nose, not quite straight, but almost. Her best feature was her hair, which was glossy black and very thick and wavy. It was the only thing about her that the girls at school had envied. She wore it long and held back with a slide. It looked old-fashioned, but Roddy liked it, and that was all that mattered.

'Has Mary started school yet?' she asked.

'No, luv. She starts next term at St Joan of Arc.'

'Hester's going to Salisbury Road. It's not that far away.'

'You're not Catholic, then?'

'No.' Laura took a sip of the tea, which was lovely and strong. 'I'll take Mary to school for you, if you like,' she offered. She felt almost glad Roddy had fallen off the ladder. It had enabled her to get to know at least one of her neighbours. They'd lived in the street for almost a year and this was the first proper conversation she'd had with anyone other than her husband. She was too shy, too unhappy, and had imagined people making fun of her posh accent.

'That's nice of you, luv, but the thing is . . .' Vera paused and Laura had an awful feeling she was going to say she didn't want a non-Catholic going anywhere near her daughter, but Vera said in a rush, 'They'll be closing down St Joan of Arc's if there's a war. It wouldn't be safe from the air raids, being so close to the docks, like. The kids are being sent miles away, to St Monica's up Orrell Park way. I don't know what's happening to Salisbury Road.'

'*If* there's a war!' Laura whispered. 'I can't imagine there being a war. I can't imagine there being air raids. It'd be total madness.'

Vera's face had lost its smile and her eyes were bleak. Laura had a feeling it was a face that people didn't see often, if at all. 'Madness,' she echoed in a voice as bleak as her eyes. 'The boys don't realise. They claim to be looking forward to it, as if it were just a game.'

'Roddy's a bit like that, though he's worried what will happen to me and Hester.'

'Men!' Vera sniffed and looked as if she might cry. 'I won't let them talk about it. It upsets me too much.'

'We won't talk about it, then,' Laura said. 'I'm sorry the subject came up.'

'I don't mind talking about it with you, luv, another woman. Women can see war for what it is, anything but a game. Would you like more tea?'

'I'd love some, thank you.'

Vera fetched the tea, which was even stronger than before, and explained that she had four lads of call-up age. 'Next March, our Victor turns eighteen, and Charlie the year after.'

'According to Roddy, it won't take long to give Adolph Hitler a kick up the backside – they're his words, not mine,' Laura added hastily. 'He thinks it'll all be over by March.'

'That's if it starts at all.'

'I pray every night that it won't.'

'Me too, Laura. Me too,' Vera said sadly.

'Oh, Albert, she's ever such a nice girl!' Vera told her husband that night. 'Only twenty-one and she talks like Queen Elizabeth. Her mam died when she was eleven and her dad sent her to boarding school. *Boarding* school,' Vera repeated, struck all of a heap. 'I've never met anyone who's been to boarding school before.'

'And you're not likely to again, not in Bootle,' Albert replied drily, not the least impressed.

'That's where you're wrong, Albert. Her husband went to boarding school too.'

'But he's not from Bootle, is he? People here have got more common sense. When they have kids, they look after them themselves, not dump 'em on other people.'

'Actually,' Vera dropped her voice, though there was no one within earshot, the older lads having gone out and the others scattered about the house, 'I suspect something went on.'

Albert raised his eyebrows. 'Went on?'

'Don't ask me what, I dunno, but they're both dead

posh. What are they doing in Glover Street, I'd like to know, when they've been to boarding school? She must've only been sixteen when she had Hester. I reckon she got in the club and her dad chucked her out.'

'You've been reading too many of them daft magazines, woman.' Albert rattled the *Daily Herald* that had been left on the tram. He would quite like to do a bit of reading himself. 'Make us a cuppa, there's a good girl, then I'd appreciate it if you kept your gob shut for the next half hour, so's I can catch up on the news.'

Across the road, in number twenty-two, Roddy Oliver sat on the sofa with his legs stretched out so Laura could nurse his heavily bandaged ankle. His thin, handsome face looked terribly worn, she thought compassionately, and the palms of his hands had been badly grazed as he slid down the ladder. Hester, more tired than usual after her activities that afternoon, had been put to bed hours ago.

'Does it still hurt, darling?' she asked.

'It throbs a bit, that's all,' he said stoutly.

He was enjoying being made a fuss of for a change. For a long time now, he'd been terribly brave, burdened by far too much responsibility for someone so young, yet never once complaining.

When they had first run away together, they'd had money. Roddy had been left five hundred pounds by his grandfather. The first thing he did was buy Laura a wedding ring. From then on, she had handled the money carefully, or so she'd thought at the time. They'd rented a flat in Islington, thinking that they were slumming it rather, and she'd bought the cheapest food. Hester had been born in a private nursing home, Laura unaware that she could have gone into a maternity hospital, which would have been considerably cheaper. Baby clothes were bought from an inexpensive High Street shop.

In retrospect, the flat had been a palace compared to the places they'd lived since. The 'cheap' food – lamb and pork chops, spare ribs – had become nothing but fond memories. The only meat they ate these days were sausages, mincemeat and streaky bacon.

Still, they'd thought they were managing wonderfully. Straight away, Roddy had got a job as a messenger with a bank – they were sensible enough to realise the money wouldn't last for ever. It was a job with prospects. He decided to forget about architecture and take an accountancy course at night school, make banking his career, but had been sacked within a fortnight.

'I thought you were too good to be true,' the manager had snarled halfway through his second week.

'I said to him, "What do you mean?"' Roddy told Laura that night, visibly shaken. 'Apparently, he wrote to St Jude's for a reference and they said I'd left, "under a cloud".'

'Oh, dear!' Laura said inadequately.

'It means there's no use applying for another job where they'll want a reference.'

'Oh, dear!' she said again. 'What will we do now?' What she really meant was, 'What will *you* do?' because she was barely sixteen, five months pregnant, terrified out of her wits, and unable to do anything other than ineffectually keep house.

'I'll just have to find a job where they don't care about references,' Roddy said grimly. Almost a year older, he had matured with astonishing swiftness over the last few months.

He'd gone to work in a menswear shop where the wages were so poor they wouldn't even pay the rent, let alone buy food. They moved to a smaller flat, then an even smaller one, just one large room. By then, Hester had been born. She was an irascible baby, always crying. The nappies had to be washed in the communal kitchen and there was nowhere for them to dry.

It was about this time, Laura remembered, as she sat on the sofa in Glover Street nursing Roddy's ankle, that he'd suggested she went home to her father.

'Do you *want* me to go home?' she'd asked, her heart in her mouth.

'Lord, no!' He shuddered. 'I love you so much, I can't imagine life without you but, Lo, darling, the five hundred pounds has virtually gone. At least your father would provide a roof over your head. You and Hester would be warm and have enough to eat.'

'My father would never accept Hester. She'd have to be farmed out, adopted. I'd never see her again, and I'd never see you, either. He wouldn't allow you near the house, and your family wouldn't allow me near yours.' Laura managed a smile. 'We're outcasts.'

'Then we'll have to stay outcasts.' He looked at her ruefully. 'I wish I weren't so hopeless, though. And helpless. At St Jude's, it was taken for granted we'd give orders when we grew up, not take them. We weren't taught to do anything sensible. I can't even knock a nail in straight.'

The mention of nails reminded her that he'd given in his notice at the shop and was starting work on a building site on Monday. He'd been told it was the best paid unskilled work, if not exactly regular. She could tell he was dreading it.

Laura had flung her arms around his neck. 'You're anything but helpless and hopeless. You're the most capable man I know and I'll love you till the day I die.'

The building site was hard, back-breaking toil and, at first, he came back to their squalid room full of cuts and bruises. The other labourers, mainly huge, fiercesome Irishmen, made fun of the fine-featured, graceful young man who'd been to public school and spoke with a cut-glass accent but, as time passed, they began to admire his tenacity and willingness to work as hard as they did, sometimes seven days a week. They became good friends, or 'mates', as Roddy referred to them. He no longer looked out of place as he wielded a pick axe or a spade. His shoulders were gradually broadening, powerful muscles were developing on his arms, and his once-delicate skin became weathered and brown from working in the open air. He was gradually acquiring skills; bricklaying, plumbing, plastering.

He seemed quite happy. After all, as he pointed out, he was working on buildings, if not designing them, as had been his ambition. 'It's all grist for the mill.' He began to get books on architecture from the library, but fell asleep after only a few pages.

They moved to a bigger room in a more gracious house in Highbury. The weekly rent was a shilling more, but they had their own sink and use of the garden where the washing could be hung out to dry. Hester was walking and able to totter over the long grass that nobody cut. Roddy's earnings were enough to start putting money in the bank, only small amounts but, for the first time, they were able to look to the future. They felt a sense of achievement that they'd managed to come so far without help from a soul. When Hester went to school, Laura would get a job and they'd be able to rent an entire house to themselves. One day, they planned to have more children, but that day seemed very far away.

In the meantime, the big room had become their home. Laura had managed to make it look quite charming. The ugly sofa was covered with a length of cheap material she'd bought from a market and she'd embroidered cloths for the sideboard and made flowers from tissue paper – there was a huge bowl of frilly red roses on the table.

From the window, they witnessed the changing seasons; admired the blossom on the old gnarled apple tree, picked the fruit when it appeared, watched the leaves fall and cover the grass with a crisp carpet. Then winter would stealthily creep in and the entire scene would become a wonderland of snow or ice.

They'd run away to be with each other and their baby, and were happy at last.

Hester was four when Roddy's brother, Thomas, appeared on the scene. The builders Roddy worked for had been renovating a row of Regency properties in Primrose Hill that were almost finished. Prospective purchasers were already being shown around. One night, Roddy came home, his face full of smiles, and described with amusement the expression on Thomas's face when he'd come into a bedroom and found his younger brother on his knees painting the skirting.

'He looked shattered,' Roddy chortled. 'But the thing is, Lo, the most amazing thing, is that I felt superior! I felt a proper man, a genuine worker, not a poncey git who spends his life buying and selling shares, like Tom does.'

'A poncey git!' Laura exclaimed, shocked. She wasn't sure what it meant, but it sounded awfully rude.

'That's mild compared to some of the names we call the people who come to view. I daren't tell you the others.'

Roddy wasn't laughing a few days later when he told Laura that his father had turned up that morning.

'What did he want?' she asked, suddenly scared.

'He'll forgive me everything if I come home, even put me back in his will. He said it's not too late for me to go to university.' He paused. 'What's the matter, Lo? Why are you crying?' he asked in alarm.

'I don't want you to leave, that's why. Oh!' She was being selfish. 'But I understand completely if you do. I'll manage on my own. I'll be all right.'

He was on his knees in front of her in a flash, his arms around her. 'You ridiculous girl! As if I'd leave. I told my father to . . . well, I won't say what I told him to do. How could you think such a thing of me?'

'You looked so serious. I thought you'd made up your mind,' Laura sobbed.

'I looked serious for quite another reason. My father has discovered our address. He's written to *your* father. I think we can expect quite a few visitors soon.'

Laura was horrified. She wasn't yet twenty-one and wasn't sure how much control she had over her life. 'They'll try to prise us apart.'

'I know,' Roddy said gravely.

'Your mother will want Hester. She refused to see me, but she offered to take the baby, remember?' His family hadn't wanted him to get involved with a vicar's daughter. They had high hopes for their youngest son. Thomas's wife was the daughter of a viscount.

'I certainly do. She was desperate to get her hands on her.'

'I think we should move.' She glanced around the room. She'd become very fond of it. It would be a wrench to leave, but the last thing in the world she wanted was to come face to face with her father. He might bring his sister with him, her domineering Aunt Caroline, who'd called her a slut when she'd broken the news that she was pregnant.

'I think we should move too, but they know who I work for and can always track us down that way. I'll have to find another job.' That would be another wrench. He would be leaving behind a whole crowd of friends – mates.

Next morning, Laura frantically began to pack their things in Roddy's school trunk, but they'd acquired so much over the years; bedding, dishes, cutlery, Hester's clothes, that not even half would fit. Not that it mattered yet; they still had to find somewhere else to live.

She decided to go out and look in the windows of sweet and tobacconists where cards were displayed advertising rooms to let and items for sale – it was how they'd found their present room as well as Hester's pram and pushchair. The pram had eventually been sold the same way.

From being an irascible baby, Hester had become a quiet, self-contained child. She rarely bothered her parents with demands. Laura often felt guilty, wondering if her unplanned daughter sensed the impact she had made on their lives. Their worlds had been turned upside down. When they'd first made love, they'd been little more than children. It hadn't crossed their minds they might be making another human being.

'Shall we go for a walk, darling?' She tried to keep the edginess out of her voice. Her father might have received the letter that morning telling him of their whereabouts. He might come looking for her straight away. Any minute, there could be a knock on the door. She wouldn't answer, and prayed there was no one else in the house who would – it was usually empty except for her and Hester during the day.

Hester was always ready for a walk. Laura dressed her in one of the pretty frocks she'd made from a scrap of pink and white gingham. It had smocking on the front and lace trimming on the collar and cuffs. She'd never been much good at needlework at school – perhaps it was necessity that had made her an expert.

They were outside the house and she was fastening the straps of the rickety pushchair, when the garden gate flew open and Roddy came in pushing a bike.

'The chaps are covering for me at work and I borrowed the bike,' he panted. 'Laura, how do you fancy moving to Bootle? It's a little town on the edge of Liverpool.'

One of the men he worked with had a brother there, Colm, who had his own property maintenance business and was looking for a partner, he explained. The pay wasn't much, but the hours were regular. 'And Colm will find us somewhere to live. He mainly works for landlords and one is bound to have an empty property. Rory, that's my mate, will even take us up there in the lorry on Sunday.'

It was a perfect solution. Their relatives would never find them so far away. 'I fancy it very much, Roddy,' Laura said breathlessly.

And that was how Roddy, Laura and Hester Oliver came to live in Bootle.

'Would you like some cocoa, darling?' Laura asked.

'I'd love some.' Roddy was blinking tiredly.

She slid carefully off the sofa, put a cushion under his feet, and went into the kitchen. It was a fine big room, large enough to hold the table where they ate and she cut out material. It had a cast iron range, but she only made a fire once a week to heat water for the washing and for them to have baths – the tin bath hung on the wall in the yard. The cooking she did on the relatively modern gas stove.

She had no complaints about their accommodation. The landlord was very pleasant, though it would be nice if the flat had been wired for electricity. Sewing by gas light hurt her eyes and she'd noticed Vera Monaghan's house had electricity. They had the entire bottom floor, comprising three rooms, a kitchen, and even an indoor lavatory, to themselves. The only common area was the hallway, which they shared with upstairs. After living in one room for so long, it seemed the height of luxury to have their own, separate bedroom. Hester slept in the smallest room at the back.

No, the flat was fine. It was its situation that she found so depressing. Glover Street must be the most miserable street on earth, added to which the woman who lived in the flat above, Mrs Tate, was truly horrible, screaming at her poor daughter every night when she came home from work, usually very late, almost midnight. The girl was a fragile little thing, who looked about twelve, with a withered arm, and was only seen on her way to and from school. Laura had tried to speak to her a few times, but the girl looked scared out of her wits and didn't answer. She didn't seem quite all there. Mrs Tate rudely ignored her attempts to pass the time of day.

The kettle boiled, she made the cocoa, and took it into the living room where Roddy was almost asleep. She sat in an armchair so as not to disturb his feet.

'Will you get paid for today?' she asked.

'There's no reason why I shouldn't. I'd finished the damn window when the ladder broke.' A rung near the top had snapped, the wood was rotten, and he'd slid down the rest, breaking more rungs in the process. 'I'll be fit for work again in a few days, and Colm should pay me for the time off. It's his fault, not mine, that the ladder broke. It should have been ditched ages ago. I'm fed up working myself to a standstill,' he said indignantly, 'while Colm sits back and takes the profit so he can drink himself into a stupor.'

Colm Flaherty's 'business' was scarcely worthy of the term. He was little more than an odd-job man, who hadn't wanted a partner, but an assistant to do the most awkward, difficult work. If Colm was sober, he might paint the occasional door. Despite this, he was the most charming of men, popular with everyone. Laura couldn't help but like him. If a landlord wanted a job done, the first person they approached was the silver-tongued Colm Flaherty. Roddy, conscientious to a fault, had been carrying him ever since he'd started. The ex-public schoolboy was frequently seen pushing a handcart loaded with ladders, paint, sheets of glass, and mysterious lengths of piping, up and down the streets of Bootle.

Thinking about it, Laura could easily have cried. Instead of adding to their small savings, since moving, they'd been using them to subsidise Roddy's appallingly low wages. She had an idea that would at least make a slight improvement.

'You could start your own business, Roddy,' she said excitedly. 'Be your own boss. I could write cards and put them in shop windows, "Odd-Job Man Available".'

'It hardly seems worth it, Lo.'

'Why not?' she asked, disappointed.

'Because any minute now the war will start and I'll be called up. Hopefully, I'll never push a handcart again.'

'When's Hester coming, Mam?' Mary demanded.

'If you've asked that question once, you must have asked it a dozen times. Her mam's bringing her over at half past ten.'

'Why is her mam bringing her? Why can't she come on her own?'

'I dunno, luv,' Vera said vaguely, 'It's the sort of thing posh people do.'

'Why does Hester call her mam Mummy?'

'It's another thing posh people do.'

'Can I call you Mummy, Mam?'

'Over my dead body, girl,' Vera threatened. 'It sounds dead soppy.'

'Can I wash the dishes?'

'What! And break the lot? No, ta, Mary Monaghan. I'll wash 'em later. You can dry.'

'Can't you wash 'em now?'

'Can, can't, can, can't! I'll wash *you* now if you don't shut up a minute. I'll dump you in the rainbutt and leave you there for the rest of the day.'

Mary giggled. 'I know you wouldn't, Mam.'

'Don't tempt me, Mary, else you'll end up very wet. Now, go and amuse yourself while I just take a glance through your dad's paper.'

The *Daily Herald* was still on the table where Albert had left it. The more she read, the more downhearted Vera felt. There'd been an air raid practice in London the other day. The siren had sounded and people had lain on the ground and pretended to be dead or injured. There was still a shortage of gas masks for children – the Monaghans hadn't received one small enough for Mary. 'If our Mary hasn't got one, then I'm not wearing me own,' Vera informed the empty room. 'The two of us'll die together.' Winston Churchill, whoever he was, was urging a military pact with Russia. Some people, the paper reported, mainly women, had started to hoard food, sternly frowned on by the authorities. Vera immediately decided to hoard her own; tins of soup and beans, sugar and tea, just to be on the safe side. They could go in the cupboard under the stairs and would be very quickly used up if the war didn't start. Vera flatly refused to bow to the inevitable.

She folded the paper neatly, having read enough, took it into the yard and flung it into the dustbin, along with the Government leaflet that had arrived that morning entitled *Masking Your Windows*, which she hadn't read.

She'd mask her windows, whatever good it would do, when the time came and not before.

At twenty-five past ten, she put the kettle on, so there'd be a pot of tea ready when Laura arrived. The women were separated by thirty years and their backgrounds couldn't have been more different, but Vera had the strongest feeling they were going to become good friends.

Chapter 2

The Black Horse had been built in Victorian times. It stood on a corner opposite Hornby Dock, an architectural gem, the elaborate mouldings and decorative tiles on the outside in stark contrast to the cheerless interior; one large room with sawdust on the floor, wooden tables scarred and worm-ridden, hard chairs and stools. The mirror behind the bar was cracked in two places and the brasses hadn't been polished in months.

The clientele usually comprised dockers who'd been working late and were reluctant to go home, a few foreign seamen, and a handful of prostitutes – it was taken for granted that no respectable woman would be seen dead in such a place.

At precisely ten o'clock, the barmaid, Agnes Tate, rang a bell and screamed, 'Time, gentlemen, *please*.'

No one stirred. Not a soul took the slightest bit of notice. The 'gentlemen' – she'd yet to meet one – continued to sup their ale and smoke their fags as if she'd never opened her mouth and the bell hadn't rung. Agnes shrugged. It was no more than she'd expected.

She returned to the other end of the bar where Derek Norris was standing. He grinned. 'Double scotch on the rocks, Aggie, and make it snappy,' he said, doing his impression of Edward G. Robinson. 'And have another port and lemon on me while you're at it. And a fag.' He pushed a packet of Woodbines in her direction.

'Ta, Derek.' Agnes poured his usual tipple, and a drink for herself. He'd only been coming to the Black Horse for about a fortnight. She liked him and could tell he liked her in return. He was much better dressed than the other customers, in a loud, tweed suit and a canary yellow waistcoat. A bachelor in his thirties, he earned his living in mysterious ways. It was rumoured he was a fence, handling stolen property, and could get anything at a price.

She fluttered her black eyelashes, stiff with mascara. 'That'll be ninepence altogether.'

Derek leant over and peered down the front of her purple satin blouse. 'And cheap at the price,' he said with a suggestive wink.

'Don't be cheeky.' Agnes twisted her lips, painted purple to match the blouse, into what she assumed was an appealing moue, then helped herself to a Woodbine.

'What's a bobby dazzler like you doing in a dump like this?' Derek enquired.

'You asked me that last night and the night before. I told you, earning me living. I'm a widder. I've got meself and a girl of fourteen to support.'

'Pity about the girl. I've been thinking, if it wasn't for her, you and me could take off and have some great times together.'

'Oh, yeah! And pigs might fly,' Agnes snorted. She heard the same sort of thing from men at least once a week. She was a good-looking woman, handsome, with big, dark eyes in a heavily painted face and a slightly too large nose. Her brown hair had been dyed blonde and was tightly permed in tiny curls covering her well-shaped head.

'I mean it,' Derek Norris insisted. 'I've had my eye on you, Aggie. We'd make a good pair. Any minute now,

I'm off to London to make me fortune. There'll be all sorts of rich pickings there once this bloody war starts.'

'London!' Agnes breathed, images of Mayfair and Piccadilly and Buckingham Palace racing through her mind.

'London.' Derek gave an emphatic nod.

'I'd love to go to a nightclub. I've only seen them on the pictures.'

'We'll go to a nightclub on our very first night.'

'You're having me on. We hardly know each other.'

'I beg to differ, Aggie. I think we know each other very well. We're the same type. We take risks, like nice clothes, a good time. Have you ever drunk a cocktail?'

'No.'

'You'd love 'em, they'd be right up your street. I can just see you walking down the Strand in a fur coat; mink or sable, the best there is.'

Agnes could see it too, very clearly. She glanced at him through lowered lids. He had a daring face; she could imagine him taking risks. His eyes were small and a bit puffy, and he had a snub nose and a rather feminine mouth but, all in all, she found him attractive. At least he was clean, he looked after himself, and evidently had a few bob in his pocket. He had ideas. He was an adventurer. And he made her laugh, the way he imitated film stars; James Cagney and Humphrey Bogart, as well as Edward G. Robinson.

'How do I know you're not married?' she asked pertly.

'You'll just have to take my word for it that I'm not. The truth is, I've never met a woman I fancied enough to take all the way to the altar.' He flashed her a sly grin, as if to say he'd met the woman now.

The landlord, Con Garrett, pushed his way past behind the bar. He put his hands squarely on her hips and pressed himself briefly against her. Agnes nudged him sharply in the ribs with her elbow. 'Gerroff!' she snarled.

'That's not what you said the other night,' he whispered, fortunately not loud enough for Derek to hear. She didn't want him knowing she was a woman of easy virtue. A barmaid's wages didn't go far when you liked smart clothes and jewellery, and an extra quid or two came in handy whenever she fancied a new outfit. Derek had kept himself more or less to himself the nights he came and hopefully hadn't heard she was willing to do a turn when she was broke. He was living temporarily with his sister in Chaucer Street, a woman she'd never heard of who was unlikely to have heard of Agnes Tate.

'What d'you say, Aggie?' Derek said cajolingly. 'About London, that is.'

Agnes sighed. It sounded wonderful. Derek was the man she'd been waiting for her entire life. She'd be off to London like a shot, except there was just one thing stopping her. 'I told you, I've got a daughter who's only just left school. I'm not free to up and go at the drop of a hat.'

'She's fourteen, you said. Some kids are left to look after themselves much younger than that. Thirteen, I was carting coal around. Two years later, I told a lie about me age and joined the Army. I fought for me country in the Great War,' he said proudly, 'and left without a scratch on me body.'

'Still . . .'

'She wouldn't be left without a roof over her head, would she?'

'No, but she hasn't got a job yet.'

'She'll get one soon. You've done your duty by your daughter, Aggie,' Derek said earnestly. 'Now it's time to think about yourself before it's too late.'

'That's true.' Queenie had been a drag all her life, holding her mother back. If it hadn't been for her, Agnes would have left Liverpool years ago.

'Pour us another Scotch, Aggie, and another port and lemon for your goodself.'

'You'll have me tipsy,' Agnes said skittishly. 'Anyroad, it's gone closing time.' Nevertheless, she poured both drinks.

'That's what I'd like, Aggie, to have you tipsy.' He leered at her, his meaning clear, and she bent forward over the bar to give him a better view of her bosom. Derek reached for her hand and said huskily, 'We'd go together perfect, girl, in every possible way. I knew that the minute I saw you. That's why I've been coming every night all this time. It sounds a bit far-fetched to say we were meant for each other, but I wouldn't be surprised if it were true.'

Agnes, rarely for her, was overcome with emotion. No one had spoken to her in quite such a way before. He sounded so genuine, as if he meant every word. Then common sense took hold. He was just another geezer trying to get her to bed in a more flowery way than usual. Perhaps he thought if he dressed it up in fine words he'd get it for free. She withdrew her hand and said coldly, 'If you don't mind, I'd like to see the train tickets to London before I agree to anything.'

'I'll have them tomorrow,' he promised.

She reckoned she'd never see him again.

Agnes slammed the front door with all her might, not caring if it disturbed the toffee-nosed couple who lived on the ground floor with their prissy little daughter.

'Queenie,' she shrieked as she ran upstairs, 'where are you?'

'Here, Mam.' Her daughter emerged from the kitchen wearing her nightie. 'I've just made a pot of tea.'

'I should think so too. I've been run off me feet all bloody night long. Did you do that washing like I told you?'

'Yes, Mam. It's on the rack.'

'Why are you in your nightie?'

'I washed me frock at the same time.'

Agnes peered into the kitchen. The rack was full of clothes, all hers apart from a faded cotton frock. 'They're dripping everywhere,' she said disgustedly.

'I couldn't wring them any dryer, Mam. That's the best I could do.'

'You're pathetic, that's why,' Agnes sneered. 'You're pathetic at every bloody thing.'

Queenie hung her head. 'I know, Mam.'

'Fetch us the tea and hurry up about it. I'm parched.'

'Yes, Mam.'

In the living room, Agnes did a quick inspection, looking for dust or things out of place. It was Queenie's job to keep the flat spick and span while her mam was at work. She was disappointed there was not a single thing to complain about.

'It's not strong enough,' she said when the tea was brought, determined to find something wrong. 'It looks like gnat's piss.'

'I couldn't make it any stronger,' Queenie said nervously. 'There'd have been no tea left for morning.'

'Why didn't you buy more?'

''Cos you didn't leave me the money, Mam.'

'And it didn't cross your stupid head to ask for it before I left?'

'No,' Queenie whispered.

'You're thick, d'you know that, Queenie,' Agnes said cruelly. 'I don't know what I did to deserve such a thick, useless daughter. You're the bane of me life, that's what you are. Get to bed, out of me sight. I can't stand looking at you another bloody minute.'

''Night, Mam.' Queenie crept out of the room.

Agnes didn't answer. The way the girl crept about got on her nerves, as did the way she spoke, in a hushed, terrified whisper, as if she were trying to pretend she wasn't there. 'If only she weren't!' Agnes muttered. 'If only she'd died at birth or, better still, I'd never had her in the first place.'

She'd never felt a shred of love for her daughter, the result of a one-night stand with a travelling brush salesman only a few months after her husband had done a bunk. George Tate had been in the Merchant Navy and hadn't bothered to return after a trip to America. Agnes didn't care. George had been a no-hoper. In her experience, most people were. For the life of her, she couldn't understand folks not wanting a good time. She reckoned it was why they'd been put on earth, to enjoy themselves and have a laugh.

Once it became obvious George wasn't coming back, Agnes set out to have the best possible time. Not that she'd been exactly a shrinking violet before, but a married woman had to be careful how she put herself about while her husband was away. In no time she found herself up the stick by a man whose name she couldn't even remember and would never see again. Although she'd done all the usual things, drunk pints of gin, immersed herself in painfully scalding baths, the baby had refused to be budged.

People were hazy about when George had last been home and assumed the baby was his. Agnes claimed he'd been killed in an accident on the New York docks, that she was now a widow, which sounded better than the truth. She'd stuck to the story ever since.

It hadn't crossed her mind to give the girl away when she was born. Agnes had always regretted it. Instead, she'd paid some woman to look after her during the day and got a job in Johnson's Dye factory. This arrangement had continued until Queenie was five, though Agnes had been forced to remove the girl several times and find someone else when the women got angry over the various bumps and bruises on Queenie's tiny body when she was brought to them in the morning.

'Where on earth did *that* come from?' they would exclaim. 'She's such a nice, well-behaved little thing. There's no need to smack her.'

There were only so many times Agnes could say Queenie had bumped into a door or fallen downstairs. The women hadn't spent all day in a stinking factory. They weren't desperate for a bit of light relief; a drink, some congenial company when work was over. Agnes resented being stuck in, night after night, with a whingeing child. It was only understandable she give the kid a clout when she wet the bed or refused to stop crying – Queenie wasn't all that nice and well-behaved at home.

The incident with Queenie's arm had given her a fright. The kid had done something she shouldn't have, or not done something she should have, Agnes couldn't remember what it was that made her give her four-year-old daughter a shove that really did send her flying halfway down the stairs. She'd screamed blue murder all night long, and was still screaming next morning when an angry and exhausted Agnes took her to the house where she was being looked after.

'What's the matter with her?' the woman had asked suspiciously.

'I dunno, do I?' Agnes growled. 'She's just in one of her moods.'

'I've never known Queenie in a mood. She's always as good as gold. What's wrong, dearie?' The woman knelt down and made to pick Queenie up, and the kid only screamed louder. 'Her arm's broken!' the woman gasped, horrified. 'You'd best get her to hospital straight away.'

'But I'm on me way to work!'

'I don't care if you're on your way to heaven, Mrs Tate. Queenie needs to have her arm set straight away. And I'd have a good explanation ready for the doctor, if I were you, else you might find yourself up on a charge.'

Agnes had had dealings with the law before; twice for being drunk and disorderly, once for soliciting, though the latter had been a misunderstanding. The last thing she wanted was the police involved. She took Queenie home, put her arm in a sling, and fed her with Aspro, cursing loudly when she thought about the money she was losing. She also lost the next day's pay searching for another woman to look after her.

The arm had managed to set itself, but the bones hadn't knitted together properly, so that for ever afterwards, from the elbow down, Queenie's right arm faced the wrong way. The sight of her daughter's crooked arm always irritated Agnes beyond endurance. It was a constant reminder of what a damn nuisance the girl had been since the day she was born.

Queenie was five, had started school, when Agnes decided to become a barmaid. At least she'd have company, could share a joke or two with the customers, be able to dress nice for work, and there wouldn't be a creepy supervisor breathing down her neck all day long. The spinster sisters who'd lived downstairs used to put the kid to bed. Both were dead by the time Queenie turned eight, and Agnes judged she was old enough to look after herself and make herself useful around the house. Despite her arm, there wasn't much Queenie couldn't do, but she'd never been able to manage the ironing, and the washing was always sopping wet when it went on the rack because she couldn't wring it out.

Agnes took a Player's Weight out of her bag and lit it. Everywhere was so quiet. She couldn't stand the quiet or being alone. If she went with Derek Norris, she'd never be alone again. What's more, she imagined London being the sort of place that was never still. It was probably buzzing with activity right now, even though it was nearly midnight. The clubs would be full, the cafés open, there'd still be people on the streets.

Could she leave Queenie on her own? Any minute now, the girl would get a job. It was her arm that had stopped her so far. She'd been for half a dozen interviews, but employers took one look and decided she wasn't up to cooking or cleaning or doing anything heavy. But something was bound to turn up soon. Agnes had done her duty. It was time she thought about herself. 'Before it's too late,' Derek had said.

Too late! She wasn't getting any younger, but then who was? Next year, she'd be forty. She'd have to get a move on if she wanted a good time. If Derek brought them train tickets tomorrow, Agnes decided she'd be off.

Laura had acquired a fear of letters. It was rare one came for her or Roddy, and they were usually about something innocuous, but she worried constantly that his relatives, or her father, had discovered where they lived.

She uttered a little gasp when, one morning in August, she heard the letter box click and the flutter of a letter on to the mat. Approaching warily, she picked it up, hoping it was for the horrid woman upstairs, but the brown envelope was addressed to Roderick Bennett Oliver, and bore the dreaded words 'On His Majesty's Service' in black print in the top left-hand corner. She knew straight away that he'd been called up.

Sometimes, if he was working nearby, he came home and ate the sandwiches she'd made for his lunch. She put the letter on the mantelpiece and prayed he'd come today. But lunchtime passed and he didn't. Laura sat on the settee, her sewing forgotten on her lap, her eyes fixed on the letter. What was going to happen to them now? she asked herself, before realising it was a stupid question. She knew exactly what would happen. Roddy would go into the forces, she and Hester would be left in Glover Street on their own. She would get a job, war work of some sort, not only because she wanted to do her bit, but she would need the money. The matter had already been discussed with Vera, who'd offered to look after Hester while Laura was at work. It was all settled and the future looked very hard, not just for her, but for the entire population.

She wondered idly how the War Office, or whoever it was who sent out call-up papers, had known where Roddy lived? How had he been tracked down to this address? They'd had no contact with officialdom since they'd come to live in Glover Street.

In the middle of her reverie, Hester came in sulking, having quarrelled over something trivial with Mary. The two girls had become inseparable, but Laura had a feeling they didn't like each other much. Hester considered Mary too boisterous, whereas Mary thought Hester not boisterous enough. They teased each other mercilessly over their wildly differing accents, and Hester's exquisite table manners were mocked, while Mary's lack of them derided.

'What's happened now?' Laura asked with a sigh.

'Mary won't let me have a go on the swing.' Hester

sniffed. The swing was merely a rope slung over a lamppost.

'She will when she's had a turn herself.'

'She's been on it for *ages*.'

Laura suggested she play with the bat and ball she'd recently bought – the hard sponge ball was attached to the bat by a piece of elastic. She quite enjoyed playing with it herself.

'The elastic's snapped.'

'I can easily mend it.'

The idea seemed to appeal and Hester returned outside with the bat and ball. Laura watched through the window. Her socks were grubby, her frock had a little tear in the sleeve, and her sandals were badly scuffed. Yet she looked happy. Much happier than Laura had been at the same age. Little girls had to be brought to the vicarage for her to play with, or she was taken to their houses. She'd never been allowed to set foot outside on her own until she was in her teens. At boarding school, a mistress had accompanied the fifth-form girls on their weekly outings to Tunbridge Wells, although being carefully chaperoned hadn't stopped her from meeting Roddy, she remembered with a smile.

She saw a little boy come hurtling along the pavement on a home-made scooter. Bigger boys, Caradoc Monaghan amongst them, were kicking a football against the grain silo wall. A hopscotch grid had been drawn outside her window. Laura fancied having a go on that, too.

Mary had stopped swinging and was watching Hester thoughtfully. Seconds later, she ran into her own house and came out with her bat and ball. Unlike Hester, who still hadn't quite got the hang of it, Mary could hit the ball in every direction, and began to slam it upwards, sideways, downwards. She was showing off, and the regular thump, thump, thump could be heard inside the house. Hester dropped her bat and made for the swing and the two girls glared at each other, which they seemed to do an awful lot.

Laura sighed and returned to the sofa. Out of habit, she picked up her sewing, but continued to stare at the mantelpiece, at the letter that was about to completely change the course of their lives.

As she had guessed, the envelope contained Roddy's call-up papers. He would be joining the Army and had been assigned to the King's Own Regiment. He was commanded to present himself at the Territorial Army Headquarters in Park Road, Bootle, at 8 a.m. on Monday, prepared for immediate departure.

'Immediate departure to where?' Laura cried.

'A training camp, I suppose.' He looked remarkably composed, but men were like that, never revealing their emotions. Inside, he would be as upset as she was. 'Not that I'll need much training. I was in the Cadet Force at St Jude's. The adjutant was a teacher who'd been a captain in the regular Army, so I've already been fully drilled in the basics.'

'Monday's only four days away.' They'd never been apart for a single night before. She wasn't sure if she could bear it.

'I know, darling.' He held out his arms. 'Come here!'

She snuggled on to his knee, determined not to cry, which would only make things worse for him. He was holding up so well. 'I'm amazed the War Office managed to find you,' she said in a shaky voice. 'And why are you being sent away so quickly? I thought you were supposed to have a medical first?'

He didn't answer for a while then, with a little shrug, he said, 'They didn't need to find me, Lo. I've already had a medical. I volunteered, that's why.'

'And you didn't tell me!' She leapt off his knee and stared at him accusingly. 'You *want* to leave, don't you? You can't wait! You don't care what will happen to me and Hester if you're killed.'

'I won't be killed,' he said confidently.

'How can you possibly know that?'

'In six months, the whole thing will be over.'

'And how can you possibly know *that*?'

'It's only common sense, my darling Lo. Come here!' Once again, he held out his arms, but this time she ignored them.

'Don't darling me, Roderick Oliver.' She stamped her foot, angrier than she'd ever been before. 'You actually *want* to fight. You're raring for it. That's because you're a man and men are stupid. They start wars, can't wait to rush off and fight them, and us women are left behind to pick up the pieces.'

Roddy looked impressed. 'Where did you get that from? You don't usually have such strong opinions.'

'Oh, go and jump in the lake, Roddy.' She went to the front door and shouted loudly for Hester. Two gulls on the roof opposite immediately took flight, and Hester arrived looking scared. 'What's the matter, Mummy?'

'Ask your father.' Laura stamped into the kitchen to get the dinner.

'Our Billy's going on Monday, too,' Vera told Laura the following day.

'I bet he wasn't silly enough to volunteer,' Laura grumbled. She'd come across to Vera's first thing for a moan. Vera appeared quite happy to leave the breakfast dishes on the table in favour of a chat. She wore a crossover pinny that had stopped crossing over a long while ago and now barely met on her chest. Hester and Mary were squabbling upstairs.

'Billy wouldn't dare. He'd have got a black eye, if he had.'

'Roddy didn't even tell me.' Laura's brown eyes shone with indignation. 'He just went and did it without a word. That's what I find so maddening. If he'd been called up because it was his turn, it would be different. We fought all night. It was our first proper row.'

'Well, there's a first time for everything, Laura, luv.'

'He said it was his duty. I said it was his duty to stay with me and Hester for as long as he could, but he can't see it that way.' She snorted contemptuously. 'I wanted to kill him.'

'That wouldn't have helped much.' Vera leaned towards the other woman and said confidentially, 'You'll never guess what my Albert's gone and done.'

Laura gasped. 'Don't tell me he's volunteered too.'

'Not at fifty-six, luv, no,' Vera hooted. 'But he's giving up the trams and going to work in a munitions factory. Mind you, the pay's good, though it's shift work.'

'Good for Albert! I want to do something like that, but when I told Roddy, he had a fit. He insists Hester and I are evacuated. He said it would be dangerous to stay in Glover Street, so close to the docks, and I said it would be less dangerous than him going off to fight.' She rolled her eyes. 'We rowed about that too.'

Vera reached for the teapot. 'Pass us your cup, luv. It sounds as if there was a right old barney going on in your house last night.'

'Indeed there was, though it makes a change. It's usually that horrible Mrs Tate upstairs making all the racket.' Laura frowned. 'It's strange, but she's been quieter than a mouse recently. It's not a bit like her.'

'Now that you mention it, I haven't seen Aggie Tate around in a while.'

*

Laura went straight from Vera's to the shops in Marsh Lane, where she bought two ounces of Emu 3-ply khaki wool. With a feeling of despair, she saw signs that war was imminent everywhere. Sandbags were stacked in front of public buildings, and a dazzling silver barrage balloon floated in the blue sky over Bootle Hospital. Lots of houses already had their windows covered with crisscross tape to stop the glass from shattering in an explosion. She must do her own soon, and put up the blackout curtains she'd made.

It was a relief to get back to Glover Street. She intended knitting Roddy a pair of socks before he left on Monday. Despite everything, she didn't want him to have cold feet. She got out the bag of needles, selected a set of four size twelves and cast on the rib. She'd made so many socks, she could now do them from memory, even turn the heel.

The rib quickly grew and she imagined it fitting snugly around Roddy's lean ankle. Oh, Lord! She loved him so much. Laura sniffed, wiped her eyes with the back of her hand, putting all her pent-up frustration and resentment into knitting an innocent sock.

She felt a sense of achievement when four inches of rib were done and she could change to size ten needles and ordinary stocking stitch. At this rate, she might manage two pairs.

There was a knock on the living room door and she nearly jumped out of her skin. It could only be someone from upstairs. Please don't let it be that dreadful Mrs Tate, she prayed when she went to open the door.

Mrs Tate's daughter was outside, shifting nervously from one foot to the other. The first thing Laura noticed was that her right arm wasn't withered as she'd thought, but twisted almost back to front.

'Me mam's gone on holiday,' the girl whispered, 'and

she hasn't come back. I don't know what to do. The rent man's called twice, but I didn't let him in. I haven't got the money to pay him.'

'Oh, dear!' Laura said sympathetically. 'Why don't you come in and tell me all about it?'

The girl shuffled into the room. She wore a threadbare frock that was much too short and ragged plimsolls that had once been white. 'I don't know what to do,' she repeated.

'I'm sure you don't. Sit down, dear. When did your mother go?' She quickly removed her knitting when the girl looked about to sit on it, giving it a regretful glance.

'About two weeks ago.'

That accounted for the silence upstairs. 'Did she say how long she'd be away?'

'She said she'd only be a few days. I don't know what to do,' she whispered for the third time. 'I've got no pennies left for the meter.'

'What about food? Did your mother leave food?'

'It's all gone.'

'When did it go?' Laura asked angrily.

The girl cringed and looked fearful. 'The other day.'

'Please don't be frightened. I'm angry with your mother, not you. What's your name, dear?'

'Queenie,' the girl whispered.

'Well, I think the first thing to do, Queenie, is get you something to eat.' Laura considered the contents of her meagre larder. There were two eggs and a two slices of streaky bacon for Roddy's breakfast next day, mincemeat and vegetables for a casserole tonight that she'd not yet started, and half a pound of broken biscuits. 'Would you like to come into the kitchen while I make it?'

'Ta.' Queenie crept out after her, making hardly any noise at all on the linoleum floor.

Laura gave her a glass of milk and she drank it thirstily,

able to hold the glass quite safely in her twisted hand, and watching her all the time with a pair of huge grey eyes, almost silver, surrounded by a frame of thick, pale lashes.

The eggs and bacon were quickly fried, along with a thick slice of bread. She put the food in front of the girl, then began to prepare the vegetables for the casserole. In no time at all, she could hear the plate being scraped.

'Ta,' Queenie muttered. The plate was clean, every trace of egg having been wiped up with the bread. The poor child must have been starving.

'Did your mother say where she was going?' she asked, when she sat down at the table with two cups of tea.

'No, just on holiday.'

'Where did she work?'

'In a pub, the Black Horse. It's on the Docky.' The Dock Road was referred to locally as the Docky.

'When my husband gets home, I'll ask him to see if anyone there knows where she is.'

'I want me mam back.' Two giant tears rolled down the girl's thin cheeks.

Laura felt her heart contract. 'You poor thing!' She reached for the girl's hand. It felt as light as a feather in her own, sensible broad one. 'You should have come down before. I feel awful, knowing you've been by yourself all this time with nothing to eat or drink.' What a perfect bitch the mother was, though there was just a chance the woman had been taken ill or had had an accident and was lying in a hospital somewhere.

'I didn't want to be a nuisance,' Queenie whispered.

'Of course you're not a nuisance.' Although the words were sincerely meant, Laura would have far preferred to have been left alone with her knitting. She had no idea what to do with the girl now. 'How old are you, Queenie?'

'Fourteen.'

She looked less than that, her slight body that of a child's, no sign of breasts beneath the cotton frock. Her white legs were as thin as sticks. On another face, her grey eyes would have looked quite pretty, but Queenie's cheeks were almost non-existent, making the eyes seem much too big and accentuating her pointed nose and little, pale mouth. Her hair looked dreadful, as if it had been chopped off with a pair of blunt scissors, though the colour was nice, a silvery blonde. It stood in stiff clumps on her tiny scalp. She looked like a half-starved elf.

'Would you mind if I looked upstairs, dear, to see if your mother's left any clues as to where she might have gone?'

'No.' Queenie shook her head. She seemed less nervous than when she'd first arrived. Perhaps she sensed Laura wasn't about to bite her head off.

'I'll give you another cup of tea first, and perhaps you'd like to finish off these biscuits before they go soft. You'll be doing me a favour.' Laura put a plate of perfectly good, if broken biscuits on the table. She had a feeling, if she told Queenie to help herself, she'd only take a couple.

'Ta.'

The first thing she noticed when she went upstairs was the strong smell of polish. The rooms were gloomy, the furniture old and well worn, as it was in her own flat. But Laura had added things to make it look like home; pictures and ornaments, embroidered cloths and flowers. Nothing had been added upstairs. The walls and surfaces were bare. Everywhere looked very drab, but immaculately clean. Queenie must have been dusting and polishing in readiness for her mother's return. The idea made Laura want to weep.

In the bedroom, a neatly made double bed was

covered with a well-worn eiderdown. On opening the wardrobe, she found nothing but half a dozen wire coathangers, jangling eerily against each other. The drawer underneath contained sheets, unironed, but clean. An almost empty bottle of bright scarlet nail polish on the dressing table indicated this must be Mrs Tate's room. In the drawers, there was a pair of leather gloves with the fingers hanging off and a few items of underwear that Laura wasn't willing to touch. She came to the definite conclusion that Mrs Tate had gone for good.

Where did Queenie sleep? she wondered. She somehow doubted it was with her mother. The small room at the back, the equivalent of the one where Hester slept downstairs, had been turned into a kitchen. She remembered there was a floor above and found the narrow staircase tucked in a dark corner next to the lavatory. The further she climbed, the stronger became the odour of damp and mould. There were wet patches on the landing ceiling. She opened the first door and her heart sank. This must be where Queenie slept, on a mattress on the floor in a room with green mould in all four corners and no curtains on the window. Beside the mattress, there was a nightlight in a metal container, matches, a cardboard box with a few pathetic items of clothing, and two magazines. Laura picked them up. Both were well-thumbed copies of Enid Blyton's *Sunny Stories*.

Earlier that day, she'd flippantly remarked to Vera that she could have killed Roddy for volunteering, but the anger she'd felt then was nothing compared to the anger she felt now. Laura had a strong urge to strangle Mrs Tate with her own bare hands.

'She's done a bunk, I'm afraid. She's gone to London

with one of the customers, a chap by the name of Derek Norris,' Roddy reported breathlessly. He'd been despatched to the Black Horse as soon as he'd finished his dinner to establish the whereabouts of their missing upstairs neighbour. 'The landlord was highly indignant because she gave him less than twenty-four hours' notice.'

'Good riddance to bad rubbish!' Laura snarled. She was washing the dishes with unnecessary vigour.

Roddy did a double-take. 'Lo! The last few days you've been quite frightening. There's a side to you I never knew you had.'

'I didn't know I had it either.'

'I quite like it.' He slid his arms around her waist. 'There's something happening tomorrow that you don't know about,' he whispered in her ear. 'Please don't be mad.'

'What?' she snapped.

'We're getting married.'

'*What?*'

'I got an emergency licence, but last night I was too scared to tell you. Tomorrow, Saturday, at precisely twelve-fifteen, you shall become Mrs Roderick Bennett Oliver at the registry office in Brougham Terrace. That's if you want to,' he said meekly, nuzzling her neck. 'Then your name will be down as my next-of-kin, not my parents.'

'So they can write and tell *me* that you're dead?' Laura said bitterly. 'Oh, Roddy!' She turned and put her wet arms around his neck. 'You know quite well I want to marry you, and of course I'm not mad. We should have done it before.'

'I know, darling. I always thought we would, one day, but now it seems sort of necessary.'

★

Hester seemed quite taken with Queenie, perhaps because she was a welcome contrast to the belligerent, bossy Mary. What Queenie's feelings were, no one knew. She looked dazed and kept glancing nervously over her shoulder, as if expecting her mother to appear and drag her away. The two girls sat on the sofa, Queenie reading *Sunny Stories* aloud to an entranced Hester. To Laura's surprise, she read well in a high, sweet voice, not once stumbling over a word.

At nine o'clock, Laura suggested the girls went to bed and that Queenie should sleep in her mother's room upstairs. Hester's bed was much too narrow, even for two small people.

'But she might come back and find me!' The girl's eyes were wide with horror.

'Just in case she does, I'll bolt the door on the inside,' Laura promised. 'Don't worry, I'll let her in,' she said when Queenie seemed just as horrified at the idea of her mother being locked out, even if she dreaded her coming back. 'You'll have plenty of time to go to your own room.' But not if I've got anything to do with it, she added to herself. She'd forgotten Queenie loved the cruel woman who had almost certainly gone for ever.

She went upstairs with the girl and tucked her in. 'Good night, dear,' she said gently, giving the clumpy hair a little pat.

Roddy had already put Hester to bed when she came down. 'What will happen to Queenie?' he asked.

'I've no idea,' Laura confessed. 'All I can think of is going to the police. I doubt if she's capable of looking after herself.'

'That seems a bit harsh,' he said ruefully. 'On Queenie, that is. She seems a nice kid. They might put her in a home.'

'I know. I'll discuss it with Vera tomorrow. I need to

speak to her, anyway, to ask if she'll look after Hester while we get married.'

'Oh, well.' He stretched his arms. 'Shall we turn in early tonight?'

'We'll do no such thing, Roderick Oliver. I'm about to have a bath and wash my hair and there isn't time to light the fire and wait for the water to get hot, so I'll have to boil pans instead. You must have a bath too. You smell of paint and it's quite disgusting. And I have a wedding dress to get ready, gloves to find, a hat. I would have liked a little nosegay too, but there's not much chance of that. At least I've got the ring.' She twisted the thin gold band around the third finger of her left hand. 'I've never had this off since the day you put it on,' she said.

'It won't be off for long. Tomorrow, I'll put it on officially, and you'll never have to take it off again for the rest of your life,' Roddy promised.

Chapter 3

The weather during August had been lovely. Day after day, the country woke to a brilliant sun shining out of a cloudless blue sky. It was hard to believe, while they luxuriated in the warmth and glory of these magical summer days, that such terrible things were about to happen to their world.

When Laura opened her eyes on Saturday morning, Roddy fast asleep beside her, the first thing she saw was her wedding dress hanging on the wardrobe door. With a little pang, she wished she were getting married in white, with all the fuss of a proper wedding; bridesmaids, flowers, an organ playing 'The Wedding March', a big reception afterwards. But if that had been the case, she mightn't have been marrying Roddy. As he was the only man with whom she wished to spend the rest of her life, what did it matter that there would be no bridesmaids, no flowers, no organ, and merely lunch in a restaurant to celebrate?

It didn't matter a bit, nor that her wedding outfit was in fact a cream silk afternoon dress she'd bought years ago off a secondhand stall in Petticoat Lane market. It had a frill for a collar and puffed sleeves ending at the elbow in another frill. She had no idea whether it was fashionable or not. Her mother had bought *Good Housekeeping* every month to keep up with the latest styles, but Laura couldn't remember when she'd last read a women's magazine.

She raised her head a few inches so she could see her hat, the straw boater she'd worn at school during the summer term. Ages ago, she'd removed the navy-blue band, and added different coloured trimmings to match whatever she happened to be wearing. Last night, she'd tied a cream georgette scarf around it, knotting it at the back, leaving the ends to trail. Her lace gloves had been mended for the umpteenth time. It was a pity her best shoes were brown and rather heavy, but they went with her only handbag.

Roddy turned over and mumbled something inaudible in his sleep. She stared at the back of his neck, thinking what a beautiful shape it was, longing to touch the short, blond hairs, wake him, lie in his arms for a while in the warm sunshine that poured through the window. They only had two more nights together. Monday night she would sleep in this bed alone. She shivered and crept reluctantly out, let him sleep a little longer.

In the kitchen, she opened the door wide to take advantage of the sun before it disappeared, put the kettle on, and wondered what to make Roddy for his breakfast, having forgotten to replace the bacon and eggs she'd given Queenie the day before – she liked him to have something more substantial than cornflakes. She was still wondering when Roddy came in, still in his pyjamas, and asked, 'Where's my gas mask?'

'Under the stairs,' she told him.

'And the suitcase?'

'The same place as the gas mask.'

'Right.' He disappeared, but was back seconds later. 'I forgot, you'll want the suitcase, won't you? I'll find something else for my things. I won't need to take much.'

'Why will I want a suitcase?'

He gave her a steely look. 'For when you and Hester are evacuated, of course.' He disappeared again, but this time she followed him.

'Roddy, I told you before, I've no intention of leaving this house.'

'You're being very selfish, Laura.' He emerged from the cupboard with a gas mask in a cardboard case. 'Once the air raids begin, Bootle docks will be one of the most dangerous areas in the country.'

'*I'm* being selfish!' She laughed sarcastically. 'What about you?'

'Please don't start that again,' he groaned. 'I would have been called up eventually. I'm just going sooner rather than later. Forget about yourself for a minute and think about Hester. It's not fair, letting her stay in a place where she could be killed any minute.'

'There's a shelter at the end of the next street.'

'I know, I've seen it, and I can assure you, if it gets a direct hit, it'll be no safer than this cupboard.' His face was dark with a mixture of anger and fear. 'And you've got some daft idea about going to work. What happens to Hester then?'

'Vera will look after her,' Laura said defensively.

'And how will you feel if there's a raid and you're at work, knowing the docks are being pounded to bits and Glover Street might not be standing when you get back?'

She shuddered. 'Oh, Roddy, don't say things like that!'

He took her in his arms. 'I don't want to frighten you, Lo, but that's the way it's going to be. I'd feel happier, knowing my family are safely out of harm's way.'

Hester came out of her room and immediately wanted

to know where Queenie was. She was despatched upstairs to fetch her in case she was too nervous to come of her own accord. She reappeared a minute later, leading a fully dressed Queenie by the hand. Laura sent the pair of them to the nearest shop for four eggs and a loaf. She'd make poached egg on toast for breakfast.

Agnes Tate's ears would have burnt to cinders had she been able to hear the insults heaped upon her dyed-blonde head when Vera was told she'd walked out and left Queenie on her own.

'The irresponsible cow!' Vera screeched. 'The bitch! She wants horsewhipping from one end of Glover Street to the other.'

'I felt like strangling her myself,' Laura conceded. 'The thing is, I don't know what to do about Queenie.'

Vera's expression changed from anger to concern. 'You're awful young, luv, to have a girl of fourteen dumped on you.'

'I feel about twenty years older, not just seven,' Laura confessed.

'As for Queenie, poor lamb. Aggie led her a terrible life. She's better off without her, not that she'll realise that for a while. She can come and live with us for now, the little pet,' she said generously. 'She'll be a sister for our Mary. Once she's got a job, she'll be able to pay for her keep.'

Mary poked her head around the door. 'I don't want a sister, Mam,' she whined, clearly jealous of her position as the only girl in the family.

'You'll have a sister whether you want one or not,' Vera barked. 'Anyroad, girl, you'd best be off if you're going into town with your Roddy.'

'I know, I've got to get changed. You don't mind keeping an eye on Hester, do you? And Queenie too, I suppose. This is the first time Roddy and I will have been out together, just the two of us.'

'And it'll be the last for a long time,' Vera said grimly. 'Stay as long as you like, I don't mind. I'll feed 'em both. 'Fact, I'll be cross if you come back much before it's dark.'

She didn't feel the least bit different when she emerged from the Registry Office in Brougham Terrace. In law, she was now Mrs Roderick Oliver, but she'd never really thought of herself as anything else. Two guests, a married couple, who had arrived early for the wedding after theirs, had acted as witnesses, and the man had taken a snapshot of them with his Box Brownie camera. Roddie had given him their address to post it to.

'You both look awfully young,' the woman had exclaimed.

'I wonder how she would have reacted if we'd told her we had a five-year-old daughter,' Roddy laughed when they were outside.

'Shocked and disgusted, I expect,' Laura replied.

'Look, there's a tram coming. It's going into town. Let's run and we just might catch it.'

They lunched in Frederick & Hughes in Hanover Street – known locally as Freddy's – one of the most exclusive department stores in Liverpool. The restaurant was like a ballroom, with soaring oak-panelled walls and an elaborately moulded ceiling from which hung three magnificent chandeliers. Stained-glass peacocks in the centre of the tall windows cast brilliant spots of colour over the room. It was like being in another world, Laura thought. There was something faintly thrilling about the subdued clink of cutlery, the murmur of voices, the sound of the white grand piano being played by a man in a velvet jacket and a bow tie. Ordinarily, they could never have afforded such an expensive place, but Colm Flaherty had given Roddy a two pound bonus when he'd left the day before. 'I don't know what I'll do without you, boyo,' he'd said with tears in his eyes.

'Let's blow the lot,' Roddy said impetuously as they studied the menu. 'That's not exactly extravagant,' he added when Laura made a face. 'When my brother, Thomas, got married, it cost over two hundred and fifty pounds. There were more than a hundred guests and an entire orchestra played at the ball that night. I bet no one had as good a time as we're going to have with our measly two, and that pianist is better than an orchestra any day.'

'A three-course meal is only half a crown. We'd have to eat four each if we're going to blow the lot,' Laura pointed out.

'But we've got the rest of the day to go, haven't we? After this, we'll do some shopping, then go to the cinema.' He smacked his lips. 'I'm having vegetable soup, lamb chops, peas and roast potatoes, followed by trifle. Oh, Lord!' He sniffed appreciatively. 'I can already smell the mint sauce. I think that's what I've missed more than anything over the last few years, lamb and mint sauce.'

'I'll have vegetable soup and *coq au vin*, only because it's something I've never had before and it makes it more exciting.'

He grinned boyishly. 'It *is* exciting, isn't it?'

'Yes, but Roddy,' she said in a small voice, 'do you mind having missed lamb and mint sauce and so many other things all this time? If we'd never met, by now you'd be a fully-fledged architect. You might be married. There'd have been more than a hundred guests and an orchestra at your wedding and you'd be living in a lovely house, like the one in Primrose Hill where you saw Thomas.'

'Laura,' he said gravely and with a touch of impatience, 'if I could go back in time, I wouldn't change a single thing. I *am* married, to the most beautiful girl in the world and have an equally beautiful daughter. And I'll have you know that, although I may not be an architect, I'm a fully-fledged builder's mate. So there!' He stuck out his tongue and she giggled. 'How about you? Would you do things differently if it were possible?'

'You know I wouldn't. What are you doing?' she exclaimed when he took the stub of a pencil out of his pocket and began to write on the menu.

'Just making a note of something.'

The waitress arrived to take their order. While they waited, Roddy said, 'Remember the notes we used to write each other in that bookshop where we met?'

'We used to leave them in Gibbons's *The Rise and Fall of the Roman Empire*.' The shopkeeper must have wondered how it became so well-thumbed, but had never been bought.

'The first time I saw you through a gap in the shelves, I said to myself, "I've got to get to know that girl properly." It was love at first sight.'

'For me too,' Laura said tenderly. 'There was something familiar about you, as if I'd known you all my life.' He was taller than her by a head, very attractive and debonair in his grey school uniform. It was Saturday and the fifth form of Burton College for Girls were on their weekly visit to Tunbridge Wells. Miss Lancing, the teacher, was keeping a sharp eye on her charges when the shop had been invaded by half a dozen boys from St Jude's whom they'd been forbidden to speak to. Roddy had written a note, put it inside the Gibbons, and placed it on the shelf in front of her. 'What's your name? I'm Roddy Oliver and I'd like to see you again,' it had said.

Laura had wandered away, clutching the note. When she was sure that Miss Lancing wasn't looking, she wrote on the other side, 'I'm Laura Conway and I'll be here at the same time next Saturday.'

It had gone on like that for weeks. Sometimes there was no sign of Roddy; he'd had a rugger match, his note would explain the following week. Other times, the girls had choir practice or there was a hockey game. Laura wasn't in the school team, she hated hockey, but was required to stay and cheer their side on. If there was no Roddy and no note, she'd leave one for him, and he did the same. When he was there, they merely stared at each other, while Laura experienced all sorts of strange, pleasant emotions. She assumed he must feel the same.

The waitress came with the soup. It was very thick, no doubt nourishing, but much too filling. 'I'll never manage the main course if I eat all this,' she said halfway through. Roddy had already finished his.

'Hand it over. I'll eat it.'

'You'll make yourself sick,' she warned. She glanced around to make sure no one was looking before passing him her bowl.

'I don't care. It's my wedding day and I'll do as I like. I'm trying to make up for six years of starvation.'

'There was a fat girl at school. We used to call her the human dustbin. She finished off everybody's meals.'

'I remember. Her name was Fiona. She came with you to that tea room and stole your currant bun.'

'She didn't steal it. I gave it her. How could I have eaten a currant bun with you sitting at the next table? But fancy you remembering that,' she said, impressed.

'I remember everything about that day. It was the first time we spoke to each other. I asked if I could borrow your sugar. You passed the bowl and our hands touched.'

'Then you passed it back and they touched again.'

He must have noticed the girls went into Hunter's Tea Room before they caught the bus back to school. He was there with another boy when they went in. It was just before the Easter holidays. 'Where do you live?' the note she had found earlier had asked. She had written her address on the back and left it in the Gibbons.

The following week, on Maundy Thursday, he'd turned up at her home, having caught a train from Guildford to Brighton, a bus to Eastbourne, then walked all the way to the village where she lived. It had taken two and a half hours.

Her father was in church, it was his busiest time of the year, and she was clearing weeds in the rose garden, which had been her mother's favourite place. It had a little iron bench in the corner where she used to sit and read. Her mother had been dead for four years and Laura still missed her badly. She felt closer to her in the rose garden than anywhere else.

She didn't know what to say when he arrived, bowled over by how handsome he looked in an open-necked shirt, tweed jacket and baggy flannel trousers. His hair was very blond, very straight, and a mite too long. That was the day when everything had started for real. Within a fortnight, they were making love. It seemed so natural, so beautiful, that she could see nothing disgraceful about going to bed with a boy she hardly knew, but felt she had known for ever. Her father was busy with his duties as a vicar, and the housekeeper worked in the kitchen, out of sight, out of mind, out of hearing of the young couple in the bedroom under the eaves of the old vicarage.

She jumped when the waitress put the *coq au vin* in

front of her. She'd been so engrossed in reliving the past that she hadn't noticed the soup bowls had been removed. To her surprise, the woman also placed a bottle of wine on the table.

'Compliments of Mr Theo,' she said with a smile. 'Congratulations to you both. I hope you'll be very happy.'

As if on cue, the pianist began to play, 'Here Comes The Bride,' Roddy leapt to his feet and kissed her, and the other diners burst into spontaneous applause. Everyone in the room was looking at her. Laura didn't know whether to crawl under the table or burst into tears. 'Who's Mr Theo?' she asked in a cracked voice.

'The owner of Freddy's, luv. He's ever such a nice man. There he is, over there.'

Just outside the entrance to the kitchen, a handsome, foreign-looking man was watching them intently. He bowed courteously in their direction. Laura gave him a little wave. 'Tell him thank you very much. It's a lovely gesture.'

'You're a lovely bride. Mr Theo said so himself. Someone showed him the menu with your husband's message and he came down to take a peek at you both. Oh, and he said the meal's on the house.'

'All I asked was for the pianist to play something special,' Roddy said later. 'I wasn't expecting wine and free food.'

To their surprise, Vera was in the living room when they got home, reading the *Silver Star*, a magazine containing tawdry tales that Laura found quite fascinating when she borrowed it.

'Did you enjoy yourselves?' she asked.

'It was wonderful!' Laura cried. 'We went to see *Jezebel* with Bette Davis and had lunch in Frederick &

Hughes. They gave us wine and the pianist played . . .' She stopped just in time.

'The pianist played what?'

'"Happy Birthday". It was someone's birthday on the next table and they gave us a glass of wine. And Roddy bought me a ring. It was only two and elevenpence, but isn't it pretty?' She displayed her right hand so Vera could see the sparkling glass stone. 'It's not a real diamond.'

'I wouldn't have expected it to be, luv, not for two and eleven.'

'After the pictures, we went for a drink,' Laura continued, her face glowing. 'I had a cherry brandy – I think I'm a little bit tipsy – then we strolled down to the Pier Head and watched the ferries sail in and out. We walked home along the Docky. It's so *foreign*, and incredibly busy, even at this time of night.' She collapsed on the sofa with a whoop of delight. 'Oh, I *love* Liverpool! I want to stay here for the rest of my life.'

'Was it you making a commotion outside the window a few minutes ago?'

Laura giggled. 'We were playing hopscotch in the moonlight. Can you think of anything more romantic? I've been dying to have a go.'

Roddy had been watching his young wife with a mixture of amusement and total adoration while she spoke. 'I think you could say, Vera, that today we enjoyed ourselves to the full.'

'Has Hester been all right?' Laura suddenly remembered they had a daughter.

'No.' Vera said grimly. 'She's been a little minx, our Mary too. They've been fighting for possession of Queenie the whole day long. The poor girl doesn't know whether she's coming or going. Don't be surprised when you find Hester's room empty, because she's upstairs. All three of 'em are fast asleep in Aggie Tate's bed.'

'They're a lovely couple,' Vera said fondly to Albert when she got home. 'They talk like books. "Today we enjoyed ourselves to the full," Roddy said.'

'In other words, they had a bloody good time,' Albert remarked drily.

'I think you could say that. You should've seen their faces! And the way they looked at each other! You'd think they had lighted candles behind their eyes.'

'Who's talking like a book now?' Albert said, impressed. 'You'll be writing poetry next, girl.'

'Did we ever look at each other like that, Albert?' Vera asked wistfully.

'I'm looking at you like that now, Vera. And there's not candles behind me eyes, but two bloody bonfires. C'mon, girl. Let's go to bed.'

Hester woke her parents early the following morning simply by bursting into their room and throwing herself on to the bed. She shook her mother awake. 'Mummy, why should Mary have Queenie for a sister?' she demanded. 'It's not fair. It was me who saw her first. She should be mine.'

'What time is it?' Laura mumbled.

'I don't know, Mummy. The big hand's on nine and the little one has just passed six.'

'I can't work that out.' Her brain was too fuggy. She'd been in the middle of a lovely sleep and felt completely relaxed. 'Go away, Hester.'

Roddy pushed himself to a sitting position. 'It's quarter to seven, it's Sunday, and we usually sleep in. What do you want?' he enquired sternly. 'And what's all this about you being a minx yesterday?' he added.

Laura sat up with a groan and they both stared at the normally quiet, uncomplaining little girl who was sitting crossed-legged between them, already dressed, her face a mask of haughty indignation.

'It wasn't me being a minx, it was Mary. She's trying to steal Queenie off me. She said she's going to be her sister. It's not fair.'

'Queenie can't be stolen, sweetheart. She's not a toy,' Roddy said reasonably. 'Where is she, anyway?'

'In the kitchen, making tea. We polished the whole of upstairs together, Queenie and me,' Hester said importantly.

'What about Mary?'

'She's gone home. I pushed her out of bed and she banged her head.'

Laura gasped. 'That's a horrid thing to do, Hester. Was she hurt?'

Hester had the grace to look ashamed. 'She cried. I didn't mean for her to cry. I was sorry afterwards.'

'I should think so too. Later, you must go over and tell Mary how sorry you are for being a very, very naughty girl. I shall also apologise to Vera on your behalf.'

'All right, Mummy,' Hester said meekly. 'Would you like some tea? It'll be ready by now.'

Roddy got out of bed. 'I'll fetch it. I don't trust you not to throw it over us, the mood you're in.'

An hour later, Laura still felt bleary-eyed, but was glad they'd got up early. There were lots of things to do. Roddy had started to stick tape on to the windows. He was measuring them carefully with a ruler, making sure the crosses were perfectly symmetrical. The curtains were taken down, and she sewed the blackout material to them so it would only be seen on the outside, otherwise the place would look like a funeral parlour.

As she sewed, she thought about yesterday. Already, it

was beginning to feel faintly unreal. It was the first time they'd had fun together, felt young and without a care in the world, the way young couples should. Now Roddy was going away, and it might be years before they would feel young and carefree again.

Queenie came in accompanied by an eager Hester waving a duster. 'We've polished the bedrooms. Shall we do in here?'

'If you don't mind, Queenie.' The girl seemed to have an obsession with polishing. 'I'll make a drink. It's about time we had a break.'

Colm Flaherty arrived, just in time for a cup of tea, bearing a wireless he'd cadged off an elderly lady who was too deaf to listen to it any more. It was very big, in a walnut casing with a gold brocade front. 'I thought you'd find it useful, Laura, me darlin'. It'll be company while your feller's away.'

'But we haven't got electricity, Colm!'

'You don't need electricity, darlin'. It's a battery set. All you have to do is get the battery refilled every now 'n' again. There's a spare to keep you going while the other's being charged. Where would you like it put?'

'On the shelf beside the fireplace, I think. Thank you very much, Colm. I really appreciate it.'

Colm began to fiddle with the wireless and everyone sat, entranced, when the room was suddenly filled with music, something passionate and classical that Laura didn't recognise. She was shown how to turn the set on and off and on what waveband to find the Home Service, then Colm said, if she didn't mind, he'd like to take her feller away and buy him a pint of ale.

'Of course I don't mind.' The taping of the windows was almost finished. The curtains merely had to be re-hung. There were a few jobs Roddy still wanted to do before he left for good, like fix the crooked shelf in the kitchen, do something about the lavatory seat that had become loose and the sideboard drawer that was too tight.

Before he left *for good*! Laura caught her breath. She was doing her best not to count down the hours. But, as she watched him pass the window with Colm, it was impossible not to think that by this time tomorrow he would have been gone for four long hours, and the hours would only get longer and longer until he came back.

She sighed and remembered it was about time she took Hester across the road to make the promised apology. There'd been no sign of Mary all morning, which was unusual.

It was very peaceful in number seventeen, apart from the sound of pans rattling on the stove. She was boiling a piece of ham and some taters, Vera said. Albert had gone to the pub with the lads, all eight of them, though half would have to stand outside and make do with lemonade and a packet of crisps, not being old enough to set foot on licensed premises.

'It's a farewell do for our Billy, though I don't doubt there'll be another tonight,' Vera said. She sniffed. 'I'm darning his socks. I'm trying to do them nice and neat, but I've ended up in a terrible ravel.' She flung the sock on to the table, looking close to tears. 'I'm useless at darning. The poor lad will march around the parade ground with a great lump of wool rubbing against his heel.'

'Here, let me do it.' Laura took the sock and began to unpick Vera's attempts at a darn. 'Where's Mary?' she asked.

'Upstairs. She's been very quiet this morning, I don't know why.'

'Hester!' Laura jerked her head in the direction of the stairs. When her daughter had gone, she explained to

Vera that she'd been very naughty and had pushed Mary out of bed. 'She banged her head. Hester's gone to say she's sorry. I'm sorry too. I've told her it must never happen again.'

'I'm sure she didn't mean it,' Vera said charitably. 'I've pushed Albert out of bed before now, but it was only by accident. Anyroad, luv, there's no need to make a fuss, coming over and apologising, all formal like. Hester and Mary needle each other all the time, yet they can't keep away from one another. Let's leave 'em to sort things out for themselves.'

'You're awfully clever, Vera,' Laura said, full of admiration for her friend's philosophical attitude to life, though it didn't prevent her getting upset over lumps in Billy's socks.

'I'm not clever, luv, just sensible. There's enough horrible things happening in the world for people to worry about. It makes sense not to tear yourself apart over things that don't matter a bit. My,' she exclaimed, 'that darn's dead neat. I couldn't have done one like that in a million years. It's you who's the clever one, not me.'

'I haven't finished yet. I'll do the other sock in a minute. The other day, I started knitting a pair for Roddy, but then Queenie arrived on the scene and I haven't touched them since. Roddy said the Army will provide them with socks, but an extra pair wouldn't go amiss.' She intended making him lots of things; more socks, a scarf, gloves. It would help to keep in touch with him in a very personal way, knowing that one day his fingers would slide inside the fingers of the gloves and the scarf would keep his neck warm when it was cold. She was too embarrassed to tell Vera this, but was sure that she, more than anyone, would have understood.

*

The dreaded time had come, the time for Roddy to leave. It was another glorious morning, absolutely perfect, the sun a dazzling golden circle in the pale sky. The air was already warm and it tingled in a way that, ordinarily, would have felt quite exhilarating.

His things were packed in two carrier bags; a few clothes, his two favourite John Buchan books, shaving gear, the writing pad and envelopes she'd bought him on Saturday, along with a cheap fountain pen and a bottle of ink that Laura had wrapped in several sheets of newspaper in case it leaked.

The minutes ticked away. Twenty minutes past seven, twenty-one, twenty-two . . . He was leaving at exactly half past. They sat in the kitchen, around the table, not knowing what to say, Hester and Queenie too. Queenie looked as upset as everyone. She'd become very much attached to the Olivers over the last few days.

'I wish I hadn't done it, volunteered,' Roddy said dully. 'At least we would have another few weeks together.'

'As you said, darling, you're merely going sooner rather than later.'

'I just wish it was later.'

'Have you taken handkerchiefs?'

'You put some in last night.'

'Did I?' She couldn't remember. 'What about nail scissors?'

'I've got some.'

Twenty-five minutes past seven.

'Write as soon as you can and let us know your address, won't you, Roddy?'

'At the very first opportunity.'

'You can use your new pen, Daddy.'

'That's why Mummy bought it for me, sweetheart.'

'Queenie's going to learn me how to write, so I can send you letters too.'

'Teach, sweetheart, Queenie's going to teach you to write, not learn. And what about Queenie writing me a letter?' he said warmly. 'The more the merrier, as far as I'm concerned.'

Queenie nodded furiously and said she'd start one that very afternoon.

Twenty-nine minutes past seven. Roddy got to his feet and threw his gas mask over his shoulder. 'Well, I'd better be off.'

The girls ran to the front door, opened it. Laura stood too, hardly able to speak. Roddy took her in his arms. 'This is it, my darling Lo. You know I love you with all my heart and always will.'

'I love you, Roddy.' She clung to him, and he had to remove her arms from around his neck.

'Bye, Laura.'

'Bye.' She followed him into the street. Billy Monaghan was coming out of number seventeen, accompanied by his entire family. Other doors opened, three other young men stepped out, and they formed a little straggly group. It probably wasn't deliberate, more an automatic reaction, that they should fall into step and march out of Glover Street on their way to war, accompanied by a chorus of tearful 'goodbyes' and 'taras'. Then the little company turned the corner and were gone.

Laura wasn't allowed to feel upset. When she returned to the house, she found Hester in tears because her daddy had gone and Queenie trying to comfort her, while looking close to tears herself. She had just managed to quieten them, when there was a knock on the door. It was the rent man, a nice, fussy little person called Edgar Binns with whom she got on very well.

'I came on Saturday, luv, but you weren't in. As I was in the area, I thought I'd call. Frankly, it's not you I'm after, I know you'd have paid the next week, but I was hoping to catch Aggie Tate from upstairs. It's three weeks since she last paid.'

'You'll be lucky. I'm afraid she's gone.'

Edgar looked understandably annoyed. 'That's a bloomin' nerve. She didn't tell us she was going.'

'She didn't tell her daughter, either. She just went, leaving Queenie behind.'

'Poor kid. What's happened to her?'

'We've been looking after her for the last few days. I didn't know Mrs Tate had gone myself until Thursday. While you're here, I'd like to show you something.' She took him upstairs and pointed out the damp on the ceiling of the top landing, then threw open the door of Queenie's room so he could see the mould in the corners.

'All she had to do was tell us and Mr Granger would have had it fixed straight away. He's very particular about keeping his properties in good repair. There's probably a few slates loose on the roof and bricks that might need repointing.'

They went back downstairs. On the way, Edgar took a look at the other rooms and remarked how spruce they were.

'That's all due to Queenie,' Laura told him. 'She's a dab hand with a duster and polish.'

She gave him the seven and sixpence rent and asked if it would be all right if Queenie slept upstairs until the new tenants arrived. Edgar said he was sure Mr Granger wouldn't mind. 'It's no skin off his nose, is it, Mrs Oliver? He won't be looking for new tenants until that damp's been sorted. Which reminds me, doesn't your husband work for Colm Flaherty? Perhaps he'd like to make a few bob on the side and do the work himself. Mr Granger would pay well.'

She was amazed at how even and steady her voice was when she replied, 'I'm afraid that won't be possible, Mr Binns. My husband has joined the Army. He only left this morning.'

That afternoon, she made sandwiches and took the girls to North Park for a picnic. Mary and Hester seemed friends again, though they argued incessantly. When they reached the park, they made straight for the swings, Queenie too. At first, she didn't quite know what to do, but in no time she was swinging higher than the others, dangerously so, a look of pure daring on her peaked face. Laura had to tell her to slow down a bit.

'You might hurt yourself, dear.'

'All right, Laura.' She'd been told to call her Laura, not Mrs Oliver. Laura preferred to be regarded as an elder sister rather than a substitute mother. Queenie was gradually coming out of her shell, getting more outgoing by the day. It must make a change, to be treated with kindness, aware that people cared, and have two little girls fighting constantly for your attention. Over the last emotional few days, Laura had grown very fond of her and wasn't too keen on letting her live with Vera. She'd very much like Queenie to stay. Mary wouldn't be too pleased, having decided, after all, that she wanted Queenie for a sister, but only to spite Hester. They seemed determined to rub each other up the wrong way. Till she'd met Mary, Hester had been a docile child. It was rare she'd played with other children, but when she had, they'd got on fine. Laura hoped she wasn't being unfair by placing the blame for the fights on Mary, who'd been completely spoiled by Vera and Albert and her eight big brothers. She seemed to regard Hester as a rival, rather than a friend.

Laura sat on a bench where she could keep an eye on the girls and wondered what Roddy was doing. He'd probably already been issued with a uniform, his worldly possessions transferred to a kit bag, and be on his way to a training camp, which could be anywhere in the country.

There was a rumbling noise from behind and she turned to see an Army lorry entering the gates. It stopped and half a dozen soldiers leapt out and unloaded a large gun. Vera had said there would be an ak-ak battery in the park, and she thought it obscene that a gun had been placed so close to where children played. It was from this very spot that Bootle would be defended when enemy planes attacked.

Laura glanced fearfully at her daughter. Hester was swinging gently, eyes closed, her face dreamy. Am I being selfish by wanting to stay? she asked herself. She didn't want to be evacuated, spend the war sheltering in the countryside with nothing to think about except Roddy. It would be much more bearable if she had a job to occupy her mind, which undoubtedly *was* selfish. She was putting her own needs before those of an innocent child. Hester would be given no say in the matter. Her safety, whether she lived or died, was entirely in the hands of her mother. Laura groaned and supposed she had no choice. She wasn't prepared to let Hester be evacuated on her own and if she stayed and was killed, she would never forgive herself and doubted if Roddy would either.

Laura had become addicted to the wireless, listening to every news bulletin, praying that war would somehow be averted, but each bulletin only seemed to bring it nearer. On Tuesday, it was announced that place names visible from the air had to be removed, including the names of railway stations. By Thursday, it appeared the country was on the very brink when the government ordered evacuation of the population living in unsafe areas to start the very next day. She ran across to see Vera, who looked very grave, having just heard the news on her own wireless.

'I haven't packed a thing,' Laura wailed. 'I don't know where to go, what to do. I don't know who's organising the evacuation, where we'll be sent. I don't know anything.' She'd put off finding out, hoping there would never be the need.

'The WVS are arranging it, the Women's Voluntary Service,' Vera said calmly. 'Be at St Joan of Arc's by nine o'clock tomorrer and they'll put you on a bus to Wales.'

'But Wales is the back of beyond!'

'That's the best place to be in a war, luv. I've a favour to ask.' Vera leaned forward in the chair, shoulders hunched. Laura sensed that what she was about to say had taken a lot of thought. 'Me and Albert talked about it last night. We'd like you to take our Mary with you. At least we'll know our girl will be safe, if not our lads.'

'Of course I will. Oh, but I'll miss you so much!' She wanted to fling her arms around Vera's neck and have a good cry.

'And I'll miss you, Laura, luv.' Vera sniffed pathetically. 'So many people leaving! It's as if the whole world's going away. One good thing, Queenie can have Mary's bed and there'll be no need to move things round.'

'She went after a cleaning job this morning, Queenie. Some doctor's house in Merton Road.' Laura wrinkled her nose. 'She could do better than that, but no one will employ her because of her arm. They think she won't be able to cope, yet it hardly bothers her at all – her handwriting is far better than mine. She's very intelligent and responsible too, though I wish it was me going after a job, not her.'

'Why not . . .' Vera paused and shrugged. 'Oh, never mind, it was a daft idea.'

'Tell me what the idea is and I'll judge if it was daft.'

'I just thought,' Vera said, slightly embarrassed, 'why not let Queenie go with the girls instead of you?'

Laura didn't answer for a moment, letting the idea sink in. 'That's not daft,' she said eventually. 'That's not daft at all. In fact, it's a marvellous idea!' Her enthusiasm mounted. 'It would solve all our problems. I mean *my* problems. I can stay in Liverpool and do my bit. Hester and Mary will be thrilled. It would be like an adventure for them – and Queenie. Oh, Vera, you're a genius! Why didn't *I* think of it?'

'Because,' Vera said smugly, 'you're not a genius like me. Mind you, you'd better ask Queenie first. She mightn't be as taken with the idea as we are.'

Queenie returned, very forlorn. She was wearing Laura's school frock that she'd long grown out of. The hem had been taken up and the waist made smaller. It was still too big, but at least she'd looked respectable for the interview if you ignored the tattered plimsolls. 'The lady didn't want me. She was very cross and said I was wasting her time.'

'She doesn't sound a very nice lady.' Laura wanted to run as far as Merton Road and give the woman a piece of her mind.

'No, but it was a job. I'll never get one at this rate.'

'Come in the kitchen. I've made tea. I want to talk to you about something.' Queenie followed, dragging her heels. Laura sat her down, put the tea in front of her, and said, 'I have a job for you, if you're willing to do it.' To her astonishment, the girl looked annoyed before she'd had a chance to explain what the job entailed.

'I couldn't take money off you,' she said stiffly. 'If you want me to clean, I'll do it for nothing.'

'It's not cleaning, dear. It's not even a proper job, and all you'll get is a bit of pocket money.' She told her what she and Vera had in mind. 'Of all the people we know, you're the only one we'd trust to look after Hester and Mary. I understand Wales is very pretty and it shouldn't be for long. They say the war won't last more than a few months and then everything will be back to normal.'

'But you won't be coming with us?'

'I'll be staying here. I want to start work as soon as I possibly can.'

Laura was startled when Queenie burst into tears. 'I'd sooner stay with you,' she sobbed. 'I don't care about the bombs. As long as I was with you, I wouldn't care.'

'But Queenie, love,' Laura put her arm around the girl's thin shoulders, 'that's not possible. If you don't go with Hester and Mary, I shall have to go myself.'

'Then why can't I go with all of you? Why can't you work in Wales?'

'Because, because . . .' It was a perfectly reasonable question and Laura couldn't think of an answer other than the plain, honest truth. 'Because, love, I don't want to. I want to do war work, not stand behind the counter of the village shop, that's if they'd have me. It's why I'm asking you to take my place. And I'd like to think *you're* safe too.'

Queenie sniffed a few times, then suddenly nodded, very grown up. 'All right, I'll go. But when we come back,' she said shyly, 'can I stay with you? I don't want to live with Vera. She's nice, but their Tommy makes fun of me arm every time he sees me. Most children do, but he's one o' the worst.'

'There'll always be a place for you with this family, Queenie. Oh, come here!' She took the girl in her arms and gave her an affectionate hug. 'Now, drink your tea. We've a lot to do if you and Hester are to be ready for Wales by morning.'

There were two more frocks in the wardrobe that she'd grown out of and had been keeping to cut down for Hester. She altered them to fit Queenie instead and wished she had a sewing machine. It would have taken a fraction of the time.

Her mind was racing as she sewed. Queenie badly needed new underwear. She only had one of everything and they were mostly in rags. And those disgusting plimsolls needed replacing. Did she have a coat? Laura picked up her purse and stared at the contents, biting her lip as she wondered when the allowance from the Army would arrive and how quickly she would get a job and earn money of her own. She could just about afford to pay for the underwear, but not shoes. It would be some time before Queenie needed a coat.

Vera arrived, panting, to ask if Laura had a suitcase.

'Only a big one. It would be too heavy to carry once it's full of clothes. I've been thinking about that myself. I suppose we'll have to make parcels and tie them with string.'

'Right. I'll sort out some brown paper.'

'We've got plenty of string.' Laura groaned and stretched her fingers, they were becoming stiff. 'I've been sewing too fast. I was just about to despatch Queenie to buy herself some vests and pants and a couple of petticoats.'

'Lord almighty!' Vera gasped. 'I'd forgotten all about

that. She needs kitting out, doesn't she? She can't possibly go wearing them old pumps. What'd people think? I'll take her along Strand Road, buy her a few odds and sods meself. I'll get our Mary some new knickers at the same time.'

'And I'll buy a bottle of Tizer and make sandwiches for them to eat on the way. Oh, and I must make a little dolly bag for Queenie to put the ration books and identity cards in.'

Two coaches stood in the blazing sunshine outside St Joan of Arc's next morning when the small party arrived, to find a queue of mothers and children slowly making its way into the school playground. Just inside the gates, two uniformed WVS women were seated behind a trestle table taking down particulars of would-be evacuees.

'Queenie Tate, Hester Oliver and Mary Monaghan,' Laura said crisply when their turn came.

'Address?'

'Queenie and Hester are twenty-two Glover Street, Mary's number seventeen.'

'I can't guarantee they'll all be put together.'

Vera pushed her way forward. 'They'd better had be,' she said threateningly. 'If they're not, then they're coming home. You'd better make a note of that on your list.' She turned to Queenie. 'If they try to separate you, you're to come back straight away. You've got enough for the fare.'

'Yes, Mrs Monaghan,' Queenie whispered. She'd looked wretchedly miserable all morning. Waves of guilt washed over Laura. She was *still* being selfish, foisting the onus for keeping her daughter safe on shoulders far narrower and weaker than her own.

'Perhaps I should go with them,' she muttered. 'We could go tomorrow instead.'

'No, luv.' Vera shook her head. 'If you're worried about Queenie, she'll be far better off in a nice place looking after two little girls than cleaning some uppity woman's house. The responsibility will be the making of her, you'll see.'

'I do hope so, Vera.'

'Will mothers kindly say goodbye to their children now, then wait outside the gates, please?' a WVS woman called.

Laura bent and kissed Hester's excited face. She looked very sweet in her straw bonnet and best frock, her gas mask over her shoulder and a little crocheted purse looped over her wrist.

'Here's your clothes, sweetheart.' Laura had plaited the string handle to make it easier to carry. She and Mary seemed to think they were going on an extended holiday. 'Look after each other, won't you? And be good for Queenie. Oh, Lord!' She wanted to weep. Something she had thought impossible had happened. Within the space of a few days, she was losing her entire family. 'I'll come and see you as soon as I can.'

'I'll be very good, Mummy. I promise. You'll tell Daddy where I am, won't you, so he can send me a letter? Queenie will read it to me.'

'Of course, sweetheart.' She gave her daughter a little shove, and put her arms around Queenie, pressing the girl's head against her breast, unable to speak. Then she went outside and joined the mothers clutching the railings, unable to take their eyes off the children who were being sent to live with strangers many miles away. She saw Queenie take the girls' hands and hold them tightly, as if determined never to let go. Vera came outside and stood beside her, tears streaming down her cheeks.

There was a shout. The children froze and began to form in lines. They shuffled towards the coaches and climbed aboard, filling both. A few mothers rushed forward and banged on the windows. 'Where are you, Johnny, lad? Wave tara to your mam,' one screamed.

The first coach drove away, then the second. Laura looked frantically for Hester.

'There they are!' Vera nudged her sharply, almost breaking a rib. 'They're all together in the back seat. Wave, Laura, wave.'

Laura waved and waved until the tiny figures grew smaller and smaller and she couldn't see them any more. It wasn't until then she realised she was still holding the bag with the bottle of Tizer and the sandwiches she'd made.

There was a letter on the mat from Roddy when she got home. She opened it listlessly. He was in a place called Catterick, but she wasn't to write back because he was about to be transferred elsewhere. 'I'm being sent for officer training,' he wrote. He finished by saying he hoped she'd made arrangements for them to be evacuated. For a while, they would have to correspond through Vera, as neither would know where the other was.

Laura folded the letter and put it back in the envelope. She must find a place to keep all his letters. One day, she might want to read them again, though this, the first he'd ever written her, was surprisingly impersonal.

The house felt unnaturally quiet and, for a change, the street was empty of children, many on their way to Wales or other parts of the country. For the first time in her life she was entirely alone and, although it was her own choice, she wasn't sure if she could stand it. She switched on the wireless for the ten-thirty bulletin, which was due soon.

When it came, the news was chilling. Hitler had marched his troops into Poland, a country that Great Britain was bound by treaty to protect. Now there was no going back. To all intents and purposes, the war had already begun.

Chapter 4

The girls' breathing was gentle now, steady, a sign that both were fast asleep. Queenie sat, fully dressed, on the bed. Her head felt very strange, empty inside, as if her mind hadn't grasped the remarkable things that had happened since Mam had gone, which was remarkable enough in itself. At first, when there'd been enough to eat, she hadn't minded being on her own, not being screamed at and told she was as thick as two short planks. Then the food had run out as well as the few bob Mam had left, and she'd been terrified out of her wits, not knowing what to do. She supposed it was because she was thick. It had taken days before she could pluck up the courage to go downstairs and tell Laura, driven there by hunger and fear.

From that moment on, she'd been glad that Mam had gone and hardly missed her at all. It was lovely being part of Laura's family. 'I'm only seven years older, so you're to think of me as your sister,' Laura had said. As for Roddy, he was the nicest, handsomest man in the whole world and Queenie was a little bit in love with him.

For the first time in her life she hadn't felt stupid. Roddy had said how well she read and Laura had admired her handwriting, whereas at school everyone had made fun of the way she wrote, her hand all twisted, and it had turned out shaky and misspelt. The teachers never asked Queenie Tate a question, assuming she wouldn't know the answer, yet she nearly always did. She enjoyed lessons and had taken everything in. She could do fractions and knew what an adjective was and that Captain Cook had discovered Australia and Elizabeth I was the daughter of Henry VIII who'd had six wives.

But the lovely life with Laura had swiftly come to an end and now she was in a strange house in Wales with two funny little girls who seemed so anxious for her to like them. It was another new experience. Until then, no one had ever cared whether she liked them or not. Now, all of a sudden, her opinion on all sorts of things was apparently very important and it made her feel terribly confused, not sure whether she was an adult or a child.

All the way to Wales in the hot, smelly coach, which felt as if it was taking four days, not just four hours, they'd been vying with each other to capture her attention.

'Queenie! Queenie! Look at that house,' Mary had squealed. 'It's pink. I didn't know houses could be pink.'

'See that tree. Queenie, see that tree!' Hester had nearly fallen off the seat in excitement. 'It's *huge*, like the spreading chestnut tree in the song.'

Mary had spied a castle, but Hester argued that it was just a big house. 'Castles have big, round chimneys on each corner.'

'Turrets,' Queenie said. 'They're called turrets.'

'That had turrets, didn't it, Queenie?'

'I didn't see it,' she'd said tactfully. She must make sure she treated them fairly. The truth was, she liked Hester best. Mary was a show-off and could be nasty if she didn't get her own way. She could imagine an older Mary making fun of her arm as their Tommy had done all the time. Hester was a solemn, gentle little girl, until

Mary provoked her, when she could very easily fly off the handle.

By the time they'd reached Caerdovey, the small town where they were to be billeted, half the children were fast asleep – Hester and Mary in each other's arms – and the rest were in tears. Apart from the WVS lady sitting at the front, there were two other women, both with toddlers too young to have come on their own. One of the women was sobbing quietly. She wished she hadn't come, she said, and wanted to go home. She didn't like Wales. 'It's too big,' she sniffed.

Queenie didn't like Wales either. The scenery was too vast, too overwhelming. The dark green hills blocked out the sky, and the deep valleys were choked with trees, untouched by the sun, not a human being, not a house in sight. She longed for Glover Street, for the safety of bricks and mortar. Most of all she longed to be back with Laura.

It had been a relief when the coach had turned off the road and they began to pass places where people actually lived, only a few at first on each side of the road; bungalows and cottages and large houses in their own grounds, but getting closer together all the time, until they came to little streets running off the main road, groups of terraced houses, shops, a church, Caerdovey Town Hall, a garage, eventually stopping in a little sun-scorched square with a war memorial in the centre.

The first coach had got there before them and was empty, most of the children having already been taken to their billets. Only a few stragglers remained, clutching their parcels of clothes and looking pathetic and lost. One little boy had wet his pants and was bawling his head off. The newcomers were shown into a hall with a plaque over the door proclaiming it had been donated to the town by Councillor Wilfred Jones in 1928. They were given a welcome drink of lemonade and a fairy cake while a lady with a lovely sing-song voice read out their names.

'Here, miss,' Queenie called, when she came to Queenie Tate, Mary Monaghan and Hester Oliver.

'You're to go with Mrs Davies, dears,' the woman said. 'She'll drive you to the Mertons' house.'

Mrs Davies came up. Her red face was streaked with perspiration and she smelled of mothballs. 'Isn't it hot?' she gasped, but didn't wait for an answer, ushering them back outside into a little black car, like a box on wheels. Queenie sat in the front; the girls, wide-eyed and plainly terrified by now, got in the back.

She was the district nurse, Mrs Davies explained when they set off, but had taken the day off to help with the evacuees, seeing as she had a car. The billets had been arranged weeks ago, Caerdovey was very well organised, she said proudly. 'Rather more children have turned up than expected, but I'm sure we'll cope. Most people are only too willing to do their bit and take evacuees, but a few have had to be forcefully told where their duty lay, including Mrs Merton. Mind you, she's not Welsh,' she added, as if this explained everything.

It didn't bode well for the future, Queenie reckoned, if they were being placed with a woman who didn't want them.

'You won't see much of her,' Mrs Davies went on. 'She owns a pottery factory on the other side of Caerdovey and she's out most of the time. Mr Merton has never put in an appearance, so she might be a widow, or she might not. No one knows, not even Gwen Hughes, the housekeeper. Gwen lives on the premises and she's the one who'll be looking after you. You'll find her a bit taciturn at first, but she'll be fine once she gets to know you.'

Queenie didn't know what tacky-turn meant, but got the drift. She noticed houses were getting sparse again. They must be approaching the other end of town.

'Here we are,' Mrs Davies sang, drawing up outside a large, grim, grey stone residence with small windows draped with blackout. Behind the rickety fence, there was a small patch of grass, yellow and parched, and there was a name, not a number on the plain, wooden door: The Old School House.

They followed Mrs Davies through a gate at the side into a large expanse of more parched grass surrounded by a high, grey wall covered with ivy. A small woman was unpegging washing off a line strung between two trees bearing hundreds of apples.

'Gwen,' Mrs Davies called when the woman appeared not to notice their arrival. 'I've brought your evacuees.'

The woman turned. Her face was as grey as the house and her hair was gathered in an untidy bun on top of her head. The escaping strands had stuck to her neck with the heat. She didn't look faintly pleased to see them, and approached, a mountain of clothes over her arm.

'Mrs Merton was hoping we'd only get one or two,' she said in a dull voice.

'Tell her she's lucky to only get three,' Mrs Davies said brusquely. She clearly had no time for Mrs Merton. 'She's got six spare bedrooms, she could have been landed with twice or three times as many. And if you'd seen the state of some of the children, in rags and bringing not a stitch of clothing with them, poor little beggars, you can also tell her she's lucky to get such nice, respectable girls. As you can see, they're all wearing hats,' she added as if this was the ultimate sign of respectability. 'Now, I hope you've got some food ready, Gwen. I bet they're starving after that long journey.'

'There's a lamb stew on the stove and I've made a fruit cake,' Gwen Hughes muttered.

'Gwen's fruit cakes are famous throughout this part of Wales, so you're in for a treat,' Mrs Davies told them as proudly as if she'd made the cakes herself. 'Two more things, a priest is coming to the Councillor Jones hall at eleven o'clock on Sunday to say Mass, though poor Councillor Jones would turn in his grave if he knew, him being strict Presbyterian like, but there isn't a Catholic church in Caerdovey. And school starts at nine on Monday in the same place.'

'Thank you,' Queenie said politely. Mrs Davies must have assumed they were all Catholics because they'd come on the St Joan of Arc bus. She didn't bother to disabuse her, and Hester and Mary seemed to have been struck dumb.

'You'd better come indoors,' Gwen said in a surly voice when Mrs Davies had gone, remarking that she'd never known it quite so hot as it was today.

Mary found her voice and whispered that she wanted to go to the lavatory, so Gwen took them through a dreary kitchen with a tiled floor and roughly plastered walls, and up a narrow wooden staircase. She pointed out the lavatory, then showed them where they were to sleep, in a long narrow room at the back of the house with only two beds, a wardrobe and a chest of drawers.

'I'll fetch another bed down from the attic,' Gwen said wearily. 'It'll only be a trestle, but it'll have to do. Would you like the stew now, or would you sooner wait till later and just have cake and a cup of tea?'

They decided they'd sooner wait for the stew, so Gwen went to put the kettle on, Mary to the lavatory, and Queenie took off her hat – Laura's straw boater that she'd worn for school, now trimmed with pink ribbon rather than the chiffon scarf, which had been thought to look too dressy. The ribbon matched her pink and white flowered frock, which had also been Laura's. She looked down in awe at the white canvas sandals on her tiny feet – Vera had given her a bottle of white powdery liquid to clean them with. The transformation of her wardrobe, from one faded, too small dress and a pair of tatty pumps, to such a grand, modish outfit, was another of the remarkable things she was having difficulty getting used to. Mrs Davies had spoken to her as if she was a normal human being, as if she was no longer the Queenie Tate whom everyone had looked down on at school, an expression of disgust on their sneering faces.

Mary invited them to come and see the lavatory. 'There's a bath in there as well and it's not tin like our bath at home.'

The bath was white enamel with claw feet and had a tap at the end. Hester recalled they'd once lived in a house that had a bath just the same. 'But Mummy said the water was hardly ever hot enough.' Her bottom lip trembled. 'I think I want my mummy, Queenie. I don't like this house.'

'*I* think it's all right, so there!' Mary made a face and told Hester she was a cry baby but, that night, after they'd eaten the cake and, later, the stew and more cake, played catch in the garden with the ball they'd brought with them, after Gwen had suggested they go to bed, even though it was only half past six, and Queenie had obediently agreed because perhaps it was the sort of thing people did in Wales, it was Mary who collapsed into a paroxysm of tears. She wanted her mam, her dad, her brothers, her dolls, her own bed. She wanted to go home, she sobbed. She hated Wales, and in particular Caerdovey. She hated Gwen. She hated the food, which had in fact been very nice, especially the cake, and she'd eaten every mouthful. She hated everything and everybody.

'There, there,' Queenie soothed, wanting to cry every bit as much. Then Hester had joined in the tears, and she'd had to flit from bed to bed, telling them they'd soon get used to it.

'Anyroad, aren't your mams coming to see you in a few weeks' time? And on Monday, you'll be going to school,' she said comfortingly, 'There'll be loads of children there from Bootle. Two girls from Glover Street were on the coach with us.'

Eventually, they fell asleep, worn out, and Queenie was left to sit on the bed with her own thoughts. Laura had given her some books to read – *The Railway Children, Little Women* and *Good Wives* – but the curtains were drawn and she didn't want to turn on the amazing electric light and risk disturbing the girls. She hugged her knees and almost wished her mam hadn't gone away, that she'd never met Laura, and her life was back the way it had always been, but the feeling quickly passed. She threw back her shoulders. From now on, she would have to be very brave, very strong, and watch over her charges, make sure they came to no harm.

She got up and changed into one of the pretty nightdresses Vera had bought. It was white wincyette with a pattern of rosebuds and rather stiff. Vera had said it would go soft when it was washed, but there hadn't been time before they left Bootle. There were no hangers in the wardrobe, so she neatly folded her clothes and put them in a drawer. About to get into bed, she heard voices downstairs, so went over to the door, making no sound in her bare feet, opened it carefully, and crept out on to the landing.

The inside of The Old School House, what Queenie had seen of it so far, was made entirely of wood. Except for the kitchen, everywhere else, the floors, the walls, the ceilings, was lined with strips of natural wood, turned darker by the years so that they were now a dingy oatmeal colour. It was like being inside a great big tree. There were no carpets anywhere, no mats, no lino, not even on the two sets of stairs; the little narrow staircase that led from the kitchen, which the girls had used, or the much wider one in the hall.

Queenie peeped through the banisters and saw a very broad woman with a tough, mannish face, wearing a severely tailored costume and heavy, lace-up shoes, talking to Gwen Hughes. Gwen's shoulders were bowed and she looked dejected, as if she were expecting a tongue lashing. Queenie knew exactly how she felt, having been in receipt of many herself in her short life.

'Three!' the woman spat. 'You should have refused to take them.'

'I couldn't very well, Mrs Merton. Edna Davies said we could have had more. And as she pointed out, they're all nice girls, well-dressed and clean, like. The older one's got something wrong with her arm.'

'I don't care how nice they are,' Mrs Merton said brutally in her hard, gruff voice. 'I don't like strangers in my house. Where have you put them?'

'In one of the corner rooms at the back,' Gwen said humbly.

'Well, make sure they're kept out of my way. They must use the back stairs and stay in the kitchen. I don't want them in this part of the house, do you understand?'

'Yes, Mrs Merton.' Gwen shuffled away, Mrs Merton disappeared into one of the rooms at the front, and Queenie went to bed, wishing she hadn't eavesdropped. It had made her feel more miserable than ever.

When she woke, it was barely light and Hester and Mary

were dead to the world. Queenie knew she wouldn't fall asleep again, she felt too wide awake. She knelt on the bed, lifted a corner of blackout, and peered through the window. To her astonishment, she could see a vast expanse of water, glistening dully in the early morning glow, stretching as far as the eye could see, and preceded by a strip of flat, golden sand.

She hadn't known that Caerdovey was on the coast. She quickly got dressed, including the hat that made her look so respectable and a cardigan in case it was chilly, and went down the narrow stairs into the kitchen.

The kitchen door was unlocked. Feeling daring, Queenie went outside and through the gate at the side, emerging in the main road. There wasn't a soul in sight. The small town was fast asleep, no one to ask how you got to the shore. She walked along the deserted road and eventually, between two houses, saw a narrow path with a thick hedge either side that she assumed was a public footpath. Queenie pushed her way through the sharp, dew-drenched branches, disturbing the birds who chirruped indignantly at being woken early, emerging in a field of rough, overgrown grass scattered with clumps of yellow dandelions and sloping slightly upwards. Ahead, the water glimmered invitingly, although, from here, the shore was invisible. The sky was pearly grey, without a cloud in sight. This vast, alien world was entirely different to the one she'd been used to, but she didn't find it frightening, not like the gloomy scenery of the previous day. There was a tingle in the air, which smelt fresh and lemony. She breathed deeply and could feel it reaching right down to her lungs.

Now she was at the back of the houses on the main road. She could see The Old School House and the window of the room where Hester and Mary still slept. At least she hoped they did. They'd be frightened if they woke up and found her gone. There was a door in the grey wall at the bottom of the garden, so she hadn't needed to come such a long way round.

The field ended abruptly in a steep incline composed of hard sand and the occasional gorse bush. It wasn't very deep, but didn't look easily negotiable until she spied, some distance away, a series of wooden steps curving down to the shore. She had just reached the steps when the sun rose, touching the water at its furthest point, and sweeping rapidly towards her, as if a dark cloak had been removed to reveal a sea as bright and as sparkling as diamonds.

Queenie gasped. She had never witnessed such a breathtaking sight before. The wet sand gleamed like satin and it met the water in a little ruff of snow-white foam. As the sun rose higher, the sea grew even brighter and the waves rippled and twinkled like stars.

She ran down the steps, tore off her shoes, and raced towards the water, her toes sinking into the wet sand, making a funny squelching noise. The water was icy cold and she shrieked, as strange, chilling sensations swept through her bones, from her feet to the top of her head, making her whole body shudder with a mixture of pain and delight. She stamped her feet and the water exploded in little silvery spurts.

'Enjoying yourself, Queenie?' said a voice.

She shrieked again, this time in fright, and looked up to see Jimmy Nicholls, who'd been in the class below her in Salisbury Road school, watching her with amusement. He was thirteen, a big lad, the biggest in the school, who always looked a bit ridiculous in his too-short trousers. There were scabs on his huge, red knees and he wore a tattered jersey and shoes with the toes almost out. He had a nice, dreamy face, and his short brown hair had been chopped off with the same disregard for appearance as hers.

'What are you doing here?' she asked resentfully. She'd liked being on her own, being herself for once.

'Been evacuated, same as you,' he replied. 'Staying over there, I am,' he jerked his head towards a row of cottages, 'with some old lady. Our Tess and Pete are next door. That's the only reason I came. Pete's only two and Mam didn't want him coming with just our Tess. She's only six. Mam daren't give up her job to come an' all, not with our dad out of work 'cos of his lungs. Me, I'd sooner have stayed home and joined the Army.'

'You're much too young. They'd never have taken you.'

'Everyone ses I'm big for me age. I'd have tried, given it a go. What's the water like?'

'Cold. Is this the Atlantic Ocean?' Ships sailed from Liverpool to America across the Atlantic, but she had no idea where it began or ended.

'Nah, it's the Irish Sea, or so my old lady ses, and she ought to know.' He was removing his shoes and a pair of socks with holes in the toes and heels. Seconds later, he joined her in the water.

'Bloody hell, Queenie!' he gasped. 'It's freezing.'

'You soon get used to it.'

'I don't think I'll bother.' He stamped out again. Back on the glistening sand, he regarded her silently for a while, then said, 'You look different.'

Queenie didn't answer. She *felt* and no doubt looked different, too.

'You don't sound the same, either,' Jimmy said baldly. ''Fact, I can't remember ever hearing you talk before.'

'I can't remember hearing *you* talk, either,' she lied. He had a boomingly loud voice, as deep as a man's, that was difficult to miss, but the new Queenie Tate wasn't prepared to be put at a disadvantage.

'Will you be going to school on Monday?' he asked.

'No. I'm fourteen. I've finished school.' She wondered what she would do with herself all day without Hester and Mary.

'I'm only thirteen, but I'm not going. I've had enough of school. Anyroad, it's Catholic and I'm C of E. I told the lady who brought us I'd left, that I was only here 'cos of our Tess and Pete.'

'I'm only here because of Hester Oliver and Mary Monaghan. I'd've far sooner stayed in Bootle.'

'Me too.'

They grinned at each other and Queenie felt as if she'd passed another milestone. She was close to making a friend her own age, something that had never happened before.

'I'll have to be getting back,' she said.

'I'm not in any rush. I'll walk with you. Where are you billeted?'

'That grey house over there.'

'It looks a grand place,' he remarked.

'It's dead miserable inside. I'd sooner be in Glover Street any day.'

'Me dad thinks it'll all be over by Christmas and we'll be home again.'

'I hope so,' Queenie said with feeling.

They strolled in companionable silence until they reached The Old School House where the door in the wall refused to budge when she tried to open it. Jimmy pushed her aside and attacked it with his shoulder and the door opened a few inches.

'It's covered with ivy, that's what's stopping it,' he announced and gave it several more shoves, eventually flinging his very large self against it. The door opened and he fell inside.

'Did you hurt yourself?'

'Nah. What's that place over there?' He pointed to a small grey building at the side of the house.

'I dunno.' She hadn't noticed it before. It was like a miniature house with the same pointed slate roof.

'Shall we have a gander?'

'I'll see if Gwen's up yet. She's the housekeeper and she mightn't like us bringing strangers back.' Mrs Merton would definitely disapprove, but was unlikely to be around so early.

'I'm not a stranger.'

'Gwen's never seen you before, has she?' Queenie crossed the wet grass and went into the kitchen, which was as dead and deserted as when she'd left it. There was no sign of Gwen. There was no sign of Jimmy Nicholls either when she returned outside.

'Oi!' he called and she saw he'd opened a door in the small building that had aroused his curiosity. 'It's a garage,' he said, 'and there's a car inside. When I grow up, I'm gonna buy meself a car and take me mam and dad out for rides.'

'It must be Mrs Merton's.' She followed him inside and saw that there was room for two cars, although the other space was empty. Jimmy had climbed into the passenger seat and was clutching the steering wheel, pretending to drive, making funny engine noises. She felt worried, half expecting Mrs Merton to throw open the double doors at the front, and demand to know what was going on.

'You'd better get out,' she said nervously. 'Someone might come.'

'All right, Queenie,' he said easily. 'I wonder what's upstairs?' He made for the staircase at the back, more like a ladder, that led to a square opening in the ceiling, and had already reached the top, his head poking through the opening, before Queenie found the breath to ask if he was always this nosy?

'Always,' he assured her. 'Dad ses if our name was Parker, they'd've called me Nosy. Come and have a decko. Someone used to live up here.'

'P'raps they still do.'

'Nah, it's full of dust.' He heaved himself upwards and disappeared.

Queenie climbed the ladder and found herself in a large, square room with a high, peaked ceiling and diamond-shaped windows at each end covered in cobwebs. It held a bed with a striped mattress, an easy chair, chest of drawers, a table and two wooden chairs, and two tea chests. Everything was covered with a thick layer of dust. It must have been a squeeze, getting everything through the opening. Jimmy was already rooting through the tea chests.

'It's nothing but rubbish,' he said. 'Old clothes and stuff. Eh, we can come up here when it's raining.'

'We?'

'You can come to my old lady's if you want. She said I can bring me friends. She makes these dead good biccies. They're called shortbreads. She didn't mind me eating the lot.' He sank into the easy chair, raising a cloud of dust.

'I think you'd better go,' she said. 'I should see if Hester and Mary are awake.'

'Okey-dokey,' he said equably. 'Will you be going to the sands later?'

'Yes.' Hester and Mary would love it. They could take the ball with them.

'See you there then, Queenie. Tara.'

'Tara, Jimmy.'

★

Jimmy was waiting, as promised, outside the row of cottages where he lived with his old lady, on Monday morning when she took the girls to school. They waved to each other. His sister, Tess, waited with him. By now, having played with each other all Saturday and Sunday, they knew each other well.

Tess was six and tall, with big bones, like her brother. She had a broad, flat face and dead straight hair, which she kept secured behind her ears with hairclips, making her look very severe. Her green frock was much too long and far too thick for such a warm day and her shoes were missing the laces. She was a moody girl who seemed to be in a permanent bad temper. Hester and Mary had decided that they didn't like her and Queenie wasn't so keen, either, though they all agreed that Jimmy was the gear; good-humoured, kind, showing immense patience with his horrid sister and his unhappy little brother. Pete was badly missing his mam.

'You're late,' Tess grumbled when they came up. 'Anyroad, I don't see why we should have to walk such a long way. They should send a charabanc for us.'

'Shurrup, sis. It'll do you good.'

'And we're not late,' Mary felt bound to point out. 'Gwen said it'd only take half an hour and we left in plenty of time.'

'What's that you've got?' Jimmy asked Queenie when the little procession set off, Tess lagging sulkily behind.

'It's a letter for Laura. I promised to write straight away. I did it last night.' She'd told Laura that Caerdovey was very pretty, that they hadn't seen much of the woman they were staying with, but the housekeeper, Gwen Hughes, made lovely food and had started off all tacky-turn, but was gradually coming round as she got to know them. It was Gwen who'd told them she'd heard on the wireless that the war had started for proper.

. . . Hester and Mary cried a bit when we first came, but they're all right now. Yesterday and today, we went to the shore and paddled in the Irish Sea. We also made sandcastles and played ball.

She described Jimmy, Tess and Pete, and mentioned that the girls were going to school next day.

Mary went to Mass this morning so me and Hester went with her. It was very mysterious. The priest didn't speak English so I've no idea what he was on about. Hester sends her love to you and Roddy, and Mary sends her love to her mam and dad and all her brothers. They are both being very well behaved.

Your friend,
Queenie Tate

'Can you write proper with your funny arm?' Jimmy enquired.

'I can write very well, thank you,' Queenie replied coldly.

'Was it like that when you were born?'

'I dunno. Me mam wouldn't talk about it when I asked.'

They arrived at the Councillor Jones Hall. She kissed the girls tara and promised to meet them at going home time, which, after asking one of the teachers, Miss Larkin, she learnt was half past three.

'I've got to buy a stamp for me letter,' she announced when only her and Jimmy were left. They found the Post Office and had to wait outside a few minutes for it to open. The stamp bought, the letter was placed carefully in the red pillar box outside. Queenie felt a glow of pride. It was the first letter she'd ever written and she imagined it being carried from Wales to Bootle by various means and eventually dropping on to the mat in twenty-two Glover Street.

'I've promised to weed me old lady's garden. She's getting a bit past it, like. Shall we walk back along the shore?'

'All right.'

'Would you like a hand with the weeding?' Queenie asked when they reached the wooden steps.

'I wouldn't say no.' Jimmy looked pleased. 'I dunno the difference between weeds and flowers.'

Neither did Queenie. The old lady turned out to have a name, Mrs Jones. (There seemed to be an awful lot of Joneses in Caerdovey.) She came outside and told them what to pull out. When they'd finished, she gave them a cup of tea and produced a plate of shortbreads, which she'd made especially for Jimmy, seeing as he liked them so much. Jimmy went next door to see how Pete was, and returned to say he was fast asleep and not to be disturbed.

'Mrs Jones is very nice,' Queenie remarked later when they were on their way to The Old School House.

'She's a decent enough old stick,' Jimmy agreed. 'Being evacuated isn't as bad as I'd thought, though I've a feeling that before long I'll be bored out of me skull. What'll we do now?'

'I've no idea.'

'Tell you what, let's give that room over your garage a good tart up. We can turn it into a den. I've always wanted a den.'

'What do you do in a den?'

Jimmy shrugged and said vaguely, 'I dunno. Read and stuff, talk, play games.'

'I'm not sure if Gwen'd let us.'

'You could ask her. It won't do no harm to ask.'

Gwen looked faintly alarmed when Queenie entered

the kitchen accompanied by the huge, shambling figure of Jimmy Nicholls. The alarm turned to surprise when she was asked if they could turn the room over the garage into a den.

'You see, there's nowhere for us to play if it rains,' Queenie pointed out. Mrs Merton had said the evacuees were only allowed in the kitchen and the bedroom, though she couldn't very well mention that and admit that she'd eavesdropped.

'Did someone used to live up there?' Jimmy asked.

'Yes.' For some reason, Gwen's sad eyes grew even sadder. 'During the war, the last one, when this was still a school. His name was Hugh Jones and he looked after the garden and did all the odd jobs. He was only a lad, not much older than you when he first came.' She nodded at Jimmy. 'I was the cook in those days and I wasn't much older than you,' she said, looking at Queenie.

'I didn't know it had really been a school,' Queenie remarked.

'Why should you?' Gwen said tiredly. 'It was a boarding school, though most of the children were orphans. The Reverend Allsop ran it. He was very strict and used to beat them. It closed in nineteen twenty-five when he died and that's when Mrs Merton came to live here. She inherited the house and kept me on as housekeeper. She was his niece or something.'

'What happened to Hugh Jones?' Jimmy asked curiously.

'He was killed in the war, in the very last month. He was only eighteen.'

'That's a shame.' Queenie sensed she'd been rather fond of Hugh Jones.

Gwen's pale lips twisted ruefully. 'A terrible shame,'

she sighed. 'The room's never been used since. I don't suppose it'd hurt, you cleaning it up a bit.'

They were given a bucket of soapy water, a collection of rags and a stiff broom. Gwen loaned Queenie a pinny to keep her frock clean and said they'd find a watering can in the garage. 'Fill it up from the tap outside and sprinkle water on the floor, else you'll have dust all over the place.'

Two hours later, there wasn't a speck of dust to be seen in the den, as they had christened it. The floor had been swept and washed, the furniture wiped with a damp cloth, the ceiling brushed, and the windows cleaned and polished. Jimmy took the mattress and the cushions off the easy chair into the garden and thrashed them to within an inch of their lives.

'We can use this as a sofa,' he said, throwing the mattress back on to its frame.

'What about when it's dark? There's no light. We won't be able to see.'

'We'll use candles. I bet that's what Hugh Jones had.'

'I'll buy some this avvy, and a box of matches.' She took it for granted Jimmy didn't have any money, whereas Laura had given her five shillings pocket money. She had no idea how long it was supposed to last.

Jimmy was delving into one of the tea chests, flinging clothes all over the place, looking for a candleholder. 'Me mam's got this tin one with a handle. We use it to take to the lavvy in the dark. Eh, Queenie, I wonder if Gwen'd mind if I had some of these.' He held up a pair of corduroy trousers. 'They look like they'd fit me. There's some decent shirts an' all. How do I look in this?' He plonked a wide-brimmed felt hat on his head.

She laughed. 'You look like an explorer.'

'D'you think Gwen'd give us something to eat? I'm

bloody starving. After all, my old lady gave you some biccies.'

Gwen had already made them each a corned beef sandwich. She gave a little shriek when she saw Jimmy in the hat. 'You look just like him, like Hugh Jones,' she gasped. She offered to wash the trousers and a couple of shirts tomorrow. 'You may as well have them. I'm surprised they're not rotten by now.' She was obviously quite smitten with Jimmy. Most people seemed to be.

At three o'clock, Queenie had a quick wash and set off to collect the girls. Jimmy said he'd better go and see how their Pete was. 'Meet you back in the den tonight,' he said casually.

The den became Queenie's favourite place. It was where she read on dark afternoons – after giving Gwen a hand with the housework – sitting in the easy chair in front of the window, a candle flickering on the table. Jimmy usually joined her, bringing his treasured motor car magazine, three years old and coming to pieces. He studied it avidly, his lips forming the words as he read, occasionally asking the meaning of certain words. His dad had been a motor mechanic and was almost as mad about cars as Jimmy himself.

Much to her chagrin, Mary was finding it hard to learn to read. Queenie reckoned that somewhere in a house that used to be a school there must be a blackboard and some chalk. One Wednesday afternoon, the day that Gwen usually went to see her sister, she explored the rooms the girls had been forbidden to enter – Gwen had been very apologetic when she told them. Mrs Merton's living room was crammed with showy, old-fashioned furniture. There were tasselled curtains on the window and a rich red carpet on the floor. Another room turned out to be a study, with a big wooden desk and glass-fronted bookcases. There was no way of knowing if Mrs Merton used it now, or if this was how it had been left by the Reverend Allsop.

Two further rooms were empty, apart from a few items of furniture and several suitcases stacked on top of one another. The final room was twice, possibly three times as big as the others. Queenie felt as if time had stood still when she saw it was still laid out as a classroom. The rows of shabby desks with their dried-up inkwells had a spooky air, as if they'd only just been vacated. She felt the hairs prickle on her neck, half expecting a bell to ring and the children to return; little ghostly figures with their heads meekly bent, terrified they might be beaten by the Reverend Allsop, whom she imagined having dark eyebrows, almost joined together, and mutton chop whiskers. She opened a cupboard, found a blackboard and a lump of chalk, and hurried away, vowing never to enter the room again.

From then on, when Hester and Mary came home, the den became a classroom. Queenie would write words on the board for Mary to read.

'I know that already,' Hester would yawn. Laura had already taught her to read a little, which only made Mary crosser.

Not long after the lessons started, Tess began to turn up regularly, eventually bringing another girl, Brenda O'Toole. Queenie felt obliged to draw the line at Brenda, worried that the den might end up with as many pupils as the school. She taught the girls how to add up and take away, the two and three times tables, the alphabet from beginning to end, though only Hester could say it the whole way through without hesitation.

They'd been in Caerdovey for almost two months when Queenie arrived to collect the girls and found herself invited inside the Councillor Jones Hall by Miss

Larkin who'd taught in St Joan of Arc's. There were only two teachers, Miss Larkin and Mrs Waters, who was very old and had come out of retirement to do her bit, a lot of the younger teachers having joined the forces, leaving schools short of staff.

The hall had been split into two with screens, the five to eights in one half, the older children in the other.

'I understand you've been teaching some of the children to read and write?' Miss Larkin said.

'Yes. I'm sorry,' Queenie stammered, worried she was doing something wrong.

'Please don't be sorry. Mrs Waters and I are very impressed. We wondered if you could spare the time to come in, say two mornings a week, and give the little ones a lesson? Of course, if there wasn't a war on, such a thing would be seriously frowned upon by the authorities, but there *is* a war on, and Mrs Waters and I are trying to do the work of five teachers. Your help would be greatly appreciated.'

Queenie felt herself go dizzy. A vision of Mam sprang into her mind, sneering at her. 'You're thick, d'you know that, Queenie? I don't know what I did to deserve such a thick, useless daughter.' What would Mam say if she knew her useless daughter had been asked to *teach*? 'All right,' she said faintly.

Laura arrived unexpectedly on Saturday carrying a large suitcase. It was her third visit, although she was usually accompanied by Vera. 'The weather's getting cold and Vera and I suddenly realised you didn't have any heavy clothes,' she said breathlessly. 'I've brought Hester and Mary's winter coats, some thick jerseys and skirts, and stout shoes. I only hope they still fit. And there's stuff for you, Queenie, second-hand, but in perfect condition. I got everything from Paddy's Market, and I've made you a pretty mohair beret.'

'Why hasn't my mam come?' Mary asked indignantly.

'She couldn't take the day off at such short notice, dear.'

Surprising everyone, Vera had got a job and now worked behind the counter of a ship's chandlers on the Dock Road. 'She'll come next time, don't worry. Only one more visit and it'll be Christmas and you can all come home for a few days.'

'Have there been any air raids yet, Mummy?' Hester enquired.

'No, sweetheart.'

'Then why can't we come home for good? Some children from school have already gone back to Bootle.'

'Daddy would skin me alive if I let you. He's already cross I'm not here as well. You're not unhappy, are you?' Laura said anxiously. 'I thought you were having a lovely time, what with that den of yours and a lovely beach right on the doorstep.'

Hester laid her head on her mother's knee. 'I'd sooner be home with you,' she said quietly.

'I'd sooner you were too, but, sweetheart, you know I've got this job in a factory. It's what's called shift work. Some weeks, I'm out all night and sleep all day. The rest of the time, I'm either gone by six in the morning, or not home till nearly midnight. Life wouldn't be the same as it was before. Mummy wouldn't be there all the time.'

'All right.' Hester sighed.

Laura remarked on how well they all looked, particularly Queenie, who'd put on some much needed weight. 'And your cheeks have filled out, your eyes are sparkling. You look incredibly pretty. Oh, I've just remembered. I've brought some scissors to tidy your hair and another five shillings pocket money.'

'I've still got loads of money left,' Queenie told her.

'That doesn't matter. I can't very well keep it just because you've been careful.'

At half past five, after they'd eaten the beef casserole Gwen had made, followed by jelly and cream, they all went with Laura as far as the Town Hall where she would catch the bus to Llangollen, then the train to Liverpool. By then, Jimmy had arrived, cutting a dashing figure in Hugh Jones's trousers, tweed jacket and oversized hat. Before leaving, Laura asked Gwen if Mrs Merton was home so she could thank her for having the children, but was told she was out.

'She's always out,' Laura complained. 'I'll never get to thank her.'

'I'll thank her for you,' Gwen promised. It had been agreed that Laura and Vera weren't to know how thoroughly obnoxious Mrs Merton was. It would only make them worry, yet it didn't bother the girls a bit.

'Anyway, Gwen,' Laura said warmly, 'it's you who does all the work. That meal was delicious and I know the children have become very fond of you.'

Gwen flushed with pleasure and said they were no bother and she loved having them. 'I don't know what I'll do when they're gone.' Her eyes rested, not on the girls, but on Jimmy Nicholls.

At first, it seemed as if they wouldn't get home for Christmas. With December came snow, several feet deep, covering most of the British Isles. The roads were impassable. As soon as it was cleared, more snow would fall, but on the Friday school broke up, Miss Larkin announced that two coaches were leaving Bootle the next morning and would hopefully arrive in the square about midday. Their families had been told to expect them. 'Let's pray it doesn't snow tonight,' she added. 'I want to be home as much as you do to spend Christmas with my parents.'

Everyone must have prayed very hard. That night, the snow remained in the heavens and next morning the road through Caerdovey was relatively clear, though snow was still banked in dirty heaps at the side and the pavements were covered with a thickly frozen layer.

As soon as they arrived in Glover Street, Mary made straight for the Monaghans, and Laura came to the door of number twenty-two. 'I thought I heard voices,' she cried delightedly. 'I've been coming out to look for you for ages. I've got the kettle on.'

'It looks dead pretty.' Queenie breathed a sigh of pure happiness. She was home! The living room was drenched with paper chains and a warm fire burned in the grate, which Laura said wasn't as big as she would have liked, but fuel was difficult to get at the moment, 'Along with all sorts of other things, tea for instance, and sugar. You can't get fresh fruit for love nor money, not that I mind. The Merchant Navy's got more important things to do than bring luxuries into the British Isles. However, months ago, I put my name down with the butcher and we've got a lovely big chicken for our Christmas dinner.'

No, Roddy wasn't coming home, he couldn't get leave, she went on, her voice faltering slightly, when Hester asked if Daddy would be there. 'You'll be pleased to know he's now a First Lieutenant in the Royal Artillary. He's sent cards – there's one for you, Queenie – and presents, but I can't put them under the tree because we haven't got one. I'll put them beside the beds with the ones from Santa Claus on Christmas morning.'

They had cottage pie and jam tart for tea. It felt strange, preparing a proper meal, Laura said. 'I make do with things like beans or sardines on toast when I'm alone, and never bother with a pudding. I'm usually too tired to eat.' Her job was very exhausting. She was a riveter in an aircraft factory in Kirkby, which was quite skilled work. 'It was murder at first, but easy now I've got the hang of it.'

Vera and Albert came over later to say hello. Vera said indignantly that Mary had complained the meal wasn't as nice as the ones Gwen made. 'I told her, if that's how she felt, she could go back to Caerdovey and spend Christmas with Gwen. Needless to say, she ignored that. She's too busy being petted to death by all and sundry.'

The Monaghans were still there when the new residents in the flat upstairs came down bearing a bottle of sherry; two brothers, Eric and Ben Tyler, both in their thirties, and Eric's son, Brian, who was fourteen. The Tylers were from Newcastle, Eric was a widower, and he and Ben were electricians who'd come to Liverpool to work on the docks. Brian had passed the scholarship to grammar school at eleven, and had transferred to Merchant Taylor's in Crosby. When they'd first come, Eric had asked Laura if she'd do their washing, but she'd refused.

'Cheek! They expected I'd look after them, being the only woman in the house. Next thing, I'd've been doing their cooking too. I told them they could do their own washing, that I worked just as hard as they did.'

Queenie saw that Ben, the younger brother, who was quite handsome, though not as handsome as Roddy, kept throwing Laura admiring little glances, but Laura made no sign that she'd noticed.

On Christmas Day afternoon, it was Queenie's turn to be in receipt of admiring glances when they went over to the Monaghan's for tea.

'You've changed,' said Charlie.

'You've turned into a proper bobby dazzler,' Victor

claimed, looking at her speculatively. He was the best-looking of all the Monaghan boys.

'You look different, Queenie,' said Tommy, who'd made fun of her mercilessly in the past. 'You'd never dream you still had a funny arm.'

'She's a teacher now,' Vera beamed. 'We're all dead proud of Queenie, aren't we, girl?'

Queenie didn't answer. Never, not in a million years, had she thought the day would come when she would be embarrassed by so many compliments.

This had been her first real Christmas, she thought in bed that night. Last year, and all the years before, there'd been no presents, nothing so grand as chicken for dinner. The day had been no different from any other, except that Mam was out much longer because the Black Horse had an extension or something, and stayed open until midnight.

This year, she'd got loads of presents; a handbag from Laura, a purse to match from Hester and Mary, which had loads of pockets, and Vera had bought her a lovely notebook with a swirly cover, a box of pencils and a silver sharpener.

'I thought it'd help with your teaching,' Vera said with a twinkly smile.

But the thing that Queenie treasured most was the scarf that Roddy had sent. It was soft blue chiffon covered with little gold moons and stars and went perfectly with the navy blue coat Laura had got her from Paddy's Market.

She'd saved enough pocket money to buy everyone presents and had had a marvellous time in Woolworths where nothing cost over a tanner, getting scent for Laura, gloves for Vera, a book each for Hester and Mary, a big white hanky with 'R' embroidered on the corner for

Roddy and the same with an 'A' for Albert. She bought a belt for Jimmy to keep up Hugh Jones's trousers, two pretty hair slides for Tess, and a wind-up car for Pete. She remembered Jimmy had promised to come and see them tomorrow and Laura thought there'd be enough chicken left to have with chips. 'And I've got a tin of peas,' she added.

Queenie supposed that before she'd met Laura she must have been very unhappy. She hadn't *realised* she was unhappy. She hadn't known it was possible to feel any different to the way she felt then, not until she'd discovered what happiness was and that the years spent with Mam had been dead miserable. She snuggled under the covers and resolved never to be miserable again, too young to realise that misery, and happiness, weren't just dependent on herself, but on other factors, including people over whom she had no control. Indeed, the very next day brought some unpleasant news she hadn't been expecting.

When Jimmy came, he had on a thick jersey and trousers even shorter than the ones he'd worn when he first arrived in Caerdovey, though he still had his hat. He was shivering and his legs were blue with cold.

'What's happened to Hugh Jones's trousers and tweed jacket?' Queenie gasped. 'Come and sit by the fire. You look frozen to death.'

'Me mam pawned them to pay for the Christmas dinner,' Jimmy replied with a brave grin. 'The pawnbroker wouldn't take me hat.'

'But that's not fair.'

'Yes, it is, Queenie. Mam got two bob and we had pigs' trotters and roast spuds and a sandwich cake for pudding, otherwise we'd have just ended up with scouse.'

'Gwen will be dead upset when we go back.'

'Our Tess and Pete are going back, it's two less mouths for me mam to feed, but I'm staying put. Mam reckons it's about time I started work. I'll be fourteen in March.'

'You can't go to work in them trousers. Oh Jimmy!' Queenie wanted to cry. 'Caerdovey won't be the same without you.'

'Bootle'll seem dead funny without you, Queenie, girl,' Jimmy said soberly. 'I'll miss our den and the shore. I'll even miss me old lady.'

Laura came in and also wanted to know what had happened to his nice warm clothes. 'The ones that you found in that den of yours?'

'His mam pawned them to pay for their Christmas dinner.'

Sensing a hint of disapproval in Queenie's voice, Jimmy immediately sprang to his mam's defence. 'Me dad hasn't worked in years 'cos of his lungs. If Mam didn't work herself to a stand-still, cleaning, there wouldn't be a penny coming in.'

'What's wrong with your dad's lungs, Jimmy?' Laura asked gently.

'It's something called emphysema. It gets worse all the time.' There was a suggestion of tears in Jimmy's kind eyes. 'Sometimes, he can hardly breathe at all.'

'I'm so sorry.' Laura squeezed his hand and Queenie rather hoped she'd offer to redeem Hugh Jones's clothes from the pawnshop, but realised it would be a waste of time. The minute Mrs Nicholls needed money, they'd be pawned again. Laura, however, had a better idea.

'Would you like me to lend you my husband's working jacket and trousers?' she asked. 'There's a couple of flannel shirts too. But I'd like them back in case

Roddy needs them once this damn war is over, so you must tell your mother they're not to be pawned.'

'Thank you, Mrs Oliver,' Jimmy said politely. 'I'd like it very much.'

Queenie gave him his belt and the things for Tess and Pete and hoped they wouldn't end up in the pawnshop, too.

At the beginning of January, only one coach was waiting outside St Joan of Arc's to take the evacuees back to Caerdovey.

'What's happened to everybody?' Queenie asked Miss Larkin, who seemed to be in charge.

'Their parents have decided to keep them in Bootle. Last September, we had over sixty children. Now we've only got twenty-five. If you must know, Queenie, I wish I was staying myself.'

Even Mary nearly hadn't come. Vera had said it was up to her. Given the choice of staying at home, her mam out at work all day, her dad putting in all sorts of funny hours, Billy in the Army, George and Dick expecting their call-up papers any minute, her other brothers all with jobs, apart from Caradoc who'd be leaving school soon and getting a job himself, Mary had decided she'd sooner be in Caerdovey with her friends.

'You'll still want me to teach the children two mornings a week, won't you?' Queenie asked Miss Larkin anxiously. It would be unbearable if she lost that as well as Jimmy.

'Mrs Waters and I won't exactly be worked off our feet this term, but some extra help is always useful. Unlike us, you can give the little ones individual attention.'

'I'll miss him,' Gwen said tearfully when she learnt

Jimmy hadn't come back. 'I'll miss him something awful.'

'We all will,' Queenie assured her. 'The den won't be the same without Jimmy.'

Caerdovey seemed to have lost a lot of its charm. It was too cold to play on the shore, where the waves rippled ominously, as if they were terribly angry about something. Their bedroom was freezing, and the only warmth to be found was in the kitchen. Gwen gave them an old paraffin stove for the den, but the heat it gave off was pathetic and the room stank. Hester claimed the smell made her feel sick.

The months dragged by. There was more snow, heavier than before, and day after day the town was muffled underneath a thick, white blanket, the silence unnatural and faintly threatening. Laura and Vera found it impossible to visit, not knowing if they'd get there and back within the day.

Suddenly, it seemed to happen overnight, it was spring. The sun came out and the snow disappeared as if by magic, revealing surprisingly lush green fields. Little shoots thrust their way bravely through the black soil of the gardens, except the garden of The Old School House where there were no flowers, though Queenie was pleased to find the suggestion of buds on the apple trees, which she found quite heartening. Soon, it would be Easter and they would be going home to Bootle and this time she was determined to persuade Laura to let them stay.

'Queenie, dear, you don't know the half of it,' Laura said earnestly. 'It's not true that nothing is happening as you said. Hitler has just invaded Norway and Denmark and you wouldn't believe the number of British ships that the Germans have sunk. Thousands of seamen have lost their lives. Russia has attacked Finland. I'm not even sure what that means, I thought Russia was on our side, but it might have been the other way around. Oh, Queenie,' she cried, joining her hands together as if she was about to pray, 'I can't make you go back to Caerdovey, it's entirely your decision, but I hope you'll do it as a favour to me. I feel so much happier, knowing you and Hester are safely tucked up in Wales – and Mary, too, of course. Now that Roddy's in France, in the thick of things, as it were, he'd be upset if I told him Hester was back in Bootle.' She paused for breath. 'We're short of so many things that you're probably not aware of; meat, eggs, butter, which Gwen manages to get from the local farms. It's nice to know you're eating properly. By the way, I'm very grateful for the things she sent. Those pork chops look lovely and juicy, and the eggs are huge. You must take Jimmy's fruit cake round later, and the shortbread from his old lady. And don't let me forget to write a note to take back, thanking Gwen for her kindness.'

'All right,' Queenie sighed.

Laura groaned. 'I'm being selfish, aren't I? Putting my peace of mind before your and Hester's happiness.' She chewed her lip worriedly. 'I tell you what, if there still hasn't been an air raid by the end of the summer term, I'll assume Hitler has no intention of bombing Bootle and you can leave Caerdovey for good. How does that suit you?'

Mrs Merton had a wireless. When she was in bed, Queenie frequently heard the subdued sound of voices downstairs, or music, singing, laughter. She began to listen daily to the one o'clock bulletin, not caring if Gwen found out or if she was discovered by Mrs Merton in her over-furnished sitting room where the wireless had its own special table with curved legs.

The news she heard was dreadful; British forces lost their bid to defend Norway and retired, defeated; Hitler invaded Holland, Belgium and Luxembourg, then entered France. At the beginning of June, there was a great evacuation from Dunkirk, when more than 300,000 British and French troops were transported across the English Channel, including Lieutenant Roderick Oliver and Private William Monaghan. The channel was all that separated Britain from the approaching enemy. A few days later, France fell and Britain stood alone.

It was a relief to switch the wireless off and take herself to the sun-kissed sands where the water, no longer angry, lapped lazily onto the shore, trickling over her bare feet, or retire to the den with one of her favourite books – she had joined Caerdovey library. Sometimes, she would sit in the kitchen and talk to Gwen, who was always glad of her company. The war seemed very far away and she couldn't imagine it shattering the peace of Caerdovey.

At the end of June, they had a party. Gwen made one of her famous cakes, using the last of the glacé cherries. June was the month the girls had their birthdays; Hester and Mary were six, and Queenie turned fifteen. The party was for them all.

The most startling news of all came, not from the wireless, but when she was in the Post Office buying a stamp for her weekly letter to Laura.

'Last night, the air raid siren went in Liverpool,' the postmistress, another Mrs Jones, told her. 'My nephew lives Childwall way and he rang and told me.'

'Was anybody hurt?' Queenie's heart did a somersault.

'No, lovey. No bombs fell, but it was the first time and everyone got a terrible fright.'

There were more air raids in July. Bombs were dropped, but in harmless places, like fields, except for one that hit a house, though the occupants weren't injured. Laura wrote to say they could come home when school finished, but be prepared to return immediately if the air raids got worse, even if it meant them going back by train.

Queenie was in Glover Street when she experienced her first air raid. Hester had gone to bed, and Laura was on afternoons and not expected home for another hour. She was listening to the wireless, to a man with the deepest voice she'd ever heard singing, 'Ole Man River', when the siren went. It was an eerie sound, an up and down wail that made her blood curdle. As soon as it faded, it was followed by the rumble of aircraft overhead. She crept into Laura's room where Hester was asleep in the double bed, and sat on the edge, thinking of Roddy who was so anxious for his daughter to be safe, imagining a bomb dropping directly on to the house, killing them both, imagining Roddy's dear face when he learnt that Hester was dead. She dithered over whether to wake up the little girl and take her to the shelter or leave her to sleep in peace, and almost collapsed in relief when the All Clear sounded.

Laura arrived home, very late, her face grim. 'Wasn't it awful? We were all pouring out of work when the siren went, so we all had to pour back and go down to the shelter.'

'I was petrified,' Queenie confessed.

Next morning, they heard that bombs had been dropped, but once again had fallen harmlessly in fields. But that wasn't the case a few days later when a woman was killed when her house in Birkenhead received a direct hit. The next night, four people died in Wallasey and another four were seriously injured.

'That's it!' Laura said when she heard the news. 'You're going back. I'll find out about the trains.'

But there was no need for Laura to find out anything. A WVS lady came to the house later to say coaches were leaving from the usual place at noon the next day.

'I don't know how many coaches there'll be, but I'd get the children there early, if I were you, Mrs Oliver, else you'll find it's standing room only. Everyone's desperate to get their children out of harm's way. And make sure they get on the right coach. They're not all going to Wales.'

It was late in the afternoon when the three girls were taken to The Old School House in Mrs Davies's little black car. To Queenie's dismay, Gwen didn't appear the least bit pleased to see them. She pushed them into the kitchen, closed the door, but stayed outside. Hester and Mary ran upstairs, but Queenie was curious to know why Gwen was behaving so oddly.

The two women seemed to be engaged in a heated argument. Queenie opened the door a crack and listened.

'I can't put them somewhere else, Gwen,' Mrs Davies was saying irritably, 'not even for a few weeks. Caerdovey's bursting at the seams. We've more evacuees than ever now the raids have started in earnest.'

'But Edna,' Gwen hissed, '*he's* still here. He's not going back to Manchester until September.'

'Don't be ridiculous, Gwen. You've always had too much imagination. That . . . that *thing* was only a rumour. There was never any proof.'

'There's no smoke without fire, Edna,' Gwen said stiffly.

'Well, there's nothing I can do. If you're all that concerned, you'll just have to keep an eye on the girls, but it's my opinion you're worrying over nothing.' With that, Mrs Davies turned on her heel and left.

Queenie was innocently staring out of the window when Gwen came in, wondering what on earth the conversation had meant. It was only then she noticed the young man sitting in a deckchair beneath the apple tree, eyes closed as he soaked up the August sun.

'Who's that?' she asked.

'That's Carl, Mrs Merton's son,' Gwen said tightly.

'I didn't know Mrs Merton had a son. Why haven't we seen him before?'

'Because he's at university in Manchester and, until now, you haven't been here when he's home. He doesn't usually stay long. Caerdovey's too quiet for him.' Gwen grabbed Queenie's arm and clutched it so tightly that she winced with pain. 'Keep well away from Carl Merton, lovey,' she pleaded. There was a raw, desperate edge to her voice. 'The girls too. You're not to let them anywhere near him.'

Queenie glanced again at the young man, sleeping innocently beneath the apple tree. At that moment, the sun disappeared behind a cloud and the garden became full of dark shadows. The leaves on the tree shook, caught by a sudden, violent wind. She shivered as Gwen's words hammered against her brain. She'd been only too glad to get back to Caerdovey after the scare of the raids, but had they returned to something even more terrifying?

Chapter 5

Gwen had been talking nonsense, Queenie decided after a few days. Carl Merton seemed perfectly harmless. She'd come back, tired after the long journey, worried about Laura being left to face the air raids on her own, and had let Gwen's hysterical outburst get to her when there was no need. Even so, a little thread of fear remained at the back of her mind.

Mrs Merton was obviously glad to have her son home. She went into her factory very late or didn't go at all, and had been heard to laugh for the first time, a high-pitched girlish giggle. She even dressed differently, in summer frocks and high-heeled shoes. Mother and son went out to dinner some evenings, to Barmouth or Harlech where they had friends. They used Carl's car, which was long and grey and didn't have a roof.

'It's called a sports car,' Gwen said. 'My brother-in-law said they cost the earth. As far as Mrs Merton is concerned, nothing's too good for her Carl.' Her face was bitter.

Carl Merton was twenty. He was a squat young man with broad shoulders and heavily muscled arms. His brown hair was very thick and his eyebrows protruded like two little shelves over eyes that never seemed properly open, so that he always looked half-asleep.

So far, he and the girls hadn't met. When he was in, he spent a lot of time in the garden, sunbathing, or hitting a ball against the wall with a tennis racquet. Gwen refused to let them out when he was there. If they wanted to go to the sands, she made them leave by the front and use the path Queenie had discovered on her first visit.

'I don't want him to see you,' she would hiss. 'You're to come back the same way.'

'Why, what will he do if does see us?' Queenie asked. She thought Gwen was being over-protective. Surely Carl Merton wasn't likely to leap up from his deckchair and attack all three of them on the spot?

Gwen merely shrugged and said it was better to be safe than sorry. 'He'll be off soon. He usually goes back to Manchester before the new term starts. There's more going on there.'

It was therefore a relief when, on the final day of August, Gwen announced that Carl was leaving Caerdovey the next day. 'He's gone to look for petrol, the black market stuff. He used up all his ration while he was home.' She sniffed. 'He couldn't possibly go on the bus and train, not like ordinary people.'

The wireless had been on all night playing music, very loud. One of the songs Queenie would never forget was 'Over the Rainbow', sung by a girl with a lovely, passionate voice. Gwen had been told to prepare an extra-special dinner and get two bottles of wine out of the cupboard where it was stored. Above the music, Mrs Merton's shrill laughter could be heard and Carl's answering guffaw. They were clearly having a good time on his last night at home.

It was late when the wireless was finally turned off. Outside, it was pitch dark and, in the distance, the Irish Sea could be heard lapping briskly on to the shore. The passing traffic had ceased. There were footsteps on the stairs, a giggle when Mrs Merton tripped – she must have drunk too much wine. She bade her son goodnight. A door closed, followed, seconds later, by another.

Queenie was used to staying up late, waiting for her mother to come home, and rarely fell asleep before midnight. The noise downstairs hadn't bothered her. She snuggled under the bedclothes, looking forward to tomorrow when Carl Merton would be gone and everything would be back to normal. Gwen had been talking through her hat, her fears had been groundless.

She didn't hear the door open or the man enter the room. The thing that woke her was the hand pressing against her mouth, so hard that she could hardly breathe. She gagged and a voice rasped in her ear. 'Don't make a sound, or I'll kill you and then I'll kill your little friends.'

She gagged again. The hand eased a bit and she drew in a hoarse, sharp breath. The smell of alcohol was strong and sickly, and she could feel little flecks of spittle on her face.

'I've been watching you, Queenie,' Carl Merton whispered. 'I watched you on the beach, paddling in the water, your skirt pulled up around your thighs. You knew I was watching, didn't you? That's why you did it,' he gave a long, deep sigh, 'for me. I saw you that first day, looking at me through the window when you thought I was asleep. This is what you've been waiting for, isn't it?' His other hand slid under the covers of the bed and began to caress her.

Queenie struggled, but he was much too strong for her. She thought about biting the hand over her mouth, drawing blood, screaming at the top of her voice, but Gwen slept downstairs and was unlikely to hear and Mrs Merton was probably in a drunken stupor – Mam had slept like a log and couldn't be roused when she'd had too much to drink. The only people who would wake would be the girls in the nearby beds and the man, Carl Merton, had threatened to kill them. In the cold light of day, she might have seen the threat as an empty one, but it was dark and she was petrified, her body melting away to liquid with fear.

What happened next, she was never sure, whether she fainted, or merely switched herself off to avoid the horror that was happening. When she returned to consciousness, or reality, Carl Merton had gone, but she knew he'd done something to her. Her tummy was hurting badly and her legs throbbed.

She didn't even try to sleep, too scared to close her eyes in case he came back. Yet despite this, she must have dropped off, because when she looked, a pale rim of light shone under the curtains. It was morning and she wondered if it had all been a dream.

'You look pale, lovey. Didn't you sleep well?'

Queenie shook her head and Gwen said she hadn't either. 'The wireless kept me awake and the noise that pair were making. Mind you, I'm not surprised. I've just collected these from the sitting room.' She pointed to the empty bottles on the draining board. 'They finished off a whole bottle of whisky between them, as well as the wine. Still, it didn't stop them from getting up early. They'll be well on their way to Manchester by now.'

'Carl's gone?' She was surprised she hadn't heard him leave.

'They both have. They left at the crack of dawn. Mrs Merton always goes back with him and stays a few days. She can't bear to say goodbye. She thinks far too much of that boy. It isn't natural.' Her lips curled. 'He can't do anything wrong. I'd like to bet she won't let him go in the Forces next year when he's twenty-one. She'll send him abroad, to somewhere like America, out of harm's way.'

Queenie found it an effort to leave the house on Monday when school started again. She had to force herself to take the girls. She'd felt the same over the weekend; reluctant to go to the shore, to Mass, to visit Jimmy's old lady who'd invited them to tea. She was actually glad it had rained and they'd been able to spend most of the time in the den, where Hester and Mary played house with their dolls, some cracked dishes and an old kettle they'd found in one of the chests. On Saturday, they argued over everything, getting on her nerves to such a degree that she lost patience and shouted at them for the very first time, then burst into tears at the sight of their shocked faces.

'Oh, I'm sorry,' she wept. 'I didn't mean to shout.'

They were beside her within seconds, stroking her hair, patting her face, both trying to climb on her knee. They would never quarrel again, they promised. Never, ever.

'We didn't mean to upset you.' Hester was close to tears herself.

'I'm not upset. I don't know what I am,' Queenie wailed. It would have been nice to talk to someone about Carl Merton, what he'd done – not the girls, of course, someone older. But she felt Gwen wasn't the right person, which meant there was only Laura and she'd have to put it in a letter and she could never write it down. And then it might never have happened at all. It might really have been just a dream, a terrible nightmare, something which she'd much prefer to believe, even though her tummy still hurt and there'd been spots of blood on her nightie, which she had to scrub off before putting it with the washing for Gwen to do. She had no idea where the blood had come from because she wasn't due a period.

'It was a dream,' she told herself. 'Just a dream.'

The raids over Liverpool were getting heavier and more frequent. As soon as she'd delivered the girls to school, Queenie would immediately make for the Post Office where Mrs Jones would regale her with the latest news; the Customs House had been hit, Edge Hill Goods Station, Dunlop Rubber Works, Tunnel Road Cinema, the list was endless. The number of casualties was increasing at an alarming rate.

'My nephew said it looked as if the entire city was on fire,' Mrs Jones declared in a dramatic voice one morning, clearly enjoying her role as the purveyor of ill tidings. 'He reckons there were at least two hundred German planes in the sky.'

Laura didn't know Queenie was being kept up to date with the bombardment of Liverpool. Her letters made it appear as if little was happening.

The siren goes nightly, waking everyone up, and we daren't go asleep again, just in case, but usually it's just a false alarm. Vera and I will come and see you as soon as we can, but we're both terribly tired, losing sleep like nobody's business, yet we still have to get up for work. We've been saving our sweet coupons and have sent a parcel of chocolate bars. To avoid an argument, the Fry's Chocolate Creams are for Hester and the Mars Bars for Mary. I've included some Turkish Delight for you, Queenie, dear, because you are so sweet!

Queenie didn't feel sweet. She felt sour and bad-tempered. Miss Larkin had to remonstrate with her for shouting at a little girl who was having difficulty learning to read.

'Losing your temper will get you nowhere,' she said coldly. 'In fact, it will only make things worse. Nora won't learn a thing if you frighten her. Teachers have to be patient, even if they want to scream inside.' Her voice softened. 'This isn't a bit like you, Queenie. You usually have the patience of Job. Is something bothering you?'

'I don't know,' Queenie said distractedly, which was a most unsatisfactory answer.

At the end of October, Laura came to see them, accompanied by Albert instead of Vera. It was his first visit.

'Your mam's exhausted, so I thought I'd take her place for once,' he told Mary, who didn't mind who came so long as they made an enormous fuss of her.

There wasn't an opportunity to tell Laura about Carl Merton and what he'd done – or might not have done. Anyway, it was almost two months ago and Queenie was doing her best to forget about it. But she was finding it awfully hard. The only place she felt safe was in the den, her head buried in a book, engrossed in a world that was completely different from the dark, dangerous one outside.

Laura said Roddy was now stationed in a place called Colchester, which was on the opposite side of the country to Liverpool. She hadn't seen him since he'd been evacuated from Dunkirk and had been given an entire week's leave. Since then, he'd only been allowed twenty-four-hour passes, not nearly long enough to come home. 'I'd go and see him one weekend, but it means getting a train to London, then catching another.' She sighed. 'Trains are so unreliable these days. Even if you manage to catch one, you're quite likely to be turfed off halfway if it's needed for the troops. I could be days late getting back to work, which just isn't on. My job's too important to lose time.'

'This war's turned people's lives upside down,' Albert said gloomily. 'Vera's a nervous wreck, worrying about the lads.' Two of the Monaghan boys were in the Army, and Dick had joined the Royal Navy. Nobody had a clue where he was.

Gwen reported, with a touch of relish, that Mrs Merton's pottery factory was on its last legs. Most of the staff, mainly young women whose job it had been to hand-paint the finished products, had left Caerdovey for better paid work. Anyway, hardly anyone went on holiday these days and the market for china replicas of Harlech or Caernarvon castle or ashtrays proclaiming they were a Present from Barmouth was virtually non-existent. In an attempt to keep the business afloat, the few remaining staff were producing mugs on which Winston Churchill smoked a fat cigar and bore the message 'Good Luck to our Boys'.

To add to her employer's woes, the petrol ration was a mere six gallons a month. 'She'd prefer Carl had the coupons,' Gwen said, wrinkling her nose in disgust, 'so she's decided to walk to work and back. I can't say I envy her, not on such dark mornings. There's no street lights and she can't use a torch.'

Mrs Merton's troubles were increased when she was knocked down by a lorry. It was only crawling along in the thick white mist that had rolled in from the sea overnight, making visibility virtually impossible. The lorry continued on its way, unaware it had hit anybody, and Mrs Merton limped back home, one side of her body badly bruised. She went to bed after telling Gwen to send for the doctor.

The mist was still there when it was time for school,

cloying and claustrophobic, turning Caerdovey into a ghost town, a place of disembodied voices and eerie footsteps. Hester and Mary tried to wave the mist away with their arms, as if it were smoke, but it stubbornly refused to move.

'Why don't you stay with us today, Queenie?' Miss Larkin suggested when they arrived at the Councillor Jones Hall. 'It seems silly to make the journey twice in this awful weather. I'm sure I can find things for you to do.'

'I'd love to, but Gwen will be worried if I don't come back.' She didn't fancy walking on her own but, with Mrs Merton having taken to her bed, Gwen already had enough to worry about.

'Nip over to the Post Office and ask Mrs Jones to give Gwen a ring.' As well as her duties behind the counter, Mrs Jones was in charge of the switchboard dealing with calls coming in and out of the town, listening in quite shamelessly and knowing everybody's business. She already knew about Mrs Merton's accident. 'She's just called her son in Manchester. Terrible bruised she said she was. Isn't this fog awful, lovey? Yet a couple of miles away there's no sign of it.'

Queenie spent a pleasant day tidying cupboards and mending damaged books, carefully sticking the loose pages back in. She kept looking at the windows to see if the mist had lifted, but all that could be seen were hazy white clouds pressing against the glass.

School let out at half past three and Miss Larkin told everyone to walk in single file and to never lose sight of the person in front. 'And stay on the pavement,' she warned.

The walk seemed to take twice as long as usual and they nearly went right past The Old School House. Mary recognised the rickety fence just in time. It looked very peculiar, stuck on its own, the house to which it was attached no longer in sight.

Mary must have thought she was entitled to a favour. 'Can we go straight to the den?' she asked. 'We can light the candles. I love it when the candles are lit and you tell us stories, Queenie.'

'All right, but first I want Gwen to know we're home. You're not to light the candles until I come.' She'd forbidden them to touch matches. They ran off, giggling happily.

There was no sign of Gwen in the kitchen. Voices could be heard upstairs, one of them a man's, which she assumed was the doctor. She hung around, waiting for Gwen, and when she didn't appear, went up to see for herself. Gwen and the owner of the voice were coming out of Mrs Merton's room. It wasn't the doctor, but Mrs Merton's son, Carl.

Terror rose like a ball in Queenie's throat. She could hardly speak, think, breathe, just wanted to scream and scream at him to go away, never come back, forgetting entirely that this was his house and he could come and go as he pleased.

'Queenie!' Gwen hurried towards her. 'You look as if you've seen a ghost. Come on, lovey, let's go downstairs. There's tea in the pot and you look as if you need it. Isn't this fog terrible! I'm glad I didn't have to go out.'

As Gwen led her away, Queenie looked back. Carl Merton was watching her across the landing, eyes half-closed and brooding. It *had* happened, it hadn't been a dream and, if she stopped blocking it out and concentrated hard enough, she'd be able to remember every single detail.

'I can't stay a minute,' she mumbled as soon as they reached the kitchen. 'Hester and Mary are in the den, waiting for me.'

'Just get this nice hot tea down you, lovey. You'll feel better for it.' Gwen rolled her eyes, unusually animated. 'You wouldn't believe the day I've had. Mrs Merton's had me up and down them stairs like a yo-yo. Then Carl arrived, only an hour ago. He must have driven like the wind. He only came to see how his mother was. He's going back later.' She cocked her ear towards the door that opened on to the hall. 'What was that?'

'I didn't hear anything,' Queenie said dully.

'I heard a creak, as if someone was outside. It's probably just my nerves. This fog would get anybody down. What did you do with yourself at school? Mrs Jones rang to say you weren't coming home. It was very thoughtful of you, Queenie. I told Mrs Merton what you'd done. I told her you were a proper little lady.'

'I'd better get to the den.' With an effort, Queenie pushed herself to her feet.

'Don't stay long, lovey. It'll be cold out there.'

'No.' She went into the garage and was surprised that the girls were being so quiet. There wasn't a peep from either of them. She'd have expected them to be in the middle of a fierce argument by now. She was about to call their names, but thought better of it. They might have fallen asleep on the bed, in which case she'd leave them. She'd appreciate being left with her own thoughts for a little while.

She crept up the ladder and had almost reached the top, when a hand reached down and grabbed her arm, pulling her upwards. She screamed, and would have fallen had not the hand been holding her so tightly.

'Hello, Queenie,' said a smiling Carl Merton. 'I got here just in time. Are you pleased to see me? Are . . .'

Queenie would never know what he was about to say next, because the smiling face, so close to hers, was no longer smiling. The sleepy eyes had opened wide and, for some insane reason, were dark with fear. All of a sudden, he toppled head first out of the cavity and on to the concrete floor, taking Queenie with him. The last thing she remembered hearing was a sickening, cracking noise followed by a bloodcurdling groan.

The nightmare was dreadful. She was lost in a thick, dark forest, where the mist swirled in and out of the trees and the leaves met overhead so that the sky was invisible. Strange, half-formed figures danced around her, getting closer and closer, until she could have touched them, until they were touching *her*, their slight bodies brushing against her skirt, nipping her arms, poking her face, tugging at her hair. Her eyes searched desperately for a way out, but there wasn't a glimpse of daylight anywhere.

'Ouch!' she cried, when there was a particularly vicious tug at her hair.

'Ah!' a voice said cheerfully. 'You're awake at last.'

Queenie opened her eyes. She wasn't in a forest, but lying in bed in a small white room where a woman of about forty wearing a white apron and a strangely shaped cap was bending over her. She had cheeks like apples and warm friendly eyes.

'I'm Sister Thomas, love. How are you feeling?'

'I dunno.' The mist had entered her head and she couldn't think. 'Where am I?' It seemed a sensible question to ask.

'Caerdovey Cottage Hospital.'

'Why?'

'For two reasons,' Sister Thomas said practically. 'First, you were badly concussed following your accident. Second, your arm was broken for the same reason. It's nicely set and there'll be someone along in a minute to put a plaster on, so try not to move till then.'

'Which arm?' Queenie mumbled.

'The right one, love. You'll be pleased to know it's nice and straight again. Doctor Owen came all the way from Llangollen to set it. He said it hadn't been set properly when it was broken the first time. He was extremely shocked. We both were.'

'I didn't know it had been broken before. You mean, it isn't twisted any more?' She must have misunderstood. It seemed too good to be true.

'That's right, Queenie.' The nurse looked pleased. 'It's just like new.'

The mist in her head was beginning to clear. Details of the 'accident' Sister Thomas had mentioned were gradually coming back. She remembered the wide-eyed, horror-struck face coming towards her, the body hitting the floor with a strange thud. 'What happened to Carl Merton?' she asked.

'I think I'll leave that for your friend to tell you.' Her knee was given a comforting squeeze. 'She's outside now. I'll call her in. Now that you've safely returned to the land of the living, I can see to my other patients. We had a new baby last night, two burns and a heart attack.'

Minutes later, Sister Thomas had been replaced by Gwen Hughes, looking very grave. 'That fog's cleared at last,' was the first thing she said.

'How long have I been here?' Queenie had lost all sense of time. She looked at the window and it was dark outside. There were flowers on the bedside cabinet; chrysanthemums with tousled heads, a lovely tawny brown.

'Just over twenty-four hours. A doctor came from Llangollen to set your arm.'

'Sister Thomas told me. She said it's straight now. I can't imagine what it'll feel like, straight.' She'd have to learn to write again, do all sorts of things the proper way.

There was a pause, then Gwen said in a terse, hushed voice, 'Queenie, did you know you were pregnant?'

'*What?*'

'You were expecting a baby, lovey. You lost it when you fell off that ladder. I cleaned you up while we waited for the ambulance. No one here knows.'

Queenie felt tears rush to her eyes. 'I didn't know, no.'

'It was Carl Merton, wasn't it? When he was home during the summer. Oh!' she cried, shaking visibly in her distress. 'I told Edna Davies it wasn't safe to leave you and the girls, not with him around. He raped you, didn't he?'

Queenie didn't know what raped meant. 'He got into bed with me one night,' she muttered. 'I was never quite sure what he did. Whatever it was hurt, but I kept telling meself it was just a dream.'

'Oh, lovey!' Gwen wept. 'You should have told me. I should've kept you all under lock and key. He's done it before, raped a girl. It was on the beach, behind the Town Hall. Someone, an old man, Ernie Preston, saw him hanging round, but Mrs Merton swore blind he'd spent the night at home, with her. The police believed her, rather than Ernie, who was never all that sober. He's dead now, poor soul,' she sighed. 'Me, I thought I heard Carl go out. I never said anything because I wasn't entirely sure.' Her eyes darkened and her face became grim. 'Then, a year later, didn't he go and do the same thing again in Manchester! I heard Mrs Merton on the phone. She got him a solicitor from London. I don't know what happened, whether he went to court or not. If he did, he must have got off, because he was home a few weeks later and Mrs Merton was full of the joys of spring.'

'He was trying to pull me into the den,' Queenie

whispered. 'He must have leaned down too far and toppled over.'

'Remember me thinking I heard a noise outside the kitchen door?' Gwen said thoughtfully. 'It must have been him, listening. He knew you were on your way and got there before you.'

'I thought Hester and Mary were there.' She remembered wondering why it was so quiet.

'No, they were in the garden, lovey, looking for something. It was them that found you. They ran into the house, screaming their little heads off. Sergeant Adams from the police came and they told him the same thing. He's coming to see you in the morning.'

'Where are they now?' she asked, alarmed. 'Is Carl still around? I don't want them anywhere near him.' She would never go back to The Old School House, whether Carl was there or not.

'Don't worry, they're with Jimmy's old lady. And Carl isn't around any more, Queenie. He broke his neck in the fall. He's dead and Mrs Merton's completely lost her mind.'

'Do the girls know he's dead?' a horrified Queenie asked.

'Me and Sergeant Adams thought it best not to tell them.'

Laura and Vera arrived late that night. Queenie had never been so glad to see anyone in her life before. They'd had a terrible journey. The train had crawled along, the bus was late. They'd thought they'd never get there. 'And we were worried to death the whole way,' a red-faced Vera gasped.

'Whatever happened, Queenie?' Laura asked gently. 'I got this garbled telephone message at work saying I was to come to Caerdovey straight away, Vera too, but the person couldn't tell me why. I downed tools and left immediately and collected Vera on the way.'

'There was an accident.' She told them the story she'd agreed with Gwen. She'd been climbing the ladder, Carl Merton, whom she hardly knew, had leant down to help her up, but lost his balance and fell. 'There's no need to mention the miscarriage, lovey,' Gwen had said. 'Just imagine the fuss there'd be. Laura, everyone, would be terribly upset, and it'd only complicate things.'

'I'll never tell anyone I was pregnant,' Queenie vowed. She'd keep it to herself for the rest of her life.

Both women were already upset enough about her broken arm and the fact that Hester and Mary had found her unconscious. 'Poor little mites,' Vera wailed. 'It must've given them a terrible fright. Was the man hurt too?'

Queenie took a deep breath. 'He was killed,' she said in a shaky voice. 'Hester and Mary don't know.'

At this, Vera proceeded to have hysterics, but Laura remained calm, although she was obviously badly shaken.

'How long will it be before you can leave hospital, dear?' she asked crisply.

'I dunno.' It could be days, it could be months, Queenie had no idea. 'A policeman's coming to see me in the morning.'

'I'll ask. If they say you'll be discharged in a day or so, I'll hang on. Longer than that, and I'll come back and fetch you.' She turned to Vera and sternly told her to calm down. 'You're to take Hester and Mary back to Liverpool first thing tomorrow. I don't want them here a minute longer than necessary. There must be a hotel in Caerdovey where us two can spend the night, hang the expense.'

'But the raids, Laura,' Vera wailed. 'They're getting worse.'

'We'll find somewhere in Southport for them to stay. In fact, I don't know why we didn't send them to Southport in the first place. It's only half an hour away by train. We can visit every weekend.'

Queenie's arm felt naked and vulnerable when the plaster was removed. It had been on for ten weeks, covering her entire arm, from the shoulder right down to her wrist.

'I can't bend it,' she said. 'I don't think I can move it either.'

'You'll do both in time,' Dr Hollis advised. He looked much too young to be a doctor, barely out of his teens. The lenses on his horn-rimmed spectacles were very thick. His poor sight was probably the reason why he wasn't in the forces. 'I'll give you a list of exercises to do three times a day. 'How's your grip? Shake hands.' He put out his hand and Queenie had to lift her right arm with the left to shake it. 'Very good,' he said. 'At least your hand is working. The arm will soon follow.'

'The doctor in Wales told me to use me hand as much as possible. I've been gripping things like mad ever since.'

'Sensible girl. You'll be as right as rain in no time. Out of interest,' he asked curiously, 'do you know why it wasn't set the first time it was broken?'

'I fell downstairs. Me mother must have thought I'd only hurt it. She put a sort of bandage on it, a sling.' Mam had *thrown* her downstairs. It had come back to her in Caerdovey hospital and she'd remembered a time in her life when she seemed to be enveloped in a cloud of pain which she thought would never go away. It wasn't long before she'd started school, and she'd put it out of her mind, just as she'd done the incident with Carl

Merton, because it had been too painful and she'd prefer to forget, particularly the angry look on Mam's face.

Dr Hollis looked at her doubtfully, but, 'Come and see me again the same time next week and we'll see how you're getting on,' was all he said.

Queenie left the hospital and walked down to the sea front where the water glinted dully in the distance and the fairground looked forlorn and neglected. Southport was an attractive town, but not at its best in January. She doubted if it was much colder at the North Pole. She shivered when she was caught in an icy blast of wind that went right through her thick coat. Shoving her left hand in the pocket, she found it hard to believe that the day would come when she could do the same with the right, now hanging, completely useless, at her side. She was scared she'd bump into a wall, or someone would knock against it, and it would break again.

She turned into the path of a well-kept detached house with 'Sea Shells' on a shell-shaped sign attached to the door. When she turned the knob, another blast of icy wind almost threw her inside.

'Shut the door, quickly now,' said Mrs Palfrey, who seemed to spend her entire time hovering in the hall waiting for someone to come in. 'Oh, I see your plaster's gone. Pretty soon you'll be able to give me a hand with the dishes.'

'I'll be looking for a job as soon as I'm fit again.'

Mrs Palfrey was the owner of Sea Shells, a bed and breakfast establishment, but business had been poor all summer and, as hardly anyone except the occasional commercial traveller wanted to stay at the seaside in winter, Mrs Palfrey took in evacuees to occupy the empty rooms. She had eight at the moment and, being a businesswoman, considered herself entitled to make a profit. The allowance from the Government, ten and sixpence for each child, wasn't sufficient to provide nourishing food *and* leave a few bob over, so the evacuees had toast for breakfast, no jam, and margarine instead of butter, despite them being entitled to a butter ration. They ate a good dinner at school, which was fortunate, as the tea Mrs Palfrey provided was more a snack than a proper meal; tinned soup, or a single sausage with fried tomatoes, or beans on toast. Puddings were strictly off the menu.

Vera thought it disgusting and was all for tearing Mrs Palfrey off a strip, but Queenie pleaded with her not to. 'She's all right. I'd sooner there wasn't any trouble.'

She'd had enough trouble. All she wanted was a quiet life and for her arm to get better. Fortunately, Vera agreed to let Mrs Palfrey alone. 'Though she's a bloody miser,' she breathed, curling her lip, 'expecting to make money out of children while there's a war on. What happens to your meat ration, that's what I'd like to know.'

'Would you like a cup of tea, dearie?' Mrs Palfrey enquired. The gesture was made only because she wanted someone to talk to. 'I bet it's cold outside.'

'It's icy. I'd love some tea, thank you.' It was almost as chilly inside as out. A small electric fire kept the dining room faintly warm while they ate, but was removed when the meal was over. If the children wanted to stay and do their homework, play cards or board games, read, or generally make a racket, they did so in an atmosphere that was close to freezing. The lounge was strictly off limits in case they damaged the furniture. Queenie sometimes took the girls for a walk along Lord Street after tea, where the shops were still open, or they went up to their bedrooms and tucked themselves in bed, fully dressed, after making themselves a jam sarnie or eating Vera's scones, sadly denuded of currants that had disappeared from the shops, like so many other things. There was a supply of food kept in the wardrobe to ward off their frequent pangs of hunger; bread and jam, Vera's scones and sausage rolls. Laura gave them her cheese ration.

Queenie was invited into the kitchen, the only place where there was a proper fire. A big pan of beans was slowly heating on the stove and she hoped they wouldn't be given the ones that had stuck to the bottom and had turned into a hard, lumpy mess. Mrs Palfrey must have been feeling generous and gave her a custard cream to have with the tea.

The landlady was a widow and reminded her a bit of Mam, with her bright blue eyeshadow, stiff black lashes and heavily painted lips, except her hair was dyed the colour of cherries and Mam's had been a curious yellow. She was fascinated by Laura, her ladylike ways and the refined way in which she spoke.

'What does Laura's hubby do?' she asked today.

'He's a lieutenant in the Army. His name's Roddy and he's in Egypt.'

Mrs Palfrey looked suitably impressed. 'Is that short for Rodney or Roderick?'

'Roderick. He writes to me sometimes.'

Roddy's letters were surprisingly dull. Laura said the same. 'He'd never written to me before. I didn't realise he was so bad at it. They've got no warmth. You'd think I was a distant friend, not his wife.'

The subject of Laura continued to occupy Mrs Palfrey until the front door was flung open, crashing against the wall, a signal that the children had arrived home from school. 'I suppose they'll be starving,' Mrs Palfrey muttered as if she was likely to do anything about it.

Before they ate their beans on toast, Queenie was

obliged to roll up her jersey sleeve to show Hester and Mary her arm, which was now completely straight.

'It looks like a new one,' Mary commented.

'I can't use it yet. Someone's still going to have to cut this toast up for me. I think it's Hester's turn.'

'I'm glad the plaster's gone,' Hester said, looking very important as she sliced Queenie's toast into squares. 'It won't remind me any more.'

'Of what?'

'Of us finding you with your arm all broke and Mrs Merton's son with a bloody head. It was horrible.'

'Don't say bloody,' Mary admonished.

'His head *was* all bloody,' argued Hester, 'and it was all twisted too. It looked awful funny, as if he were dead.'

'He wasn't dead. Carl Merton's alive and well and living in Wales.' It had been decided not to tell them the truth, one of the reasons Laura had whisked them away as soon as possible. It was the first time either had spoken about the day the mist had swirled around Caerdovey and what had happened in the den, and there was a question Queenie had long wanted to ask. 'What were you looking for in the garden?' She'd wondered how they could expect to find anything in the thick mist.

Both girls appeared bemused. 'We weren't in the garden.'

'But Mary, you told Gwen – and the policeman – that you were looking for something, then you went into the garage and found . . .' She didn't finish. They already knew what they'd found. It seemed odd to be talking like this in the rowdy dining room among children whose main objective seemed to be to demolish their food in record time.

'We only said that because we were scared,' Hester admitted.

'Scared of what?'

'Of what we'd done.' Mary looked at her uneasily. 'Will you be cross if we tell you?' Queenie shook her head, though was beginning to feel uneasy herself at the turn the conversation was taking. 'We were lying on the bed in the den,' Mary said gravely, 'when Carl Merton came up the ladder. It was dark and we were whispering, so he didn't know we were there.' Queenie's heart missed a beat, imagining what Carl might have done had he known.

Hester took up the story. 'I'd already told Mary about the night he'd come into our bedroom and hurt you.'

'Why didn't you tell me you were awake?' Queenie gasped.

'I thought it best to wait until you said something first. That's why I didn't tell Mummy, only Mary, 'cos she's my friend.'

'I'm your *best* friend.'

'She's my *best* friend,' Hester concurred. 'Did he hurt you badly, Queenie?'

'He didn't hurt me at all,' Queenie lied. 'He was drunk, that's all, and he came into the wrong room. I soon put him right. What happened that night in the den?' She tried not to sound as anxious as she felt.

'We could see Carl Merton bending down over the ladder. Then you came and you screamed, so we crept over and Mary took one foot and I took the other and we tipped him up and he fell down. Then we felt frightened and told Gwen we'd been in the garden in case she got cross. Was that wrong?' she asked nervously

'I don't know,' said a horrified Queenie. 'Perhaps it'd be best not to breathe a word to a soul about what happened. Let's keep it a secret between us three.'

The girls were happy to agree. Mary said she'd sooner

not think about it any more and Hester said she'd hardly thought about it all. It was only Queenie's plaster that had reminded her.

Queenie tried to imagine what Laura and Vera's reaction would be if they learnt their daughters had killed Carl Merton. It was a feat of imagination that was quite beyond her.

The movement in her arm was improving with each day, just like the weather. She could hold a knife and fork and cut her own food, fasten the hooks and eyes on her clothes, tie shoe laces. Dr Hollis was very pleased with her progress.

'You've done wonderfully well,' he told her one balmy day in March. 'One more visit and you won't need to come again. Your shoulder's a bit stiff, but that's all. What are you going to do with yourself once you're better?'

'Get a job,' Queenie said promptly. 'I'd like to do some sort of war work.'

'I don't think that's such a good idea.' He gave a wry smile. 'We'd all like to do our bit towards the war, but you're very young, only fifteen, and it'd be best not to strain your arm for a few months yet. Take it easy, you'd be better off with a nice, pleasant job, in a shop, for instance. Lots of women have either joined the forces or are working in factories, so you'd be welcomed with open arms. Anyway, off you go, Queenie. Have a nice Easter.'

'The same to you, doctor.'

When Laura came on Sunday, she thought Dr Hollis made perfect sense. 'You've been through a hard time, Queenie,' she said, though she didn't know the half of it. 'A nice, pleasant job is exactly what you need.'

Three weeks later, Queenie started work in the children's clothes section of Herriot's, a small, dead posh department store in Lord Street, in itself one of the poshest shopping venues in Lancashire. She was interviewed by the manager, Mr Matthews, a friendly man in his sixties with lovely silver hair. He'd been on the point of retiring, he explained, when the war had started and the assistant manager, Mr Mackie, who'd been about to take over, had been called up straight away as he was already a sergeant in the Territorial Army.

'Do you have any retail experience?' he enquired, peering at her through his half-moon glasses.

'No. I've been working as a governess since I left school and I did some part-time teaching in a school in Wales.' The governess idea had been Laura's. 'It's true, in a way,' she insisted. 'If they want proof, tell them to write to me. I'll give you a glowing reference.'

Mr Matthew's lips twitched with amusement. 'That's rather an achievement for someone so young. What did you teach?'

'Reading, writing and arithmetic.'

'Although retail experience would have been desirable, such an amazing knowledge of the three Rs is good enough for me, added to the fact that you're very presentable, even if your accent is a bit rough. Can you start on Monday?'

She was told she had to wear black, an eventuality Laura had already foreseen and had given her the money to buy an outfit. 'And you'll need shoes, your first grown-up pair. You'd better get stockings and a suspender belt too.'

On her way out of Herriot's, Queenie glanced at the prices in the Ladies' Clothes Department and was shocked to the core. Two pound, ten and sixpence, just for a skirt! The same for a blouse, even though it was very smart; black georgette with lace inserts on the front. On the assumption that not everyone in Southport was a millionaire, she went outside, turned off Lord Street and found herself by the station. Nearby, she came across a street of inexpensive shops where she bought a gaberdine skirt for seventeen and six, a black satin blouse with pearl buttons for thirteen and elevenpence halfpenny, a pink brocade suspender belt and two pairs of rayon stockings. Shoes proved more difficult, she hadn't known there was a shortage, but eventually she found a pair of black court shoes with daringly high heels.

'You're lucky, only taking a size three,' the assistant said. 'We've a few eights in stock, but are completely out of the sizes in between.'

Back in Sea Shells, she managed to avoid Mrs Palfrey who had trapped one of the few real guests in the hallway. She went upstairs, put on on her new outfit, though it took a while to understand the suspenders, and examined her reflection in the wardrobe mirror.

It was hard to believe she was looking at the same person who had nervously knocked on Laura's door almost two years ago because her mam had gone away and she didn't know what to do. Her silvery blonde hair was thick and smooth and she wore it shoulder length; sometimes loose, sometimes tied back with a ribbon. The black outfit – she'd never worn black before – made her slim body look even slimmer, and the high-heeled shoes accentuated the curves of her legs. She felt quite tall.

'You're pathetic!' Mam used to say, but she didn't feel pathetic now. She wondered where Mam was, and what she would say if she knew about all the things that had happened and the job she was starting on Monday. Most importantly, what would Mam think about her arm, now perfectly straight, exactly the same as the other?

Also, she would like to ask Mam exactly how her arm had been broken the first time and why she hadn't been taken to the hospital to have it set.

The transformation, from the pathetic little girl she used to be, to the pretty, smartly dressed young woman she was now, was so great, so astounding, it was almost as if a miracle had happened and she had become a completely different person.

'Oh, hello. Can't you sleep either?' It was a young woman who spoke, one of Mrs Palfrey's guests.

'I don't feel the least bit tired.' Queenie was sitting on an iron bench in the back garden of Sea Shells, her eyes fixed on the blood red cloud suspended over Liverpool.

'It's well past midnight, but I can't stop thinking about my husband. Do you mind if I sit with you?'

'Of course not.'

'My name's Madge. What's yours?'

'Queenie.'

'Have you got family back there, Queenie?' Madge nodded towards the red cloud, then took a puff of her cigarette.

'Not exactly. Just some close friends, but they're almost family.'

'I've loads; Mum and Dad, a brother and two sisters, in-laws and, of course, Paul, my husband. He's a voluntary ARP warden.' She sighed. 'If it weren't for the children, I would have stayed, but John's only six months old and June's two. It didn't seem fair to risk their lives.' Madge had arrived at about six o'clock that evening with her two small children. The baby was teething and she'd gone straight to her room.

May had brought air raids the likes of which no one in Liverpool had known before. For two nights in a row, the bombs had rained mercilessly down. The dull sound of the deadly explosions could be clearly heard miles away in Southport. Now, the third night, and the Luftwaffe weren't letting up. The onslaught had begun a few hours ago.

'It looks as if the entire city is on fire,' Queenie murmured.

'They drop incendiary bombs first to start fires and to help identify targets,' Madge told her. 'It's like being in hell. We weren't the only ones to leave today. Paul brought us in the car and we passed hundreds of people on their way out carrying bundles of bedding. We gave a woman and her little girl a lift. They were going to sleep in a field, anywhere to escape the raids. We're lucky, being able to afford a hotel.'

Despite Madge's words, Queenie almost wished she were in Bootle, underneath the blood red cloud, not miles and miles away. So far, she'd avoided the worst of the war, but since coming to Southport, they'd been back to Glover Street a few times and witnessed the devastation wrought by German bombs. She'd felt, most unreasonably, that she was missing out on all the excitement.

Laura said she was crazy to think like that. 'You're best out of it,' she advised, but Laura had made no attempt to get out of it herself. She actually enjoyed her job as a riveter, being in the thick of things, queuing for food and making do.

She gasped when there was an extra-loud bang and the red sky lightened for a moment. 'That's the *Malakand*,' Madge explained. 'It was lying in Huskisson Dock with a thousand tons of ammunition on board when it was hit. Every now 'n' again, there's another explosion. Honestly, Queenie,' she said impatiently, 'I think the world's gone mad.'

'That's what me friend, Laura, always ses.'

Madge lit another cigarette. 'I'm smoking meself to death. I never smoked until this bloody war started. I didn't swear either. Would you like a ciggie? I didn't think to ask.'

'No, thank you.'

'It dulls my brain, or so I tell myself. Stops me worrying about Paul quite so much.' There was the suggestion of a sob in her voice. 'Perhaps I should start drinking, too.'

Queenie supposed she should tell her not to worry, that Paul would be all right, but what did she know? Many people would already have died that night beneath the red cloud. One of them could be Paul and another could be Laura, who had a vitally important job to do and couldn't get away.

'I wish I could get in touch with me friends,' she said. 'I've been worried about them all week.'

'Where do they live?'

'Bootle.'

'We live on the other side of Liverpool, by Sefton Park, otherwise I'd ask Paul to find out for you. He promised to ring in the morning.'

'Thanks, anyroad. If I've not heard by Sunday, I'll go and see if they're all right. I'd go before if it wasn't for me job.'

'Where do you work?' Madge asked.

'Herriot's. It's a big shop on Lord Street.'

'I've heard of it, but I've never been in. It's like Freddy's in Hanover Street; dead posh, quite beyond the pocket of a schoolteacher's wife. Oh, did you hear that!' She threw her cigarette to the ground and stamped on it. 'John's crying again. If that bloody tooth doesn't come through soon, I don't know what I'll do. It didn't help, me forgetting to bring his teething ring. He's been using my finger instead. It's nearly gnawed right through. Goodnight, Queenie. I'll see you tomorrow.'

'Goodnight, Madge.'

Next day, Queenie bought a teething ring for John, the last one in the shop, but when she got home, Madge and her children had gone. 'Her dad came for her this morning and took her and the kids away,' Mrs Palfrey said. 'Apparently, her hubby was killed in the raid last night, poor chap.'

There were no trains running to Liverpool on Sunday morning. 'Marsh Lane Station was wrecked last night,' the woman in the ticket office said when Queenie asked for three tickets to Bootle. 'It was the heaviest bombing yet. I'd be surprised if there's anything of Liverpool left. You can get the bus as far as Seaforth, but you'll have to walk the rest of the way.'

Hester and Mary insisted on coming with her. She hadn't told them about the raids, but there'd been talk in school and they were aware something odd and very worrying was happening.

They held hands on the bus to Seaforth and hardly spoke. Queenie's tummy had tied itself in a knot and a pulse in her throat was throbbing madly. She stared out of the window. It was a lovely day, sunny and warm, and the gardens of the houses that they passed were full of flowers. People, in their best clothes, were on their way to and from church. Only the numerous gas masks gave any sign the country was at war.

The bus stopped by the railway bridge where Seaforth ended and Bootle and the docks began. Here, the air smelt different; acrid and smoky. They got off the bus, walked under the bridge, and into a completely different world, of jumbled bricks and flat landscapes where people's homes had once stood, of gaping roofs on skeletal houses, broken windows with tattered pieces of curtains fluttering through. Everywhere was thick with dust and men were tearing away at the rubble.

For a while, they stood silently, unable to take in the horror that faced them, until Hester said timidly, 'What are they looking for?'

'I dunno,' Queenie said. Bodies, she supposed.

Mary, who always pretended to be so brave, started to cry. 'I want me mam and dad.'

'In a minute.'

They walked on, stepping over someone's front door, avoiding the craters, the scattered bricks, the charred pieces of wood. The landmarks of a lifetime had disappeared and Queenie was no longer sure where Glover Street was. She made for the Dock Road where a fire still blazed amongst the remains of a building that she vaguely remembered had used to be a pub. Half a dozen firemen were standing around the engine, hoses limp on the ground.

'No water, luv,' one of the men said, shrugging helplessly, when they passed. 'No water, no gas, no electricity. There's nothing left.'

They reached Glover Street, but it was a Glover Street they'd never seen before. Both ends had disappeared; the little shop on the corner where Laura had bought her groceries, along with the first three houses on both sides had been reduced to a jumble of bricks, and the wall of the grain silo at the far end was now no more than a few feet high. Incredibly, halfway along, an elderly woman was sitting in the doorway, sunning herself. Another woman was scrubbing her step, not the sort of thing usually done on a Sunday, but the everyday standards of normal life no longer applied.

'Our house is still there,' Hester said in a quivery voice.

'So's ours.' Mary started to run.

'Mind the crater,' Queenie shouted. The bomb had left a deep, wide hole and there was very little pavement left.

Mary disappeared into the Monaghans'. Hester ran ahead, pulled the key to her own house through the letter box, and unlocked the door. Ben Tyler came into the hall. He gasped when he saw them. 'How did you get here? I didn't think there was any transport running. Laura's been threatening to walk all the way to Southport this afternoon, despite the state she's in.'

Laura was lying on the settee when they went in, her head heavily bandaged. 'Don't look so alarmed, both of you,' she said, laughing. 'It looks much worse than it is. I fell down that damn crater in the dark, that's all. Ben's been looking after me. Isn't he kind?'

'You should be in hospital,' Ben chided.

'I've been in hospital, but last night people were being brought in who'd been hurt far worse than me. I felt ashamed to be taking up a bed. I came home and not long afterwards the hospital was bombed. Come along, sweetheart,' she held out her arms and Hester fell into them, 'Mummy's not an invalid and she'd appreciate a hug. And from you, too, Queenie.'

Ben offered to make everyone a cup of tea until he remembered there was no water and no gas to boil it on. He went upstairs to look for lemonade, and Queenie told Laura she'd been watching the raids from Mrs Palfrey's garden. 'I was dead worried,' she said. 'Is everyone all right?'

'Not really.' Laura made a face. 'Billy Monaghan has been captured in Egypt and is now officially a prisoner of war, and Dick has been reported missing at sea – his wife, Iris, is expecting a baby any minute and Vera's almost out of her mind with worry. I haven't heard from Roddy in ages. But,' she sighed, 'that's not all. Quite a few people we know have been killed. Remember Edgar Binns who collected the rent? And Jimmy Nicholls's mum and dad died last night when a land mine fell on Salisbury Road.'

'Oh, poor Jimmy!' Queenie gasped. 'He thought the world of his mam and dad. I'll go and see him later.'

'You might not be able to find him, dear. Lord knows where he is now. One other thing, not nearly so important, a letter came for you the other day from Caerdovey. It's on the mantelpiece, probably from Gwen.'

The letter was from Gwen. She read it on her way to look for Jimmy.

My Dear Queenie,

I'm about to leave Caerdovey for Cardiff where I've got a job as a cook in a munitions factory. I'm very much looking forward to it.

There was an inquest into that business with Carl Merton. The verdict was 'Accidental Death'. I was very relieved as Caerdovey was awash with all sorts of rumours. As for Mrs Merton, she disappeared one day and The Old School House is up for sale. Don't answer this letter, lovey, and I won't write to you again. I'm sure you'd sooner not think about that dreadful night and a letter from me will only remind you. You must try to put it to the back of your mind and not let it spoil your life. I hope everything goes well for you in the future, my dear Queenie. You deserve it.

With all my love,

Gwen Hughes

Jimmy was sitting on the heap of bricks that had used to be his home. His eyes lit up when he saw Queenie approach. 'Hello, girl. You're a sight for sore eyes and your arm's looking good.' The light quickly faded.

'I'm sorry, Jimmy. Laura's only just told me.' She climbed the bricks and sat beside him, not caring about her pretty summer frock.

'They'd have gone to the shelter, but me dad couldn't manage the stairs – we lived on the top floor. Anyroad, some people in the shelter smoked like bloody chimneys and he couldn't breathe. They always made me go though, else I'd be dead an' all.' He kicked morosely at a heap of rubble. 'I'll never buy me dad a car now.'

Queenie never knew what to say on these occasions. 'Never mind, Jimmy' just didn't seem enough. 'You can still buy one and take your Tess and Pete for rides,' she said encouragingly. 'I wouldn't mind a ride meself.'

'Wouldn't you?'

'No, Jimmy.'

'I always wanted to work in a garage, but they've mostly shut down, with there being no petrol, like. I've got this job with the Corpy clearing rubble. I wish I was old enough to join the Army. A chap in Chaucer Street joined and they're teaching him to be a motor mechanic.'

'One day, Jimmy.' She patted his arm and asked if he'd like to come to the British Restaurant, which, according to Ben Tyler, had been set up in a giant tent in North Park. 'Me and the girls are going. The food's for free.'

'Thanks, girl, but I'd sooner stay here.' He turned over a brick. 'I keep finding things. The other day I found me dad's best tie, though he hadn't worn it in years. Yesterday, I came across one of mam's pearl earrings, not real pearl,' he added hastily, just in case Queenie thought it might have been.

It was awful, having to go back to Southport, to Sea

Shells and Mrs Palfrey, leaving behind a distraught Vera and an injured Laura who was determined to return to work next day. The only good thing about Southport was her job, which she loved.

Herriot's was a haven of normality in a war-torn world. Once inside its doors, it was almost possible to forget about the horrible things happening outside. It was a comfortable cocoon, where the lights were always bright, there was carpet on the floor, never too much noise, and the atmosphere genteel.

The staff, mainly women, got on well. They felt as if they were all pulling together to keep the shop open for the people of Southport, even if it was only those able to afford Herriot's sky-high prices.

Every morning, Kate on Cosmetics let Queenie have a quick dab behind the ears from one of the demonstration bottles of expensive scents, and Ellen on Hosiery would let the others know when a delivery of silk stockings had arrived. Mr Matthews had taken a shine to Queenie. 'How's our little governess today?' he would enquire with a twinkling smile when he did the rounds before the shop opened and the staff were standing to attention behind their various counters.

'Very well, Mr Matthews,' Queenie would say demurely. She would always be grateful to Dr Hollis for suggesting she work in a shop.

Perhaps Hitler had decided Liverpool was on its knees and there was no need to attack it further. The city centre had been devastated, the docks, the lifeblood of the city, put out of action. But not for long! What Hitler didn't know was that the morale of the inhabitants was sky high. The main services were speedily reconnected, accommodation found for those who had lost their homes and, in no time at all, it was business as usual on the docks. All over the country, people were willing to put up with the most appalling inconvenience if it meant winning the war.

There were a few more raids at the end of May, but nothing as severe as those during the first horrendous week. June and July saw only a handful of attacks and in August there were none at all. One Sunday, Laura came to Southport and announced she and Vera thought it was time they all came home.

'You've been been away for two long years. Any longer, and we won't know each other any more. Hester and Mary will be just in time for the new term at school and, Queenie, there's no need to leave Herriot's. I know how much you love it and you can go by train.'

'When can we come?' Hester was jumping up and down with excitement.

'Why not today?' Laura said with a smile. 'Now we've made up our minds, there's no point in putting it off another minute. Get your things packed, say goodbye to Mrs Palfrey, and we'll be on our way.'

Chapter 6

'Queenie!' Laura shouted. 'Which of the silk stockings on the rack are mine?'

'The ones over the towel,' Queenie shouted back. 'Be careful how you pull them off.'

Laura came into the living room, wearing a smart blue frock with a sun-ray pleated skirt, the tops of the stockings held carefully between finger and thumb. 'When Hester was a little baby, she wasn't treated as tenderly as these. I'm terrified they'll snag.'

'You look nice,' Queenie remarked.

'It's only the second time I've been to a dance with Winnie and I've no idea why I'm bothering to look nice. I don't want to "cop off with a feller" like she does, yet I suppose my pride would be hurt if no one asked me up. You don't think I'm being unfaithful to Roddy, do you?' she asked anxiously.

'Would you mind if he went to a dance?'

'I've thought about that, and I'm *almost* certain I wouldn't mind a bit.'

Queenie raised her eyebrows. 'Only almost?'

Laura frowned and looked a tiny bit doubtful, imagining Roddy with another woman in his arms. Her face cleared. 'No, *absolutely* certain. I don't expect him to behave like a monk.'

'That's all right then. Let's hope he feels the same

about you. I'm sure he does,' she added quickly when Laura began to look anxious again.

'Shall we put the decorations up tomorrow?' Laura wondered aloud. 'Or is it too soon? Christmas is a whole fortnight away.'

'Me, I'd have them up all year round. I love decorations.'

'But they'd lose their novelty. I think I'll leave them for another week.'

Eric Tyler popped his head around the open door. 'Can I borrow a tablespoon of sugar?'

'Only if you lend us a tablespoon of tea,' Laura told him. 'We're completely out.'

'It's a deal. Let's make it a swap.' Eric vanished, returning minutes later with the tea in a paper bag. 'I heaped as much on the spoon as I could.'

'I hope you know the difference between a tablespoon and a dessertspoon,' Laura said severely when Eric followed her into the kitchen.

'A tablespoon's the biggest,' he said, leaning against the door jamb. He was a big man, ruggedly handsome, with dark eyes and dark curly hair, comfortable with himself. Given the choice, she preferred his younger brother. Ben was quieter, less brash, a gentle person. Eric's wife had died not long after Brian was born and he'd had a long time getting used to being a widower. He'd had quite a few lady friends since coming to Bootle, although he never brought them to the house.

She put the tea in the empty caddy and measured sugar carefully into the bag. 'Will that do? It's about time you learnt to live without sugar.' He and Ben drank that ghastly Camp coffee needing mountains of sugar to disguise the taste.

'I could say the same to you about tea. Why are you all dolled up?' he asked curiously. 'Are you going out with your friend, the glamorous Winnie?' Winnie was a frequent visitor to Glover Street.

'We're going dancing at the Grafton. Queenie's off to the pictures with your Brian and Jimmy Nicholls. I didn't feel like staying in on my own on Saturday night. Hester's over at the Monaghans'. Sammy's six months old and having a party. I presume you and Ben are going out.' Ben was upstairs, singing along to the wireless at the top of his voice. 'When you wish upon a star,' he crooned manfully.

'We'll probably go for a pint later. Another Saturday, you can always come with us rather than stay in by yourself.'

'Thanks, but I wouldn't be seen dead in the sort of pubs you frequent.'

He pretended to look hurt. 'There's nothing wrong with them.'

Laura grinned. 'There is if you're a woman. I've got my reputation to consider.'

'OK, Miss Stuck-Up, we won't invite you.' He grinned back.

'You'd better go and make your disgusting coffee. I haven't finished getting ready for the dance.'

She went to collect her stockings and gave a little scream when she found Brian in the living room, sitting on them. 'Stand up, young man, very slowly,' she commanded. The stockings had stuck to his trousers and she carefully peeled them off.

'Men!' she huffed in the bedroom, sitting on the bed while she rolled the featherlight silky material on to her legs, stretching them to examine the soft, shimmering effect. 'I should really be keeping these for when Roddy comes home,' she told herself. 'Lord knows when Herriot's will get more in.' But then only the Lord knew when Roddy would be home.

It was a year last June since she'd seen him, right after Dunkirk. He'd arrived exhausted, his feet swollen after the long march to the French coast. While home, he'd hardly spoken, refusing to talk about his experiences in France, and too weary to make love or travel to Wales to see Hester. He hadn't noticed she'd had her hair cut short and Laura had felt she was getting on his nerves, asking too many questions, fussing over him. She'd felt awful when he'd refused to have anything to do with the Tylers, who'd offered to take him for a drink.

It had been frustrating, all the months he'd spent in Colchester. It wasn't exactly the opposite side of the world, yet they'd been unable to meet, not even at Christmas. She'd suggested they try to catch up with each other in Birmingham, roughly halfway between, but he'd reminded her that with a twenty-four-hour pass he couldn't guarantee getting back to base on time. When, in the New Year, he'd told her he was being posted to North Africa of all places, she'd written to say she thought it most unfair that he wasn't allowed leave to see his wife before being sent so far away.

He'd written back in one of his impersonal letters, saying many wives came frequently to Colchester to see their husbands. 'You could say it was unfair your job doesn't allow you to take time off to do the same.'

It would have been easy to engage in a written argument, emphasising how important her job was, how essential to the war effort, and that she was surprised he was reduced to making such a trivial point. 'For goodness' sake, Roddy, I'm helping to make *aeroplanes*.' But she'd held her tongue – or perhaps she should say her pen – and sent him the usual cheerful letter in return, full of local news and gossip and saying how much she missed him. He would be in Africa by the time he read it, and how could she write any other way to the man she loved who was risking his life for his country? He was still annoyed she hadn't gone to Wales with Hester and it could only be because he loved her so much and why he resented her job. In Dunkirk, he had probably witnessed suffering she could only imagine and it had changed him. Once the war was over and they were together again, everything would return to normal.

Upstairs, Ben was now singing 'The Last Time I Saw Paris', and doing his best to sound like Maurice Chevalier. Listening, Laura smiled. The Tylers had taken the edge off what she'd expected to be a lonely, painful period, turning the house into a place full of laughter and good humour. The two older men, with their warm Geordie accents, were kind and generous to a fault. Brian was nice, if rather full of himself, and was obviously keen on Queenie, but Ben and Eric made her smile when she didn't feel a bit like smiling, and she'd been instructed to come upstairs if ever she felt miserable and they would cheer her up, though they hadn't been any use at all during the air raids, she remembered, having slept right through the fiercest, Brian too. Not even the bomb that had dropped at the end of Glover Street had woken them. With the landlord's permission – readily given – Ben had wired both flats for electricity, which was a boon.

Occasionally, she felt guilty for having such a good time, putting aside the terrible raids and the worry over Roddy. There was a wonderful camaraderie at work and the girls often went out together in a group, to the cinema or a pub. They'd arranged to go for a meal on Christmas Eve.

There was a knock on the front door, but Laura didn't move. Someone else would answer it. A minute later, the bedroom door was flung open and Winnie Corcoran came breezing in, waving a cigarette, bracelets jangling, exuding wafts of cheap scent, and wearing a fluffy jacket over a black, crêpe frock, liberally decorated with sequins. Her nails, including her toes, were painted brilliant purple.

'You bitch!' she snorted. 'You've got your silk stockings on. The first thing men look at is a woman's legs. You'll be asked up before me every time.'

'I somehow doubt it,' Laura said drily, glancing at her friend's half-exposed bosom, visible under the jacket, despite it being December and terribly cold outside. Winnie had natural blonde hair, very long, and combed over one eye like Veronica Lake. Her curvaceous figure and long tanned legs – the tan came out of a bottle – were the target of many a lascivious glance from the men at the factory where they both worked. Even in her overalls, her lovely hair hidden under a scarf tied with a jaunty knot, Winnie could attract a chorus of wolf whistles. Had she been regarded in the same way, Laura would have died a thousand deaths, but Winnie adored every minute.

Both women were twenty-three and their men were away at war, but there the similarity ended. Winnie was determined to enjoy her husband's absence to the full.

'I married Joe when I was eighteen,' she'd told Laura when they'd first got to know each other. 'I should have realised someone who was still an altar boy in his twenties wasn't exactly normal. Joe's got this thing about sex. He thinks it's sinful, whereas I quite liked it, even with Joe, who went at it dead half-hearted.' She sniffed contemptuously. 'I used to wonder what it'd be like with someone else and the war gave me the perfect opportunity to find out.'

Laura often wondered how she could make a friend out of someone so lacking in morals, who was unfaithful to her husband on a regular basis, drank too much, smoked like a chimney, and whose language was outrageously coarse. She had never discovered an answer, only that she liked Winnie Corcoran very much, despite her numerous faults. Usually, they went to the pictures together, but Winnie had persuaded her to go dancing again, claiming she felt lonely on her own.

'You won't be lonely for long,' Laura had pointed out. 'Last time, you found someone you liked after the second dance. From then on, I felt in the way.'

'You had a nice time, though, didn't you, Laura?'

'I suppose,' Laura said grudgingly. It had been quite flattering, as well as a new experience, to be asked for every dance and turn down repeated requests for dates and pleas to take her home. She had missed that particular part of growing up, not that she minded, she hastily told herself. Life with Roddy had been tough at times, but she wouldn't have changed it for the world.

'You know what I'd like?' Winnie said now, sitting beside her on the bed.

'How could I? I'm not a mindreader.'

'What I'd like,' Winnie continued, ignoring the remark, 'is a regular feller, someone I really got on with. I'm sick of copping off with different blokes all the time when most turn out dead hopeless. I'd only want him for the duration, like. Once Joe's home, I'll just have to teach him a few of the tricks I've learnt.'

'What sort of tricks?' Laura enquired, interested.

Winnie winked lewdly. 'You won't have heard of 'em. Christ knows what you and your Roddy got up to in bed. I'm amazed you managed to produce a child.'

Laura hadn't the faintest notion what she was talking about. What else was there to do in bed other than make love, and there was only one way of doing it.

'I'm ready,' she said. 'Shall we have a cup of tea before we go? And I want to call on Vera on the way.'

'Ready! But you haven't got any lippy on.' Winnie was aghast. 'You look as if you're off to milk a bloody cow, not go dancing.'

'You know I never wear make-up.'

'Well, it's about time you did. Would you like to borrow me lippy?'

'Not if it's the one you're wearing. I thought lips were supposed to be red, not purple.'

'Oh, well, please yourself,' Winnie said with a heavy sigh. 'Let's forget the tea and go now.'

'It's only seven o'clock. Won't we be too early?'

'I thought we could go for a drink first, a proper one. Get ourselves in the mood, like.'

Laura glared at her with exasperation. 'You know I'm not prepared to go into a pub with you again.' She didn't mind with a crowd, but the time she'd gone with Winnie every man in the place had tried to pick them up.

Winnie groaned. 'In that case, you can make us that tea. I'm bloody parched. I like it strong with loads of sugar.'

'In your dreams, Winnie Corcoran.'

It was the stupidest party Mary had ever been to. It had all been Iris's idea. Iris was Dick's wife, who had come to live with them just after Dick went missing and Sammy was born. Dick had almost certainly been lost at sea, but Iris refused to believe it. He was probably stranded somewhere on a desert island, she claimed, or floating around in a lifeboat, eking out the food so it would last until he sighted land.

Even Mary could see both ideas were daft, particularly the second one. They made Mam all confused and upset. 'Iris is stopping her from grieving,' Dad said, annoyed. The Monaghans had always thought Dick's wife a little bit touched and since she'd come to live there, she'd proved it. She was often to be found kneeling on the mat in front of the fire, her eyes fixed on the crucifix on the mantelpiece, praying aloud that Dick was still alive. All the Monaghans prayed for the same thing, but more privately, before they went to bed, though there was a feeling of hopelessness about it. They also prayed that their Billy would return, unharmed, from the prisoner of war camp, and the other lads, George, Frank and Victor, would be kept safe.

In January, Charlie was due to turn eighteen and his call-up papers would arrive. Mary would only have two brothers left – one, if the war lasted another two years and Tommy was called up, and none at all if it went on for another four and it would be Caradoc's turn to go. It was such an awful thought that a sob formed in her throat. She swallowed it quickly before it turned into a sound.

She tried to concentrate on the jigsaw she was doing with Hester. It was the first time she'd done a jigsaw at a birthday party. People usually played statues or musical chairs or pinning the tail on the donkey, which she was particularly good at. But you couldn't play those sort of games when there were only the two of you.

Seven of them had sat down to tea, not counting Sammy, but Dad had done a bunk as soon as he'd finished eating the triangular-shaped sarnies and the burnt blancmange. He'd wanted to check his football coupon, he said, which apparently demanded total privacy. That was ages ago and he still hadn't come back. Then Tommy and Caradoc had made excuses and left. Charlie was out with his girlfriend and had refused to come at all.

The trouble was no one could stand Iris, apart from little Sammy, and even he seemed to prefer his grandma.

'I can't find the woman's head,' Hester complained, sorting through the pieces of jigsaw.

Mary had the woman's head in her left hand. They were having a race. She'd bet Hester she would finish the man before Hester finished the woman and was making sure she won. She fitted a piece of the man's check waistcoat, found one of his shoes, quickly found the other, put the woman's head on the table when Hester wasn't looking, and declared herself the winner.

'I can't be bothered doing any more,' she announced.

'Oh, there's the head, right by you.' The head was clicked into place and Hester said she couldn't be bothered doing any more either. 'What shall we do instead?'

'Dunno. It's too cold to go upstairs. Shall we go over to yours?'

'Everyone's going out.'

'Including Queenie?'

'She's going to the pictures with Brian and Jimmy.'

'Lucky beggar.'

'Mary!' her mother said sharply. Iris rolled her eyes.

'I said beggar, Mam, not . . . not the other word.'

'I should hope not. Put the kettle on, there's a good girl, and I'll make us all a cup of tea.'

It was strange, Mary thought, running water into the kettle, but when she'd first met Hester, the house over the road had seemed dead miserable. Aggie Tate had lived upstairs and Hester's mam and dad were always looking worried about something. In contrast, her own house had been very different; her eight big brothers making loads of noise, the wireless on most of the time, Mam and Dad always laughing and joking with each other.

But now she'd sooner be in Hester's house than anywhere. The Tylers were dead funny and she had a bit of a crush on Brian, even if he never noticed she was there. Since clothing coupons were brought in last June, Laura and Queenie, stretching ingenuity to its limit, had been making loads of things, like dirndl skirts out of blackout with a band of flowered curtain material or rick-rack braid around the hem, coats from old blankets, skirts from old coats, dissolving into helpless giggles when sometimes things went hopelessly wrong, like the time Laura had tried to bleach a length of blackout and it had turned out all mottled. Afterwards, she'd sewn pieces of patchwork over it and had made Mary a frock, which looked fine.

Back at her own house, Mam hardly laughed these days, and Dad hadn't cracked a joke in ages, what with Dick missing and Billy being in the prisoner of war camp. Iris didn't help. She suffered from terrible headaches and everyone had to creep around like mice. The least noise, and she would groan and cast an accusing glance at whoever had coughed too loudly, or returned their cup to the saucer with rather more force than necessary. She winced when the lads ran upstairs, their boots thumping on each step. Mam would shout at them to shush and Iris would wince again.

'Can't they take their boots off in the house, Vera?' she would complain. 'I've got one of me heads.' She complained all the time about more or less everything. The tea was too hot or too cold, too weak or too strong. The pastry was too soft or too hard. Mam had put too much salt in the spuds. The meat was underdone or overdone. She felt cold in bed, but when Mam gave her an extra blanket, she felt too hot.

If Iris hadn't been Dick's wife, mother of Dick's son and the Monaghans' first grandchild, she would have been given her marching orders a long while ago, but Sammy was the most beautiful, intelligent, captivating baby in the world and the entire family would have been prepared to put up with ten Irises to keep him. When Mary had returned from being evacuated and discovered she was no longer the centre of attention, she didn't mind having her nose knocked out of joint by little Sammy.

The kettle boiled. Mam was nursing the adorable Sammy and made to hand him back to his mother while she made the tea, but Iris irritably waved him away. 'Oh, lie him on the floor, Vera. I've got one of me awful heads.'

Hester immediately knelt on one side of the baby and Mary the other. Sammy gurgled and waved his arms and legs, his sparkling eyes shifting from one to the other.

'Who's lovely?' Hester poked his fat tummy.

'I am, I am,' Sammy's delighted expression seemed to say.

'He knows I'm his auntie. He always recognises me straight away, don't you, Sammykins.' Mary was excessively proud of being an aunt at only seven.

They continued to play with the baby, until Mam came in with the tea and insisted on picking him up. 'There's draughts on the floor,' she said, glancing at Iris, who didn't apparently care.

'I think he needs a new nappy, Mam. He smells a bit.' The nappies were airing over the fire guard.

'I'll change him in a minute,' Mam said with another glance at Iris who never felt well enough to do much for her son, or give a hand with the laundry, the cooking, washing the dishes, or going anywhere near a mop and bucket.

The girls returned to the table where Hester stuck another piece in the jigsaw. 'Perhaps we should finish it,' she said in a desultory tone.

'It's boring around the edges, nearly all the same

colour. I only like doing the man and the woman. I think,' Mary said in a whisper, 'we should go to your house, even if there's no one in. We can listen to the wireless and play cards or something. Even hide and seek.' Needless to say, Iris couldn't stand the wireless. There was nothing on but rubbish and it gave her a bad head. Everyone was dreading Christmas when she would be given a golden opportunity to have a monumental moan.

'Mummy's coming in a minute to say goodbye before she goes to the dance.'

'OK, we'll go after then.'

'Let's say we're going to fetch something, and then just not come back. Otherwise, it'll look rude.'

Mary nodded. Mam wouldn't be too pleased about being left alone with Iris.

'What are you two whispering about?' Vera enquired.

'It's rude to whisper in front of people,' Iris said tartly.

'We weren't whispering,' Mary said loudly, causing Iris to wince. 'We were just talking quietly, wondering whether to finish the jigsaw or not.'

'I hope you both have a nice time,' Vera said wistfully. 'I can't remember the last time I went dancing. I had this black frock trimmed with feathers. It looked dead glamorous.'

'Why don't you and Albert go to a dinner dance at Christmas? It's only a few weeks off,' Laura said.

'Oh, I don't know about that.' Vera looked doubtful. 'We're a bit old for that sort of thing.'

Iris sniffed disdainfully, as if she'd never heard such a daft suggestion.

'There's no age limit at dinner dances. I'll make you a new frock for a Christmas present,' Laura said encouragingly. 'Or at least I'll turn one of your old ones into something more fashionable. But I'll have to do it soon, there isn't much time. I'll even see if I can find some feathers.' Vera wasn't exactly a shadow of her former self, but she'd lost three stone over the last few years. Food rationing was doing wonders for people's figures.

'You can't turn down an offer like that, Vera,' Winnie said chirpily.

'She can if she wants.' Iris looked even more disdainful.

'We'll just have to see,' Vera said, clearly not entirely opposed to the idea.

'I'll have a quiet word with Albert,' Laura said as she and Winnie walked down Glover Street. The crater had been filled in, but Laura still felt nervous walking over it. 'It's about time Vera had a treat. At least her job got her out of the house, took her mind off the boys, but she gave it up when Iris landed on them and she had to look after Sammy.'

'Why can't Iris look after Sammy herself?'

'She's in poor health, or so she claims. Personally, I think she's just pretending, taking advantage of Vera's kind heart – and you couldn't find a kinder heart than Vera's.'

'And she's a miserable cow, an' all, that Iris,' Winnie growled. 'She looks at me as if I were no more than a piece of dirt. I'd like to give her arse a good kicking.'

'Yes, well . . .' Laura wouldn't have minded joining in the kicking, but was too ladylike to say so.

Perhaps it was about time she started wearing make-up, she thought, when they arrived at the Grafton and she contemplated her scrubbed, rosy face in the mirror in the crowded cloakroom.

Winnie must have read her mind and grinned at her

through the mirror. 'I told you, you should've brought your milking stool.' She spat on a block of mascara and began to apply another coat, turning her already stiff lashes into a row of little black spikes. The girl on Laura's other side was dabbing her cheeks with rouge and looked for all the world like a clown. Laura supposed there was a happy medium; a little touch of powder to take the shine off her nose wouldn't hurt, a smear of pale pink lipstick.

And her woollen frock seemed awfully sensible compared with the other girls' – and she was probably the only person there in flat shoes. Still, she hadn't come to 'cop a feller', and only her feelings would be hurt if no one danced with her.

To her surprise, and Winnie's, she was asked to dance the very second they entered the ballroom where the orchestra was playing 'Kiss The Boys Goodbye'. Laura was a good dancer, she had been pleased to discover, and she enjoyed being swept around the floor by a young soldier called Jack who said she reminded him of his sister.

Jack asked her for the next dance and the next, until she felt obliged to bring up the subject of husbands and told him hers was in North Africa, just in case he got ideas.

Winnie was being pestered by a chap she didn't like and suggested they move to a different part of the ballroom. 'It'll put him off the scent. I don't like to turn him down, 'case he gets nasty.'

They retired to a corner, the orchestra struck up, 'We'll Meet Again', one of Laura's favourites, when a laughing voice said, 'Can I have this dance, Winnie?'

Winnie gasped, 'You bugger! You followed us,' but didn't sound as if she minded in the least, as Eric Tyler led her on to the floor.

Ben Tyler looked at Laura, clearly uncomfortable. 'I'm sorry, but he insisted. He's got a thing about Winnie. I hope you're not cross.' He began to edge away. 'Don't worry, I'm not going to cramp your style. I'll make myself scarce.'

'Don't be silly.' Laura spied Jack on his way towards her. He'd obviously tracked her down. 'I'd love to have at least one dance with you. There's a young man about to ask me who I'd sooner not dance with again.' Jack was very nice, but she didn't want him monopolising her all night.

'Actually,' she said, when she was on the floor in Ben's arms, 'I find dances rather difficult. You can get stuck with people and it's hard to get rid of them without being rude. It's all right for men, they can pick and choose. I don't think I'll come again. Anyway, it hardly seems fair, when I've no intention of acccepting a date or letting anyone take me home.'

'Not even me?' Ben raised his eyebrows. He was a smaller, slighter version of his brother, his hair not quite so dark, his skin a tiny bit paler, which made him look rather delicate. He had an attractive, whimsical smile.

'Oh, you can take me home, of course. I'll be glad of the company. Will Winnie and Eric be coming with us, too?'

'Not if Eric's got anything to do with it. He has plans for Winnie that involve going back to her house, not ours.'

Laura felt embarrassed. She was well aware that Winnie slept around, but there was something different, she couldn't quite put her finger on what, about her sleeping with someone like Eric whom Laura knew well.

The music ended. Ben said, 'Would you like a drink? But please say no if I'm being a nuisance.'

'I'd love a glass of lemonade.' It was getting very

warm. 'Though I don't want to stop you from dancing with other women.'

'To tell the truth, I don't like dances either,' Ben confessed. 'I can't remember when I last went. Asking girls to dance takes a certain sort of courage that I don't have.'

'I like the atmosphere,' Laura said when they were sitting at a table on the balcony looking down on the dancers. 'It's very emotional and romantic, moving in a way. All these soldiers, sailors and airmen. Who knows where they'll be this time next week?' For some, it might be the last time they would hold a woman in their arms. She spied Winnie's blonde head. Eric seemed to be holding her unnecessarily close as they danced to 'Two Sleepy People', not that Winnie appeared to mind. 'I'd love to come with Roddy. Is there someone you'd like to come with?' she asked curiously. He was thirty-two, very presentable, and she felt sure he must have a girlfriend back in Newcastle, though he'd never mentioned anyone.

Ben didn't answer for a while and she regretted asking such a personal question. She was about to apologise, when he spoke. His voice was strained.

'There was. Jennifer – Jenny. We were engaged, about to be married, when she decided to give me up for someone richer and better-looking.'

'Gosh. I'm so sorry. I shouldn't have asked. It was very rude of me.' She wished the balcony floor would swallow her up.

'That's OK.' His smile was a touch bitter. 'I'm all right now, though it took a long time to get over the feeling of betrayal.'

Laura squeezed his hand. 'You're bound to fall in love with someone else one day.'

Ben looked at her directly. His eyes were very bright. 'I already have.'

'Oh,' she cried, delighted. 'Is it someone I know?'

'It's someone you know very well.'

'Not Winnie!' It would cause dreadful complications as Eric already seemed badly smitten.

'Not Winnie, no.'

'And not Queenie. She's far too young for you.'

'Not Queenie either, but you're getting close.'

He was staring at her oddly and she could feel herself going very red. She clapped her hands to her cheeks. They were burning. 'Not me,' she said in a strangled voice. 'Not me, surely.'

'Don't worry,' Ben said calmly. 'I won't make a pass. I know how much you love Roddy and I'd like us to stay good friends. I shouldn't have told you, but I suppose the romantic atmosphere got to me, loosened my tongue.' He stood. 'I'll get you another lemonade and after I come back we'll never talk about it again.'

Queenie was having trouble with her men. She hadn't been back in Glover Street long before Brian Tyler invited her to the pictures. She went willingly because she liked him. Behind his rather haughty exterior, she sensed he was quite shy. When he suggested Saturday night, she told him she'd already made arrangements to go out and asked if they could go Friday instead.

'Friday it is.' Brian looked pleased.

They went to the Palace in Marsh Lane and saw *They Drive by Night*, with George Raft and Ann Sheridan. Brian held her hand on the way home.

The following night, Saturday, Jimmy Nicholls arrived to take her to the pictures. They'd already been out about half a dozen times. '*They Drive by Night*'s on at the

Palace,' Jimmy said, rubbing his hands together gleefully. 'It's all about lorries.'

'I'm sorry, Jimmy, I've already seen it.'

'Eh? Who'd you go with?'

'Brian Tyler from upstairs.'

'But you're *my* girlfriend!' Jimmy said indignantly.

'No, I'm not.' Queenie was equally indignant. 'I'm nobody's girlfriend.'

'I thought, after the war, once I'd got a proper job, like, we'd get married.'

'That's the first I've heard of it.' She was sixteen and had no intention of getting serious with anyone, though felt awful when Jimmy looked terribly hurt. He was probably the nicest lad on earth, living in a disgusting lodging house on the Dock Road and spending most of his pitiful wages buying clothes for Tess and Pete who were still living in Caerdovey, virtually the only evacuees left. He went to see them at least once a month. Laura sometimes knitted jumpers for Pete, and Queenie had made Tess a dirndl skirt out of blackout material.

She felt so guilty, she told him she'd enjoyed *They Drive by Night* so much that she wouldn't mind seeing it again.

'Are you sure?' he asked pathetically.

'Absolutely.'

'Are you seeing that Brian Tyler again?'

She wasn't prepared to lie. 'We're going into town on Wednesday afternoon. It's me half day off, and he's still on holiday from school.' Brian was in the sixth form at Merchant Taylor's. 'We're going to the matinée at the Forum.'

'What's on?'

'*Gone With the Wind*. It's nearly four hours long.'

Inevitably, Brian discovered she was seeing Jimmy and said he didn't want to share her with another chap. 'I hope you don't mind, Queenie, but I'd like you to be just *my* girlfriend.'

'I've no intention of being anybody's girlfriend,' she said huffily. 'You'll just have to put up with Jimmy, and he'll have to put up with you. Either that, or we won't go out.' She'd be perfectly happy without both of them. She loved her job at Herriot's, she loved living in Glover Street with Laura and Hester. She didn't need one boyfriend, let alone two.

'But I like you!' Brian wailed. He was very clever and very spoiled, used to getting his own way.

'I like you, but I like Jimmy as well.'

Each became so jealous when she went out with the other, that she suggested they went in a threesome. It had been funny at first, both vying for her attention the way Hester and Mary had done in Wales, but they'd only been five years old, whereas Brian was seventeen, Jimmy two years younger. She told them she found them extremely childish.

Eventually, to her relief, somewhat grudgingly, they began to get on. Both avid football fans, they went to see Liverpool or Everton play on Saturday afternoons when Queenie was at work. By the time December came, they had become good friends.

They took turns choosing what to see. Jimmy liked cowboy pictures best, Brian thrillers, and Queenie anything that made her laugh or cry. Tonight had been Jimmy's turn and they'd seen *Destry Rides Again* with James Stewart and Marlene Dietrich.

'See what the boys in the back room will have,' they sang on the way home, linking arms, Queenie in the middle.

Halfway down Marsh Lane, Brian who, unlike Jimmy, was inclined towards introspection, stopped. It was a lovely moonlit night and they could see as clear as day.

'I wonder where the people are who used to live there?' Brian nodded towards a row of half-demolished houses. The moon peered through the spaces where windows had once been, through rafters that had once supported a roof. 'They look like corpses. The flesh has been removed and only the bones are left. It's strange how we get used to things,' he said in an awed voice. 'This time last year, they were perfectly ordinary houses, now they're wrecks. Half of Bootle has been obliterated, yet we've stopped noticing. We can actually walk along the road and sing. I'm surprised anybody, me included, is able to enjoy themselves after everything that's gone on.'

'I've not stopped thinking about me mam and dad,' Jimmy growled, 'but as me old lady said in a letter, "Life goes on".'

'I suppose that's it,' Brian said thoughtfully. 'Life goes on. Either you go on, or you go under.' He began to walk again, more slowly now. 'You know, I'll never forget this, being with you two, living in Glover Street, the war, the raids. Everything. It's been the high point of my life. I can't imagine things ever being *real* again.'

'You mustn't think like that.' Queenie felt quite shocked. 'It's as if you don't expect anything exciting will ever happen again.'

'Maybe it won't,' Brian said in a flat voice.

'Things'll seem real to me when I get a car,' Jimmy said.

'Oh, come on, both of you.' Queenie forged ahead, dragging them with her. She was glad to be alive, to be who she was, where she was, and wasn't prepared to listen to such talk. Laura had said there was enough tea to make a pot when they got back, 'But only have a cup each. There isn't much milk left.' Everyone was out, so they could sit around talking till they came home, listen to Radio Luxembourg, which played all the latest songs.

Jimmy wouldn't go home until Brian went upstairs, and Brian wouldn't go upstairs until Jimmy had gone, and she'd have to pretend to go to bed to get rid of them.

She was surprised to hear voices when she opened the front door, and found Hester and Mary in the living room lying on the mat in front of the fire reading a book together, Vera relaxing in an armchair, and Sammy, like a little angel, fast asleep on the sofa. The wireless was on and Anne Shelton was singing 'Night and Day'.

'I thought there'd be no one in,' she exclaimed.

Vera groaned and stretched her legs. 'Iris went to bed, so me and Sammy followed the girls over here. It's nice, sitting in someone else's house for a change and listening to music. I didn't think Laura would mind. I'm sick to death of our place. If I so much as breathe, it gives Iris a headache. What was the picture like?'

'Much better than most cowboy pictures,' Brian said.

'It was the gear, Mrs Monaghan,' Jimmy enthused. 'Can I pick Sammy up? I used to nurse our Pete when he was little.'

'Go ahead, luv. Shall I make everyone a cup of tea? I brought some with me, as well as some cheese scones.'

'You stay there, Vera. I'll make it.'

Queenie was setting out the cups and saucers, singing, when there was a knock on the door. 'Who can that be?' she asked herself.

She switched off the kitchen light so it wouldn't show when she opened the door. A man in khaki wearing a peaked cap was standing outside, clearly visible in the light of the brilliant moon.

'Good evening.' He courteously touched his cap. 'I seem to have mislaid my key. I'm Roddy Oliver, Laura's husband. Can I please come in?'

Chapter 7

'Roddy!' she cried. 'It's me, Queenie. Oh, come in, come in. Laura's out, but she'll be back soon.'

He removed his cap and stepped inside. She closed the door and turned on the light. He was every bit as handsome as she remembered, though older, thinner, very sunburnt, extremely weary, but nevertheless he managed a smile that made her heart turn over.

'So it is!' he said with a warmth that she could tell was an effort. 'Laura told me in one of her letters that I'd never recognise you and she was right. You look marvellous, Queenie. The little duckling has turned into a beautiful swan.'

'Daddy!' The living room door was flung open and Hester appeared. 'I heard your voice. Oh, Daddy, Daddy, Daddy!' She flung herself at him.

Roddy picked her up. 'Lord, you're a weight. And so tall. How old are you now, fifteen?'

Hester giggled. 'No, I'm only seven, but much taller than Mary. Daddy, are you home for good?'

'No, sweetheart. I'm afraid not.' He carried her into the room. 'Hello, Vera, Mary. Ah, I see we have acquired a baby. She looks very sweet.'

'She's a he, Roddy. His name's Sammy and he's six months old today,' Queenie said in a rush, praying that Laura would come soon, wishing she'd gone to the pictures, not a dance, or hadn't gone out at all, wishing

Roddy had given advance notice he was coming home. 'This is Jimmy Nicholls. He was evacuated with us to Wales, and that's Brian who lives upstairs. You might have already met him.'

Jimmy said hurriedly he'd better be going. Brian wished everyone goodnight and left. Vera gave Roddy a hug and said she'd finish making the tea Queenie had started, then take Mary and Sammy home. 'He's me first grandchild,' she said proudly.

'I was sorry to hear about Dick, Vera. And Billy too, of course.'

'Ta, luv.' Vera gave him a little welcoming pat as she went past.

Five minutes later, there were only three of them left; Roddy, Hester and Queenie. Hester was sitting on her daddy's knee, his chin resting on her blonde curls. Feeling in the way, Queenie announced she was going to bed.

'You'll do no such thing,' Roddy said, smiling again in the way that always did something to her heart. 'You're family now. I'd like you to stay. What time will Laura be home?'

'Any minute now.' She wondered if he was only asking her to stay because he wanted to question her about Laura.

'Is she at the cinema?'

Hester raised her head. 'No, Daddy. She went to a dance. She wore the silk stockings Queenie got her from Herriot's.'

A frown flickered across Roddy's smooth brow. 'And who did she go to the dance with?'

'Winnie. Winnie's beautiful, Daddy. She has purple fingernails. I'm going to have purple fingernails when I grow up.'

'It's only the second time she's gone dancing,' Queenie put in. 'Winnie talked her into it.'

'Laura's told me all about Winnie.' Roddy said stiffly. 'I didn't realise they went dancing together.'

'As I said, Roddy, it's only been the twice.' She changed the subject. 'Will you be staying for Christmas?'

'No, only for a few days. Then I'm off to Kent for special training.'

'Is Kent in this country, Daddy?'

'Yes, sweetheart.' He kissed the top of the blonde head.

'Then you'll be able to come and visit us often.'

'We'll just have to see,' Roddy said in what Queenie thought was a rather offhand way.

He told them a little about his time in North Africa. When he'd first arrived, the British forces under General Wavell were on top, then the Germans, led by a General Rommell, had driven them back. 'Last month, November, we regained some ground, but I'm not sure if we'll be able to hold on to it.'

'Was it hot, Daddy? Mummy said it would be terribly hot.'

'Terribly, terribly hot, sweetheart.' He looked impatiently at his watch. 'Mummy's late. It's almost midnight. Now, what about this marvellous job of yours, Queenie?' he said with an effort. 'I worked in a shop for a while, but I'm afraid I found it deadly dull.'

They went to bed at last. It was past one o'clock and Laura was exhausted. Her head throbbed, her throat ached with talking, trying to explain that the dance meant nothing, that coming home with Ben Tyler meant nothing either.

'We didn't go together. I went with Winnie. It was Eric's idea to come to the Grafton after us, only because he fancies Winnie. Ben just came along with him. I was already fed up by then.'

'So why didn't you come home?' he said accusingly.

'Ben was fed up too. He doesn't like dances. We just sat on the balcony and talked.'

'Till midnight?'

'No, we left at half ten, but had to wait ages for a tram. In the end, we gave up and walked to the Pier Head and caught one to Bootle. Roddy,' she said desperately, 'you know, you must know, in your heart, that I would never be unfaithful.' She tried to put herself in his place, imagine coming home after an absence of eighteen months, finding your wife was at a dance and she didn't return until very late accompanied by another man. She would be equally upset, but felt sure she would have believed him had he sworn, as she had sworn, that it was all completely innocent. The other way around and, by now, they would be laughing about it. No, not laughing; in bed in each other's arms.

'So, where's Eric?'

'I've no idea. He and Winnie didn't leave with us.'

'I haven't heard him come in. Presumably, he's still with Winnie. Some friends you have, Laura.'

She squirmed at the contempt in his voice. He'd never spoken to her that way before. This wasn't the Roddy she'd fallen in love with, the man she'd married only days before the war had begun, a war that had changed him, turned him from a boy into a man, an angry, unreasonable man she hardly recognised. 'I'm sure not all your friends are angels, Roddy,' she said quietly. 'Let's go to bed. I'm tired and you must be too.' Once in bed, he would become the Roddy she knew. She couldn't wait to feel his hands on her, for them to kiss. Incredibly, they still hadn't kissed, yet they'd been in the same room, just the two of them, for more than an hour.

The bedroom was flooded with moonlight. She left the curtains undrawn, so that she could see his face when they made love, see his eyes soften, so that he could see her.

'You haven't asked why I'm here,' he said as he took off his clothes.

She didn't say it was because she hadn't had the opportunity. He'd been too busy accusing her of all sorts of things for her to ask anything. 'I thought you'd come to see us, me and Hester.'

'There's a war going on in North Africa, Laura,' he said, as if she didn't know. 'Troops aren't normally allowed to come thousands of miles just to see relatives when they're in the middle of a crucial fight.'

'But they let you?'

'I'm being transferred to SOE, the Special Operations Executive, that's why. A notice came round, anyone who could speak fluent French was urgently required to help the Resistance movement over there. I was always top in French at St Jude's, so I put my name forward, passed the test, and was accepted.'

'Good.' She saw he was putting on his pyjamas, when she'd expected him to get into bed naked, so felt obliged to put her nightdress on. It was made out of an old sheet, not exactly glamorous to wear when they hadn't slept together in such a long while. He got into bed, but didn't lie down. Instead, he sat, leaning against the bed head. She got in and sat beside him. Neither spoke for several minutes.

'Roddy,' she said eventually. 'The thing with Ben . . .'

'It doesn't matter.' His tone was brusque.

'Yes, it does. We're just good friends. It's impossible *not* to be friends when we live together in the same house.'

'We weren't friends with Agnes Tate when she lived upstairs.'

'But this is different, surely?'

'I know it's different. Don't worry about it, Laura. I don't know why I made such a fuss.'

'But . . .' She stopped, not knowing what to say. He was acting very strangely.

'Laura.'

'Yes, Roddy?'

'I can't put off telling you any longer. I've met someone else. We'd like to get married after the war. I'll provide you with all the evidence for a divorce.'

It took ages for the words, spoken so matter-of-factly, almost brutally, to sink in, to make sense. There was a rushing sound in her ears, as if she were drowning, sinking deeper and deeper into the water, unable to breathe, her chest expanding, feeling as if it would burst.

'*What*?' Now she was choking, could hardly speak.

'I've met someone else.'

'Who?' she choked. 'Where?'

'Her name's Katherine. We met in Dover, after Dunkirk. I told you this chap, Jack Muir, brought me over in his boat and I stayed at his house a few days to recover. Well, Katherine is his daughter. Believe me, Laura,' his voice softening a little, 'I truly didn't mean to fall in love. It was the last thing I expected.' He shrugged. 'But I'm afraid I did. And she with me.'

She got out of bed and began to walk around the room. 'When you came back from Dunkirk, when you hardly spoke to me, hardly touched me, were you in love with Katherine then?'

'Yes,' he conceded, slightly shamefaced. 'I couldn't bring myself to tell you.'

'Did you see Katherine while you were in Colchester?'

'She works in London, it was easy.'

'Roddy.' She stopped walking and stared at him intently. 'Tell me truthfully, did you ever get longer than a twenty-four-hour pass?'

'Yes, I did, Laura. I'm sorry. It just seemed so completely over between you and me.'

'In your mind, not mine.'

'As I said, I'm sorry.'

She couldn't believe she was having this conversation, not with Roddy. The words 'completely over' cut like a knife in her heart. 'Why did you decide to tell me now?' she asked.

'Because at times, when I'm not in France, I'll be in Kent. You'd be expecting me to come home, come here, to Liverpool. I didn't want to tell lies.'

'You mean *more* lies?'

He sighed. 'All I can think to say is how sorry I am.'

'What about Hester? Are you divorcing her too? Will she never see you again?'

In the next room, Hester gave a little cough, as if to remind him that she existed. The bed creaked as she turned over.

'Of course she will. Hester will always be my daughter.' Though I won't always be his wife, Laura thought bitterly. 'Katherine has a little flat in Chelsea. After Christmas, maybe, Hester could come and stay with us. We could take her to the pantomime.'

It was the 'us' that did it, the 'we'. Until then, she'd been in a trance-like state of calm. But Roddy was referring to himself and another woman as 'us', when it should have been, she had thought it always would be, Roddy and her. There was an explosion in her head and she imagined him lying with this other woman, touching her, making love. The vision was too impossible, too improbable, too cruel. She couldn't accept it, she wouldn't.

She began to scream, not saying a word, just screaming hysterically, banging the wardrobe with her fists, screaming and screaming.

Roddy leapt out of bed and shook her. 'Laura, you'll wake the whole house.' He led her back to bed.

'I don't care if I wake the street.' She was still screaming. 'I'm not divorcing you. You told me you would love me for ever, that we were made for each other, that we'd be together our whole lives.' She paused for breath. 'We made plans for the future. We were going to have another baby, a little brother for Hester. Oh,' she collapsed on the bed, 'I think I'm going to die.'

There was a soft tap on the door. 'Laura? Are you all right?'

'Yes.' Her voice was muffled in the eiderdown. 'I was having a nightmare. I'm sorry I woke you, Queenie. Go back to bed, dear.'

'Laura.' Roddy sat beside her, stroked her neck. 'Darling, please don't take it so badly. Somehow, I thought perhaps we'd grown apart, that you wouldn't mind all that much.'

'I think of you every minute of every day,' she sobbed. 'At the dance tonight, I said to Ben how much I wanted you to be there. I told him I'd never go to another dance unless it was with you.' She remembered the fuss he'd made when she came home and suddenly felt angry. 'How dare you suggest we were having an affair, Ben and I, considering what you've been up to. You're a hypocrite, Roddy.'

'I was half hoping you were having an affair,' he said ruefully. 'It would have made everything so much easier, yet I felt genuinely upset at the idea of you sleeping with another man.'

'That's because you're a hypocrite.'

'You're right.' He turned her over and began to kiss her face, her lips, her ears. 'I think I'll always love you, Lo,' he murmured.

Desire, hot and fiery, shot through her like a bolt of lightning. She put her arms around his neck and held him fiercely, pressing against him. If she reminded him what it was like when they made love, perhaps he'd stay, forget about Katherine. She began to touch him with hot, eager hands. And he responded, entered her, and they made love with a passion that was almost desperate in its intensity, at least on her part.

Roddy collapsed back on the bed, gasping. 'I'm sorry,' he said. 'I shouldn't have done that.'

And Laura realised that she'd failed. He didn't love her enough.

He stayed for three days and offered to sleep on the sofa, but she said someone would notice and think it very odd. She didn't want people knowing, particularly Hester, that he was leaving and never coming back, not until she was ready to tell them.

They lay in bed with their backs to each other, as far away as they could. But Laura found it impossible to sleep. In the end it was her who ended up on the sofa when everyone had settled down and the house was silent, getting up very early before anyone woke. She didn't cry. She felt too cold, frozen. The tears that fell would have been tears of ice. She pretended that nothing had happened.

Roddy was being tremendously kind, very gentle and sympathetic, which she hated. She found it helped to be aggressive, but only when there was no one else there, throw his kindness back in his face, otherwise she might have pleaded with him to stay, grovelled. She positively refused to give him a divorce. 'You'll just have to live with Katherine the way you lived with me.'

And there wasn't a chance of Hester going to London after Christmas, she told him bluntly. 'Perhaps another Christmas. That's if she wants to.'

'I suppose you'll make sure she won't.'

'That's a horrible thing to say. In good time, I'll tell her what's happened and she can make up her own mind. I've no intention of trying to turn her against you.'

'I'm sorry.' He sounded it. 'I should have known you'd never do such a thing.'

'To be frank,' Laura said. 'I'd sooner Hester didn't know the truth until absolutely necessary, even if it means waiting until after the war, whenever that is. She's going to be terribly upset; the older she is, the better.'

'Whatever you think best, Lo.'

'*Please* don't call me Lo!' It was too familiar.

'I'm sorry, it just slipped out.' He smiled drily. 'All I seem to do is say I'm sorry.'

'You can say you're sorry till the cows come home, Roddy, but it doesn't mean a thing.'

It didn't help that he looked so handsome; leaner, fitter, sunburnt, more sure of himself than she remembered, no longer a labourer, but a First Lieutenant in the Royal Artillery, a leader of men, who carried himself proudly. She reminded herself that she'd always been proud of him, of the way he'd struggled to keep them together when he'd been no more than a boy. She remembered all sorts of things; the notes they'd left for each other in *The Rise and Fall of the Roman Empire*, bringing Hester home from the nursing home and staring down in wonder at the baby they'd made. The memories always ended with the day they got married, in Freddy's restaurant where the pianist had played 'Here Comes

The Bride'. Everyone had clapped and Roddy had looked at her, his face brimming over with love.

But now it was all over and he loved someone else.

He left early on Wednesday. Laura wished she'd been on the morning shift, so she could have walked away from *him*. Instead, she was on afternoons.

'I'm off now, Laura,' he said, coming into the kitchen where she was staring at a pile of washing, wondering where to start. He looked very sad, close to tears. 'Goodbye, Lo . . . Laura.'

'Goodbye, Roddy.' This was it. This was all that was left.

'Don't let Hester forget me.'

'That's up to Hester. And I meant what I said about not divorcing you, so don't bother to try.'

'I'd sooner we didn't part on such a sour note.'

'What did you expect, Roddy? For me to throw my arms around you and wish you good luck?'

'I'd like to wish you good luck in the future.'

'Thank you.' She turned away and began to sort through the washing. Seconds later, the front door closed, and it was only then she was able to cry.

Queenie knew something was badly wrong. She'd never known Laura have a nightmare before. And she hadn't just heard screams, she'd heard words, like 'divorce', and, 'you told me you would love me for ever'. She was convinced it was nothing to do with the dance. Always sensitive to the slightest inflection in a voice or the expression on a face so she would know when it was time to get out of Mam's way, she could tell it was Roddy who was at fault. He seemed as charming as ever, but he didn't look at Laura the way he'd used to. And Laura was so tense, as if she was holding herself together by a thread. The photo of them together with Laura wearing the hat Queenie had taken to Caerdovey, had disappeared from the mantelpiece.

After Roddy had gone, Laura threw herself into preparations for Christmas, frantically roaming the shops in search of presents, jars of mincemeat, tins of fruit. 'See what I've got,' she cried gaily, waving a jar of Pomphrey's lemon curd at Queenie when she came home from work. 'I got some prunes too. I'm going to put them in the Christmas cake.' She made Vera a smart frock out of two old ones, though was unable to find feathers. At her urging, Albert bought tickets for a dinner dance at the Blundellsands Hotel on New Year's Eve.

The Tylers were invited to dinner on Christmas Day if they contributed some food. Eric said he'd ordered a chicken and had won a tin of assorted biscuits in a raffle and would Laura mind very much if Winnie came? Jimmy Nicholls was invited, but had to refuse. He was spending three days in Caerdovey with Tess and Pete, staying with his old lady.

'You won't go out with Brian while I'm away, will you, Queenie, girl?' he asked anxiously, and she promised faithfully that she wouldn't.

Laura had never smiled so brilliantly as when they sat down to dinner on Christmas Day. Queenie kept glancing at her guardedly, worried that the thread was about to break, because Laura was laughing and talking far too much – and drinking glass after glass of sherry. Ben Tyler watched her with undisguised admiration, unable to avert his eyes.

At five o'clock, Laura, Hester and Queenie went over to the Monaghans' for tea, taking with them heaps of sandwiches made from the remnants of the chickens. Everyone was relieved that Iris was spending the day with her sister, but sorry that she had taken the adorable Sammy with her.

The thread broke after they'd finished tea. Laura leapt to her feet. 'Excuse me, Vera. I need to lie down a minute,' she said in a strangled voice. She ran upstairs.

Vera groaned. 'Oh, Lord! I've been so busy, I haven't made a single bed.'

'I wonder if she's all right,' Vera said when half an hour had passed and Laura hadn't come down. 'I'd better go and see.' The girls and Caradoc had gone into the parlour where, this one day of the year, a bright fire burnt, to play Monopoly, a present from the Tylers to Hester. Albert said it was about time he went for a drink. Charlie went to see his girlfriend. Tommy told Queenie about the pictures he'd been to see and she could tell he was leading up to asking her for a date. She'd refuse – she would never forget the way he'd used to make fun of her arm.

The two women were upstairs for ages. Vera came down briefly, looking very grave, and disappeared again with a glass of water and a box of Aspros.

When Vera came down for good, she was alone and so was Queenie. Tommy had gone into the parlour in a huff when she'd told him she wouldn't go out with him.

'She's asleep', Vera said. 'I don't think she's slept much for quite a time.'

'Roddy's left her, hasn't he? He's not coming back to Liverpool.'

'I promised not to say anything, but seeing as you seem to know . . .' Vera sighed. 'Yes, luv. Roddy's met someone else and Laura's just cried herself to a standstill. I think she's just a little bit unhinged. You must tell her you've guessed so she doesn't have to go on pretending in front of you. It's the bloody war that's done it. It sends everybody crackers. One of these days, he'll regret it. If ever I saw two people so completely in love, it was Roddy and Laura Oliver.'

The Tylers threw a party on New Year's Eve, but when the clock struck midnight, Laura was nowhere to be seen. She missed Eric's little speech.

'Some people said the war would be over in a few months but,' Eric said a trifle drunkenly, while Winnie hung possessively on to his arm, 'but here we are, two and a half years later, and there's no sign of an end. In fact it's got worse and we seem to be losing the battle on all fronts. Here's hoping nineteen forty-two brings a change of fortune and we start winning for a change. Let's drink to that; to victory. We can't let Hitler win.'

'To victory,' everyone chorused.

Herriot's was holding its annual winter sale. The shop was heavily over-stocked with women's and children's clothing. Coupons had been introduced suddenly, without warning, and they'd been left with loads of garments slightly out of fashion, they couldn't sell, not because their clientele couldn't afford them, but because they didn't have the coupons. Prices were slashed, to half or less, in the hope of clearing old stock. But, as Mr Matthews said logically, 'If people haven't got the coupons, they haven't got the coupons.'

With Laura being so clever with a needle, neither she nor Queenie had used many of their own coupons. Laura was saving hers to buy towels and replace the bedding that was coming to the end of its life, but Herriot's hadn't reduced their household linens nearly as much as the clothes.

'I was thinking of buying a coat,' Queenie said. 'There's this lovely one half-price, black with a little fur collar.'

'You should snap it up before anyone else,' Laura advised. 'I might get Hester one of those frocks you told me about, the ones with embroidery on the bodice – I'll let her choose. The poor girl's never had a frock from a shop before. Until now, they've all been made out of scraps or my old things. We'll come to Herriot's on Saturday, take a look around.'

Laura had looked surprisingly serene since the New Year had begun. When Queenie told her she knew Roddy had gone for good, she'd looked at her blankly, as if she'd never heard of Roddy Oliver. She moved about very slowly, eyes dreamy, her face calm and composed. She'd obviously got over things much sooner than everyone had expected.

Herriot's was always extra-busy on a Saturday, but the crowds had almost doubled with the winter sale. Queenie had hardly stopped all morning. The most popular item in the children's department was the Wolsey V-necked pullover in black or grey. It was the sort of thing that would never go out of fashion and had only been reduced by ten per cent.

Laura arrived on the second floor just before one o'clock, accompanied by Hester and Mary who screamed with excitement and made straight for the rack of girls' frocks, all heavily reduced.

'What time do you have lunch?' she asked.

'Not until two,' Queenie replied.

'I know you have a nice staff restaurant, but would you like me to treat you to a meal somewhere else?'

'I'd like it very much. Thanks, Laura.'

'Mary wanted a frock as soon as she heard Hester was getting one. Vera said I'm not to go over thirty shillings, though she's never spent nearly that much on a frock for herself.'

'There's plenty for thirty shillings, some only a pound.'

Together, they went over to the rail. Mary had been drawn to a bright red velvet creation with a ruched bodice and a white lace collar, but Hester couldn't see anything she liked. 'They're all too fancy,' she claimed, and eventually settled on a brown jumper and a fawn pleated skirt.

Laura was slightly shocked. 'I wonder if she's never liked the pretty things I've always made her?' she said to Queenie.

'Maybe she just wants a plain outfit for a change.'

'I suppose I was really making them for myself.' She made a face. 'I enjoyed sewing on the lace, adding bows and embroidery, the smocking. Poor Hester ended up looking like a Christmas tree. Can we go into a cubicle and try everything on?'

'Only if you join the queue.' There were at least a dozen mothers with children waiting to use the cubicles.

'I don't mind, I'm used to queues. After this, we're going down to the first floor to look at Ladies' Fashions.' Laura gave her a little shove. 'You've got a customer waiting, Queenie – no, two. I'll get out of your way. See you later.'

Queenie had on her hat and smart new coat and was ready to leave promptly at two o'clock. She went down to Ladies' Fashions on the first floor and found the girls admiring the ball gowns, also going cheap in the sale. Laura emerged from a cubicle, somewhat breathless, a strawberry pink garment over her arm.

'I thought, if I'm going to look like an elephant, I may as well look like a pink elephant,' she said gaily, then laughed at Queenie's look of incomprehension. 'Oh, Queenie, love. I'm having a baby. Roddy and I . . .' She paused and went as pink as the frock. 'Oh, it doesn't matter. Grown-ups can be very complicated – you'll find that out for yourself one day.'

'How can you be so sure you're pregnant?' It was only just over three weeks since Roddy had been home.

'I was due a period on Boxing Day, ten days ago, but it didn't happen. I'm always as regular as clockwork. I've only been late once before, when I was having Hester. And it's not just that,' she went on, starry-eyed, 'I just *know*, know in my heart that I'm pregnant.'

'Congratulations.' Queenie threw her arms around Laura's neck and kissed her. 'I'm dead pleased. Oh, it's going to be lovely, you having a baby.' She contemplated the fact that she had carried a baby for two whole months, but hadn't known a thing about it. For the first time ever, she wondered what it would have looked like, had it been a boy or a girl? 'You'll leave the factory, won't you?' she said worriedly. 'You don't want to risk having an accident.'

'Oh, yes. Anyway, I doubt very much if they'd want a pregnant riveter. But I'll get another job, a sitting down one. I don't want to hang around the house, getting bigger and bigger, and bored out of my mind.'

Roddy had got out of North Africa just in time. In January, it appeared that nothing could stop the German advance under General Rommell. Even worse, the next month saw more than 60,000 Allied troops in Singapore surrender to the seemingly all-conquering Japanese, who were bombing Australia and had Borneo next in their sights.

'Will we ever win anything?' Laura wailed.

It didn't do to dwell on the things that were happening overseas. There was nothing anyone in Glover Street could do about it, other than to send its young men in the hope they would help to save their country.

That year, two more left with that object in mind, though in most people's minds, they were little more than children. First, Charlie Monaghan became a private in the Army then, in June, Brian Tyler turned eighteen and joined the RAF. He asked Queenie, very soberly, for a photo, 'To keep next to my heart.'

Queenie had two copies made of the photograph taken at Herriot's Christmas party, cutting off the other women who'd been sitting at her table. The second copy was for Jimmy Nicholls, just in case the war lasted another horrific two years and he was called up too.

Brian had only been gone a week when Winnie Corcoran moved in upstairs. 'Eric didn't like to ask while Brian was there,' Ben told Laura. 'The thing is, they're in love. Madly in love. I dread what's going to happen when Winnie's husband comes home.'

Laura missed the camaraderie of the factory and rather liked the idea of having Winnie live upstairs. She was now employed in the laundry department of Bootle Hospital: repairing sheets, re-hemming frayed towels, patching the hospital-issue nightclothes, using an elderly sewing machine in a little room all on her own. It was even more boring than being at home, but at least it meant she was still doing her bit and earning money at the same time. Not that she would be exactly hard up when she was no longer working. She'd saved up quite a bit over the last few years and would still get an allowance from the Army for being Roddy's wife.

'Thank goodness I didn't agree to a divorce, otherwise the allowance would have stopped.' No, she didn't miss Roddy the slightest bit, she said when Queenie asked. 'I'll soon have a replacement, won't I? At least *he* won't fall in love with another woman and leave me.' She was convinced the baby would be a boy.

Queenie didn't say he would, one day. It wouldn't happen for a long time and perhaps Laura would be resigned to the idea by then. 'Have you decided on a name yet?'

'No. One of these days a name will hit me and I'll know it's the right one.'

Hester couldn't wait for her little brother to arrive, but couldn't understand why she was forbidden to mention the forthcoming baby when she wrote to her daddy. Roddy sent his daughter a letter about once a month.

'It's because I want it to be a surprise,' Laura told her. 'And I don't want Daddy worrying about me when he's being sent on dangerous missions to France.'

Mary was beside herself with jealousy. *She* wanted a little brother like Hester, but when she demanded her mother have a baby, Vera merely dissolved into gales of helpless laughter, setting off a delighted Sammy who was on her knee. 'I'm sorry, girl. It's just not on.'

'Why not?'

'Because I'm too old, Mary. At fifty-six, I'm well past it.'

'It's a disgusting suggestion, anyroad,' Iris said with her usual disdainful sniff. 'As if your mam and dad would get up to *that* sort of thing,' the sniff said.

Vera grinned. 'There's nothing disgusting about it, I may be past having babies, but that's the only thing I'm too old for.'

Laura's baby arrived on 1 October, early in the afternoon. A glorious sun shone out of a clear blue sky, though it was unusually cold for the time of year. The last few weeks, Vera had been sitting with the heavily expectant mother when everyone was out, which Laura claimed unnecessary, although she welcomed the company.

The contractions were coming every half hour when the women decided it was time to catch the tram to the maternity hospital, Laura in the pink elephant dress, which she already had plans to alter in time for Christmas. At 3.15 p.m., after a relatively pain-free delivery, she gave birth to a six-and-a-half-pound baby boy.

A beaming Vera came back with the news only minutes before Queenie arrived home from work. 'He's a smashing little chap,' Vera enthused. 'She's still not sure what to call him.'

'I'll go and see her straight away.'

'Can I come with you?' Hester asked eagerly.

'Can she?' Queenie looked at Vera who shook her head.

'I'm sorry, luv, but children aren't allowed on the ward. I don't know why. I suppose the hospital has a good reason.'

'I'll give Mummy your love,' Queenie promised the dejected little girl who was longing to see her new brother.

She sat on the tram, watching the cold sun sink down in the sky, unable to stop thinking about the baby she herself had carried inside her body for eight whole weeks. Since Laura had become pregnant, her own baby had assumed a sort of identity. It had been a girl, it *had* to have been a girl; a boy might have looked like Carl Merton. She hated having to admit, even to herself, that it might have been for the best that the baby had been killed, just as its father had been killed, in an accident. An accident in name only; it had been a murder carried out by two small girls.

Yet, sometimes, she wished she hadn't lost the baby. But then what would she have done? How could she have admitted to Laura, to everyone, that something she'd convinced herself was a dream had actually happened? They would have thought her dead stupid. She would sooner have run away, brought up her daughter on her own, had someone of her own to love, except the daughter might have been a son, and how could she raise a child who would have been a constant reminder of the man who'd raped her?

The thoughts of what might have been chased each other round her head until she felt dizzy and nearly missed her stop.

When she reached the hospital, visiting time hadn't started. She stood in the queue and shortly afterwards was joined by Ben Tyler, who'd also heard the news when he came home from work.

Laura was sitting up in bed, nursing her son. If only Roddy could see her now, Queenie thought. She'd always thought Laura pretty, but now she looked quite beautiful, her wavy hair tumbling over her large, brown eyes, her cheeks glowing rosily. A look of quiet happiness radiated from her face. She smiled when she saw her visitors.

'Isn't he lovely?' She held out the sleeping baby for them to see, to admire. 'Isn't he absolutely perfect?'

'Perfect,' Queenie breathed. The tiny boy was very pale, long lashes quivering slightly on delicate white cheeks. His short hair was the colour of pure gold.

'Very handsome,' Ben agreed. 'Has he got a name yet?'

'Yes, Augustus.' Laura stroked a miniature white hand.

Queenie and Ben looked at each other in horror. A name like Augustus would be a burden the child would have to carry for the rest of his life. It was almost as bad as having a twisted arm. Everyone would make fun of him at school.

'Mummy's name was Augusta,' Laura went on, 'but

she never liked it. People used to call her Gussy, so I shall call him Gus.'

'Gus is nice,' Queenie said, relieved.

'Gus is OK,' agreed Ben.

Three weeks after Gus was born, the tide of war at last began to turn in favour of Britain and its Allies. In North Africa, the battle of El Alamein was being fought. Allied troops, under the leadership of a new commander, General Montgomery, had sent the enemy into full retreat, while the Australians retook ground in New Guinea.

'Now is not the end,' Winston Churchill said on the BBC in response to this heartening news. 'It is not even the beginning of the end, but it is perhaps the end of the beginning.'

Chapter 8

Tuesday, 8 May 1945. VE Day.

At long last the war in Europe was over and the jubilant population poured out on to the gaily decorated streets to celebrate. They cheered every faded Union Jack, ate too much, drank too much, and sang 'When The Lights Go On Again', 'Rule, Britannia!', and every other song they could think of. On that never-to-be-forgotten day, many millions of hands were shaken and millions of cheeks were kissed. Next morning, there were a record number of hangovers.

But not everyone felt like celebrating. On some windows, the curtains were tightly drawn; the war would never be over for those inside who had lost their loved ones.

Vera and Albert Monaghan sang and danced as loud and as long as anyone in Glover Street. Seven of their lads had gone to war and seven had survived, but wouldn't come home until Japan had been defeated. They were to return eventually, one at a time, thinner, a bit harder, and with bitter memories that would stay with them for the rest of their lives, fading a little with the passage of time. Billy, who'd spent four years in a German prisoner of war camp, would find it more difficult than his brothers to readjust to civilian life.

It was in 1943 that something unexpected and quite miraculous had occurred. A telegram had arrived at number seventeen sent via the Red Cross. Vera had opened it with dread in her heart, too upset to notice that the envelope was addressed to Mrs I. Monaghan, not to herself and Albert.

'Am fit and well,' the message read. 'Love, Dick.'

'Iris!' Vera screeched. '*IRIS*!'

'What?' demanded a weak voice from the bedroom where Iris was lying down with one of her heads.

'There's a telegram come to say our Dick's alive. He's *alive*, Iris.'

'What?' The voice was no longer weak. Iris appeared at the top of the stairs. Her face had never looked so animated since the day she'd married Dick. All of a sudden, she was pretty again, the headache gone or forgotten. 'I *knew* he was alive,' she croaked. 'I just knew. I could feel it in me bones. Oh, Vera!' She ran downstairs and threw herself in Vera's arms and the two women hugged as they'd never done before and took turns to dry each others' eyes.

Later, it turned out that when Dick's submarine had been torpedoed in the Ionian Sea, he and two other seamen had escaped through the hatches, lungs bursting as they rose to the surface, and found themselves close to the Greek island of Cephalonia. One of the men drowned during the long swim towards land, but Dick and the other man survived, dragging themselves on to the shore, where they were found by a Greek woman, Melania. The island was occupied by the Italians, they learnt. Melania and her friends bravely hid the two sailors from the enemy, cared for them, fed them out of their own meagre rations.

It was almost two years before the Resistance was able to smuggle the men off the island. They were taken by boat to Turkey, a neutral country. After reporting to the

British Embassy in Ankara, arrangements were made to take them back to England.

From the day the telegram came, Iris never had another headache, and discovered she had a beautiful son, whom she'd sadly neglected. Never again was she heard to complain – the wireless could be on full blast, but Iris didn't care. In fact, it was Albert's turn to have a moan. He was thrilled to pieces his eldest son was alive, but did Iris really have to go around the house singing hymns at the top of her voice?

'We always knew she was a bit odd,' Vera reminded him.

'I'm not sure if I didn't prefer her the way she was before,' Albert grumbled. 'At least she was quiet.'

Vera said there was no pleasing him. Dick was alive, Iris was happy, and that was all that mattered.

Just as people had quickly become accustomed to the war, they just as quickly got used to the peace. Many women were angry to lose their well-paid work in factories when the men came home, wanting their jobs back. They found it hard to get used to being housewives again, no longer the breadwinners. Men found it equally hard to return to wives who'd become far too independent in their absence, not prepared automatically to do their husbands' bidding or be regarded as second-class citizens because they were women. In some families, a private war had to be fought before they could become adjusted to peace.

In July, Eric and Ben Tyler returned to Newcastle. Brian was still in the RAF and no one knew when he would be demobbed. It was more than a year since Brian had come home on leave and told Queenie that he'd met someone else, a girl called Ellen. He hoped she wasn't too upset. Queenie wasn't the slightest bit upset. She wrote regularly to Jimmy Nicholls, now a private in the Army, and one of the troops who'd stormed the Normandy beaches on D-Day. Jimmy was in Berlin, a member of the British Army of Occupation of the Rhine. His letters back were misspelt and badly written, but each one was more passionate than the last. He loved her, missed her. Could they please get engaged as soon as he came back?

'I suppose I do love him in a way,' Queenie had to concede. 'He's so incredibly kind and generous. Responsible too, and very mature. Look at the way he cares for Tess and Pete. He'd make a marvellous husband.'

Laura wasn't sure if that was a good enough basis for marriage. But no one could have loved each other more than she and Roddy, and look how they had ended up.

'I'll tell him I will marry him,' Queenie said. 'In fact, I'll write this very minute. After all, so far, I've never met anyone half as nice.'

'You're a peach of a girl, Laura Oliver,' Eric told her on his last night in Glover Street. 'We couldn't have found anyone better to share a house with if we'd tried. Roddy's a very lucky fellow. I suppose he'll be back any minute?'

'He's in Paris,' Laura lied, 'trying to link up families who were separated during the German invasion.'

'I think I read something about that in the paper.'

Laura had read it too. It seemed an ideal excuse to explain Roddy's non-appearance. Only Vera and Queenie knew the truth, although she would have to tell Hester soon that her daddy wasn't coming home.

'It was through you I met Winnie,' Eric said. 'I'll always be grateful for that.'

Winnie was going back to Newcastle with Eric, and

Joe Corcoran was destined to return to an empty house. Winnie had paid a couple of months' rent so it would be there for him.

'Do you think I'm awful,' Winnie had asked, 'leaving Joe in the lurch?' Her conscience was obviously bothering her, but not enough to make her stay.

'I don't know. It's not something I could bring myself to do.'

Roddy had done it to her and she would never have got over it if Gus hadn't come along. Her heart went out to Joe Corcoran.

'That's because you're too respectable.'

'It's because I can't bear to hurt people.'

She'd hurt Ben though. Not deliberately. She'd done nothing to make him fall in love with her. He looked quite desolate when they said goodbye for the last time.

'I'll never forget you,' he said dully.

'Nor me you.' She wanted to tell him that one day he'd fall in love with a woman who would love him back, that they'd get married, have children, and live happily ever after, except, in her experience, life wasn't like that.

Not long afterwards, Iris Monaghan and Sammy moved in upstairs so the small family would have a place to themselves when Dick came home. In no time at all it was hard to believe the Tylers had ever lived there.

Laura had spent the years since Gus was born quietly at home. Gus would be four in October, a well-behaved, rather solemn little boy, with Roddy's fair hair, blue eyes, and fine features. He had a sharp, curious mind. On one occasion, Laura had had to take him outside in the pouring rain so he could watch the water gushing through the grid into the drain.

'What happens to it now?' he wanted to know.

'It goes into the sea,' Laura replied vaguely.

'Can we go and see where it comes out?'

'I don't know where that is, sweetheart.' Neither did anyone else she asked.

When Gus was taken to Seaforth shore, he dug holes, as deep as he could, with his little tin spade, in the hope of reaching the other side of the world. He took the eyes off his teddy bear to discover what lay behind and was disappointed to find just more brown fur.

'What's behind my eyes?' he asked his mother who had to confess she wasn't sure, other than the rest of his head.

'Can I take one out and see?'

'*No*!' She gave him a stern lecture, worried he might try.

One of his main ambitions in life was to take her alarm clock to pieces and she had to keep it on top of the wardrobe, out of reach. An awful lot of things had to be kept on top of the wardrobe, including her handbag, the scissors, the whisk – he had once tried to whisk the fingers of his left hand – the mincer, Hester's dolls – her favourite, Gracie, had to be taken to the dolls' hospital to have its arms and legs put back on.

Not that Hester cared. She adored her little brother who, so far as she was concerned, could do no wrong.

Any minute now, the allowance from the Army would stop and Laura had to think what to do with the rest of her life. She had two children to support and no intention of marrying again – anyway, she was still married to Roddy – and didn't want to spend the next thirty-three years, until she was sixty, in and out of ill-paid jobs, scrimping and scraping to make ends meet. She couldn't type, in fact there was very little she could do, and had no qualifications. She'd been studying for her

School Certificate when Roddy, then Hester, had come into her life and her education had stopped dead. Though it had been a good education. She'd taken subjects that didn't appear on the syllabus of state schools. Neither Queenie or Vera's boys had been taught Latin and French, Physics and Chemistry, Greek and Roman History.

Try as she might, though, Laura couldn't think of a single job where a smattering of knowledge in all these subjects would be of any use. And Queenie's inability to quote a string of Latin verbs hadn't done her any harm. Last year, at only nineteen, she'd been made head of the Children's Clothing department in Herriot's, though that might have been due to the manager, Mr Matthews, having taken a shine to her right from the start. It was such a pity he was retiring and the recently demobbed assistant manager was about to take his place.

Staff who'd known Gordon Mackie before the war said he hadn't been well-liked then, but after his time in the Army, where he'd been a sergeant-major, they liked him even less. A tall, red-faced man with a bristly moustache, an unusually broad chest and hardly any neck, he spoke to them as if he were addressing his troops, in a loud, barking voice, expecting no argument.

On his second day back at Herriot's, he called a meeting in the staff restaurant after the shop had closed. They were told to address him as 'Sir', and warned to prepare for a massive re-organisation, of both themselves and the shop itself.

'Things have been allowed to get very slack in my absence,' he boomed, 'And there have to be some changes made. It keeps people on their toes, knowing that things aren't going to stay the same for ever.'

When he wasn't marching around the shop, standing

to attention in front of various counters, rocking back and forth on his heels, regarding the assistants thoughtfully, he could be found in his office drawing up charts, writing down names, then crossing them out and putting them in another column.

Herriot's, once such a happy place to work, became full of ugly rumours and the staff divided into two camps: those who were willing to suck up to Gordon Mackie in the hope of emerging from the re-organisation in a better position than before, and those who weren't.

Queenie, who couldn't stand the man, fell into the latter camp. She was polite, but distant. She didn't wish him 'Good morning, Sir,' in a sycophantic voice accompanied by a simpering smile. She didn't admire his tie, ask how he was today, utter a single word of criticism against Mr Matthews and say how pleased she was *he* was back and in control. Nor would she stoop to flirting, fluttering her eyelashes at his stern, red face in the hope of influencing his decision.

At the beginning of December, when Herriot's was gearing up for Christmas, employees were ordered to stay behind after the shop shut. It was Wednesday, half-day closing.

Once again they gathered in the staff restaurant where they were addressed by the new manager in clipped, curt tones. He began with some very unwelcome news. After Christmas, the staff restaurant would close, he announced, and be replaced with a new Music department.

'Are you allowed to do that, sir?' Mr Briggs from the Furniture department enquired in a shaky voice. He had worked there for almost forty years. 'I'd always understood the restaurant was the idea of Grenville Herriot himself to provide cheap meals for the staff. I can't imagine he'd agree to it being shut down.' The Herriot family lived in Chester. Although they took no part in the running of their shop, Mr Herriot always sent the staff a pound bonus at Christmas. Everyone had wondered why they didn't get one last year. Gordon Mackie supplied the answer.

'You're obviously not aware, Briggs,' he snapped, 'that Grenville Herriot died eighteen months ago. Ownership has now passed to his daughters who have given me free reign to do as I please. In future, profit will be the first consideration, not the cosseting of staff. The rest room will remain. You can bring sandwiches and eat them there.'

They were then treated to a little pep talk more suitable for troops about to go into battle than shop-workers; urged to all pull together, proudly, shoulders back. Finally, 'There's a chart on the wall showing your new positions from the first of January. In order to be fair, every single employee has been moved elsewhere. Kindly stand in an orderly queue while waiting your turn to examine the chart. If anyone wishes to question my decisions, my mind is made up and I am not prepared to listen.' He marched away, his back ramrod stiff.

A few people got up straight away to look at the chart, while the rest sat in stunned silence, which quickly turned into a mutinous rumble.

'I'm not sure if I still want to work in his bloody shop,' Mr Briggs said indignantly.

'Don't worry, Geoff, you won't have to,' shouted a white-faced Reg Barnes from Men's Wear. 'You and me have got the push. There's a big list at the bottom. It looks as if everyone over fifty is on their way out.'

There was a rush for the chart. Josie Mellor, Perfumerie, lit a cigarette, now strictly forbidden, and said loudly that 'Sir' could stuff his stupid job where the monkey stuffed its nuts. 'I'm leaving. I'm getting married in

January, anyroad. Frank would far sooner I stayed at home, so he'll be pleased.'

'You'd have been in the new Music department,' someone said.

'I don't care. In fact, I think I'll leave now. Tara, everyone. I hope you enjoy working for another Adolf Hitler.' With that, Josie gave a little wave and was gone.

Queenie wished she could do the same when she discovered she had been transferred to Ironmongery in the basement, where she would never see the sun, and which she knew, instinctively, that she would loathe.

The vacated jobs were filled by Gordon Mackie's friends and relatives. Young men from his regiment took over Furnishing and Men's Wear, Mrs Matilda Mackie, his wife, appeared behind the counter of Ladies' Accessories, assisted by his daughter, Ann. Mrs Mackie seemed quite nice and no one could understand what she saw in her fearsome husband.

A handful of the old staff left in disgust at such blatant nepotism – mainly women with husbands already working. But few people were able to give up relatively well-paid employment at the drop of a hat. All they could do was grin and bear it, which Queenie, for one, was finding extremely difficult.

Ironmongery smelt: of bricks, though Herriot's didn't sell bricks, and washing powder, which they didn't sell either. Perhaps it was the chemicals in the cast iron fire baskets and shiny grate fronts, the tin buckets, the spades and rakes, tools, stone hot water bottles, metal door stops in the shape of animals, that gave the corner in which she worked such an unpleasant odour. The best-selling item was buckets, which had been as hard to get as fruit during the war.

The department only needed one assistant. It had been

Mr Brownlea, long past sixty, and perfectly happy to sit behind the till, only getting up when a rare customer approached – there were never more than twenty a day. But Mr Brownlea had been sacked, the chair taken away, and Queenie's legs ached from standing, though they'd never ached when she'd been on Children's Clothing. She was isolated from the other assistants and had no one to talk to. Every morning, she woke up with a heavy heart, dreading the day ahead, when she'd used to look forward to it.

Laura pressed her to leave. 'There's plenty of other shops that'd be happy to have you.'

But a stubborn Queenie refused. She was also a tiny bit scared of moving somewhere new and strange. Herriot's had become as familiar to her as the house in Glover Street. It was like a second home. She didn't join in the hope expressed by some of her fellow workers that Gordon Mackie would fall under a bus, but she prayed something would happen and she'd be transferred. Anywhere would be be an improvement on Ironmongery.

In fact, two things happened, one of them really horrible, but the outcome was to change her life for ever.

Christmas was a quiet, rather sober affair without the Tylers upstairs. Iris took Sammy to her sister's on Christmas Day and the house felt abnormally quiet. It seemed odd, slightly unsettling, only four of them sitting down to dinner. They were, as usual, going to tea at the Monaghans' – by now, three of the lads were home – but that was hours away.

Months ago, Hester had been told about her father. She'd taken the news calmly. She was eleven and, apart from one short visit four Christmases ago, her daddy had been absent for more than half her young life.

'You can always go and stay with him and his –

friend,' Laura told her. 'Her name's Katherine. They'd both be thrilled to have you.'

'I don't want to, thanks,' Hester said coolly. 'I don't think I want to see Daddy any more. I shan't write to him again, either.'

'It's up to you, sweetheart. I'd prefer you and Daddy to stay friends.'

Hester merely shrugged but, on Christmas Day, after dinner, when Laura and Queenie were washing the dishes, Gus came into the kitchen and announced gravely that Hester was sick. 'Her head's fell on the table.'

'Oh, my God!' Laura flew into the living room and found her daughter weeping copiously, her face buried in the white damask cloth. 'Sweetheart! What's the matter?'

'Daddy's *horrible*. I hate him. I wish he'd died in the war. After Christmas, I shall send him back his card and tell him so.'

'I'm sure you wouldn't really do such an awful thing, Hester, love.'

'Yes, I would,' Hester wept. 'Why isn't he with us? Why is he spending Christmas with some other lady?'

'Where is *my* Dad?' enquired Gus who'd followed them. 'Sammy's got a dad. Vera said he fell into the sea off a big, black boat, but the sweet Lord Jesus saved him and he's coming back soon.'

'Mummy, if Daddy knew about Gus, he might have come home,' Hester said accusingly.

'He knows about you, sweetheart, and he didn't come.' Laura could easily have cried herself at this unexpected turn of events. There'd been a time when she'd looked forward to the first Christmas after the war, when they'd all be together again, a family, though then there'd been no Gus on the scene. Now there was, and it would have been even better.

Gus was still watching her curiously, waiting for an answer as to the whereabouts of his father, and she had no idea what to tell him. Queenie rescued her by suggesting they play I Spy, a game he loved. A sulky Hester joined in, but recovered her usual good spirits when Gus spied something beginning with H and, after they'd spied every H in the room and had to give up, he said triumphantly, 'Horner.'

'Horner?' Laura and Queenie said together.

Hester broke into peals of laughter. 'He means corner. "Little Jack Horner sat in the corner . . ." Oh, Gus, you're such a funny little boy. Come here and let me give you a kiss.'

Late that night, when everyone had gone to bed, Laura re-read the letter Winnie had sent with the Christmas card from herself, Eric and Brian. She loved Newcastle and she and Eric were very happy.

. . . And you'll never guess, I'm having a baby! It's due in July. Brian's home, very grown-up. I was worried he wouldn't fancy having me for a step-mother, but we get on fine and he's looking forward to having a little brother or sister. He'd planned on going to university when the war ended, but he likes the idea of becoming a teacher and is going on something called the Education Training Scheme instead. He's got this little booklet. You'll never guess, it says there's a teacher training college in Kirkby, not far from where we used to work. Have you seen anything of Joe? Me and Eric were wondering if he'd divorce me so we can get married and the baby would be legitimate when it comes.

Laura had seen nothing of Joe Corcoran and it was the

Education Training Scheme that had caught her attention. After Christmas, she'd find out more about it. She quite liked the idea of becoming a teacher, too.

Whenever Queenie lifted a heavy object, her right arm gave a little twinge of protest, as if to remind her it had been broken twice and she'd better be careful.

It ached badly one day in Herriot's when she picked up a fire basket, which she'd already wrapped in several sheets of brown paper and tied with string, and handed it to the large autocratic woman who'd just bought it.

The woman looked at her, astounded. 'Would you kindly carry it to the door for me? My car's parked outside.'

There wasn't a male assistant in sight. Queenie tucked the bulky package under her left arm and made for the stairs. The woman followed, grumbling that she'd once had servants to shop for such mundane household items as fire baskets.

'But nowadays the working classes think they're too good to fetch and carry for their betters.'

Her burden was threatening to slip away. Queenie seized it with both arms, worried it might drop on to her feet. They reached the top of the stairs, the woman was complaining that the wages people expected were disgracefully high. 'You'd think they'd be grateful to be given a job,' she was saying when Queenie's right arm gave way altogether and the fire basket fell with a loud clatter, right in front of Gordon Mackie who happened to be talking to his wife. Queenie jumped back, just in time, and her heel caught the customer's toe.

The customer screamed. The manager opened his mouth to say something, though Queenie would never know what it was, because Matilda Mackie rushed around the counter and put her arm around her shoulders.

'Are you all right, dear?' She turned to her husband. 'Gordon, I don't know what this little girl was carrying, but it sounded like a ton of bricks and it shouldn't be allowed. Come, dear. I'll take you to the rest room and you can have a sit down. Gordon can see to this lady.'

Gordon Mackie requested Queenie's presence in his office first thing next morning. 'It seems to me you're not fit to be on Ironmongery,' he said with his usual bluntness.

'I'm fit enough, just not strong enough.' Queenie said defiantly. There was no chair in front of his desk and she had to stand, as if she was about to be put on a charge and thrown into the glasshouse. She didn't know what to do with her hands and clasped them loosely over her stomach. 'It's usually a man on Ironmongery, anyroad.'

'I suppose I'll just have to move you.' He sighed heavily. 'I hadn't planned on moving staff for a while yet. Which department do you fancy?'

Queenie blinked. Was she being given a choice? 'Anywhere would do, though I'd prefer not to stay in the basement. Mr Matthews only put new staff there and they worked their way up, as it were.'

'Did you work your way up from the basement?'

'Well, no,' she conceded. 'Mr Matthews thought I'd be ideal on Children's Clothing.'

'Then don't you think it's about time you took your turn?'

'If you insist.' The Wool and Fabric departments were in the basement, as well as China and Cutlery, Children's Toys and Stationery.

A strange, almost sly smile flitted across Gordon

Mackie's red face. 'You're a snotty little madam, aren't you?'

Queenie blinked again. The words weren't only offensive, but there was something familiar about the way they were said.

'I was expecting that something like this would happen,' he went on. 'That you wouldn't be able to stick it out and'd come crawling, asking to be transferred.'

'I haven't come crawling.' Queenie gaped. 'And I haven't asked to be transferred, either.'

'You would've, eventually.'

'No, I wouldn't.'

'I like a girl with spirit.' He winked. 'How d'you fancy the new Bridal Room? It's due to open on St Valentine's Day. You'll be twenty-one soon, old enough to be in charge.'

'I'd love it, but . . .'

'But what?'

'I dunno.' It seemed too easy. There must be a catch. One minute she was on Ironmongery, next the new Bridal Room, which all the women coveted and for which Queenie assumed she would be last in line.

'All you have to do is be nice to me.'

'Have I been horrible?'

'No. But I can't recall you being nice.'

'I don't understand.' Queenie felt bemused.

'Here, let me show you.' He got up from behind the desk and came and put his arm around her shoulders, as his wife had done the day before, except Mrs Mackie hadn't stroked her breast with her other hand. 'That's what I mean by nice,' he whispered.

She had vowed to never let anyone take advantage of her again. Queenie roughly shoved the hand away, slapped his red face, and fled.

★

'And his wife's so nice!' she wailed that night.

'He sounds a beast,' said a wide-eyed Laura. 'I wonder if she knows what he gets up to?'

'Perhaps she knows, but doesn't care.'

'Perhaps *he* wouldn't care if she did. Anyway, what are you going to do now?'

'I've got no choice,' Queenie said miserably. 'I'll have to leave.'

'You're right, you've got no choice.'

'He'll give me a terrible reference, I just know.'

'Mm.' Laura tapped her fingers thoughtfully on the arm of the chair. 'When you go for interview, tell them to approach Mr Matthews for a reference. It'd be best to ask him first. Do you know his address?'

'No, but I can find out.'

Ena Heron, Ladies' Footwear, knew Mr Matthews's address. 'It's The Nook, Wellington Avenue, Birkdale. We sent a card from all of us when his wife died, it must be about ten years ago now. Lord, I don't half miss him!' she said with feeling.

That night, Queenie wrote Mr Matthews a little note saying she was about to apply for a new job and would he mind if he was asked for a reference?

His reply came by return of post. He wasn't surprised she was leaving. He'd heard about the incident with the fire basket – 'I have my spies' – and thought it disgraceful she'd been put on a counter where no selling talents were required, no awareness of the customer psychology. 'People either want a tin bucket, or they don't.' He would be pleased to supply a reference, but could do even better than that.

. . . If you wish, I will contact my old friend, Miss Patricia James, who is Personnel Manager at Frederick & Hughes in Liverpool – known locally as Freddy's – and

recommend she give you a job. Perhaps you would let me know if this suits you. (I worked in Freddy's for over twenty years, starting in the stock room. I was just about to be made assistant manager, when the manager's job in Herriot's became vacant. I've often felt sorry that I took it.)

'Freddy's!' Laura breathed when she read the letter. 'It's a beautiful shop. The architecture's Victorian, so Roddy said. We had lunch in the restaurant only a few days before he went into the Army. There was a man playing a white grand piano and you should have seen the chandeliers, three of them, like cascades of diamonds.' She paused a moment, her face very still, remembering. 'You were here then, Queenie. I asked Vera to look after you and Hester. The manager – no, I think he was the owner – I can't recall his name, but he sent us a bottle of wine. He was terribly nice, very handsome. I'm sure you'd enjoy working there.'

'Laura, what's customer psychology?'

'I've no idea. Ask Gus, he's more likely to know than me.'

Miss Patricia James was fiftyish, beautifully slim and terribly smart. She wore a black, pin-striped costume with a frilly white blouse underneath, and a pearl necklace and earrings. An overwhelmed Queenie tried hard not to show how nervous she felt as she faced Miss James in her rather cramped little office on the sixth floor of Frederick & Hughes. Queenie had worn her best black coat for the interview, a white angora beret with gloves to match, and her highest heels. She had brushed her creamy hair till it shone and felt she looked her best.

'You obviously made an impression on Richard Matthews,' Miss James said. 'He wrote, praising you to the skies. You want to leave Herriot's, he said, and I was to snap you up before another big shop got to you first. Mind you,' she smiled, 'Richard always had a weakness for a pretty face, though that's as far as it went. I understand the new manager of Herriot's isn't quite so restrained.'

'How did you know?' Queenie gasped.

'These things get around. Did he make a pass at you?'

'Yes,' Queenie said indignantly.

'Well, you weren't the first. From what I hear, no woman under thirty is safe from Gordon Mackie's roving hands. Now, I'm going to give you a form to fill in. Stay where you are and I'll leave you in peace. I have one or two things to do in the shop.'

Queenie quickly completed the form in her small, neat handwriting. She sat, twiddling her thumbs, taking in the dark green filing cabinets, the faded carpet, the Venetian blinds, through which she could see flakes of snow being blown around outside. Miss James's camel swagger coat hung on a satin hanger behind the door, a pair of suede gloves poking out of one of the pockets, and there was a beige velvet hat with a speckled feather on top of a filing cabinet. She quite fancied a camel coat, the belted sort, except her small, trim figure suited fitted styles best. Belts made her look all bunched up, like a Christmas cracker.

She was giggling to herself at the comparison, when the door opened and a man entered the room.

'I was looking for Miss James,' he said in a soft, gentle voice.

'She's doing something in the shop,' Queenie informed him.

'Excuse me, but why were you laughing?' the man enquired courteously. He had the most beautiful eyes, large and brown, a touch sad, she thought, and wasn't very tall, about five feet seven. Although soberly dressed, somehow he managed to look rather flashy. Perhaps it was because his black hair was a mite too long, his grey silk suit a touch too shiny, and he was showing too much white cuff. She noticed a pin sparkling in his pale grey tie.

'I was just thinking about something funny,' she explained.

'Would you care to tell me what it was?'

'Lord, no! It was funny, but at the same time dead stupid.'

'I might not think it stupid.'

'Oh, all right. I was comparing meself to a Christmas cracker. Me shape, that is. There! It's not a bit funny, is it?'

The man looked at her gravely. 'You're right, it's not. Why are you here?'

'I've come for an interview for a job. I've just filled in the form. Do you work here?'

'Yes. Goodbye, Miss . . .?' He raised his eyebrows questioningly.

'Tate. Queenie Tate.'

'Queenie Tate,' the man repeated as he closed the door.

'Did you get it?' Laura demanded the minute Queenie came in.

'I don't know, Miss James is going to write to me. I think, I hope, I made a good impression, and I filled in a form and put that I understood customer psychology. Oh, and I met this smashing chap, incredibly good-looking, though awfully old, at least forty. I should have asked his name. He looked sort of foreign and reminded me of Charles Boyer.' She'd been unable to get the man out of her mind all the way home on the tram. He'd brought with him an all-enveloping warmth that had made her feel at ease straight away. She hoped she'd meet him again when – if – she got a job at Frederick & Hughes.

'Now we're both waiting for letters. I filled in a form too, for the Education Training Scheme. I'm still waiting to hear if they'll have me.'

Queenie's letter came first. Miss James requested that she commence work a week on Monday. She gave in her notice at Herriot's in writing, putting it on Gordon Mackie's desk when she knew he was at lunch, feeling sorry, but at the same time excited that she was about to start work in a shop four times as big and posher than Herriot's by a mile.

On the day of the interview, after she'd left Miss James's office on the sixth floor, she'd taken a look around the floors below on her way down the circular marble staircase, starting with the restaurant, where she treated herself to a cup of coffee and admired the three dazzling chandeliers suspended from the ornate ceiling, the satinwood walls and the stained glass peacocks in the enormous windows. She was disappointed that no one was playing the white grand piano.

The Furniture department was on the fourth floor and she was impressed by the elegant bedroom and dining room furniture and big, cushiony three-piece suites that stretched as far as the eye could see – Herriot's were having difficulty getting the same department fully-stocked, factories were only slowly getting back into production following the war.

A male assistant approached and regarded her hopefully. 'Can I help you, Miss?' He was very old with rheumy eyes.

'Not really. I was just wondering where all this lovely furniture came from so soon after the war?'

'Mainly South America, Miss. You'll find some very nice jewellery on the ground floor from the same place, handbags and gloves too. Mr Theo has a cousin who owns a shipping company in Greece. It's him who fetches the stuff. Same with carpets from India and rugs from Persia. We're very lucky in Freddy's, not like some shops, still waiting for the same goods to come in.'

'Who's Mr Theo?'

'The owner of Freddy's, Miss.'

'Thank you for the information.'

'It's a pleasure, Miss.' He gave her a little, old-fashioned bow.

She gave Kitchenware, Household Linens, Curtains and the small electrical section only a cursory look. The same with Gentlemen's and Children's Clothing on the floor below, where goods were merely more plentiful and more expensive than in Herriot's. She went down another flight of the circular stairs to the thickly carpeted, rosily lit second floor. 'Ladies' Exclusive Fashions' proclaimed the sign over the door. The air smelt sweet and flowery and a number of well-dressed women were searching through the racks of clothes, pausing occasionally in front of one of the gold-framed swing mirrors to hold one of the delectable garments against them, before deciding whether or not to try it on. A few bored-looking men occupied some of the cream upholstered chairs, waiting for their partners to make up their minds. There was a large bridal section, another devoted to evening wear, a room within a room containing furs.

The furthest wall was a series of narrow recesses, individually lit, just big enough to hold a single plaster mannequin, each wearing a spectacular outfit: a mink coat, a sable jacket over a soft brown jersey frock, a severe black cocktail frock softened by a spangled lace bolero, a slinky white evening frock with narrow shoulder straps encrusted with diamonds. Queenie paused in front of a powder blue bouclé costume, the skirt gently flared, the fitted top completely plain except for a collar faced with paler blue silk.

She desired it instantly. It would make a perfect going-away outfit for when she married Jimmy. Laura had offered to make her a wedding dress, so it wouldn't hurt to splash out on a costume to go away in – where to, she had no idea. Jimmy wasn't due to be demobbed until March and they hadn't got round to discussing the honeymoon in their letters.

The clothes in the recesses didn't show a price. Queenie knew for a fact that Jaeger costumes cost as much as thirteen guineas, more than three weeks' wages. But I'll only get married once, she reasoned. Unlike a wedding dress, a costume could be worn over and over again. It would be perfect if she was invited to a christening or someone else's wedding. She could think of a dozen reasons why she should buy the costume, and not a single one why she should not.

'How much is the blue costume over there?' she asked an exquisitely made-up blonde assistant who was watching her with interest.

'That's a Jacques Fath model, not long in from Paris, part of their spring collection. Smart, isn't it? It's priced at seventy-five guineas. Would you like to try it on?'

Queenie gulped. 'No, thanks. I'll think about it.' She made her way regally towards the exit. *Seventy-five guineas.* She would expect to buy a car for that much, even a house. It was a relief to reach the first floor where she recognised most of the lines; the Jaeger costumes, Slimma slacks, Hart blouses, Dereta skirts, the Robert Pringle jerseys, which, until now, she'd always considered way beyond her means, but seemed quite reasonable when compared to the prices upstairs.

On the ground floor, she searched around for something to buy as a souvenir of her first visit to Freddy's, but the handbags and gloves were leather, the jewellery gold or silver and set with real stones, the scarves either silk or cashmere. In the end, she bought a nail file in a suede case with her initial on in gold.

'We don't often sell a Q,' the assistant remarked. 'I bet your name's Queenie.'

Queenie agreed that it was, pleased that Freddy's sold at least one thing she could afford.

Gus always insisted on picking up the letters off the mat. Perhaps he thought he was doing his mother a favour, saving her the effort of walking down the hall and bending down. He studied each letter carefully, front and back, upside down, remarking on the stamp, thrilled if the sender had used more than one, while Laura gritted her teeth, longing to snatch the letter out of his helpful little hands.

'I'd like to be a stamp when I grow up,' he said on the morning Queenie had started work at Freddy's, at last handing over the letter that had slid through the box and been subjected to a thorough, clinical examination.

Laura ignored the comment. She had been able to see it wasn't from the Education Training Scheme – the envelope with the form in had been long and brown with her name and address typed. This envelope was square, white and handwritten. She felt herself grow cold when, on closer examination, she recognised Roddy's sloping script – and he was writing to her, not Hester. It was postmarked Dover.

She didn't open it immediately, just held it, stared at it, aware her hands were shaking, unable to think of anything Roddy might have to say that she'd want to know.

Eventually, because she knew she had no choice, it might be something important, she tore the envelope open.

Dear Laura,

In another few weeks, I shall be discharged from the Army and you will no longer be in receipt of an allowance. My future employment has already been arranged with a stockbroking firm in London. The salary is good and I am very much aware of my responsibilities to you and Hester. I propose to send a monthly allowance and would be grateful if you would let me know if £20 will be sufficient for your needs?

I hope that you and Hester are well – I don't seem to have heard from Hester in a long while.

I beg you to reconsider your decision to refuse me a divorce. Surely it would be best for all concerned if we were both free? I would, of course, furnish the necessary evidence and pay all legal expenses. You would then be entitled to alimony.

Yours,
Roddy

Laura flung the letter on to the fire and wished she could do the same with Roddy. Why would it be best for her to be free? So she could marry someone else when she'd promised to stay with him 'till death do us part'.

So, he was going to be a stockbroker! His brother, Thomas, had had something to do with stocks and shares. Perhaps they'd meet up, become friends again, and Roddy would be welcomed back into the bosom of his family. His father would put him back in his will, Katherine would be invited to meet them, and Laura would be called every name under the sun because, due to her, the loving couple couldn't get married.

And they never would, she swore, not over my dead

body. Well, they could, obviously, if she were dead, but while she was alive, they'd just have to live in sin. As for the money, the huge sum was very tempting, but he could keep it. She'd manage on her own.

She leaned back in the chair, watched the letter curl and burn until it was a little heap of white ash, and thought how much she hated him. Except she knew in her heart that it wasn't true. He was the love of her life and always would be.

A few days later, it was Laura's turn to go for an interview. A Mr Bailey-Oliphant, North-West Area Manager of the Education Training Scheme, wrote to request that she attend his office in Dale Street at midday the following Thursday.

'What swung it for you,' Mr Bailey-Oliphant said in a voice that Vera would describe as sounding as if he had a plum in his gob, 'is not just your excellent education in such a wide range of subjects, but on top of that you spent two and a half years engaged in war work. A riveter! I'm very impressed.'

'I loved it,' Laura said. 'I only left to have a baby.'

'Is your husband behind your decision to become a teacher?'

'I'm afraid he's – he's not coming back.'

'Oh, I say, I'm awfully sorry.'

Laura shrugged. He obviously thought Roddy was dead, and as far as she was concerned, he was. 'It can't be helped. I expect the same thing's happened to lots of women.'

'About the baby? Have arrangements been made for him or her to be taken care of while you're at teacher training college? Naturally, you'll attend the college in Kirkby.'

'Gus is three and a half. A neighbour will look after him.'

'Good. Well, Mrs Oliver, you have been accepted on the Government's Education Training Scheme starting in September.' He stood and extended his hand. Laura did the same. 'Good luck! I'm sure you will make a wonderful teacher.'

'Thank you, Mr Bailey-Oliphant. I shall do my very best.'

Chapter 9

Freddy's occupied an entire block in Hanover Street, just around the corner from Bold Street, which was full of small, expensive shops such as Aquascutum and Mappin & Webb. It was a splendid, dark red terracotta building, its most outstanding feature being the rows and rows of arched windows with a stained glass peacock in each one, and mock, cast iron balconies that, from a distance, gave the appearance of black lace frills.

There were three customer entrances, two set at angles on the front corners, the main one in the centre. Set back by about twelve feet to form a lobby with a Roman tiled floor and walls, it had four swing doors and a doorman in a black and green uniform to help people out of their chauffeur-driven cars and, later, help them and their purchases back in.

The shop was much wider than it was deep. After passing through the elegant, dazzling white cosmetics and perfume departments, customers would quickly find they'd reached the rear of the shop when they came to a circular marble staircase. The inner circle contained an ancient, very noisy lift, as splendid as the shop itself with its alternate bars of iron and shining brass. There were more lifts at the far ends of the shop, but none were so grand as this one.

On her first day, Queenie was disappointed to find herself in the basement on the book department. And

Miss James, who'd been so friendly when they first met, seemed rather cold when she arrived at the Personnel Office at eight-thirty on Monday morning as instructed.

'You're on Books,' she said shortly. 'Frances, my assistant, will take you down.'

'Thank you,' Queenie said, but Miss James had returned to reading something on her desk and didn't look up when she left.

Her disappointment was tempered rather when she met her co-worker, a dark-eyed, exuberant, well-spoken young man called Steven who explained he wasn't long out of the Air Force and had only been there a few months himself.

'But there's nothing complicated about selling books. Fiction is the most popular and they're on the wall at the back.' He pointed out the biggest sellers; 'Eric Ambler – have you read *A Coffin for Dimitrios?* It was made into a film with Peter Lorre and Sydney Greenstreet. I loved it. John Buchan – they made a film out of *The 39 Steps*, too. Agatha Christie, Dorothy L. Sayers, and so on. Mills and Boon romances have a section all to themselves, as do the classics; Trollope, Dickens, Austen, and those Russian chappies – I can never remember their names.'

Four large bookcases stood at right angles to the wall. Steven showed her the children's section. 'Have you read any of the *Just William* books by Richmal Crompton? I loved them when I was young.' Without waiting for a reply, he indicated where the atlases were kept, the travel books, dictionaries and encyclopaedias, educational, biography, gardening and cookery. 'Other than those, we don't stock much non-fiction, just one or two books on each subject, so if a customer wants a book on chemistry, say, or films, there'll be something on the shelves, arranged alphabetically by subject. I say, would you like a sweet?' He produced a sticky paper bag out of his pocket. 'I've got a thing about pear drops.'

'No, thanks. I like them too, but I'd sooner not be sucking a pear drop in front of a customer.' A bell had just rung, signalling the shop had opened and customers could arrive any minute.

The department was surprisingly busy. A lot of people spent ages browsing before making a choice. Steven seemed quite happy to leave her to do most of the work, disappearing frequently, coming back smelling of cigarettes and sucking a pear drop. He kept looking at a rather fine gold watch and asked if she'd sooner have an early lunch or a late one. 'Eleven in the morning, or two in the afternoon? The staff restaurant's on the fifth floor. Only a tanner for a meal and threepence for the pud.'

'Which would you prefer, early or late?'

'Me? Oh, I'd like both. I'm already starving, but if I go early, the afternoon stretches ahead with only a twenty-minute break and it's terribly boring. But then, if I go late, the morning's just as boring.'

Queenie laughed and suggested they take turns. She paused to sell a copy of *Gone With the Wind*, remembering she'd always meant to read it herself, then said, 'You go early today, and I'll go early tomorrow. That might make things a bit less boring.'

'Good idea.' Steven grinned. He had lovely white teeth and was altogether a most attractive young man. She didn't know much about men's clothes, but could tell his well-cut grey suit had been expensive. 'Old Rollinson,' he went on, 'always insisted on lunching in the afternoon. He'd been here since before I was born and I wasn't given a choice.'

'Who's old Rollinson?'

'Chap who's been in charge of books since the year

dot. Poor thing, he got the hump when Miss James sent him upstairs to the wilderness of Gentlemen's Footwear.'

'When did this happen?'

'Last Saturday. Mind you, I was glad to see the back of the miserable sod. You're a terrific improvement. You're coming to Lila's birthday party next week, aren't you? We can have a dance together.' He winked. 'Or two or three.'

Could it be that old Rollinson had been moved to make way for her? If so, it seemed very unfair. As to the party invitation, she felt confused. 'I've no idea who Lila is, or why she should invite me to her party.'

'Lila's my sister. She's twenty-one a week on Saturday. Dad always invites the staff to our birthday parties. This year, Lila was dead set against it, but Dad insisted. He told her, ten o'clock, she can go home and have another party with her smart friends, but he wasn't prepared to do the staff out of theirs. I had my demob party upstairs last November and the staff clubbed together and bought me a silver lighter and cigarette case. I was in the RAF on my twenty-first. It was a rowdy old do, I can tell you.'

Queenie felt even more confused. 'Upstairs?'

'In the restaurant. It's used for functions a couple of nights a week; parties and dinner dances, mainly.'

'Who exactly *is* your father?'

'Theo Vandos, owner of this damn place.' He looked glumly around the shop. 'One of these fine days, all this will be mine. Trouble is, I don't want it.'

'He wants to be an actor,' Queenie told Laura that night. 'Gosh! It was a really peculiar day. There was never a day like it in Herriot's. Fancy me working side by side with the son of the owner! I love being on Books. People are so friendly. They discuss plots and authors – I felt dead stupid, hardly knowing a thing. I'm going to join Bootle library and read and read. This afternoon, old Rollinson – I've told you about him, haven't I? – came and just stared and stared, as if he hated me guts. I felt dead uncomfortable, not that it's *my* fault I've been given his job. Though it seems a funny thing for Miss James to do, seeing as I'm so ignorant and Steven's not there half the time. He's in the Gents having a ciggie. Someone asked for a book on bats and I was looking in the sports section for one on cricket, and it turns out he meant the animals – or are they birds? I dunno. Before I knew it, there was a queue and I got meself into quite a tizzy.' She paused for breath. 'Anyroad, me invitation to the party arrived this avvy. Frances, the girl from Miss James's office brought it down. I'm going to wear that purple frock you made me for Christmas. It's not exactly a party frock, but it'll do with that diamond necklace I got from Woollies. Oh, and there's *another* funny thing. Miss James was dead unfriendly when I reported in. I can't think why. She was so nice before.'

Laura remarked that it all sounded very interesting, and Queenie agreed it was interesting all right, and also just a tiny bit mysterious.

Next day, Steven Vandos suggested she be his guest at the party. 'That means you can come to the house when it finishes upstairs.'

'I wouldn't dream of it,' she told him, annoyed. 'The other staff would hate me if they knew I'd had special treatment. I've already made one enemy in old Rollinson.'

'No one would know.'

'They might. Anyroad, I've got a boyfriend, a fiancé. He won't mind me going to the party, but not with another man.'

'So why aren't you wearing a ring?'

'Because Jimmy's in the Army. He's being demobbed the week after next. There hasn't been a chance to look for a ring.'

Steven didn't look too bothered by the rejection. He wanted to know when she was getting married and Queenie said she didn't know. 'I've still got to get used to being engaged.'

Try as she might, she found it impossible to imagine being married. It was nice to think about the wedding, discuss with Laura what style of dress she'd like, but beyond that her mind refused to go.

'I hope you're not marrying Jimmy for his sake rather than your own,' Laura said when Queenie tried to explain her feelings.

'I don't think so. It's probably because I haven't seen him for such a long time. It's bound to work out all right in the end.'

'I suppose lots of wives are finding it hard to get used to their husbands again, let alone boyfriends.' Laura sighed. 'Me, I wasn't given the chance.'

Half the tables in the restaurant had been removed, leaving enough space in the centre for people to dance. Four musicians in red satin shirts and black trousers were playing, 'The Way You Look Tonight', and a few couples had already taken to the floor when Queenie went in, all women dancing with each other. Partners hadn't been invited. Freddy's employed over three hundred staff and there wouldn't have been room. Having only been there a fortnight, she hardly knew a soul, so stood at the back of the crowd standing awkwardly inside the entrance, admiring the way the chandeliers cast little sparkling spots of light on to the wood-panelled walls. The atmosphere was stiff and rather formal.

A woman said, 'Excuse me, luv,' and was about to push past when she paused. 'I remember you! You asked the price of that Jacques Fath costume. I admired the way your face didn't even flicker when I said seventy-five guineas.' It was the blonde assistant from Ladies' Exclusive Fashions. 'I didn't realise you worked here,' she said.

'I didn't then. I'd just had an interview that day. I'm still trying to work out how a costume could possibly cost so much.'

'It's the label,' the woman explained, 'and the fact it's from Paris. The style is new, setting a trend. The skirt's about five inches longer than usual, the jacket's fitted instead of boxy and it hasn't got shoulder pads. And it's an original. Whoever buys that costume will never see another woman in the same outfit. Get one from C and A or Marks and Sparks, and you're likely to go somewhere like a wedding and come face to face with a woman in the same thing.' She smiled. 'It can be dead embarrassing, particularly if she's got a better figure than you. Anyroad, this time next year, the High Street shops will be bursting with costumes just like the one you wanted, but they'll only cost seven guineas, not seventy-five. What's your name, luv? And what department are you on? I'm Judy Channon, by the way.'

'I'm Queenie Tate and I'm on Books.'

'With the boss's son, eh? I understand he smokes about a hundred fags a day.'

'Something like that,' Queenie admitted.

'Have you had anything to eat, luv?'

'Not yet.'

'The buffet's over there. Help yourself before it all goes. There's wine an' all, red or white. I was just on me way to the Ladies when I saw you, but I'm sitting with me friends on the table nearest the band. Come and join us if you want.'

'Thanks, I'd love to.'

Judy Channon was back at the table by the time Queenie arrived with an assortment of sandwiches, a sausage roll, and a glass of white wine. She was introduced to the other women there. 'This is Edie, that's Gladys – she thinks she's better than us 'cos she works in Accounts – that's Brenda wearing the glasses, and Mona's the one with the grey hair. We're known as the War Widows' Club. Our husbands were killed in the war, so we always have plenty of shoulders to cry on when one of us feels low.'

'Couldn't you pick something better than me grey hair to point me out by?' Mona complained. 'Me nice blue eyes, for instance, or me nails. I had a manicure yesterday. What d'you think?' She flared her hands and everybody admired the bright pink nails. 'Did you know the female staff can use the hairdresser's and the manicurist for free, Queenie? The beauty salon's on the fifth floor. It stays open till eight o'clock three nights a week, just for us. They'll even do you in your lunch hour if they're not busy. Not only that, the staff restaurant stays open till seven, so's you can get a cheap meal if you want to go out straight from work.'

'Miss James told me.'

'You couldn't get a better boss than Theo Vandos,' Mona said fondly. 'He doesn't deserve that cow of a wife, or those two bitchy daughters.'

'Is he here?' Queenie asked. So far, she hadn't set eyes on Mr Theo or the man she'd spoken to in Miss James's office whom she'd very much like to meet again.

'Not yet. Oh! Here he is now! Come on, girls. Give

him a big cheer.' Mona jumped to her feet and started to clap.

The music stopped and a man entered the room, a small, dapper man in evening dress, very slim, with luminous eyes and black hair. His bow tie was perhaps a mite too big and he showed too much white cuff. Queenie felt herself go cold. Mr Theo and the man she'd already met were one and the same. He'd asked why she was laughing, and *she'd* asked if he worked there!

'Yes,' he'd said modestly, not admitting he was the owner.

She comforted herself with the thought that he would have forgotten her by now, that he wouldn't even recognise her if he saw her again. He had a girl on either side, linking their arms, whom she took to be his daughters – his bitchy daughters, according to Mona. The tallest was outstandingly beautiful, with a great mane of jet black hair, big dark eyes, and a perfect mouth painted scarlet. She wore a stiff cream taffeta frock, ankle-length, with a swirling skirt, and an emerald green velvet bolero. A diamond necklace glittered around her slender neck, which Queenie would like to bet hadn't come from Woollies as had her own.

Perhaps it was because her sister was so lovely that the other girl appeared so nondescript. She looked about fifteen, round-shouldered and very thin. Her hair had been cut unflatteringly short, and she would have looked much better in a plain frock, rather than the frilly pink creation she wore.

Neither girl was smiling. The tall one, whom Queenie presumed was Lila, looked downright sulky. Steven had said she hadn't wanted her party held in the shop this time.

Steven followed his father and sisters, accompanied by a striking woman in royal blue chiffon who could only be Mrs Vandos. Her black hair was drawn severely back from her haughty face and twisted into a tight knot on top of her well-shaped head. She looked no more pleased to be there than did her daughters and reminded Queenie of the wicked queen in *Snow White and the Seven Dwarfs*, which she'd taken Hester and Mary to see when they'd lived in Southport. In pleasant contrast, Steven grinned at everyone in sight. He caught Queenie's eye and winked. She pretended not to notice.

Theo Vandos made a short speech. People had to strain to hear his soft voice. He said he was glad to have the opportunity of sharing another family celebration with the staff of Freddy's. 'I like to think of us as one big happy family. Now, if everyone would like to stay where they are, the waiters will come round with a glass of champagne. Could we please have the cake?'

An enormous white and silver cake was wheeled in, white candles fluttering. With ill grace, Lila blew out the candles and cut the first slice, to the accompaniment of polite applause. Waiters swiftly distributed the champagne, while two others deftly cut the cake into small pieces and took them round to the guests. The band were playing 'Happy Birthday to You', but not very loudly. When everyone had been served, the elderly man with rheumy eyes who served in the Furniture department, presented Lila with a gold chain from the staff. Theo Vandos raised his own glass of champagne. 'Many happy returns, Lila,' he said with almost a sigh in his voice. The band burst into a rowdy version of 'Twenty-one Today', and the guests joined in, more for Mr Theo's sake than the surly Lila's.

'No wonder he wants us all to be one big happy family, when his own are such a shower,' Mona said. 'Steven's all right, but he's a bit of a playboy.'

Queenie didn't want to betray what might have been

a confidence and tell them that Steven wanted to be an actor. 'Vandos is an unusual name,' she said. 'I've never heard it before.'

'That's because it's Greek, luv,' Brenda explained. 'Mr Theo's dad came to Liverpool from Greece at the turn of the century. He started off with a market stall and within ten years had taken over Freddy's. He died just before the war.'

'I believe you promised me a dance, Queenie.' Steven was by the table, hand outstretched. The band were playing 'You Were Never Lovelier'.

'Excuse me,' Queenie muttered to the women. 'I wish you hadn't asked,' she said to Steven when they were on the floor.

'Why not?' He looked surprised.

'I don't like being made to look special, dancing with the boss's son, like.'

'In that case, I'll ask that grey-haired woman who was sitting by you next. What's her name?'

'Mona. She's a widow, so be nice to her.'

'I'm nice to everyone. Is it all right if I ask you for every other dance?'

She rolled her eyes. 'Can't you share yourself out a bit more?'

'The truth is, Queenie,' he said meekly, 'I'm basically terribly shy and you're the only person here I know.'

'Liar! You've been here months. You must know loads of people.'

'You're the only *young* person I know.'

'That's not true, either.'

'You're the only young, *pretty* person I know. What's more, you're a girl. Have I convinced you yet?'

'I suppose.' She knew he was only flirting and his words meant nothing. When he got home, where the party would continue, he would probably say the same things to someone else.

'What do you think of the family?' he asked.

'They seem very nice.'

'Nice! Who's being the liar now? Dad apart, they're a ghastly crew. It must be obvious that Lila and Stephanie hate each other and Mum hates Dad.'

'Why? Oh, I'm sorry. I shouldn't have asked.'

'That's all right,' Steven said cheerfully. 'In its own way, it's something of a Greek tragedy. Lila is jealous of Steph's brains, and Steph envies Lila's looks. Mum hates Dad for too many reasons to list.'

'That's terrible. Mind you, my mam hated me.' It must be the wine mixed with the champagne. Ordinarily, she wouldn't have dreamed of revealing anything so personal.

'Whatever for?' he asked, shocked.

'For being me. I was ugly, useless, stupid. In her eyes, anyroad.'

'Your mother must be mad. Introduce me to her and I'll tell her how mad she is.'

'She's not around any more. She went away when I was fourteen and I've been dead happy living with Laura ever since.'

'Good for Laura, whoever she may be.'

Queenie described Laura and told him she had, sort of, met his father many years ago. 'She and her husband Roddy were having lunch here and he sent them a bottle of wine. It was only days before the war began.'

'I'll remind Dad. He'll probably remember. He remembers everything to do with the shop.'

They had danced past his father several times. He watched them with dark, brooding eyes. The family were sitting together on a table in the corner, not speaking to each other. Steven seemed the only one having a good time.

The dance finished. The atmosphere had warmed up considerably, and there was no longer an awkward crowd inside the door. It was announced that the next dance would be the Gay Gordons and people poured on to the floor, stamping their feet enthusiastically, enjoying themselves. Steven dutifully asked up a flustered Mona, then returned to Queenie for the next dance.

'If you play your cards right,' Judy said some time later, 'you could end up married to the next owner of Freddy's.'

Queenie explained there was no chance of that because by this time next week her fiancé would have been demobbed. Steven had charm, but he hadn't an ounce of Jimmy's character.

When the war ended, Tess and Pete Nicholls had returned to Liverpool from Caerdovey and gone straight into a children's home in Fazakerly. Tess was now twelve. For Pete, eight, Liverpool was just a far-off memory.

Vera Monaghan, all heart as usual, had wanted to take the 'poor little mites', but Albert had put his foot down, reminding her that once the lads were home she'd have a houseful, that she would be sixty next year and it was about time she put her feet up and, finally, that Tess Nicholls was anything but a little mite and he'd heard she was a difficult girl to get along with.

'I don't want a repeat of the situation we had with Iris when she first came. Anyroad, the home's only temporary. Once their brother's back, he'll have them out like a shot.'

This came as a relief to Mary, who couldn't stand

Tess. Even Hester was pleased that Tess wouldn't be living across the street, temporarily or not.

Mr Iles, who now collected the rent in place of the sadly missed Edgar Binns, had been asked if he would please let Queenie know if a property should fall vacant. Once Jimmy was back, he wanted his family together again as soon as possible. Mr Iles promised to do his best, but Bootle had lost so many houses in the raids it was rare anything became available. If it did, it was snapped up straight away.

Queenie had been to see Tess and Pete once a month on Sunday afternoons. She would have gone more often if it had only been Pete. He was a nice little boy with a sweet disposition but, with the years, Tess had become even more belligerent. Her mousy brown hair was plaited into two stiff pigtails, which seemed to bristle when her anger was at its height. Always needing somone to blame for her misfortunes, her rage was, most unreasonably, directed at her brother, as if it were Jimmy who'd started the war, bombed the house in which her parents had been killed, then joined the Army to avoid looking after her and Pete, so they'd been left to rot in Caerdovey for years, until being put in a home, which she hated.

'Jimmy had no choice but to join the Army,' Queenie told her angrily, wanting to wrap the pigtails around her neck and give them a good tug. Jimmy loved his little brother and sister and had always done his very best by them. What's more, although Tess had had a hard life, at twelve, Queenie's own life had been far harder. She had little patience with the girl. Her mind crept forward, just a little, beyond her wedding day, and she tried to imagine what it would be like, living with Tess and her tantrums. At least her own presence would make things easier for Jimmy.

When Queenie came home from Freddy's on the Monday after the party, Laura told her that Mr Iles had been to say a flat had fallen vacant over a baker's shop in Pacific Road.

'The old tenants did a moonlight flit, owing a month's rent. Mr Iles said it's been left in a bit of a state, but he's having it cleaned up. After tea, we can go round and have a look, see if you think Jimmy will like it. I've got a key. You have to go in through the back yard.'

'Jimmy's sure to like anything so long as it's got a roof. You should have seen the place he lived in on the Dock Road. It was horrible.'

The flat was tiny and very dirty, the furniture cracked and chipped, showing its age. The front bedroom had been turned into a living room with an elderly gas fire in the tiny grate and a meter in the corner to put pennies in. The smallest room had become the kitchen where an outside door had been installed opening on to a set of iron stairs leading to the yard and the outside lavatory. There was a double bed in the remaining room.

'It'll be a bit of a squeeze,' Laura said doubtfully. 'Jimmy and Pete can share the bedroom. Tess will have to sleep on a camp bed in the front.'

'She won't like that,' Queenie said ominously. 'Even so, I think we should take it. Jimmy'll be back on Saturday. He'll be thrilled to have a place of his own. When you consider the shortage of accommodation, he's very lucky.'

'I'll tell Mr Iles tomorrow. In the meantime, I'll take down those filthy curtains and give them a wash.'

Laura and Vera raided their linen cupboards and enough old bedding was unearthed to do the Nicholls until they could buy their own. The same with dishes and a couple of dented saucepans. Vera would let them have a camp bed, but it was only on loan.

On Friday night, Queenie went round to the flat in Pacific Road with a bunch of daffodils she'd bought off a stall in St John's Market. Laura let her have a vase, though she wanted it back. The flowers were merely hard green heads with only a glimpse of yellow petals showing, but she'd been told to put them in slightly warm water and they might be recognisably daffodils by tomorrow. She heated the water in the freshly scrubbed, if extremely shabby kitchen, and put the vase in the middle of the round table in the front room. Everywhere had been thoroughly cleaned, the lino polished, and the double bed made. The windows shone and the curtains had been washed, ironed, and re-hung. It looked cosy and welcoming. The folded camp bed was on the settee, waiting to be set up for Tess. Queenie sat down beside it. Now that Jimmy was due home in a matter of hours, she longed to see him. She knew that she would always be safe with Jimmy Nicholls, that he would look after her and love her dearly till the day she died – or he died, she thought with a sigh.

Next morning, it seemed as if every person in Liverpool had decided to buy a book and the first place they thought of was Freddy's. Queenie was run off her feet. Perhaps it was the extra work that made Steven disappear even more frequently than usual for a ciggie in the Gents.

'What happens if you become an actor and you're in a play?' Queenie snapped when he returned after about the sixth time. 'Are you going to flit off the stage every five minutes for a smoke? I've had queues a mile long and you've been no help.'

Steven grinned. 'You've no right to tell me off, Miss Tate. I'm the boss's son. I might report you to Dad.'

'What for? Working too hard?'

'Working too hard's a sin in my book.'

'Working at all is a sin as far as you're concerned.' Queenie burst out laughing. Steven was irrepressible. It was impossible to stay angry with him for long, but she doubted if old Rollinson had felt the same.

'Could you possibly look after things for five minutes while I make a note of the books I've sold?' she asked caustically. A record had to be made in a ledger of all sales, so replacements could be ordered. It was sensible to write down the names immediately, but Steven's absence had made it impossible.

'I'll do my best, Miss,' he lisped.

She was dredging her memory for titles, when a voice said, 'Hello, Queenie, girl,' and when she looked up Jimmy was smiling down at her. He wore a blue-striped, ill-fitting demob suit and clutched a grey trilby hat to his chest. At his feet, stood a cardboard suitcase with all its corners badly squashed. The stitching was coming out of the handle.

'Jimmy!' she breathed. 'Oh, Jimmy!' She wanted to run round the counter and give him a hug, kiss his lovely, innocent, shining face, but the shop was crowded – it wouldn't have been the proper thing to do even if it were not. She recalled the first morning in Caerdovey, on the shore, when he'd spoken her name, just as he'd done now.

'You look a proper bobby dazzler, Queenie.'

'You don't look so bad yourself.' The war had done him good, physically, at least. He stood taller, erect and dignified. 'I thought you were going straight to Laura's to get the key for the flat?'

'I've only just got off the train at Lime Street and I preferred to come and see you first, girl.'

Steven was watching them curiously. She introduced the men to each other. 'This is Steven who I work with. Steven, this is my fiancé, Jimmy.'

'How do you do?' Steven courteously extended his hand. 'I understand you were in the Army. Myself, I was in the RAF. I'm still not sure whether I'm glad to be home or not.'

'I'm sure, and I'm glad an' all,' Jimmy said steadily. He glanced at Queenie. 'If you want the truth, I couldn't wait.'

'Ah, well. Unlike me, you had someone to come home to.' Steven's face was sober for once.

'If you can hang on for an hour, Jimmy, we can have lunch together,' Queenie said.

'No, ta, girl. I'll call on Laura for the key, then I'll collect our Tess and Pete, show them the new place. I'll see you tonight.'

Not caring about the customers, Queenie leaned over the counter and stroked his face. 'Tara, Jimmy.'

'What's happening tonight?' asked Steven. Queenie was watching Jimmy march smartly towards the exit. He had lost his awkward, shambling gait.

'He's bringing Tess and Pete to Laura's for a meal. A homecoming. Some people from across the street are coming too.'

'Who are Tess and Pete?'

'His younger brother and sister. Their mam and dad died in an air raid and Jimmy's looking after them.'

'So, you'll be starting married life with a ready made family, eh?'

'It looks like it,' said Queenie.

Everyone had anticipated that Tess would hate the flat, but perhaps she was too pleased to have left the home to care that she was about to sleep in the living room on a camp bed. She was unbelievably sweet-natured throughout the meal.

Food rationing was still in force and the meal was no

different to the sort they'd had in war time; scouse, followed by jelly and custard, but Jimmy declared it was the best he'd eaten in a long while.

'It's nice to have you back, lad,' Albert said jovially. 'Our own lads have been coming home in dribs and drabs. They'll be over later, by the way, to take you for a pint.'

'Can I go for a pint, Mum?' asked Gus.

'No, sweetheart. Not for another fourteen and a half years.'

'Will you come with me?'

'If you like. While I'm waiting, I'll make a cup of tea.'

Mary asked Jimmy if he'd killed any Germans during the war and Jimmy said he'd sooner not talk about the war, not just now.

The meal over, he asked if anyone would mind if he took Queenie for a little walk. He promised to be back in time for a pint with the Monaghan lads.

'Of course no one minds,' Laura cried. 'So far, you haven't had a minute to be alone together.'

Queenie blushed. When Jimmy had gone away, they'd just been friends, as far as she was concerned, anyroad. Now he was back and they were an engaged couple. She wondered how she would feel if he kissed her. It was a relief when Jimmy just took her hand and tucked her arm inside his.

'The flat looks great, girl,' he said warmly, 'a real home from home. You've done us proud.'

'It wasn't just me. Laura and Vera helped too.'

'I suppose we should set a date for the wedding soon.'

'But Jimmy,' she said alarmed. 'We'd need somewhere bigger to live, where there's a room of our own.'

'You and me can sleep in the big bed and we can get a camp bed for Pete an' all. He and Tess can sleep together.'

'It would be a terrible squash. Besides, Tess will soon be thirteen. She needs her privacy. And where would we sit at night?' They'd have to go to bed terribly early, not long after tea, if the living room was to be used as a bedroom. And what would happen if they had a baby? This was another of the thoughts Queenie had resisted. The truth was, she liked working at Freddy's and didn't want to leave so soon.

Jimmy, bless his heart, was nodding understandingly. 'You're quite right, girl. I didn't think. We'd be living on top of one another. No, when we get married, we're going to live in a nice big house with a room each for our Tess and Pete. In the meantime, I'll get you an engagement ring out of me gratuity – they gave us twenty quid when I left the Army.'

'I say, Queenie, Dad would like a word with you,' Steven said when he appeared, late, on Monday morning.

'Oh, yeah!' It was 1 April, April Fool's Day, and she thought he was having her on.

'I'm serious. He wants you in his office straight away.'

'What have I done wrong?' she cried, panicking. 'I hope he's not going to give me the sack.'

'Dad never gives staff the sack. That's Miss James's job. He wants to talk to you about your friend, Laura. Go in the big lift, you'll find his office easier that way.'

Queenie's heart continued to race as she stood in the lift taking her to the sixth floor where Mr Theo's office was situated, along with a big apartment where, according to Steven, he often stayed, sometimes for weeks on end, if things were particularly bad at home.

'Which they usually are,' he'd added gloomily.

The lift stopped and she stepped out on to a thick

brown carpet in a corridor where the walls were covered with brown and gold mottled paper, almost as thick.

'That's it, the door at the end,' said Eustace, the lift man. He was a veteran of the First World War and his green uniform trousers hid a wooden leg.

The door had a little brass plate indicating the office was occupied by Theodore Vandos. She knocked nervously and a quiet voice said, 'Come in.'

Mr Theo was sitting behind a huge desk. Figures that looked very much like the twelve apostles were carved on the front. The maroon leather top had a fancy gold border and held a sheet of virgin white blotting paper in a matching leather holder. A fat diary bore the figures '1946' in gold and there was a sparkling glass inkwell with a silver lid. The room was large, at least thirty feet square, filled with equally large furniture, all as elaborately carved as the desk; cupboards, bookcases, a massive table full of papers and magazines. She noticed *Vogue* was one. In the white marble fireplace, which resembled a miniature Greek temple, a warm fire burned, emitting waves of heat. Nothing could be seen through the arch-shaped windows except a watery grey sky. None of the adjacent buildings were as tall as Freddy's.

'Good morning,' Queenie whispered, then wondered if she should have waited for him to speak first.

'Good morning, Miss Tate. Sit down.' He indicated the chair in front of his desk, which squeaked when she sat on it. There was a long silence while they just stared at each other, Mr Theo with his great, dark, brooding eyes, Queenie unsure whether it was her turn to say something. 'You wanted to see me,' she said at last.

'Ah, yes.' He looked slightly startled, as if he'd forgotten he'd asked and she was there of her own accord. 'Steven told me about your friend, Laura. I remember the occasion distinctly. They'd just got married. The young man – what is his name?'

'Roddy.'

'He sent a note, asking if the pianist would play 'Here Comes the Bride'. The waitress told me and I asked her to present them with a bottle of wine. Laura smiled at me. She looked a delightful young woman, starry-eyed, the way a bride should look on the day of her wedding,' he said eloquently.

'Oh, but they couldn't have . . .' They couldn't have just got married, Queenie was about to say. By then, Hester was five and she'd always assumed Laura and Roddy had married years before. But perhaps not. Perhaps there were secrets Laura wasn't prepared to tell anyone, not even her.

'Couldn't have what?' Mr Theo asked in his gentle voice.

'Nothing, it doesn't matter. I was just a bit confused about something.'

'I would very much like to offer them another meal, meet them personally this time. I take it Roddy survived the war?'

'Oh, he survived all right,' Queenie tried not to sound bitter, 'but he's left Laura for another woman. She hasn't seen him in years.'

'But they looked so happy.' He appeared distressed by the news. 'I couldn't see the young man, he had his back to me, but I could tell by the way he was bending towards her that he had eyes only for his new wife.'

'They were madly in love. I'll never understand how Roddy could fall for someone else.' It seemed a strange conversation to be having with the owner of Freddy's, but by now she'd concluded that Mr Theo was a strange man altogether. She liked him the first time they'd met and now she liked him even more.

'Can we ever trust people when they say they love us, Miss Tate?' he said despairingly.

Queenie didn't answer. It had sounded like a cry from the heart and she had no idea what to say.

Mr Theo gave himself a little shake and said in a more normal tone, 'How are you getting on in Books?'

'I love it,' she cried. 'I learn something new every day and I've been reading like mad. I finished *Pride and Prejudice* last night. It's just like a Mills & Boon, though better written.'

'I'm glad you think so.' He smiled. It was the first time she'd ever seen him smile and she thought it very sweet, if a little sad, like his eyes. 'Miss James tells me that there's often quite a big queue. She doesn't think you're managing all that well.'

'Oh, but there's only a queue because . . .' She stopped just in time from telling him it was because Steven spent half his time in the Gents with a ciggie.

'I know the reason for the queue, Miss Tate. You're very loyal. Mr Rollinson complained bitterly – and frequently – about the irresponsible way my son behaves.'

'Steven's very nice,' Queenie said defensively. 'He's just finding it hard, that's all, settling into a job after being in the RAF.' She felt as if she'd just been tested, to see if she would be loyal, and felt cross with Miss James for saying she wasn't managing, when she must surely know that she often looked after the department on her own.

'Next week, you'll be moving to another department,' Mr Theo continued, dropping a bombshell.

'Which one?' Visions of Ironmongery passed through her mind.

'Ladies' First Floor Fashions. This coming Friday, I would like you to accompany Miss Hurst, our fashion buyer, to the Adelphi Hotel where some of the lesser known labels will be showing their autumn lines. All you have to do is take note of the items Miss Hurst wishes to order.'

'But why are you sending me?' she asked, startled.

'Why not, Miss Tate?'

'I've only been here a month.'

'I consider you an excellent worker, having coped so admirably on Books.' He leaned forward and folded his arms on the white blotter. 'You might like to consider a career in the retail trade,' he said earnestly. 'As a fashion buyer, for instance. They lead very interesting lives. Miss Hurst travels to Paris several times a year to view the latest designer shows; Fath, Balenciaga, Dior, Cardin. Would that interest you? Or are you set on getting married very soon? Steven tells me you're about to get engaged.'

'We haven't set a date for the wedding.' What a strange thing for Steven to tell him! 'It'll be ages before we can afford a house. I'd love to be a fashion buyer,' she breathed.

He gave her another of his sweet, sad smiles. 'Then let's see how you get on on Friday.'

Queenie couldn't understand it. Mr Theo's words buzzed around in her mind for the rest of the day, but it wasn't until she got on the train at Exchange Station that she was able to think about what he'd said without being interrupted by someone wanting to buy a book. It had seemed mysterious before and now it seemed even more so. Why had Miss James turned against her? Had she disapproved of her being put on Books with Steven while poor old Rollinson was transferred to Gentlemen's Footwear? Even Queenie could see it would have been wiser for her to have been put in Steven's place and *he* be moved elsewhere. Did Miss James know she was about to be transferred to Ladies' First Floor Fashions, and that, on Friday, she was actually going to a fashion show at the Adelphi, the biggest and poshest hotel in Liverpool? Could it be Mr Theo who was deciding the departments in which she would work and not Miss James, whose job it actually was?

If so, why?

'It's obvious why,' Vera hooted about four hours later. 'He fancies you.'

Queenie and Jimmy had been for a walk, only as far as the Docky and back. It was a lovely spring evening with only a slight chill in the air. He told her about the job interview he'd been for that afternoon. It was in a garage, working on his beloved cars. 'I learnt to drive in the Army,' he said proudly.

'I know. You told me in a letter.'

'I hope I get it, the job, that is. Me gratuity won't last long if I'm not working.'

'Perhaps it'd be best to forget about an engagement ring for now,' she suggested. She didn't mention the startling improvement in her own job prospects.

'Not on your life, girl. I want you wearing me ring on your finger, particularly in front of that smart young feller you work with.'

'I hope you're not jealous, Jimmy.'

He shuffled his feet uncomfortably and his cheeks went red. 'I might well be.'

'There's no need,' she assured him kindly. 'I'm not the least bit interested in Steven.'

'I know you're not, girl, but I'd like other fellers to know you're engaged to me.'

They returned to Pacific Road, and just managed to have a cup of tea before it was time for Pete to go to bed.

He was finding it hard to settle in his new home and a different school. Tess was being awkward. She'd made friends at her own school and spent most evenings in other girls' houses, coming home at all hours. As Jimmy didn't want Pete left on his own, it wasn't possible for him and Queenie to go to the pictures or a dance.

'You don't mind, do you, girl?' he asked anxiously in the grubby little backyard when she was about to leave.

'Of course not.' He was only twenty, much too young to be landed with so many troubles. But it was proving an awfully dull courtship.

Vera was relaxing in an armchair when she got back to Glover Street. She'd come for a bit of peace and quiet, she claimed. The lads were driving her potty. They were bored witless after the excitement of the war and were finding it difficult to get used to civilian life. Victor was drinking too much, Billy was having nightmares, waking up thinking he was still in the prisoner of war camp, Frank's girlfriend had jilted him and he was going out with a flamer called Connie McBride who was the scrapings of the gutter. It was all Hitler's fault and she was glad he was dead.

'Anyroad, luv, how's the job going?' she asked, when she'd finished explaining for Queenie's benefit exactly what she was doing there.

'A strange thing happened today,' Queenie began, but Laura interrupted to say that, since she'd started at Freddy's, strange things seemed to happen every day.

'Today was stranger than ever.' She said nothing about the lunch invitation. If Laura realised Mr Theo had remembered sending the wine, he would also have remembered it was her and Roddy's wedding day, something she clearly preferred people not to know. She backtracked a bit and told Vera about old Rollinson,

Steven's smoking, the party, what a tragic family the Vandoses were, Miss James's change of attitude, all things Vera had heard already from Laura, but enjoyed hearing again from the horse's mouth. Queenie came to that morning, Mr Theo sending for her, telling her she was about to be moved to Ladies' First Floor Fashions, the fashion show at the Adelphi and, finally, his advice that she make a career in the retail industry and hinting that she might possibly become a buyer.

'There was a fashion buyer in Herriot's, Miss Ferris,' she told her rapt audience. 'She had her own little office and dressed like a film star. Rumour had it a lot of the clothes she got for free, just for placing an order. All the other women were dead envious. I can't think why Mr Theo should single me out. I mean, I've hardly been there five minutes.'

And that's when Vera had burst out laughing and said it was obvious – Mr Theo fancied her.

Chapter 10

The first and second floors of the Adelphi had been taken over for the fashion show. Some labels, with a wide range of autumn lines to exhibit, had hired an entire suite. Others that concentrated on a single line, such as wedding or ball gowns, rainwear or country wear, occupied just a single room.

Queenie met Miss Hurst in Freddy's restaurant where she was having breakfast and had reached the toast and marmalade stage. She was very friendly and asked the waitress to fetch another cup so Queenie could share her pot of tea. Going on for sixty, with a long, narrow, heavily made-up face, she was exquisitely attired in a lilac wool suit and matching turban, with a silver fox fur draped around her narrow shoulders. She had the mere trace of a Liverpool accent.

Breakfast over, she handed Queenie two fat briefcases to carry – neither of which were opened the entire day – and insisted on calling for a taxi to take them the ten-minute walk to the hotel. Friday was the second day of the show, she said on the short journey. 'I could have gone yesterday, I was invited, but I chose to come today instead. Freddy's is one of the biggest buyers and it keeps them on their toes if they think I'm not interested enough to view their wretched clothes immediately.' She had a dozen appointments, one every half an hour until five o'clock, with a break for lunch. Queenie had the list.

A company called Evangelina Fashions would be their first port of call.

'I doubt if I'll buy anything. Their clothes are usually at least a year out of date, but I must pay them a visit, just in case they've come up with something remarkable this time.'

The show was like a travelling circus, she said as she alighted from the taxi and swept into the hotel, Queenie staggering behind with the briefcases (she was rather glad about the taxi, which had seemed an extravagance at first). It toured the country, setting up shop, as it were, in half a dozen major cities. Buyers would then come from all over the surrounding area, from very big stores like Freddy's, George Henry Lee's and Lewis's, to the very smallest, usually managed by the owner.

The Evangelina label was represented by a rather sweaty, anxious young man called Mr Travis, who greeted Miss Hurst effusively and led her to a comfortable chair, then asked if she would like tea or coffee, or 'something stronger'.

'I wouldn't mind a glass of sherry,' she graciously agreed. 'And I'm sure my assistant would appreciate a cup of tea. This is Miss Tate, by the way.'

'Pleased to meet you.' Mr Travis gave her a worried nod. He snapped his fingers and a woman appeared from behind a rack of clothes and he requested she fetch the drinks.

'While we're waiting, Miss Hurst, may I show you a few of our overcoats?'

'Why not!' Miss Hurst said breezily.

'This style is going to be very big this autumn.' He took a double-breasted, bright red jersey coat from the rack. At first glance, it appeared to sport at least a hundred big, gleaming brass buttons, but when Queenie counted, there were only sixteen. 'We call this model Patricia.'

Miss Hurst contemplated the garment thoughtfully. 'Mr Travis,' she said.

'Yes, Miss Hurst.' Mr Travis jumped.

'That red is far too red. And what makes you think women want military-style clothing when the war has not long ended? They want softer styles, more feminine. In a coat like that, I might feel tempted to challenge you to a duel. What else do you have?'

Mr Travis then produced a fitted coat called Daisy that was far too green, in which Miss Hurst said she would feel like a tree. 'A bottle green would be so much nicer. I might have bought it had it been bottle.'

'We can make it up for you in bottle,' Mr Travis said eagerly. 'I have a swatch of material right here and can give you a special price if you buy a dozen, say six guineas each instead of seven,' a statement that caused Miss Hurst to give him a look of such disdain that even Queenie winced.

'Mr Travis, I'm from Frederick and Hughes. We would never, *never* stock a dozen garments all the same. I'll take two in bottle, size thirty-six and thirty-eight inch hips.'

Queenie made a note of the order in the exercise book with which she'd been provided: 'Two Daisies, bottle green, size 36" and 38", 7 gns each from Evangelina.'

Miss Hurst graciously accepted another glass of sherry while proceeding verbally to demolish every garment she was shown. They left when their half-hour was up, having ordered two bottle green Daisies and leaving Mr Travis even sweatier than when they'd arrived.

Outside in the corridor, Queenie was told to cross the

order out. 'I only made it because I felt sorry for the poor fellow. I'll cancel it next week.'

The next appointment was with Pierce & Skinner, where Miss Hurst drank two more sherries and ordered three outsize pleated skirts in different plaids. 'I can't understand outsize ladies wearing pleats – or plaids,' she sighed, 'but they do. Have you any jumpers to match?'

'Who's next?' she asked at eleven o'clock when they were back in the corridor.

Queenie studied the list. 'Fleur.'

'Ah!' For the first time she showed some enthusiasm. 'Fleur is a new label. They only do frocks. I've heard good things about them. Very clever that, using a French name.'

Fleur's representative was a tall, very pale and effeminate young man who introduced himself as Wilfred Carter. He wore a black and white polka-dot cravat instead of a tie and had a pronounced cockney accent.

Although he had hired only a small room, Wilfred Carter had brought with him his own model, an incredibly thin, incredibly tall young woman with a gaunt face and bones protruding sharply from every part of her body. Her eyelids were painted midnight blue and her thick black lashes were at least an inch long. Her name was Rosa and she looked very exotic, emerging from behind a screen wearing an off-white frock of the very finest jersey, plain, form-fitting, the only adornment being the fluting on the hem and on the edge of the long, tight sleeves that almost reached her thumbs.

'So elegant and beautifully cut,' Miss Hurst breathed. 'Only the minimum amount of material has been used, yet the fluting makes it look quite extravagant.' Material still remained in short supply. 'Do you have this design in other colours?'

'Black and grey. I would describe it as a misty grey. I'll

show you.' He took two similar garments off the rack. 'Like all the frocks, it comes in three sizes only, from a thirty-four- to a thirty-eight-inch hip, and all are priced at seven guineas each.'

'I'd like three, one of each colour. Oh, and make them different sizes too. Does this item have a name?'

'Pearl.'

Queenie was furiously writing the order down when Rosa appeared in another tight-fitting frock made from crêpe the colour of blackberries. It had a floppy flower from the same material attached just below the left shoulder.

'We also have this model in very dark blue, almost navy, but not quite, and jade. We call this our Diamond model.'

'I'll have one of each, as before. What else do you have?' she asked eagerly.

The other designs were just as impressive. Miss Hurst went quite mad and ordered eighteen frocks altogether in six different styles, and also extracted from Wilfred Carter that he designed the clothes and cut them, that Rosa was his sister, and that she, his mother and his aunt sewed them in the cellar of their house in Camden.

'That makes the whole day feel worthwhile,' she said to Queenie later. 'Pretty soon, Fleur will only show in London and Mr Carter won't need to travel the country with his lovely designs. In the meantime, he needs encouragement. That's why I didn't barter over the price.'

'The styles were very slimming. Why doesn't he make them in the larger sizes?' Queenie asked curiously.

'Because women with thirty-six hips consider themselves a different breed from those with forty-six hips. They wouldn't be seen dead in anything that was also available for the larger figure. Come on, dear. Who's next? Mr Carter didn't offer us a drink, did he?'

By one o'clock, Miss Hurst had consumed thirteen glasses of sherry, yet was still able to walk and talk like a perfectly sober human being, though her mascara had smudged and her nose was shining like a beacon. She'd been asked to lunch in the hotel dining room by one of the manufacturers, but Queenie hadn't been invited. 'You can pop along to Lyon's for a bite to eat. Have you enough money?'

'Plenty thanks.' Queenie couldn't have eaten so much as a biscuit. She was too excited. The day was turning out to be the best of her life. In the Adelphi lounge, crammed with little groups of buyers and designers all jabbering away to each other at ten to the dozen, she sank into an armchair and thought blissfully about the morning. She'd met so many interesting people and had learnt things about the fashion trade she'd never known before. She hadn't realised that, mainly in London, hundreds of firms beavered away in cellars and attics, paying their seamstresses peanuts, only managing to stay in business by the skin of their teeth, going to the wall if they misjudged a trend and ploughed a large part of their capital into lines such as military-style coats that women wouldn't want.

Evangelina's coats wouldn't go to waste, Miss Hurst had said. Eventually, they'd be sold at half-price to small, out-of-town shops whose clientele knew nothing about the latest fashions and just wanted a new coat. But it meant the firm's expected profit would be grossly reduced. 'It's their own fault. They just don't think ahead.'

'Are Fleur's frocks fashionable?' Queenie asked.

'No, but they're not unfashionable either. They have their own distinctive style. They'll be bought by women who want to look different, stand out from the crowd, but can't afford the latest Parisian designs. It's something a buyer has to take a chance on, ordering from a designer no one's heard of, yet he or she is bucking the trend and coming up with clothes that are quite unique. Mind you,' she sniffed, 'I've come a cropper more than once, bought things I thought would sell like hot cakes, but it turned out I was quite wrong.'

'I'm sure Fleur's frocks will sell like hot cakes.' She wouldn't have minded one herself.

'If they don't, I'll kick myself, and Mr Theo won't be too pleased. If a few haven't sold within the first fortnight, they'll be put in the stockroom for the winter sales. He won't have clothes left hanging around that customers clearly don't like.'

Mr Theo! She caught her breath. 'It's obvious, he fancies you,' Vera had said.

'Don't be silly,' she'd laughed, and Laura had accused Vera of having a dirty mind.

'Then why has Miss James got all snotty with her?' Vera demanded.

'I don't know,' Laura said. 'You tell me.'

'Because she's jealous, that's why. She'd know, more than anyone, if Mr Theo's taken a special interest in our Queenie. Why did he chuck this old geezer off the book department and put Queenie with Steven?'

'I don't know that, either,' Laura said stiffly.

'So he could pump Steven for information about her.'

'Oh, Vera! Pump Steven! Your imagination knows no bounds.'

'How else did he know about Jimmy?'

Laura fell silent and regarded Queenie solemnly. 'You'd better be careful,' she said after a while.

But now, sitting in the Adelphi lounge, gradually emptying as people went to lunch, Queenie was experiencing a desperate ferment in her stomach, as if little puffs of smoke were swirling around inside, getting hotter and hotter at the idea that Mr Theo might find her attractive. It was a delightful, incredibly pleasant sensation.

Added to which, that morning, a door had opened through which she'd glimpsed an entirely different world from the one she'd always known; a busy, enthralling, colourful world that she was determined to be part of. 'But what about Jimmy?' a little voice asked.

There wasn't the opportunity to answer the question as the disturbing, turbulent thoughts were interrupted by a glum voice saying, 'Hello.'

She looked up and saw Mr Travis of Evangelina Fashions standing in front of her. 'Hello,' she said.

'I invited a buyer to lunch, but she's let me down, gone with someone else. As I've booked a table for two, would you care to share it with me?'

At the offer of a free meal, her appetite returned like a shot. 'I'd love to. Thank you very much.'

'I know we were introduced, but I've forgotten your name.'

'Queenie Tate. Call me Queenie.' He wasn't much older than she was.

'I'm Geoffrey Travis.' They shook hands and proceeded into the dining room, where they ordered tomato soup followed by steak and kidney pudding with new potatoes.

Over the soup, he complained he'd had a miserable morning. His job was to buy the material for men's suits. The woman who should have come to the showing had caught something ghastly like chicken pox and he'd been sent in her place. 'I thought those coats looked all right, but then, what do I know about such things? I haven't sold a single Patricia and your Miss Hurst is the only person to order any Daisies. None of the other stuff has gone well, either.'

'You know what I'd do with the Patricia?' Queenie said, imagining how he would feel next week when the order was cancelled.

'Don't tell me.' He shuddered. 'It's bound to be rude.'

'It's not rude at all. What I'd do is take off the epaulettes, remove the brass buttons, and put self-coloured buttons in their place, though not on the sleeves. Then it'll be just an ordinary, double-breasted coat with nothing about it to remind women of the war. Meself, I thought it rather a nice, cheerful colour, perfect for autumn when the nights start drawing in and people feel a bit low because winter's coming.'

'You're obviously an expert at this sort of thing,' Mr Travis said appreciatively. 'Any ideas for the Daisy?'

Queenie put a hand to her brow and closed her eyes. 'I see it,' she said in a deep voice, 'with a dark green collar – a *velvet* collar and velvet buttons.'

'Oh, I say. That sounds marvellous.' He put down his spoon and looked thoughtful. 'You know, I've brought a seamstress with me, mainly to take measurements for special orders, though we haven't had a single one. She could make those alterations in a jiffy. She'd only need to do two coats to show people.' His face fell. 'Except we haven't got the materials.'

'Lewis's department store is only across the street. They've got a big haberdashery department.'

'Queenie Tate, you are an absolute genius. Would you mind terribly if I left you to eat lunch alone? I'll pay on my way out, of course.'

'I wouldn't mind a bit. I'm only too pleased to help.'

She watched him almost run out of the dining room, leaving her feeling extremely pleased with herself. She clearly possessed a talent she hadn't known she had.

Mr Travis had been gone only a matter of seconds when his place at the table was taken by a most unexpected figure.

'Good afternoon, Miss Tate,' Mr Theo said. 'I wanted to speak to Miss Hurst about something, but she seems otherwise engaged.'

Across the room, the wine waiter was refilling Miss Hurst's glass. Her lilac turban was askew and her face looked slightly longer and narrower. The thirteen sherries, coupled with the wine, were having an effect at last.

'Has she been drinking much?' Mr Theo asked.

'I hadn't noticed,' Queenie said evasively. Did he really want to speak to Miss Hurst? Or was she going mad, thinking that a married man, old enough to be her father, the owner of the biggest shop in Liverpool, might actually have come to see *her*?

'You're very discreet, Miss Tate. By the way, the young man whose fortune you seemed to be telling when I came in, has he gone to throw himself in the Mersey?'

'Why, no. He's gone to Lewis's haberdashery department to buy some materials.'

'What a relief! I thought that maybe you'd predicted something awful was about to happen.' His dark eyes twinkled at her across the table. Today, he looked relaxed and quite at ease.

'I was just telling him what to do with his coats.'

'In the nicest possible way, I hope?'

'It was meant in the nicest possible way.'

A waiter arrived with two plates of steak and kidney pudding. 'I didn't order this,' he told the man.

'It's all been paid for, Sir.'

'Oh, well. It seems foolish to let it go to waste.' He

tucked in with obvious enjoyment and Queenie had to kick herself to make sure it was really happening.

Laura didn't answer Roddy's letter offering to send her money and repeating his request for a divorce. She was surprised, when, a few weeks later, an envelope arrived containing four five-pound notes. There was no message enclosed.

'Oh, well,' she said to Gus. 'I won't bother looking for a job.' Once September came and she started the teacher training course, he would be put into Vera's care. The year after he would be old enough for school. These few months were the last she'd have him to herself for the entire day. 'You and me are going to have a good time,' she told him.

'Will we go to pubs for pints?' he asked longingly.

'No, sweetheart. I'll think of nicer places for us to go.'

She took him for walks along the Docky, where his bright, curious eyes took in all the wondrous sights; the great funnels of ships looming over the high dock walls, the peculiarly dressed seamen from foreign lands, the endless lorries of all different shapes and sizes, the magnificent carthorses, hooves clip-clopping loudly over the cobbled surface. He remarked on the strange smells, wanted to know why he sometimes couldn't understand what people were saying.

'Because they're not speaking English. I don't know what they're saying either.'

On nice days, they went to Southport on the train and had a lemonade in Herriot's restaurant, the shop where Queenie used to work. She showed him Sea Shells where Hester had lived with Queenie and Mary during the war.

'Why didn't I live there too?'

'Because you weren't born then.'

'Why wasn't I born?'

'Because, because – oh, look, I can see the fairground from here. Shall we have a go on the bobby horses?' Some of his questions were unanswerable.

His favourite place was New Brighton. They would sail across the Mersey on the ferry, Laura would make sandwiches and a flask of tea, and they'd picnic on the beach. She took him to the Walker Art Gallery and caught the tram to Sefton Park where he played on the swings and in the fairy glen. Wherever they went, he never ceased to ask questions: What was the sky made of? Why did that man have no hair? But Mum, how could anyone possibly *lose* their hair? His own was secured to his head quite tightly and there was no way it could get lost. Why couldn't babies walk when next door's kittens had walked within a week? Why couldn't they have a tree in the yard at home? When Laura told him it was because there was no soil, he demanded she got some.

On rainy days, she took him to matinées at the cinema. They saw *Meet Me in St Louis* and *State Fair* and other films suitable for children – and Laura thoroughly enjoyed them herself.

She loved Gus so much it hurt, quite literally caused an ache in her chest when she thought how much he meant to her and how devastated she would be if anything happened to him. She realised she was much closer to her son than she had ever been to her daughter, which saddened her. Although Hester had been a self-contained little girl, perhaps she'd had no choice because Laura and Roddy had been too preoccupied with each other. Without realising, they may even have resented the baby girl who'd turned their lives upside down and, somehow, Hester had sensed it. She hoped it wasn't too late to do something about it, but when the summer holidays came and she tried to arrange days out for just the three of them, Hester insisted Mary come too. At twelve, the two girls were just as inseparable, though there was still resentment between them. Mary was jealous that Hester had a little brother. At the same time she never missed the opportunity of pointing out that *her* dad hadn't gone away and never come back, as Hester's had.

Roddy continued to send twenty pounds each month and she wondered how long it would last – till Hester was old enough to go to work? Till he and Katherine had children and the money was needed for school fees and other expenses? She couldn't bank on it coming for ever.

She had a letter from Mr Bailey-Oliphant of the Education Training Scheme advising her which books to buy and listing the things she would need; notebooks, pencils, a sharpener, a geometry set and half a dozen cardboard folders. Gus immediately appropriated one in which to keep his important collection of tram, bus and train tickets, and the magnifying glass out of a Christmas cracker through which they were regularly examined.

It was September at last. Laura had her hair cut very short so it would be more manageable, bought a handbag somewhat similar to a school satchel, and made herself a plain black suit and an assortment of blouses so she would look smart at college.

One cloudy, miserable Monday morning, she took her son across the road to Vera's and kissed him goodbye. She could hardly hold back the tears on the bus taking her to Walton Vale where she would catch another bus to Kirkby, something she would do for the next two years. The thought that at the end of that time she would emerge a fully trained teacher, comforted her somewhat. With a regular wage coming in, her children would never go short of anything. She could leave Glover

Street, rent a proper house, perhaps in the countryside, though it would be upsetting to leave Vera. Queenie would come with them, of course, if she wasn't married to Jimmy by then, though at the rate Jimmy was going, earning a pittance in that garage, it would be years before he could afford to rent a place big enough for the four of them. Not that Queenie seemed to mind the delay, yet it was obvious she loved Jimmy very much. Laura had never known her look so blissfully happy as she'd done over the last few months. She felt quite envious. She knew what it was like to be in love and badly missed it.

The college was situated by Kirkby railway station, a large assortment of buildings that had, until recently, been a hostel for workers in a nearby ammunitions factory.

It had started to drizzle and she got lost immediately, which she felt was a very poor start to her training. She was glad to come across another lost soul, a jolly woman about ten years older than she was who introduced herself as Isobel Cartwright and said she'd been a map reader in the WAAF.

'So if anyone should feel ashamed at getting lost, it's me,' she lamented. 'I wouldn't mind, but I'm actually *living* in the damn place. I'm sure I'll never remember which is my block.'

'We're meeting in the theatre. Maybe it's that building over there. It's taller than the rest.'

'Good thinking, Laura. Let's make our way towards it through this maze of huts.'

When they arrived, a trifle damp, a hundred or more prospective teachers, predominantly male, were gathered in the theatre being addressed by the principal, Mr Worrage. They crept in, sat at the back, and discovered that the morning would be spent listening to various speakers, the afternoon collecting timetables and other important bits of paper, and being shown around the various classrooms and other facilities. Mr Worrage said he wanted to encourage extramural activities – a debating society perhaps, or any hobby group that people wished to start – he himself was a keen aero-modeller and took part in amateur dramatics. 'After all, we have our very own theatre.'

He spoke for more than an hour, and was followed by a woman who made a stirring speech, telling them that in two years' time they would be trusted with the nation's most treasured possession; its children. 'Their future, our country's future, will be in your hands. It is up to you to ensure the future works.'

They broke for tea and biscuits, and were then delivered a stern lecture by the Domestic Supervisor, Mrs Roberts, aimed at the resident students, and concerned with ration books, bedding, not stubbing out cigarettes on furniture, cleaning baths after use, and always having a reserve of their own lavatory paper in case the college ran out.

After a lunch of lamb chops and roast potatoes, followed by treacle pudding and custard, the rest of the day passed in a blur. Laura went home with her bag crammed with papers, reports and books, and her head in a whirl. Vera had boiled the kettle in readiness for her return, and made a resuscitating cup of tea.

'Are you a teacher now, Mum?' enquired Gus.

'Lord, no, sweetheart. It's going to take two whole years.'

'Less a day,' Vera grinned.

Laura grinned back. 'Less a day.'

Within a fortnight, things had settled down. She knew what was happening next without looking at the timetable; that Thursday afternoon they did PT for half an hour, not only to keep fit but it was something they might be called upon to take at school if there was an emergency. The same went for music on Tuesday morning. Anyone who could play an instrument was encouraged to do so, the rest just formed a choir and sang. 'My Bonnie Lies Over The Ocean', 'Bobby Shaftoe's Gone To Sea', and 'Greensleeves' were all songs Laura remembered from her own years at school.

Twice a week they had lectures on child psychology; problem children, damaged children, backward children, bright children. So far, they hadn't been taught anything about *teaching* children, but Laura supposed that would come eventually.

By December, she was loving every day. Her brain seemed to have blossomed, like a flower, and she was soaking up information the way a flower soaks up water and thrives. Even so, she was looking forward to the Christmas break. She, and her brain, needed a rest.

They broke up at lunchtime and Laura and Isobel went with a big crowd to the pub by the railway for a celebratory drink. Close friendships were beginning to develop between the students on the course. They were the first to take part in a great experiment and had felt the pressure during their first term. Now it had come to an end and there was a feeling of relief that they had coped.

The atmosphere in the pub was rowdy from the start. Men, nearly all of whom had been in the forces, and who until now had seemed so stiffly formal, lost all inhibitions after a single drink, offering tearful renditions of 'Lili Marlene' and 'Keep The Home Fires Burning'. Laura drank only half a pint of cider and couldn't stop laughing for some reason.

After about an hour, she left, rather reluctantly because she was having such a good time, but Vera and Gus were expecting her and would be worried if she was late. She wished everyone Merry Christmas, and found herself inundated with kisses in return, which only made her laugh even more.

'Don't forget,' she said to Isobel, 'if you feel lonely, you're always welcome at our house. You have my address.'

She felt dizzy and lightheaded and was still giggling when she got to Glover Street. At Vera's, she pulled the key through the letter box, unlocked the door, and shouted, 'It's only me.'

Gus came into the hall, his face unusually serious. He looked so adorable in his brown jersey and little grey shorts, that Laura couldn't resist giving him an enormous hug. 'Have I ever told you how much I love you?' she cried.

'Yes, Mum. Loads of times.' He frowned and looked even more adorable. Laura was about to hug him again, when he said, 'Mum. A man's come to see Vera and he ses he's my dad. Come and look.'

But there was no need to look. The man had come to the door; tall, fair-haired and as handsome as ever, though much older than she remembered.

'Hello, Laura,' said Roddy.

'I knew he was mine straight away,' he said a few minutes later when the three of them went home. 'There's a photograph of me at the same age and he looks exactly the same. Don't you, Gus?' He ruffled Gus's hair, only a shade lighter than his own. The little boy was leaning on the arm of his father's chair, staring at him intently.

'I don't know,' he said solemnly.

'How can he know without seeing the photograph?' Laura said tartly. The dizziness and lightheadedness had gone in a flash the minute she'd set eyes on him, and she no longer felt like laughing. Instead, she was shaking with a mixture of shock and anger. How dare he descend upon her without warning? What did he want? Was it just a social visit because it was Christmas? How could he just turn up, disturbing the calm rhythm of her life, distracting her thoughts, upsetting her, making her heart race so fast she could hardly breathe, but only because she was surprised to see him, not glad. She'd managed to live quite well without Roddy for the last five years and had got used to the idea of living the rest of her life without setting eyes on him again.

'What time will Hester be home?' he asked.

'About four o'clock. She's at senior school now.'

'Hester's my sister.'

'I know that, Gus. She's also my daughter, and you're my son.' He looked at Laura. 'Why didn't you tell me about him?'

'I didn't think, under the circumstances, that it was any of your business. Look, could we have this conversation some other time?' She nodded at Gus, who was listening avidly. 'Now hardly seems appropriate. Would you like some tea?'

'Vera nearly drowned me in tea, but I wouldn't mind more.'

They sat making stilted conversation for about half an hour. He seemed fascinated by the fact she was training to be a teacher. 'You could have knocked me down with a feather when Vera told me you were at college.'

'Why, didn't you think I was capable enough?'

'Laura, I think I know what you're capable of. We had some pretty tough times over the years, but you never let the worst of them throw you.'

She didn't say the toughest time of all was when he left

her for another woman and she resented being reminded of the life he'd turned his back on.

There was a knock on the door. Laura answered and found Vera outside, looking rather furtive. 'I didn't like to let meself in, luv, because – well, you know,' she hissed. 'I'm about to collect our Sammy from school and wondered if Gus'd like to come with me? We could buy some sweeties on the way home.'

'Yes, please,' said Gus. No one was allowed to knock on the door without him coming to see who it was.

'Go and fetch your coat, there's a luv.' Gus trotted away. 'It'll give you and Roddy a chance to have a chat in private before Hester comes home.' The hiss became a whisper. 'You might like to know he's left a load of luggage in our front parlour. Came in a taxi, would you believe! Must have money to burn.'

'Where's Gus?' Roddy asked when Laura went back.

'He's gone with Vera to meet Sammy from school.'

He looked hurt. 'I thought he'd prefer to stay with me. We've only just met.'

'For goodness' sake, Roddy. He's only four. You can't expect him to accept you as his father within five minutes.'

'I suppose not.' He sighed. 'He's a great kid. I wish I'd known about him.'

'What would you have done, left Katherine and come home? You've never seemed in much of a hurry to see Hester. Oh!' She flung herself into a chair. 'This is childish. What are you doing here, Roddy?' She thought about the luggage in Vera's parlour. 'Is this just a passing visit and you're on your way somewhere else? I hope you don't want to stay the night, because there's nowhere to sleep. Gus has his bed in our – in *my* room.'

He looked at her for a long time without speaking. She regarded him steadily back. He was twenty-eight and there was nothing remotely boyish left about him. Although he looked fit and healthy, his skin had lost its youthful bloom and become coarser, his neck thicker. His hands weren't quite so slender as before. But his eyes were just as blue, his mouth still as firm, and his smile when he smiled just as sweet. All these things she noted quite dispassionately. This man was her husband and he'd betrayed her. She felt nothing for him any more.

'I want to come back,' he said.

'I don't want you back.'

He winced at the certainty in her voice. 'I still love you.'

'I find that hard to believe. The last time we spoke, you told me you were in love with someone else.'

'Will you listen while I try to explain what happened? You might feel different then.'

She folded her hands together on her knee, interested even though her mind was quite made up. She wouldn't feel the slightest bit different, no matter what he said.

'I've told you before about Jack Muir who rescued me from Dunkirk and took me back to his home in Dover,' he began. 'Jack's house was similar to the one where I'd grown up, except it was smaller. When I arrived, the French windows were open and the scent of roses drifted in. A piano was being played in another room – it turned out to be Katherine playing. There were carpets on the floors, paintings on the walls, expensive cars in the drive. They had a cook, a maid. After the horror of Dunkirk, it was like heaven, exactly what I needed. I had nothing to worry about and was waited on hand and foot. I stayed a few days and felt very much at home. On the second night, when I'd more or less recovered, a dinner party was held in my honour. I was the only person not wearing evening dress.' His eyes narrowed. 'I remember the occasion perfectly; the sheen on the women's frocks, the way their jewellery sparkled, their perfume. Katherine wore cream lace and smoked cigarettes in a silver holder. The chap on her other side would light them for her and I noticed the way her earrings swung to and fro like little lanterns whenever she bent forward. It grew dark, and the only illumination was the candles on the table. Everyone quietly got rather drunk. It was like a scene from a film, a sophisticated gathering of wealthy people. Quite out of the blue, I felt that this was where I belonged.'

'I never thought of you as sophisticated,' Laura murmured.

'I'm not surprised,' he said, smiling wryly. 'I didn't think it myself when I was working on building sites or for Colm Flaherty – what happened to Colm, by the way?'

'He went back to Ireland when the bombing started and never came back.'

'Sensible chap. Anyway, back to Dover . . .'

'Where you belonged.'

'So I thought. I returned to my unit and was immediately granted a week's leave, so I came home, here, to Glover Street, except it didn't feel like home.' He glanced around the shabby, homely room. 'I was like a stranger in a strange land. By then, I had convinced myself I was in love with Katherine and she said she felt the same about me. She had a part-time job in Whitehall and went to work dressed like a model, while you looked rather like a navvy in your overalls and boots and you smelt of something terribly unpleasant.'

'It was the Swarfega, to take the oil off my hands.'

'Whatever it was, it was horrid. I managed to stick it out for the week, then discovered I'd been posted to Colchester, no distance from London. I was able to see Katherine every weekend. One of her friends was usually throwing a party. If not, we'd go to the theatre or eat out. Sunday, we'd drive down to Dover in her car. It was the life I would have been leading if I hadn't met you.'

'My own life would have been rather different if *I* hadn't met *you*,' she reminded him. 'Though not quite so glitzy,' she added caustically.

'Darling,' he said plaintively, 'I'm trying to explain things. I've been the biggest fool the world has ever known and I want you to know why. It was the excitement, the danger – North Africa was pretty hairy. My brain felt as if it had been ratcheted up several gears. Our life together seemed very dull.'

'It *was* very dull,' she agreed. 'For me as well as you, but when people marry, have children, it's usually the way life is.'

'Except it wasn't enough for me, not then. The idea of returning to Glover Street appalled me. I needed something else, something extra, particularly when I joined the Special Operations Executive, by which time Katherine and I had set up home together in London. I took my life in my hands every time I went to France, then I'd come home to a round of parties, which was exactly what I needed.'

'Did you introduce Katherine to your family?' she asked curiously.

'Yes, they loved her. She was exactly the sort of girl my parents had wanted me to marry.'

'As they always refused to meet me, they never discovered what sort of girl I was. What does Katherine's father, Jack Muir, do for a living?'

'He's a stockbroker.'

'And my father was an Anglican vicar. Is a vicar lower down the social scale than a stockbroker?'

'Darling,' he cried. 'What does that matter?'

'It doesn't matter a bit. I was just wondering, that's all.'

'Anyway,' he went on, 'the war ended. In February, I was demobbed, Jack fixed me up with a job in a stockbrokers, but from then on London was a frightful wash-out. The excitement had gone, the atmosphere of danger and romance, Katherine's job went, and her friends had dispersed to wherever they'd come from. We ate out a lot, went to the theatre, but it wasn't the same. London had lost its buzz. Before, it had seemed as if half the population had been in uniform, but now there were none. My brain returned to its normal gear and I became my old, normal self. I realised how much I missed you, *loved* you – and Hester – and badly wanted to come home. It had all been a moment of madness – a long moment, I concede.' He gave her a wan grin. 'So that's it. I've been a louse and I'm sorry and beg you to forgive me. And before you ask, I've got a job. I discovered myself quite a whizz at playing the stock market. My firm, Glyn & Michaelson, has an office in Liverpool and they're putting me in charge. I start the first of January. The salary's not to be sneezed at and they've even given me a loan to buy a house. We can move from Glover Street to somewhere nicer, say Crosby or Blundellsands. What do you say, Lo?'

'You mean, you were so confident I'd take you back you actually fixed up a job in Liverpool?' she said, outraged.

'I assumed you still loved me.' His voice faltered slightly.

'I don't love you, Roddy. I haven't loved you for a long time. Despite what you've just said, I don't want you back. Stay in Liverpool, if that's what you want, buy your*self* a house in Crosby or Blundellsands, because you're not living with us. Oh, and by the way, please don't call me "darling" again, or "Lo".'

He did live with them until after Christmas, sleeping on the sofa, which Laura thought a bit of a comedown for a stockbroker. Gus, who bore him no animosity, quickly got used to having a father on the premises. Hester, who did, only gradually came round, no doubt influenced by the fact that Roddy was less than half the age of Mary's dad and better looking than every one of her brothers. She boasted endlessly about Daddy's daring exploits in France.

Every day he went to look at houses and asked if Laura would come with him. 'I'd like your opinion.'

'What does my opinion matter? I won't be living there.'

'Would you mind if Gus and Hester came to see me at weekends?'

'Of course not. They're your children as much as mine.' She was glad he was back for their sake, if not her own.

On Christmas Day, he produced expensive presents for them all; a bike for Gus, which had been hidden in the Monaghans' parlour, a leather shoulder bag for Hester, a seed pearl necklace for Queenie, who'd swiftly succumbed to his charm and hoped Laura would soon do the same. There was even a lovely marcasite brooch for Vera, 'For being such a wonderful friend to Laura over the years.'

'Well, there's been times when she's badly needed a friend,' Vera said pointedly, though she was too nice to bear a grudge. 'Life's too short,' she said to Laura. 'He made a mistake, but it's all in the past. It's you he loves. Don't turn down happiness, luv, when it's handed to you on a plate.'

But Laura was having none of it. He'd hurt her too much, and if he could do it once, he could do it again. It was possible that, somewhere in London, Katherine was hurting as badly as she had. She hadn't asked if the break-up had been mutual.

'And this is for you,' he said on Christmas morning, handing her a velvet box.

'They're beautiful,' she said coolly when she found the box contained a gold locket encrusted with turquoise stones and drop earrings to match. They looked very old and rich, and she loved them immediately.

'They're antique.' He watched her face anxiously. 'Are you sure you like them? You don't think them too dressy? You never used to wear jewellery, but that was because we hadn't the money to buy it.'

'As I said, they're beautiful, though it's a pity the earrings are clip-on, when my ears are pierced.'

'I hadn't noticed they were pierced.' He looked so downhearted that she felt sorry for him, though she had no intention of showing it.

'I had them done during the war. One of the girls in the factory did it with a red-hot darning needle.'

He gasped. 'That sounds painful.'

'I hardly felt anything.' In fact, it had hurt like blazes and she'd been in agony for days. Then the ears had festered and the agony had stretched to weeks.

'Perhaps I could change the earrings,' he muttered.

'I do hope so, Roddy.' She took pity on him. 'They really are lovely.'

On Boxing Day, he took the children to the Empire in Liverpool to see *Puss in Boots*. Laura refused to go. She had homework to do for the course, which hadn't been touched because of him. Queenie was spending the day at Jimmy's and the house would be empty for a change.

After everyone had gone, she spread the papers on the table in the living room and set to work, half dreading Vera would come and interrupt, half hoping that she would because she was finding it impossible to concentrate and would have quite liked a good jangle.

Roddy had found a house he liked. It was down a leafy road in Crosby, a spacious turn-of-the-century semi with four bedrooms and gardens front and back. He'd put down a deposit and his firm were organising the loan. As the place was empty, the estate agent was agreeable to him moving in straight away, before the contract was finalised. 'His son was in North Africa at the same time as I was.'

He showed her the estate agent's details. She glanced at them briefly, pretending indifference.

'Why do you want somewhere so big?' she asked. 'You'll be living there alone.'

'The children might like to stay overnight occasionally. There's plenty of trees at the back for Gus. He seems to be obsessed with trees.'

'Gus is obsessed with an awful lot of things.'

Later he said, 'Remember you wanted us to have a velvet three-piece suite when we were better off? I thought I'd get one for the house. What colour do you think?'

'Whatever colour takes your fancy, Roddy. I won't be sitting on it.' She realised what he was up to. He was trying to wheedle his way back into her life, offering the house and the contents as a bribe. Any minute now, he'd ask what sort of curtains he should buy. He'd remind her that she'd always wanted a willow pattern dinner service and recall her longing for a radiogram. But she was adamant that nothing would move her. She shook away the pictures that kept flashing across her mind, of them all living together in the house in Crosby, going for walks on Sundays as they'd used to before the war, but this time Gus would be with them.

She wasn't prepared to give in so easily. Roddy had to suffer, as she had.

He left on New Year's Eve, having bought loads of furniture in Freddy's sale, including a velvet three-piece. 'A sort of russet colour,' he told Laura.

'Sounds nice,' she said carelessly. She would have chosen russet herself.

Straight away, the flat felt empty without him. Gus mooched around with his hands in his pockets, wanting to know why he'd gone away. 'Bert and Vera live together. Why can't my mum and dad?'

'Because,' said his mum.

'Because what?'

'Just because.'

If Roddy's arrival in their midst had been a bombshell, Queenie's departure was another.

'Laura,' she said one morning when January was only a few days old, 'this might come as a bit of a shock, but I'll be moving out shortly.'

'Queenie!' Laura clapped her hands delightedly. 'It's a shock, a terrible shock – what on earth will I do without you? I'm glad you've set a date with Jimmy at last, but does it have to be so soon? There won't be time for me to make that dress we always planned on.' It crossed her mind that this was a terribly tactless thing to say and the reason for the rush was that Queenie *had* to get married. She felt her face redden.

'I'm not marrying Jimmy,' Queenie said in a steady voice. 'I told him so last night. He was dead upset. The reason I'm leaving is I'm going to live with Theo Vandos in his apartment in Freddy's.'

June, 1954

Chapter 11

'*Please* can I open my eyes?'

'Not for another few minutes.'

'But where are we going?' Queenie wailed.

'You'll see soon enough.'

She caught her toe and stumbled. 'I nearly fell over,' she complained.

'I'm holding your hand, aren't I?' Theo gave the hand a little shake. 'You can't possibly fall.'

It was Sunday, scorchingly hot. The sun shone like a torch out of the blue sky. They were on the coast of North Wales not far from Colwyn Bay, which she hoped was nowhere near Caerdovey. Jimmy had asked, more than once, if she'd go with him to see Tess and Pete when they'd lived there, but she'd always refused. She would never go near the place again.

Theo had stopped the car at a boatyard. When they got out, he demanded she close her eyes. 'I have a surprise for you,' he'd said.

'You can open them now,' he said about five minutes later.

Queenie opened her eyes and saw a row of boats moored by the quayside, from the very small to the very large, some with sails, some without. A few people were about; painting hulls, rubbing them down, sunbathing on the decks. This was the first hot spell of the year and they were already more than halfway through June. The water shone so brilliantly it hurt her eyes, 'What's the surprise?' she asked.

'The boat in front, it's for you, a present for your birthday.' She would be twenty-nine next week.

Directly in front, a dinghy languished on the concrete, half the planks missing. It seemed a very peculiar present. 'That won't last a minute in the water. It'll sink straight away.'

Theo laughed. 'I should have said the boat in front of the boat in front; the one with the dark blue hull, painted white above the waterline, the one with the little black funnel and varnished wheelhouse and a man inside wearing a peaked cap. That's the skipper and his name is Trefor Jones. He's Welsh.'

'You've bought me a boat?' Her voice was subdued. She could hardly believe it. He was always generous, but a *boat*! 'It's huge,' she said.

'Eighty feet long, a motor yacht. I didn't exactly buy it, I had it built. Have you noticed the name?'

'*Queen of the Mersey*. Oh, Theo! Fancy doing something like that for me,' she cried, close to tears.

He put his arm around her waist. 'You know I would do anything on earth for you. It's to show how much I love you.'

'There's no need to buy a boat to tell me that. I already knew.'

'I like buying you things. Shall we go on board?' He squeezed her waist. 'Or are we going to stand here for the rest of the day, just looking?'

'Let's go on board. I'm dying to see inside.'

'I'll introduce you to Trefor first. Look, he's noticed us, he's coming out. Let's go on deck.'

As well as a white, peaked cap, Trefor Jones wore a white, short-sleeved shirt and white trousers, all beautifully pressed, making an attractive contrast to his dark, sunburnt skin. There were deep wrinkles around his sharp blue eyes, as if he'd spent his life peering into the sun. His jaw was square, his mouth thin and stern.

'Good afternoon, Theo.' They were obviously on first name terms. He was respectful, but not toadying, the way some people were when they spoke to Theo Vandos.

'Trefor supervised the construction of the boat,' Theo said. 'It was built here, in this very yard. He used to be in the Merchant Navy, joined when he was fourteen, the year the war started. He left with his Extra Master's Certificate and now, my darling, he's going to captain your boat.' That meant Trefor was only the same age as herself, but looked much older. 'Trefor, this is my friend, Queenie Tate.'

They shook hands. As she had expected, Trefor's grip was very firm. 'Would you like me to show you round?' he asked.

'Not just yet. I'd like Queenie to see the living quarters first. Later, we can all have a drink, make a toast to *Queen of the Mersey*. What is it they say when a ship is launched? "Good luck to all who sail in her." Come along, Queenie. This is the lounge.'

He led her through a door, down a few steps, into a long, narrow, luxuriously appointed room with a royal blue carpet and windows on both sides, which rounded to a curve at the front. Half a dozen squashy plush armchairs, a silvery colour, were placed around a circular coffee table with an inlaid top patterned with a star. At the far end, where the room tapered, there was a full-height fitted table with plush-covered benches either side. Under the windows, there were cupboards with the same inlaid star as the coffee table on the fronts. Theo smiled and opened one, revealing a radiogram. The next was a cocktail cabinet, next a refrigerator with a few bottles of orange juice inside. In the ceiling, above each window, there was a pink half-globe. Queenie looked for a switch, pressed it, and the globes emitted a subdued, pink glow.

'Where does the electricity come from?' she asked.

'A generator. Don't ask too many technical questions, darling, because I can't answer them.'

'Is this called a cabin or a room?'

'I think it's called the lounge.' He didn't look very sure.

'It's beautiful, Theo,' she said seriously, a slight throb in her voice. 'I can't believe it's mine.'

'Let's go down below and I'll show you where we'll sleep.'

They descended a highly polished staircase with brass rails either side, and went through a door at the bottom.

She gasped. The carpet here was dark cream, the fitted furniture paler and edged with a fine gold line, and the four-poster bed was covered with flounces of creamy lace. The wall lights were giant white seashells, the windows small and round – portholes, she remembered they were called.

'I can't imagine us carrying passengers but, just in case we do, there's another bedroom at the stern,' Theo said.

'What happens if there's a storm?' She giggled. 'Will the bed slide across the floor when we're asleep?' Though she couldn't imagine sleeping in a storm.

'Everything's screwed down, even the chairs. Nothing can move.'

'It's very impressive,' she marvelled. She couldn't find the words to describe how impressive it was.

'The crew's quarters and the galley are at the front,' Theo said. 'Trefor can show us them later. Shall we go upstairs and have a drink?'

'Yes, please. I'd love some orange juice.'

In the lounge, she sat in one of the squashy armchairs. It was like sitting on air. Theo handed her the drink and helped himself to a brandy. He leaned on the back of her chair and caressed her face. She bent her head, so that her cheek rested perfectly in his hand.

'I love you, Queenie,' he murmured, kissing her hair.

'And I love you, Theo.' She sighed, utterly content. 'Will we be sailing anywhere in my boat?' she asked lazily.

'But of course, my darling. Trefor is getting a crew together and later this year, when things aren't so busy at Freddy's, we shall sail to Kythira, the island where my father was born. His family were very poor, and he returned, many years later, to build a beautiful villa overlooking the Mediterranean.'

'Is that where we'll stay?' He'd told her about the villa in Kythira before.

'Yes.' He gave her hair one final kiss, before sinking into the chair beside her. 'When we've finished our drinks, we'd better let Trefor show us around. He's prouder of this boat than I am.'

'But not as proud as me.'

It must be the heat that was making her feel so tired. She followed Theo when he went to look for Trefor, who took them to the engine room, which looked incredibly complicated, the second bedroom, not quite so grand as the first, the neat galley, his own tiny, scrupulously tidy cabin, the other cabins for the crew, the fo'c'sle where the anchor was kept, the mess deck. When they'd seen everything there was to see, and Theo and Trefor had become engrossed in a map of the Mediterranean, she excused herself. 'I think I'll lie down for half an hour.' Trefor glanced at her inscrutably. She wondered if he disapproved of women who lived with married men.

She collapsed on the lacy, four-poster bed, which smelt of lavender. She hadn't noticed before that the boat was moving, ever so slightly. The tide must be coming in or going out. The gentle motion was very soothing. She lay with her arms outstretched, as if she were floating, and thought about her wonderful present, and how much she would like to be Theo's wife, not his mistress.

Irene positively refused to give him a divorce. When Theo had told her this, Queenie had said she didn't blame her. 'Laura wouldn't divorce Roddy. She wasn't prepared to give him up just because he loved someone else.'

'Yes, but Laura still loved Roddy,' he said emotionally. 'Irene hates me. We only married for our fathers' sakes.' Their fathers were old, childhood friends who'd achieved riches beyond their wildest dreams, he explained. 'Irene and I were only twenty, young enough to go along with their wishes. Older, and I, for one, would have refused.' The marriage had been a failure from the start. 'She acted as if *I* was the one who'd forced her into it and claimed to have been in love with someone else. I offered her a divorce then, but she turned on me like a wild animal.' He sighed. 'She is the most unreasonable of women. I am at a loss to understand her. Nothing I say is right. Everything I say is wrong.'

'Poor Theo.' She remembered rubbing her face against his. 'Never mind.'

It had been inevitable that they would come together one day. She hadn't been working on Ladies' First Floor Fashions long, when one of the women, Breda O'Neill, had remarked it was odd, but normally they didn't see Mr Theo for months on end, yet he'd visited the department three times that week. 'I can't think why.'

'Perhaps he's got a crush on you,' laughed Judy

Channon, a member of the War Widows' Club, with whom Queenie ate lunch in the staff restaurant.

'I only wish.' Breda rolled her eyes. 'Actually, Queenie, it was you he spoke to each time. What did he want?'

'He wants me to go to London with Miss Hurst on Friday. There's this new label, Fleur. He'd like her to see their winter designs before anyone else, so Freddy's can put in an advance order. He's been back a few times to tell me about train times and where to meet Miss Hurst, that's all.' Although this was the exact truth, even to Queenie's ears it sounded as if she'd made it up.

'Fleur? I've never heard of them.'

'Miss Hurst ordered some lovely frocks for autumn,' she explained. 'Mr Theo was very impressed. He hopes, if he buys enough from them, they'll promise not to sell to the other Liverpool stores.'

'But why send *you* with Miss Hurst?' Breda demanded hotly. 'You've hardly been here any time. Me, I'd go to London with Miss Hurst like a shot. Anyroad, why does she need a nursemaid?'

Judy laughed. 'Because she drinks like a fish, that's why. By afternoon, she's not totally *compos mentis*. And Queenie may only have been at Freddy's a short while, Breda, but she's had far more retail experience than you. She was at Herriot's for five years.'

'Still . . .' Breda looked sulky.

Queenie wasn't all that surprised when Mr Theo had turned up at their hotel in London on Friday night. He'd had business with the representative of an Argentinian furniture manufacturer who was only in London for a few days. It was a pity he'd had to come the day before, otherwise they could have travelled down together on the train. 'Never mind, we can keep each other company going back tomorrow. And, of course, since I'm here, I'd like to take you both to dinner.'

'How nice of you, Mr Theo,' Miss Hurst said in a distinctly wobbly voice.

They had only just finished the first course, when she complained of not feeling well and fell asleep in front of their eyes. Mr Theo and a waiter helped her to her room.

They'd met Wilfred Carter of Fleur in the foyer of a modest hotel in Victoria. He obviously didn't believe in plying buyers with drink and had bought them just a coffee each. It had been left to Miss Hurst to order whisky after whisky for herself. By the end of the meeting, she was glassy-eyed.

Mr Theo returned, looking grave. 'She's past retirement age. I think it's time I found her a comfortable job in the office where she can drink as much as she likes, but it won't matter. How did you get on with Wilfred Carter?'

'He had some wonderful designs,' Queenie enthused, feeling quite at ease in his company. 'He only had one sample, the rest were sketches, because he's dead busy with the autumn lines.' She told him that Rosa, his sister, had been working in Paris as a model for Christian Dior. She was sworn to secrecy not to reveal the designs, but naturally she told Wilfred about a completely new look that no one else would know about until Paris Fashion Week in July. 'Long, full skirts, almost ankle-length, tight waists, very soft and feminine. Wilfred likes to be original but, as he said, it's silly to buck what will almost certainly be a trend, so he's adding his own individual touches. He's ordered bales of wonderful cloth from India; flowered velvet and corduroy. He showed us swatches. I've never seen material like it before.' Her eyes shone, remembering. 'The model he brought was navy-blue corduroy patterned with rosebuds. It had a lace collar and cuffs and a petticoat underneath with the lace showing. It was incredibly pretty.'

'And did Miss Hurst order many of these incredibly pretty garments?' Mr Theo asked with a smile.

'Well, no.' Queenie felt uncomfortable, as if she were telling tales. 'She thought they were a bit *too* experimental, *too* different.'

Mr Theo frowned. 'Didn't Wilfred Carter inform her that the designs came straight from Dior?'

Wilfred Carter had, but by then Miss Hurst had been too hungover to take it in. 'I can't remember,' she said.

'I see.' His tone of voice told her he could see very well. 'I think it might be a good idea if we met Mr Carter tomorrow and had another look at his designs. Do you have his card?'

'Yes, he works from his home in Camden. We met him in a hotel.'

'Tomorrow, we shall meet him in *this* hotel,' Mr Theo said firmly. 'It seems to me that Mr Carter is in need of a backer, someone to pay for factory premises, more staff, an office and showroom in the West End. Tomorrow, I shall ask if he'd like a sleeping partner.'

After they'd finished the meal, they went into the bar where he ordered champagne. After a single glass, Queenie felt quite tipsy and, with a feeling of horror, wondered if that had been his intention, that he was about to make a pass, as Gordon Mackie had done in Herriot's. She refused a second glass, saying she was tired and would like to go to bed.

'I'll take you to your room,' Mr Theo said.

Her heart was in her mouth as they went up in the lift, but outside her door, Mr Theo merely shook her hand, said how much he'd enjoyed the evening, and wished her goodnight.

'Goodnight,' she murmured.

She was unlocking the door and he was walking back towards the lift, when suddenly he turned.

'Miss Tate?'

'Yes, Mr Theo?'

'Did you mind my turning up and taking you to dinner? If the truth be known, I very much enjoy your company, but don't want to become a pest. Please say if you'd prefer it didn't happen again.'

Queenie stared at him along the corridor. His dark eyes burned into hers and his face bore an expression of naked pleading. For a moment, she felt so dizzy that she had to hold on to the door knob for support. The words had held a meaning that was all too obvious. In a roundabout, very tactful way, he was asking if she was willing to have an affair, become his lover. Much depended on her answer, which could possibly change the course of her entire life. Was this what she wanted?

He took a step in her direction, then stopped. 'Forgive me, Miss Tate. That was an impertinent question for someone so old to ask of someone so young. Forget I spoke.' He turned again towards the lift.

'Mr Theo?'

'Yes, Miss Tate?'

'I would very much like to have dinner with you again.'

'Then I shall arrange it very soon.' He bowed. 'Goodnight, Miss Tate.'

Her thoughts were disturbed by the sound of voices outside the cabin. A few minutes later, the door opened and Theo came in. 'Trefor's gone to buy sandwiches from the pub. Have you had a nice rest?'

'Mm. It was lovely. The bed's so comfortable. I love my boat. I wish I could take it home with me.'

He lay beside her on the bed and began to stroke her breasts. Her body became alive with desire in an instant. Without a word, she sat up and untied the halter of her white frock, slipped it off, removed her strapless bra and pants, and turned to him, completely naked. Theo uttered something that sounded almost like a sob and removed his own clothes. He kissed her with long, slow kisses, made love to her with long, slow movements, until she wanted to scream because it was so deeply thrilling, so utterly wonderful. They came together in a rush of tenderness and passion, and he said gruffly, 'It gets better and better.'

Queenie was too exhausted to speak. They lay in silence for a long while. 'Are you sure,' Laura had said, years and years ago, 'that you're *really* in love? That you're not influenced by the fact he's a very rich, very good-looking man who loves *you*?'

'That's rubbish.' Later though, Queenie had wondered if perhaps Laura was right. It was all part of Theo's attraction. It was who he *was*. She was flattered beyond belief that, out of all the women in the world, she was the one he'd fallen in love with, whereas Jimmy's love felt more like a burden, a responsibility she felt obliged to shoulder.

Jimmy! She could still cringe, all this time later, at the memory of his shattered face when she'd said she wasn't going to marry him. She had given him back his ring, and he'd looked at it sadly, unbelievingly, then put it in the pocket of his shabby jacket. Of course, she should have told him sooner, but she'd felt as if she was leading two entirely different lives – one with Jimmy, the other with Theo – and the two lives would never coincide. Except they had, when Theo had asked her to live with him in the apartment at the top of Freddy's, be his partner for all time. He would have preferred her to be his wife, but that wasn't possible.

A year later, Vera had told her that Jimmy had taken Tess and Pete to live in Australia. It made her feel better about things, but not much.

'I love you,' she said to Theo now. '*Really* love you. I don't think I could live without you.'

'One day, my darling,' he said gently, his face sad, 'you will have to. I am twenty-four years older than you and when I die, you will still be a relatively young woman.'

She buried her head in his shoulder and said in a muffled voice, 'Please don't die. I won't be able to bear it.'

There were footsteps on the deck. Theo got off the bed and began to get dressed. 'That's Trefor back with the food – why didn't we think to bring some? Come along, my darling, it's time we made our toast to *Queen of the Mersey*.'

It was ten o'clock by the time they got back to Freddy's and Theo's vast apartment on the sixth floor, with its enormous furniture that had belonged to his father. It was from Peru, and covered with swirls and whirls, carved angels, carved animals, carved flowers, mother-of-pearl knobs and handles. There were secret cupboards, secret drawers, false bottoms, pretend keyholes.

Theo went to bed immediately. The drive and the fresh air had tired him, but Queenie felt wide awake. After a restless hour, she did what she often did on such occasions, got out of bed and went downstairs to the fifth floor, where there was usually a whiff of either food from the restaurant or the creams and lotions used in the hairdresser's. Tonight, though, the only odour was the highly perfumed disinfectant that the cleaners used, which would be gone by morning.

She entered the restaurant. Soon it would be the longest day and it was still faintly light outside. A soft tinkle came from the chandeliers, glittering dully in the dusk. There must be a draught somewhere. In another twelve hours, the room would be full of customers having their morning coffee or tea – hard to imagine as she stared at the empty tables and chairs, which, as far as she knew, might be occupied by the spirits of customers long departed.

The furniture department on the floor below was the eeriest place of all. She kept expecting a figure to step out of one of the big wardrobes, or find someone asleep in a bed, or an entire family sitting around a table, eating, yet not making even the slightest of sounds. She wandered around, until fear forced her down to the third floor, where she was met by plaster mannequins; wooden-jawed men with false smiles and expressionless eyes, some exquisitely dressed, others showing off their Wolsey vests and underpants and their harlequin patterned socks, looking slightly pained at the indignity, or so Queenie thought, her imagination stretched to the limit on her nocturnal trek through the normally bustling, crowded Freddy's, which felt so different late at night. Why she came, she had no idea, because she found it terrifying, but she was like a child in a fairground, drawn to the ghost train, yet knowing it would frighten her out of her wits.

The men's shoes, which seemed to be floating in the air, but were in fact on a perspex stand, invisible now, could well take off any minute and tap dance around the store. This is where old Rollinson had been despatched when parted from his beloved books.

'He needed to be taught a lesson,' Theo had told her,

much later. 'He was getting above himself, being rude to customers if he considered them less clever than himself.' Old Rollinson had returned to Books, a chastened man.

The second floor was Queenie's favourite. It was where she'd foolishly asked the price of the blue costume that would have made a perfect going-away outfit when she married Jimmy. From here, the latest Parisian fashions were sold and other clothes quite beyond the pockets of the ordinary women of Liverpool – there was a whole rack of Fleur summer frocks, each costing three or four times the seven guineas Wilfred had used to charge, adding to Theo's wealth because he had a half share in the company. These days, Wilfred Carter wafted around his London salon dressed in velvet suits and handmade shoes. Rosa had married a French man and they lived in Paris with their four children.

Outside, the sky had darkened and was now midnight blue, but the street lights were on and she could just about see the models, all alone in their little recesses on the far wall. She ran her fingers along a rack of fur coats – minks and sables, chinchillas and long-haired, wolf fur coats from Russia, slightly coarser than the rest – and wondered what trick of fate had made it possible for her to have any one of these beautiful coats, more than one if she wanted. If she hadn't worked in Herriot's, if she hadn't broken her arm and had to leave Caerdovey for Southport, if she hadn't met Laura who was responsible for sending her to Caerdovey in the first place, if Mam hadn't abandoned her . . .

Which meant it was all due to Mam that she was at liberty to choose anything she fancied, because she was the mistress of the fabulously rich man who owned the shop, who had just presented her with a boat for her birthday. Though 'boat' hardly seemed an adequate word to describe the miniature liner that was now hers.

Yet there'd been a time when she couldn't get a job, not even cleaning other women's houses. The change in her fortunes was so remarkable that it worried her. If things could go so far one way, they could go the other.

There were footsteps on the stairs and she nearly jumped out of her skin. Theo came through the door in his dressing gown. 'Queenie, are you there?'

'Yes.' She walked quickly towards him. 'Oh, Theo, I'm worried everything will go wrong and one day I'll be poor and ugly again.'

'You silly girl,' he said fondly, taking her in his arms. 'I flatly refuse to believe you were ever ugly. As to being poor, that will never happen.' He gave her a little shake. 'I don't understand why you wander around this place when it's empty and so dark. You always return to me with bad thoughts.'

'I feel drawn to it,' she confessed. 'I don't know why.'

'Next time you feel drawn to it, we'll come together.'

'Yes, Theo.' She laid her head on his shoulder. They weren't just lovers; he was also the father she'd never known, and she had taken the place of the daughters he badly missed.

Next morning, Queenie had hardly been in her office five minutes, when there was a knock, the door opened and Steven came in. She uttered a cry of delight, jumped to her feet, and they gave each other a hug.

'What are you doing here?' she asked. 'Oh, your father will be so pleased you're home.' He was the only one of Theo's children not to give a damn when Theo had left their mother to live with Queenie. The girls had scarcely spoken to Theo since, not even Lila when he'd given her away at her wedding or attended the christenings of her own two children. The way his daughters had turned against him upset their father terribly.

Steven grimaced. 'Yeah, but he won't be pleased by my news.'

'What have you done?' she asked, dismayed.

'I haven't done anything yet, but next week I'm off to America – Hollywood!' His face glowed. 'I've got a part in a film.'

'You haven't!'

'Don't look so astounded, Queenie.' He pretended to be annoyed. 'I'm an actor, it's what actors do. Oh, I know parts have been pretty thin on the ground so far, but not everyone becomes a star overnight. I've only been in the business nine years, bloody long years, as it happens, but there's still time for me to hit the heights.'

'Theo will miss you badly. Me, too.' He often came to stay with them and always had the grace to visit his mother and sisters while he was there.

'And I'll miss you. I've decided that if I haven't made it in show business by the time I'm forty, I'll come back and be the dutiful son.'

'I'd love you to come back, but would far rather you became a successful actor.'

He grinned. 'That's the perfect thing to say. Where's Dad, by the way?'

'In his office.'

'I'll go and break the news. Perhaps we could have lunch together later?'

'I'd love that.'

Steven gone, Queenie returned to the task she'd only just started when he came, reading a list of last week's sales of ladies' clothing. It was important to keep track of stock, to see what had sold best, and what had hardly moved. She saw the cream linen Lanvin costume had gone and the tailored, high-waisted Dior frock, so different from his New Look that had swept the world, thrilling women with its soft, flowing lines. But now skirts were gradually getting shorter and tighter, lapels wider. Women's fashion was a wondrous thing, unpredictable and full of surprises.

She went through the list, ticking items that would have to be re-ordered – not the Lanvin or the Dior as Theo refused to sell two identical designer garments. 'If a woman pays eighty or ninety guineas for an outfit, it wouldn't be fair if she met another woman wearing the same,' he said.

The telephone on her desk rang. She stared at it for a while before answering. It rang every Monday morning at about the same time and she knew who it would be. The strange thing was she never expected it and it always took her by surprise. She picked up the receiver, feeling sick.

'Call for you Miss Tate,' the switchboard operator sang. 'Just putting you through.'

'Did you enjoy yourself yesterday with my husband?' Irene Vandos screeched. 'Did you have a nice time in Wales?'

She'd had them followed again! Queenie felt even sicker. She didn't speak, just let the woman rant on and on, telling her she was a bitch who deserved to die, that one day she *would* die, and it would happen when she least expected. Queenie had ruined her life. She and Theo had been happy until she appeared and spoilt everything.

The screaming stopped and she began to moan like an animal in pain. 'I want him back. Let me have him back. *Please*! If you have a kind bone in your body, you will give my husband back to me.'

Still Queenie didn't say a word. The inhuman noise was turning her stomach, but she'd learned, a long time ago when the phone calls had first started, that it was wiser to stay silent.

'I'm going to kill myself,' the voice said menacingly. 'When Stephanie comes home, she'll find me hanging from the banisters. Do you want *that* on your conscience, Miss Queenie Tate?'

She'd listened to this nonsense long enough. Queenie put the receiver back in its cradle. Irene had been threatening to kill herself for years, long before Theo had left. She was unstable and badly in need of treatment. Occasionally, she called back if she felt she had more to say. Queenie glared at the telephone, willing it *not* to ring, then gave a sigh of relief after five thankful minutes of silence. She'd never told Theo about the calls. There was nothing he could do to stop them and he'd only be upset.

Just after Christmas, Irene had turned up in the shop and created an unpleasant scene at the glove counter when told she no longer had an account with Freddy's, something she already knew, but chose to forget. Theo had cancelled the account when it had reached four figures and not a penny had been repaid. Irene had been left a small fortune by her father and was a rich woman in her own right. Theo paid her an allowance that would have fed and clothed half of Glover Street. But it wasn't enough. She always wanted more.

The young assistant on the glove counter had dissolved into tears, Theo had been called, and things had turned even more unpleasant. He'd been left with the choice of physically ejecting his wife from the premises, or waiting until she'd run out of steam. He chose the latter and Irene proceeded to wash his dirty linen in public. What she didn't realise was that sympathy for Mr Theo only increased with each scene. 'With a wife like that,' Queenie had once heard Eustace, the lift man, say, 'no one can blame Mr Theo, bless him, for turning to another woman.'

Queenie returned to the list, but couldn't concentrate.

She could still hear Irene's shrill, desperate voice in her ears, and wondered if the phone calls would ever stop. She could imagine the woman on her death bed, demanding a telephone so she could abuse her husband's 'bit on the side', as she'd called her once.

She felt pleased when there was another knock and Mary Monaghan's pretty, cheerful face appeared. Mary had come to work in Freddy's when she was sixteen and was now on the cosmetics counter.

'Thought you'd like to know our Caradoc's wife had her baby on Saturday,' she said in a conspiratorial whisper for some reason. 'It's a boy. You'll come to the christening on Sunday, won't you, Queenie? It's two o'clock at St James's.'

'Of course.' She always liked to have a reason to go back to Glover Street or visit Laura and Roddy in Crosby. 'How many grandchildren does your mam have now? Sit down a minute, Mary. I feel like talking to someone normal.'

'Twenty-three.' Mary plonked herself in the chair in front of Queenie's desk. 'She's thrilled to pieces. It was bedlam in our house yesterday. The whole tribe turned up. Fortunately, they brought their own food, but we had to eat in stages.'

Vera's grandchildren, whose numbers increased regularly by two or three a year, had been her main comfort when her beloved Albert had died peacefully in his sleep five years before. The house was never without a gang of children; their mams were at work, doing a bit of shopping, having yet another baby for their fond grandma to look after.

'Has the new baby got a shawl?' she asked Mary. 'What's he going to be called, by the way?'

'Daniel Albert. That makes three boys called after me

dad. I think Iris has given Sarah an old shawl, but I'm sure she'd like a new one.'

'We've some lovely hand-knitted, lambswool shawls in stock,' Queenie said thoughtfully. 'I'll get Daniel Albert one of those.'

'Will you have to pay for it, Queenie? Or do you just help yourself?'

'No, I do *not* just help myself, Mary Monaghan. I pay, like everybody else. Honestly, you haven't changed a bit. You're as cheeky as you ever were. Anyroad,' she looked at her watch, 'what are you doing here? It's only quarter to ten, not nearly time for lunch.'

'I told Mrs Grim I had to go to the lavvy because I'd started a period. I only came because I thought you'd be panting to know about our Caradoc's new baby.'

'It's Mrs Prymme, not Grim. Have you started a period?' Queenie asked, trying to look stern.

'No, when I go back I'll say I made a mistake.'

'Well, you'd better go back soon, otherwise she'll come looking for you.'

'Only if she can get someone else to look after the counter,' Mary said pertly.

Queenie jerked her head towards the door. 'Off you go, Mary. And don't forget, be nice to the customers.' It was no longer a joking matter. Mary was inclined to take advantage of the fact she'd known Miss Tate virtually all her life. She was also inclined to get impatient with customers who dithered over their purchases. The Personnel Officer, Roger Appleby, who'd taken over Miss James's job when she'd retired, had mentioned it quite a few times.

'Have a word with her, please, Queenie. If she doesn't pull her socks up, she'll lose her job. I know she's the friend of a friend or something.'

'She's the daughter of a very good friend. I'll talk to her, don't worry.' Vera would be dead upset if Mary lost her job.

Every few months, she was obliged to call Mary into her office and read the riot act. 'The customer is always right. I know it's irritating when they take for ever choosing a lipstick or deciding what shade of powder would suit them best, but you must never let your irritation show.'

'Some of them take so long,' Mary had replied in a pained voice the last time they'd had a confrontation, 'I feel as if I'd like to strangle them.'

'We make it a rule in Freddy's never to strangle the customers, Mary.'

'What if there's other customers waiting?'

'Just say nicely, "I'll serve this other lady while you're making up your mind." They'll understand.'

'I should hope so.'

'Mary!' Queenie said sharply. 'I'm a buyer. I have nothing to do with staff. If you're rude again and Mr Appleby decides to sack you, there's nothing I can do about it.' Mary gave her a look that said Queenie only had to speak to Mr Theo and she could work in Freddy's until she was ninety. 'I've no intention of asking for special favours,' she said pointedly in response to the look. Anyroad, although Theo might agree to keep Mary on, it wouldn't be behind a counter. She'd be banished to the stockroom or some other place where she had nothing to do with the customers.

Mary usually behaved herself for a few months and then it would be time for another confrontation. Queenie loved the girl, but hoped she'd get married soon and leave. She was twenty and always had half a dozen young men chasing after her. Hester too, although, as had always been the way, Mary was far more interested in Hester's boyfriends than her own.

Theo never accompanied her on her visits to Bootle or Crosby. 'I'd feel in the way. They're your friends, not mine. You share a history I've played no part in.' To make sure no one thought he considered himself too grand, he would collect her in his car, coming into the house to shake hands and have a few words. The impressive dark blue Mercedes always drew an admiring crowd when it was parked in Glover Street.

The christening of Daniel Albert Monaghan was utter chaos. Even in church, where the new baby was as good as gold and didn't raise a peep when water was poured over his downy head, the other babies present set up a wail of sympathy. Toddlers chased each other up and down the aisles, the older children looked bored and talked amongst themselves. The once angelic Sammy, now fourteen and not even faintly angelic, was discovered playing cards with Gus in the back pew. Vera wept uncontrollably because Albert wasn't there. The priest looked annoyed. Mary, who'd invited her latest boyfriend, Paul, to the christening, seemed embarrassed by the way her nieces and nephews were behaving. Laura and Roddy looked amused, and Duncan Maguire, Hester's boyfriend, with whom, according to Laura, she was madly in love, could hardly keep a straight face. A lovely young man with a boyish smile, a broad Scots accent, ginger hair, and a face covered with freckles, he taught at the same school as Laura; he and Hester had met at a concert the previous Easter.

It was even more chaotic later, when approximately sixty adults and children squeezed into the house in Glover Street and attacked the mountains of sandwiches that had been made earlier.

‘To think,’ Vera panted, ‘that me and Albert had planned on moving somewhere smaller when the lads grew up. And I’m sure that christening cake’s not big enough to go around.’

After quickly stuffing themselves with sandwiches, the men went to the pub, leaving the women to cope with the queue of children waiting to be fed or use the lavatory.

Queenie and Laura, unable to hear themselves speak amidst the noise, went up to Vera’s bedroom for some peace and quiet. The ructions downstairs sounded very far away. They removed their shoes and sat on the bed.

‘Thank the Lord I only had two children,’ Laura said with a sigh of relief. ‘It’s hard enough coping with Hester and Gus.’

‘Hester’s never given any trouble, has she?’ Hester had always seemed the mildest of girls.

‘No, but she’s still a worry, particularly now she’s so smitten with Duncan. She walks around with a sickly look on her face and never hears a word anyone says. She can’t eat, she can’t sleep – I don’t know how she copes at work.’ Hester was a copy-typist with an insurance company in Southport.

‘Is Duncan equally smitten?’

‘I think so – I *hope* so, for Hester’s sake. Otherwise, she’ll end up with a broken heart. Trouble is, he’s very young, only twenty-two, and I don’t think he’s had a girlfriend before. His family back in Scotland are very religious. I get the feeling he left home because he felt it was time to spread his wings.’ Laura made a horrified face. ‘If they get married, I might be a grandmother before I’m forty.’

‘You had Hester when you were very young, that’s only to be expected.’

‘I suppose,’ Laura said with another sigh. ‘At Duncan’s age, Roddy had been a father for years.’ There was a noise outside, as if several bodies had tumbled downstairs. They waited for the screams, but there were none. 'I wonder what that was?'

'Who knows? I'm glad you two are back together.' Queenie gave her friend a little affectionate shove. 'I remember Vera saying once she'd never known two people so much in love as you and Roddy.'

Laura gave her an odd look. 'It's not the same as it used to be, you know. I was so innocent in those days, there was something pure about the way we loved each other. I hadn't a single doubt that we'd spend the rest of our lives together. But Roddy spoilt all that. I still love him, but it's a rather cynical love these days. I'm always holding back, scared he'll hurt me again, despite how passionately he wanted me to come and live with him in Crosby.' She smiled, rather sadly. 'When we first met, we'd leave each other little notes in this bookshop we used to meet in. We had our own special book, Gibbons's *Decline and Fall of the Roman Empire*. One day, after he'd been in Crosby a few months, I found a copy in the flat over the road. Roddy had put it there and there was a note inside. From then on, whenever he brought Hester and Gus home from their weekend visit, I'd find another note. I couldn't bring myself to play the game and leave notes for him. I was holding myself back, you see. But in the end, I gave in and went to live with him. It seemed foolish not to, and it was what the children wanted. Since then, I've been happy, but not blissfully happy the way I used to be, despite us being so poor.' She gave Queenie a searching look. 'Are *you* happy, Queenie?'

'*Bliss*fully happy, Laura,' she breathed. 'I wish things were different, naturally, that I could be Theo's wife, that people wouldn't look at me as if I were a scarlet woman. Even today, I noticed some of the lads' wives giving me funny looks – "Isn't she the one who lives with a married man? Fancy Vera inviting someone like *that* to the christening." In Freddy's, I never use the staff restaurant or go into the shop itself, except when it's empty, because I know everyone's staring at me. I stick to my office. It's only when we go away that Theo and I can pretend to be man and wife. I have a few friends, women I got to know when I first started. We sometimes go to the pictures together, but that's all.'

'I've never known anyone who looked less like a scarlet woman than you do, love.' Laura gave her an affectionate look. 'Theo is a lovely man and I'm so glad you're happy – *bliss*fully happy!'

'He bought me a boat for my birthday,' Queenie said shyly. 'Actually, he had it built especially.'

Laura's eyes popped. 'A *real* boat?'

'It's a motor yacht, eighty feet long, called *Queen of the Mersey*.'

'You lucky devil, Queenie Tate. On *my* birthday, Roddy bought me a powder compact.'

'Never mind, Laura. I'm sure your powder compact came with as much love as my boat.'

Theo was very quiet when he drove her back to Liverpool. They were almost there when Queenie realised she had completely dominated the conversation, describing the turmoil at the christening, the events afterwards in the house. 'Some of the children took a pram upstairs. They wanted to see if it would turn over when they let it roll back down.'

'Did it?'

'Twice. Is something wrong, Theo? You've hardly said a word.' Perhaps it was because Steven had gone away yesterday and didn't know when he'd be coming back. But the silence had nothing to do with Steven.

'I've been thinking,' Theo said quietly. 'You were

almost the only woman at Vera's without a child. It hardly seems fair that you should be denied a baby because of me, our situation.'

'If we had a baby, it would be illegitimate. It would have on the birth certificate that we weren't married.' All of a sudden, out of the blue, she remembered Carl Merton getting into bed with her, though not the thing he'd done. She'd deliberately switched herself off and it wasn't until years later that she accepted she'd been raped. She was still switching it off, denying to herself that it had happened. 'Did you know you were pregnant, Queenie?' Gwen Hughes had asked. 'You were expecting a baby, lovey.'

Queenie shuddered. Theo glanced at her and misinterpretated the shudder. 'There are worse things than being illegitimate, darling. Not being born at all, for instance. And don't forget, rich bastards have a far better time of it than poor ones.'

'I like being a buyer,' she said weakly. 'I'd hate to give up Paris Fashion Week and the London shows.'

'You wouldn't have to give up anything. We'd get a nurse – there's plenty of room in the apartment. Or, if you prefer, I'd buy us a house on the outskirts somewhere.'

They had reached the back of Freddy's. He sounded the horn and, Bill, the nightwatchman-cum-caretaker, came out of his cubby hole, made the thumbs-up sign, and unlocked the padlock on the big roll-up door that led to the garage where Freddy's green and black delivery lorries and vans were kept and where Theo parked the Mercedes. The door made a terrible grating sound as it slowly opened.

Theo reached for her hand. 'You know, darling, I think you're actually frightened of having a baby. I won't mention the subject again. I'll leave it entirely up to you.'

Chapter 12

'What are you doing here?' asked Vera Monaghan.

The little girl giggled. 'Me mam left me, Nana, while she went to get hair done.'

'I don't remember that. 'Fact, I don't remember seeing you before. What's your name?'

'Carmel.'

'Carmel what?'

'Carmel Monaghan, Nana.'

'Of course!' Vera cried. 'You're our Victor's little girl. Come and give your nan a nice big hug.'

Mary watched as Carmel hurled herself into Mam's arms and felt a little niggle of jealousy. She knew it was ridiculous, being jealous of a four-year-old child, but she missed being the apple of everyone's eye. Now the lads had kids of their own who were far more important to them than their little sister. And Mam, with swarms of grandkids to kiss and cuddle and generally make a fuss of, seemed to forget she had a daughter. Mary felt very unloved and badly missed her dad.

It was Wednesday, half day closing, and she wished she'd stayed in town and had a wander round, except there wasn't much point when the shops were shut and Liverpool was as dead as a door nail. When was she supposed to buy things for herself? It was only after lunch when, if she hurried, she could snatch quarter of an hour in C & A or Lewis's. Even with staff discount, the clothes in Freddy's were far too expensive.

Should I look for another job? she wondered. In an office, maybe, where I'd have Saturday off, like Hester, and we could go round the shops together. Then she remembered that since Hester had met Duncan Maguire they spent virtually all their free time together, so *that* idea wasn't on.

'Do you fancy a cup of tea, Mam?'

'I wouldn't say no, luv,' Mam said. She was too busy letting Carmel examine her shrivelled elbows to look up. Mary remembered she'd been fascinated by Mam's elbows when she was Carmel's age. Now they were more shrivelled and possibly even more fascinating.

What she needed was a boyfriend who worked in a shop, she thought as she ran water into the kettle, and they could go out together on Wednesday afternoons. In fact, what she needed was a boyfriend, full stop. The supply had dried up all of a sudden, the reason being she no longer went dancing with Hester, the favourite way of meeting fellows. She thought it a bit lousy of Hester to drop her like a hot brick the minute Duncan came along, entirely forgetting she'd done the same to Hester loads of times.

The chap, Paul, whom she brought to Daniel's christening, hadn't been in touch since, put off, she felt convinced, by the little Monaghans' bad behaviour in church. She felt hurt, because she'd slept with him, and had visualised *her* giving *him* up, not the other way round.

She was uncomfortably aware that Paul was the fifth chap she'd slept with – she daren't think what Mam's reaction would be if she knew. She hadn't told Hester, who was a virgin; at least had been a virgin when she met Duncan and might not be now. Mary thought it most unfair that making love, which was a very enjoyable experience, was out of bounds to people who weren't married. She wondered idly if she was over-sexed and rather liked the idea. The trouble was, if she slept around *too* much, she'd get the reputation of being a slag, which she'd hate. The obvious solution was to get married as soon as possible so she'd have someone permanent to sleep with, but it would have to be someone very nice, very attractive, with whom she felt at least a little bit in love. As there wasn't a man on the horizon at the moment, not even one who was hideously ugly, the chances of getting married soon were remote.

'Actually, Mam,' she said when she went in with the tea, 'I'll not bother with a cuppa. I think I'll go for a walk instead.' It was July and lovely and sunny outside, whereas inside the house was terribly dark and gloomy. It was about time Mam got some new furniture and had the place done up a bit.

'All right, luv,' Mam said absently.

Mary changed out of the black frock she wore for work into a red and white polka-dot three-tiered skirt and a white blouse with a drawstring neck. She put on a pair of white canvas sandals, powdered her nose, renewed her lipstick, brushed her thick brown curls, and inserted a pair of dangly bead earrings. She examined the final result in the mirror and felt pleased with her appearance – Dad used to say she was 'as pretty as a picture' – but wished her nose was a fraction longer. It was occasionally described as 'snub', which sounded a bit like a pig.

Why she was taking so much trouble when she was going for a walk around Bootle, she had no idea. She was unlikely to meet the man of her dreams and wouldn't recognise him if she did.

She walked as far as Marsh Lane where, as expected,

the shops were shut apart from the sweet and tobacconist's, where she bought a Mars Bar. She had a weakness for chocolate, particularly Mars Bars. 'You'll get spots,' Mam warned every time she saw Mary tucking into a bar of chocolate, but so far Mary hadn't had a single one.

Oh, Lord! This was boring. Perhaps she should catch the train to Southport and meet Hester when she finished work. She looked at her watch; nearly half-past two. If she went now, she'd have three hours to kill, though at least Southport wouldn't be dead, but packed with holidaymakers. She could stroll along the front, treat herself to a cream tea somewhere. But I don't like doing things like that by myself, she thought piteously. She liked company. If Mam hadn't had millions of grandkids, they could have gone together.

I know, I'll go to Crosby and see Laura! The schools had broken up last week for the long summer holiday, so Laura would be home. Gus might be there, which would be even better as they got on well. Gus had passed the Eleven-Plus and had gone to Merchant Taylor's, as Brian Tyler had.

Laura looked taken aback when she opened the door and found Mary on the step. She was wearing the glasses she'd recently acquired. They had horn-rimmed frames and looked very smart, if a bit stern.

'Hester's at work,' she said when they went into the living room. 'She's not on holiday till the week after next, and then Duncan's taking her to Scotland to meet his parents – it looks as if things are getting serious.' She must think Mary had got her dates confused and had expected Hester to be there.

'Actually, I came to see you and Gus.'

'What a lovely surprise!' Laura's smile couldn't have been warmer. 'I'm afraid Gus has gone to Formby with some friends; you'll just have to put up with me.' She began to pick up the papers and books scattered on the floor. 'We only finished school on Friday, and I'm already working on next term's timetable.'

'I'm sorry to interrupt.' Mary wasn't sorry at all, although despite Laura's warm smile, she sensed she would have preferred to be left alone with the timetable. She sat on the russet velvet settee. The room was very long and had windows both ends. With the pale furniture, the watercolours done by an artist friend of Roddy's on the creamy walls, the bookcases, the flowers in a big vase on the hearth and more flowers visible in the gardens front and back, the sunny room presented a sharp contrast to the Monaghans' living room in Glover Street.

'How's your mum?' Laura asked politely. 'She looked awfully tired at the christening. Are the grandchildren wearing her down?'

'They are a bit, even if she loves having them.'

'I don't think children take account of the fact their parents reach an age when they should be taking things easy. Your mum's sixty-eight, but I don't think your brothers have noticed. I bet Albert would have put his foot down if he were still around.'

'I'm sure he would.' The conversation might have continued in this stiff, rather formal way, had not Mary felt two tears trickle down her cheeks. She sniffed and only just managed to control a sob. 'I don't half miss him, me dad.'

'Mary!' Laura was beside her on the settee in an instant, full of sympathy. 'Oh, love! I didn't realise you were still missing Albert – mind you, in my own way I miss him myself.'

'He *loved* me,' Mary said tremulously. 'Now there's no one left who does.'

'But everybody here loves you, Mary. Me and Roddy, Hester and Gus. And I bet your mum doesn't love a single one of her grandchildren as much as she loves you.'

'She doesn't show it.'

'Maybe she doesn't think she needs to, that you just *know*. Now dry your eyes and I'll make us some tea. Or would you prefer a cold drink?'

'Tea would be nice.'

Laura went into the kitchen and had hardly been gone a minute when the doorbell rang. Mary thought she'd make herself useful and went to answer it. She was ever so glad she'd come. Laura had made her feel *wanted* for a change. She rubbed her cheeks with her hands to get rid of the tears and opened the door.

'Hello, I didn't expect to find you here,' grinned Duncan Maguire. He wore a white open-necked shirt, cotton trousers, and a wide-brimmed straw hat. 'Excuse the headgear,' he said, taking the hat off, 'but I catch the sun easily and my skin turns as bright red as my hair.'

'You look a bit pink.' The pink went oddly with his lovely green eyes, guileless eyes, which looked as if they'd never seen anything nasty since the day they'd first opened on to the world.

'Pink's okay, it'll have gone by tonight. Red, and I'll simmer for days while resembling a creature from outer space. I terrify the children at school.'

'I'm sure you don't.' Mary giggled, loving his broad Scots accent. 'Laura's making tea.'

'Then I've come at just the right time.'

Laura was obviously pleased to see him. He'd brought some books she wanted, but had no intention of stopping – except for the tea – because he knew she wanted to get on with the timetable for next term. 'I thought I'd drive as far as Southport, mooch around a bit, then collect Hester from work.'

'Why not take Mary with you?' Laura suggested. 'She's feeling a bit down, aren't you, love? Hester will be pleased when she finds you've both come to pick her up.'

Duncan thought that a great idea. 'I'd sooner not mooch around on my own. Hey! We can go on the fairground. Hester hates fairgrounds.'

'Me, I love fairgrounds,' Mary cried, though it was something she'd never had an opinion on before. The afternoon was turning out immeasurably better than expected.

Duncan Maguire had found the courage to put his foot down when he'd emerged from St Andrews University, Fife, with a First in English Literature and found his father had already begun to approach schools in the area to arrange a teaching post for his son.

If his father was successful, then there'd be no need to leave home when he started work, just as there'd been no need to leave when he'd gone to St Andrews, which was merely a long bus ride away from the small, isolated community where he lived with his parents and two younger sisters.

He'd been hoping, when he left grammar school with the top marks in his class, 'perfect university material' according to the headmaster, that he'd escape then, get a place in Glasgow or Edinburgh, both highly thought of establishments. But his father, a minister in some obscure branch of the Scottish Reformed church, was having none of it. These places were hotbeds of sin, he thundered. What's more, they took women, and once young people set foot inside their doors, they lost all inhibitions and went completely wild. Not for a moment did he think his son would do the same, but he didn't want him associating with people who would. 'Sons and daughters of the devil,' he roared during one of his own wilder moments. St Andrews would be no different, but Duncan's association with his fellow students would be minimal as he could come home every night.

At barely eighteen, Duncan felt too intimidated by his overbearing father to protest. What's more, had he found the nerve, it would have upset his mild, browbeaten mother whom he dearly loved, and who would have been left to bear the brunt of her husband's anger.

He had spent a miserable four years, missing most of the enjoyable aspects of university life, present only for lectures and the very occasional evening event. The other students looked upon him as a cissie, a judgement with which Duncan was inclined to agree. He left St Andrews at twenty-one, determined to be a cissie no longer, faced his outraged father, and told him he wished to leave home, teach elsewhere, even in a school as far away as England. His mother would be sad, but now he was an adult and couldn't stay at home for ever.

Each week, he bought *The Times Educational Supplement* and applied for posts. He was particularly interested in the vacancy in Liverpool. Liverpool was a port and, apart from his mother and sisters, the only thing he would miss when he left Scotland was living within sight of the sea. He was invited for an interview, offered the job, and accepted on the spot. He decided to stay a few days, look for somewhere to live, and found a top-floor flat in The Esplanade, Waterloo, overlooking the Mersey.

Now Duncan had reached the end of his first year as a teacher. It had been a liberating, illuminating year. One of the best things about it was discovering he was quite a likeable chap. People wanted to be his friends, men and women alike. He enjoyed their friendship, became less shy, found he had a sense of humour and could even crack the occasional joke. On a more practical level, he learnt to drive and bought a car, a blue Ford Popular, discovered the theatre, the cinema, jazz clubs, television – his father had refused to have even a wireless in the house – began to drink and smoke, but only in moderation. For a while, there'd been one problem; girls. They frightened him. He had no idea how to treat them and could never tell if they were flirting with him or not. The women friends he made were usually teachers, older than him – Laura was one.

Then, a few months ago, Laura had introduced him to her daughter. Hester was tall and willowy, with soft blue eyes and fair hair that could look like pure gold in a certain light. Quietly spoken, rather withdrawn, she was the loveliest girl Duncan had ever met. They hit it off immediately and had been inseparable ever since. It had even reached the point where he was seriously considering marriage and was waiting for the right moment to propose. In a few weeks, he was taking Hester to meet his parents. His father was bound to disapprove, but at least she wasn't a Catholic, which would have put her quite beyond the pale.

'Why are you feeling down?' he asked Mary, Hester's friend, when they set off for Southport in the car. At first, Mary, whom he'd met only a few times, had made him nervous; she was too pushy, too loud, wore too much make-up, her clothes were too flamboyant for his taste, but soon he realised it was only because she was very different from Hester, who was so ladylike and demure.

'It was nothing much. I'm OK now,' Mary said dismissively.

'Why aren't you at work?'

'Because I work in a shop and shops close on

Wednesday afternoons. Hester brought you to see me one Saturday, but you've obviously forgotten.' She sounded a bit annoyed.

'I didn't forget *you*,' Duncan said hastily, 'just the shop. Nobody could forget *you*,' he added in the hope of making amends. It seemed to work.

'Oh!' She preened herself. 'That's all right, then.' She wriggled comfortably in the seat. 'It must be nice having a boyfriend with a car.'

'It can be very useful,' he replied, thinking about the times he'd kissed Hester in the back. Kissing was as far as they'd got, though recently he'd felt a strong urge to go further, but was worried Hester wouldn't like it. She'd had boyfriends before, but Duncan would have sworn on his father's well-thumbed Bible that they'd got no further than he had. Mind you, even Hester's limited experience with men was greater than his with women.

Mary explained she was between boyfriends at the moment and he asked what had happened to the chap who'd been with her at the christening?

'I dumped him,' she said briskly. 'I didn't like the way he kept tut-tutting at the kids, the noise they made.'

'I thoroughly enjoyed that christening.' He'd never come across a family like the Monaghans before and thought them great fun. And it had felt very daring, attending a Catholic church. He smiled. He was going to the dogs, just as his father had threatened he would in Papist Liverpool.

They arrived in Southport and he parked the car on the front, close to the fairground. Mary said she felt like a drink, so they stopped at a refreshment stall and she had a chocolate milk shake and he had orangeade.

'What do you want to go on first?' he asked when they reached the crowded fairground.

'Anything! Anything daring and dangerous.'

'You're a girl after my own heart,' he said, but wished he hadn't when she gave him a sly, come hither look. She had chocolate on her mouth from the drink – she'd spooned the thick mixture out of the bottom of the glass with the straw – and he didn't know whether or not to tell her. 'What about the big wheel? Is that daring and dangerous enough?'

'It'll do for now.' She seized his hand and began to drag him towards it. On the wheel, her screams got shriller and shriller the higher they climbed. When every seat was full and it began to turn full circle, quite fast, she clung to his arm, which he found irritating.

She clung to his arm on the waltzer and the figure eight, in the ghost train and on a fiendish ride called the corkscrew, which actually turned upside down several times on its descent. On the way, her red flouncy skirt blew up, entirely covering her face, exposing a pair of plump, shapely legs and white, lace-trimmed panties. He tried, but couldn't stop himself from staring. He'd never seen a girl's legs above the knees before, except his sisters', a long time ago.

It might have been this delectable sight that made Duncan decide he quite liked Mary and was very much enjoying her company. She was only behaving the way girls were supposed to behave at fairgrounds and he no longer minded. In fact, he was feeling quite exhilarated, almost drunk. 'Come on, let's have another go,' he cried when they'd spent five minutes getting their breath back after suffering the tortures of the corkscrew. This time it was him who took Mary's hand.

Afterwards, they caught the train to the end of the mile-long pier, then walked back, pausing only for a drink when Mary claimed to be thirsty again. She ordered another chocolate milk shake and this time Duncan had the same. It was delicious.

'Now you've got more chocolate on your mouth,' he said when she went through the ritual of trying to pick the dregs with the straw.

'Whereabouts?'

'In the corners, like whiskers.'

Instead of using a hankie, she stuck out her tongue, and he watched, fascinated, as it wriggled, like a little pink worm, in an unsatisfactory attempt to remove the chocolate. 'Here, let me do it for you.' He wiped the corners of her mouth with his hankie, and noticed how red and full her lips were. He felt the desire to kiss them.

'Thank you, Duncan,' she said demurely. 'You know, we must do this again sometime.'

A warning bell rang in Duncan's ear, but he ignored it. What harm was he doing? It wasn't as if he was engaged to Hester. It was a pity he hadn't gone out with loads of girls before settling on just one. Playing the field, it was called. It was just that he and Hester had seemed so perfect for each other – still were.

'We could meet next Wednesday after you've finished work,' he said, his heart somersaulting in his chest, almost hoping Mary would refuse and his conscience would be left clear. Yet pretty soon there would be no going back with Hester, not that he wanted there to be, but it would mean he'd never again have the opportunity of going out with a girl like Mary. Again he told himself he wasn't doing any harm. Just one date, that was all, and she would be out of his system.

Mary was saying he could pick her up outside Freddy's at one o'clock. She was already looking forward to it. 'We'd better not mention it to Hester. It doesn't matter her knowing about today, it was all Laura's idea.'

Duncan felt obliged to agree but, later, when they went to collect Hester from work, he felt a terrible sense of betrayal when she emerged from her office looking rather tired, but as serenely beautiful as ever. She was dressed in a plain black skirt and a white blouse. Her slim arms glistened with perspiration.

'Gosh, it was hot in there today and we were awfully busy. I feel washed out.'

The sense of betrayal deepened when she looked so pleased to see Mary and said she thought it marvellous that they'd been to the fairground. 'You've done me a favour, Mary. I detest those places. Now I don't feel so guilty for refusing to go with Duncan.'

She felt guilty! And over such a trite little thing. His own feeling of guilt washed over him in waves. He'd tell Mary he couldn't go next Wednesday, think up an excuse.

When they got back to Crosby, Roddy and Gus were there and Laura had made a lovely tea for them all, Mary included; crab salad followed by trifle, home-made lemonade in a glass jug with little pebbles of ice floating on top. He tried several times to get Mary on one side, even offering her a lift when she said she was going home. But she gave him one of her sly looks and said she'd prefer to catch the train, as if she guessed he was looking for an opportunity to cancel the date.

The next few days were agony. During that mad afternoon in Southport, he'd forgotten how sweet Hester was, how much she loved him, how much he loved her. She was the woman he wanted to spend the rest of his life with. He thought of writing to Mary, but it would be too risky. In a fit of pique, she might show the letter to Hester. He looked in the telephone directory, but the Monaghans weren't on the phone.

When Duncan woke on Wednesday, rain was hammering on the roof and, through the window, he could see the sky was black. The fairground was out. With a huge sense of relief, he realised Mary wouldn't expect him in such awful weather. The date was off. He lay in bed, which had never felt so comfortable, feeling as if a great burden had been lifted from his shoulders and praying the rain wouldn't stop, at least not until after one o'clock. He wished it were possible never to see Mary again but, as Hester's best friend, it would be inevitable – she would almost certainly be a bridesmaid at their wedding.

It was time he started to prepare for the trip to Scotland on Saturday. He leapt out of bed, feeling like a new man, and spent hours sorting out his socks, actually darning some, which he always found an extraordinarily painful procedure. He pressed a couple of ties, ironed shirts, even ironed half a dozen hankies and his best pyjamas, which hadn't seen an iron since he'd left home. He was sorting through his cuff links, trying to find the pearly ones his mother had given him for his twenty-first, much to the disdain of his father who disapproved of adornments of any kind, when the doorbell rang three times, an indication it was for the person who lived on the third floor; in other words, him. It was probably Gus, whom he'd promised to help with a holiday project – 'Shakespeare's Ten Most Evil Characters'.

Duncan ran downstairs and came as close to fainting as he'd ever done, when he found Mary Monaghan outside in a nylon mac, under a striped umbrella.

'You didn't come like you promised,' she pouted. 'I came to see if you were sick or something.'

'I'm . . . I'm fine,' Duncan stammered. 'I didn't think you'd want to go to Southport in the pouring rain.'

'We could have gone to the pictures. *Vera Cruz* is on in town with Gary Cooper and Burt Lancaster. I'd have loved to see it. Aren't you going to ask me in?' she asked, eyeing him coquettishly. 'Me feet are soaking and me hair's all wet, despite the umbrella.'

'Of course.' Duncan courteously stood aside. 'I'm on the top floor.' They climbed the stairs in silence, and he could have kicked himself for noticing the shapely ankles in front of his nose, her strong perfume.

'This is nice,' she cried when they went into his room. She took off her mac and hung it behind the door. 'I like the view.' She noticed the clothes maiden, full of shirts. 'Oh, you've been ironing! I didn't know men could iron.'

'It's a case of having to when you live alone,' he said stiffly.

She kicked off her shoes, smiled, and said, 'Have you got a towel, Duncan, for me hair?'

He fetched a towel and she rubbed her head vigorously, emerging with her dark curls like a wild halo around her face. He couldn't help thinking how pretty she was. With a feeling of horror, he realised Mary appealed to his dark side – he hadn't been aware he had one until now. In his mind, he was investing her with all sorts of characteristics she almost certainly didn't have, turning her into a temptress, a seductive siren, when she was merely a silly little girl. She couldn't help the way her soft, silky frock clung to her breasts, and probably didn't know that the top button was undone, so that he could see the soft curve where the breasts began, giving him an unwelcome little thrill.

'Do you mind if I take me stockings off? They're sticking to me legs and feel dead uncomfortable.'

'Of course not.' He turned away, when he should have gone into another room, but staying meant he could see, out of the corner of his eye, Mary raise her skirt and undo her suspenders, peel the filmy stockings off her legs, and put them over the clothes maiden with his shirts, while his heart thumped crazily in his chest and ugly thoughts he'd never had before swirled through his head. Hester was forgotten. He wanted Mary, yet at the same time he wanted her to go, leave him in peace, stop tempting him.

'All done,' she sang. 'You can look now.' He turned to face her, and she said very slowly and very softly, 'But you were looking all the time, weren't you, Duncan?'

He felt the blood rush to his face. 'No, I wasn't.'

'Oh, Duncan. I could see you.' She came towards him and slid her arms around his neck, pressed herself against him, and he felt himself harden. 'No one will know,' she whispered. 'No one will know if we do it just this once. I'll never mention it to a soul. It'll be our secret.'

Duncan's mother and his sisters, Megan and Bryony, took to Hester straight away, and even his father had to grudgingly agree that she would make his son a perfect wife. Hester was modest, had perfect manners, didn't argue or use make-up, wore her hair in a bun at the nape of her neck and managed to convey the fact it wasn't dyed. She helped Mrs Maguire with the baking, made her bed each morning, listened, eyes closed, to the long, drawn-out grace said before every meal, giving no hint she minded the food was getting cold. Apart from her religion, or lack of it – Hester was an indifferent Protestant – Reverend Maguire couldn't fault her.

Hester was undoubtedly a nice, rather old-fashioned girl, but nothing like the saintly creature the Maguires thought. She had agreed with Duncan it would be sensible if his father was led to believe she was some sort of paragon. 'It'll only be for a week. As soon as we leave, you can put your lipstick on and comb your hair out of that awful bun. You see, if he doesn't like you, he'll only take it out on my mother.'

The week passed quickly by. He took Hester to St Andrews and showed her the university, they went for walks on the hills and lay on the grass and kissed, went for rides in the car with his mother, stopping at the occasional café for morning coffee or afternoon tea. His mother enjoyed these little treats so much that he felt dreadful when it was Saturday and it was time for them to leave.

It was dark when they got back to Crosby and the Olivers' house. 'Would you like to come in for a drink of something?' Hester enquired.

'No, thanks, Hes. It's time I went to bed. That was an awfully long drive.'

'I thought I might take driving lessons.'

'That's a good idea. I'll buy you a car for a wedding present, as long as you don't mind if it's secondhand. Which reminds me,' he took her in his arms, 'I still haven't asked you to marry me.'

'There's no need to ask, Duncan,' she said soberly, resting her cheek against his. 'I just took it for granted that we would. You see, I knew, the minute we met, that we were meant for each other.' Her voice was husky with emotion. 'I think I want to cry,' she whispered.

'If you do, I'll cry too.' This moment was one he would remember all his life, sitting in the front of the little car, proposing marriage to Hester Oliver, who had known all along that they were meant for each other. He kissed her, and lost himself in the kiss that became more passionate with each second. Before he knew it, he was stroking her breasts, squeezing them, pressing his thumbs against her nipples. 'I'm sorry, so sorry,' he mumbled, when she pushed him away.

'Don't be sorry.' She cupped his face in her hands. 'Just don't let's go any further, not here, where someone might see. Tomorrow, I'll come to your flat and we can do whatever we like and no one will see a thing.'

From the next day on, Hester Oliver and Duncan Maguire lived in their own, private little world, discovering each other's bodies, taking delight in each new discovery, getting to know each other as two people had never done before, so they both thought. Duncan had never seen anything so beautiful as Hester, completely naked, lying beside him, the sun shining on her gleaming skin. In the space of a few, short weeks, he had moved from boyhood to manhood.

When they weren't making love, they discussed who they would invite to the wedding. Everyone they knew, they decided. How many children would they have? Four; two boys and two girls. Where would they buy a house? Crosby seemed the obvious choice.

Duncan felt almost drunk with happiness when he considered the golden future that lay ahead for him and his darling Hester. He rarely thought about Mary. That was all over. It hadn't been even faintly nice while it lasted, more squalid in a way. He would always be ashamed of the way he'd behaved. He resolved his dark side would never show its ugly face again.

The phone call came on his third week back at school. September was coming to an end and he could already feel the tingle of autumn in the air. Leaves had started to fall, the nights were drawing in, Christmas would soon creep up on them. He was staying with the Olivers, and it would be the best he'd ever known.

'It's a young lady,' the school secretary said when she came into the staff room to tell him about the phone call. 'She sounds a bit distressed.'

'Hester!' He almost ran to the secretary's office. She stayed tactfully outside. He picked up the receiver. 'Darling! What's the matter?'

'It's me, Mary. Something awful's happened, Duncan.

I'm going to have a baby and it can only be yours. Can we meet somewhere tonight? Oh, Duncan! I don't know what to do. I suppose we'll just have to get married.'

'Sorry, I'm late.' Roddy Oliver threw his briefcase on to the seat. 'Something came up in the office just as I was leaving.'

'You're not late,' Duncan said, his voice sounding very thick, as if it belonged to someone else, 'it's me that's early. I've been here ages.'

'What are you having?'

'Double whisky, please.'

Roddy gave him a surprised glance; he usually drank beer. 'Won't be a sec.'

Duncan watched the man he'd expected to be his father-in-law go to the bar. He'd considered it a bonus getting Laura and Roddy as in-laws. They were both so young, not yet forty, and Roddy, with his thick blond hair and lean body always looked very boyish and could have passed for ten years younger. He'd phoned him at the office straight after school and asked if they could meet. He had no one else to talk to and Roddy might possibly be able to help him out of the mess he'd got himself into, even understand. Hester had told him her father hadn't been around during the war. 'It wasn't just because he was in the Army. He left Mummy for another woman.'

'The Wig & Pen in Dale Street at six,' Roddy had said. 'See you then, old chap. Hope nothing's wrong.'

'How many of these have you had?' Roddy slid the whisky in front of him. He'd bought himself a beer. 'You're looking slightly the worse for wear, if you don't mind my saying.'

'I've had three.' Duncan's head was splitting. He

wanted to die. At that moment, death would have been most welcome.

'What's up, Duncan?' Roddy asked kindly.

'I don't know where to begin.'

'At the beginning, old chap. It's the obvious place.'

It took a few minutes for him to remember how it had begun. 'During the holidays,' he said hesitantly, 'I think it was the first week, I went to Southport with Mary Monaghan.'

'I remember,' Roddy said encouragingly. 'Laura told me.'

'The next week, I met Mary again, and . . .' He paused and took a sip of the whisky. It didn't burn his throat as the first few had. 'And we, we . . .' He couldn't think how to describe what he and Mary had done.

'Fucked?'

Duncan nodded, shocked to the core. He'd heard the word before, but had never thought it would be spoken by someone like Roddy Oliver.

'It's not the end of the world, old chap.' Roddy slapped his knee. 'These things happen. You weren't engaged to Hester then. Has this been preying on your conscience all this time?'

'No,' Duncan said truthfully. 'I hadn't exactly forgotten about it, but the thing is, Mary rang the school today. She's going to have a baby.'

'Jesus!' Roddy's face went pale. 'Jesus! What are we going to do now?' He picked up Duncan's glass and drained it. 'I think I need another one of these.' He left, returning minutes later and slammed a whisky on the table. 'I didn't get one for you. I think you've already had enough. You're a bloody idiot, Duncan. Didn't you use anything?'

'Use anything?' Duncan looked at him blankly.

'A condom? A French letter, or whatever the hell you

call these things in that wasteland you come from. Christ! Don't tell me you don't know what a condom is?' he snapped when Duncan continued to look blank.

'I've never heard of them. What am I going to do, Roddy?' he asked piteously. He got the bewildering impression that it was OK to have sex, but only if you used one of these mysterious condom things. It seemed very hypocritical.

Roddy's blue eyes narrowed. 'If it turns out Mary really *is* pregnant, you have three choices: the first is to run away and never come back; second, you can deny the child is yours and tell her to get stuffed; lastly, you can get married, live happily ever after, and break my daughter's heart. Which is it going to be, Duncan?' he asked bitterly.

When Roddy arrived home, very late, Laura looked at him suspiciously. 'Are you drunk? Is that why you couldn't get your key in the door?'

'I'm exceedingly drunk, darling,' Roddy said carefully. He was having difficulty forming words. 'Drunker than I ever got in the Army. I'll tell you why in a minute. First of all, where's Hester?'

'She rang earlier. Apparently, Duncan called her at work and cancelled tonight's date, so she's gone to the pictures with some of the girls. Gus is at a friend's.' Laura folded her arms and regarded him severely. 'Now can you tell me why you've got yourself almost legless?'

'Because Mary Monaghan is pregnant and our daughter's fiancé is the father. He told me tonight in the Wig & Pen.'

'*What?*' Laura flinched, as if he'd struck her.

'The little bitch seduced him – honestly, darling, that boy is an innocent abroad. I knew more about women when I was twelve. He's never even heard of condoms.'

Roddy sat down suddenly with a thump. 'Christ Almighty! Do you think he's been screwing Hester?'

'Probably, but a few weeks ago, I took her to a birth control clinic. She's got a Dutch cap.'

'Sensible girl, but you should have taken her a few months ago, not weeks. If he'd had our daughter to screw, he mightn't have looked twice at Mary.'

'There's no need to be so crude,' Laura said thinly. 'Anyway, what does that matter now? Does this mean the wedding's off? It'll kill Hester!'

'It's killing Duncan. He's made the biggest mistake of his life and he knows it.' Roddy sighed. 'And yes, the wedding's off. I suggested several choices and he picked the only honourable one, marrying the damned girl.'

Laura must have noticed the television was on without the sound. She turned it off. 'What do you mean, she seduced him?' she asked, puzzled.

'They went to Southport, to the fairground. She said something about they must do it again, so they arranged to meet the next week, but he regretted it straight away. He was relieved when the day came and it was raining and he didn't have to go.' Roddy went over to the cabinet where they kept the drink and helped himself to a glass of whisky. 'I feel as if I want to drink myself senseless as well as legless. Do you want one?'

'No, I'll make tea in a minute.'

'Anyway, Mary only turned up that afternoon, soaking wet, and proceeded to entertain him with a bloody striptease. She beguiled him, he said. Beguiled! Have you ever heard anyone use that word in your whole life? I asked if she was a virgin, and he wanted to know how you could tell. It turns out she was his first woman, and it was nothing to do with love, just sex.'

Laura was close to tears. 'Oh, Lord, Roddy. This is awful. And it's all my fault! It was my idea they go to

Southport together. I wanted Mary out of the way so I could get on with the timetable.'

'Darling,' Roddy said in a voice that was becoming increasingly slurred, 'you couldn't have expected to happen what did happen – does that make sense?'

'But I knew what Mary was like. She always had to go one better than Hester, have the things she had. Now she's got Hester's fiancé.' Laura drew in a deep, ragged breath. 'Does Vera know about this?'

'I've no idea who knows. Neither does Duncan. After he left me, he went to meet Mary. You know what he said before he went? "I love Hester. I love her more than life itself." '

Mary had never meant things to go so far. Hester was as close to her as a sister, though they'd drifted apart when Duncan came on the scene. The same thing probably happened with real sisters when one started courting, but she'd resented not being the first. For some obscure reason, it didn't seem fair. Hester always managed to sail through life without even trying. People only had to look at her to like her. She didn't even have to open her mouth. At dances, Hester, in her neat, unfussy clothes, no jewellery, hardly any make-up, her hair brushed smoothly back from her face, not in any particular style, was nearly always asked up first, while Mary, who'd taken ages getting ready, was left to hang about, though not for long. Sometimes, her partners would ask, 'Who's your friend?' as if they would have preferred to dance with Hester but hadn't got there in time and Mary was their second choice.

'I would never forget *you*,' Duncan had said on the way to Southport, and she was convinced there was an invitation in his eyes. He fancied her! It wouldn't hurt to egg him on a bit, see what happened. She wouldn't feel so bad about Hester courting, if she could convince herself that Duncan might have preferred *her* if he'd met her first.

All afternoon, she'd kept pressing herself against him, clinging to him on the rides, pretending to be terrified. When he'd wiped her mouth, she could tell he would have very much liked to kiss her.

'We must do this again sometime,' she'd said, and he'd jumped at the idea. She'd been quite pleased the following Wednesday when she discovered it was raining. They could go to the pictures, have a good old neck in the back row, Mary would have proved something to herself, and Hester could have her boyfriend back.

When she'd come out of Freddy's, she'd been seriously narked to find Duncan wasn't there. She knew where he lived and had gone to Waterloo to tear him off a strip, but when he'd opened the door, he'd looked so terrified, she realised she scared him. It could only be for one reason; he found her irresistible. He didn't want them to be alone.

In his room, things had got out of hand. She hadn't meant to go so far, but had been quite turned on when she noticed he was peeping while she took her stockings off. What followed had been a disaster; he'd come straight away and looked dead embarrassed, and she'd felt dead embarrassed too, as well as a bit ashamed.

She'd hurried away, wishing it were possible never to see Duncan Maguire again. Not long afterwards, one Sunday afternoon, a starry-eyed Hester arrived at Glover Street to show off her lovely engagement ring and to say she and Duncan were getting married next July on her twenty-first. Duncan would have come with her to break the news, she said, but the night before he'd eaten something that had disagreed with him and felt quite poorly. He sent his apologies instead.

'You'll be my bridesmaid, won't you, Mary?' Hester had asked, and Mary had no choice but to say she'd be thrilled.

'Duncan's sisters will be bridesmaids too, least we hope so. He's not sure if his father will let them. Something to do with the church.'

At least it was a relief to know she hadn't spoilt things for Hester. The episode in Duncan's flat she put to the back of her mind in the hope she'd never think about it again.

Then her August period was late. Every morning, she woke up and prayed frantically to God that she'd started during the night, only to find she hadn't. At Freddy's, Mrs Prymme became so cross with her frequent trips to the lavatory to check if the longed-for period had arrived that she reported her to Mr Appleby, who reported her to Queenie, who requested her presence in her office.

'Have you started smoking?' Queenie wanted to know. 'That's usually the reason why staff visit the lavatory a dozen times a day.'

'No,' Mary said sullenly.

'Then you must have developed a weak bladder. You should see a doctor about it, Mary.'

At that point, Mary had burst into tears and told Queenie she had a horrible feeling she might be pregnant. 'I've never missed a period before,' she sobbed, 'but I'm three weeks late and it's almost time for the next one.'

'Oh, dearie me!' All of a sudden, Queenie was no longer the elegantly dressed businesswoman, 'friend' of Mr Theo, and the source of much gossip in the store, but the Queenie who'd taken them to Caerdovey and looked after them so tenderly. She dried Mary's eyes, gave her a hug, asked someone to fetch tea, and made her sit in a more comfortable chair.

'Would you like to take some time off?' she asked.

'No!' Mary shook her head vigorously. 'I wouldn't know what to do with meself and Mam'd only want to know what was wrong. I suppose you think I'm awful,' she sniffed.

'I'm hardly the person to pass a judgement like that, am I?' Queenie said drily. 'Look, it's a bit soon to get so worked up. The time to worry is if you miss the next one. Until then, come and see me every day for a little chat in the lunch hour, but please cut down on the visits to the lavatory, dear, or Mrs Prymme will only start complaining again.'

Mary wasn't all that surprised when September came but her period didn't. By now she was convinced she was pregnant, a belief only strengthened when one morning she had to rush to the lavatory to be violently sick. Some of her sisters-in-law had suffered from morning sickness so she knew this was a sign.

Later, she presented herself at Queenie's office, shaking with fear.

'Right,' Queenie said briskly. 'I haven't asked before, but who's the father?'

'Some chap I met at a dance.' She couldn't bring herself to tell the truth, not even to the understanding Queenie.

'Does he know you're in the club?'

'I haven't told him, no.'

'Is he the sort who'll marry you, or the sort who'll run a mile?'

'I think he'll marry me.' A feeling of nausea swept over her at the idea of marrying Duncan Maguire, not because of who he was, but *what* he was; Hester's fiancé. She imagined all the ripples it would cause.

'Do you want to marry *him*? What's his name?'

Mary shuddered. 'John, John Smith. I've no choice,

have I, but to marry him?' She'd have married any-old-body rather than have an illegitimate baby. Her name would be mud throughout Bootle and it'd kill Mam.

'Then you'd better tell this John Smith straight away. The sooner you get married, the fewer eyebrows will be raised when the baby arrives early.'

Next day, she'd rung Duncan at his school and they'd met in the waiting room on Marsh Lane Station the same night. He arrived, as drunk as a lord, his green eyes, no longer guileless, sunk in their sockets, empty of all expression. He asked if she was quite sure she was pregnant and she said she'd already started to be sick and was quite positive.

'It'll have to be a registry office,' she said, 'because you're not Catholic and the priest will never agree to marrying us in church.'

Duncan nodded numbly and muttered that he'd see about the licence.

'You'd better make the date as soon as possible. Have you told Hester yet?'

'I'll tell her tomorrow.' It hadn't seemed possible for his eyes to look any emptier, but they did.

Queenie went through Freddy's staff entrance and caught the lift straight up to the sixth floor.

'Lovely day out there,' Eustace said amiably, when they were on the way.

'Perfect!' she enthused. 'Not too hot and not too cold.' She wondered how he knew what sort of day it was when he spent all his time riding up and down in the lift. Perhaps the customers told him.

'You know,' she said, when she entered Theo's office, 'I think you should give Eustace a raise. That's a terribly boring job he does, yet he's always so good-humoured. How long has he worked here?'

Theo was smiling at her from behind his desk. 'For ever,' he said.

'That's even more reason for giving him more money.'

'All right. How much shall it be?'

'At least five pounds a week.'

'There'll be terrible ill-feeling if other staff find out.'

'Tell Eustace one of the conditions of the raise is he mustn't tell a soul. If anyone finds out and complains, say they can have the same as soon as they've been here for ever.'

'Right, that's done.' Theo made a note in his diary. 'Eustace will be one of the best paid employees in the shop.'

'Good!' Queenie collapsed in the chair in front of his desk. She wore a cream, lightweight tweed suit, a cream hat, like an inverted plantpot. Her beige shoes, gloves and handbag all matched. 'I felt terribly over-dressed,' she said. 'Me and Vera were the only guests. Poor Vera, she looked completely bewildered. She'd always looked forward to their Mary getting married, the first and only time she'd be the mother of the bride. But that was a joke of a wedding. Duncan couldn't have looked more miserable if he'd been on his way to the scaffold, and Mary came with a suitcase, worried he'd scarper back to his flat after the ceremony – if you could call it a ceremony – without her.'

She'd only gone for Vera's sake, still cross with Mary, lying to the last, telling her the father's name was John Smith when all the time it had been Duncan Maguire. Had she known the truth, she wouldn't have been so sympathetic during the weeks Mary had been worried she might be pregnant. No doubt Mary had guessed as much and it was the reason she'd lied.

'Imagine what the atmosphere in the flat must be like now?' Theo said.

'I'd sooner not.' Queenie shuddered delicately. 'It'd only depress me.'

Hester Oliver had forgotten how to breathe. At least, that's how it felt, as if, ever since the day Duncan had told her they couldn't get married and that he was going to marry Mary Monaghan instead, she had drawn in a quick, sharp breath, and waited for him to say it was a joke, if not a very nice one, and she could let the breath out again. But it hadn't been a joke, and the breath was still there, like a big lump in her throat, waiting to be released.

Since that day, she hadn't been to work. She didn't care if she never went again. On the day her fiancé married her best friend, Hester lay on her bed, the lump in her throat throbbing painfully, torturing herself, imagining them together; touching, kissing, making love, just *looking* at each other. The thought was so dreadful, so completely and utterly unbelievable, that her brain felt as if it were actually breaking up in a vain attempt to accept that what had happened really had happened.

She clutched her head with both hands and began to scream. It was all right to scream. No one would come. Mummy had taken the day off school to be with her, but had gone to do some shopping, thinking Hester was asleep – she'd only *pretended* to be asleep – Daddy was at work, Gus at school. She screamed and screamed until her throat felt sore and her body ached all over, then began to cry, long, wretched sobs that made her heart break into even more pieces. Each time she cried, the pieces got smaller and smaller. Any minute now, she'd have no heart left.

Chapter 13

On 1 November, *Queen of the Mersey* made her maiden voyage. Trefor Jones had hired a crew of three for six weeks, but the boat was returning to England without its two passengers who were flying back from Athens. Theo wanted to be back in Liverpool well in time for Christmas, December being Freddy's' busiest month. He had never been away from his precious shop for such a long time before and had spent weeks preparing the senior staff for his absence. All had been given the telephone number of the villa in Kythira should an emergency arise that they were incapable of dealing with themselves – something he visualised happening every day – and he could be contacted on the boat by radio telephone. A ship-to-shore set had been installed in his office, and Ronnie Briggs, one of the clerks, had been taught how to use it, much to his delight.

Queenie hadn't envisaged deserting Liverpool and leaving behind everyone close to her, apart from Theo, when they were all so desperately unhappy. Laura and Vera hadn't spoken to each other since the wedding. A bitter and unforgiving Hester had returned to work, but had sworn, understandably, that she never wanted to see her best friend or her ex-fiancé again. Mary and Duncan, also understandably, weren't getting on at all well. Mary had left Freddy's and was stuck in the Waterloo flat by herself when Duncan was at school, stuffing herself with chocolate and gradually becoming covered in spots. She felt too listless to take herself as far as Bootle to see her mother. According to Laura, the other staff, aware of what Duncan had done, hardly spoke to him, and he seemed to have lost all interest in teaching. Twice the headmaster had felt obliged to advise him to pull his socks up. Vera said he hardly opened his mouth at home and slept on the settee in the front room, leaving Mary to sleep alone.

While she packed her clothes, made arrangements for her own job to be covered while she was away on what should have been the holiday of a lifetime, Queenie felt nothing but sadness that the friends, once so close, were friends no more and she had become merely the link between them. She longed to stay and try to put things right, though there was little she could do. It seemed nobody wanted to speak to each other.

Queen of the Mersey had been brought from its permanent mooring in Wales to Gladstone Dock, where the gleaming hull and polished decks provided a stark contrast to the rusty tankers and elderly cargo boats that were its neighbours.

On the day they set sail, Queenie felt a sensation of foreboding when she and Theo got out of the Mercedes – Roy Burrows, Theo's right-hand-man, was driving it back to the garage – and saw the boats were rolling violently in the choppy water. Theo must have noticed her expression and explained it was only because the tide was coming in. 'It'll be calmer out at sea.'

But it didn't feel calmer, not to Queenie. The rolling was slower but just as violent when they ventured into the Irish Sea. She stood on the deck with Theo, aware that land was getting further and further away, that they were surrounded, not just on both sides, but underneath as well, by millions of gallons of water. *Queen of the*

Mersey, which had seemed so big, suddenly seemed very small, and her stomach started to heave along with it. She pulled her hand away from Theo's, rushed downstairs into the bathroom of their pretty cabin and, just in time, vomited in the lavatory.

'Darling!' Theo said behind her. 'I never dreamt you would be seasick!'

All Queenie could manage in reply was a groan.

She spent three days in bed, unable to move except to crawl to the lavatory, unable to eat, too ill to talk. Trefor Jones provided her with a bucket to be sick in. Theo slept in the other cabin as she preferred to be by herself, to fling her wretched, aching body all over the bed without having to care if he was being disturbed.

They had reached the Atlantic by the time she emerged; still aching, still wretched, extremely pale and weak. She managed a bowl of clear soup for lunch and a sandwich for tea. Next day, she ate more, but didn't feel much happier. The water was a dirty grey, it was very cold, the sun was invisible, and she had no wish to go up on deck. There was nothing to see except endless miles of nasty-coloured water. Trefor kept appearing to say they were abreast of somewhere she'd never heard of or, on one occasion, to report they were just leaving the Bay of Biscay, an enormous relief, as she would have been horrified to learn they were in it. She seemed to remember, from the books she'd read, that it was where pirate ships usually came to grief. The weather was relatively calm, though she found even the slight swell quite terrifying.

The fact she found sailing so unpleasant only made her feel more wretched, though in a different way. She *hated* her boat and everything about it and longed to set foot on dry land, yet Theo had had *Queen of the Mersey* built specially for her, had even named it after her, and she badly wanted to love every minute, but all it did was make her feel sick.

They reached the coast of Spain, took an entire day passing Portugal, then Spain again – she couldn't understand why, her knowledge of geography was non-existent. She went to bed, feeling better physically, but fed up to the teeth.

Next morning, Theo woke her with a kiss. 'There's a surprise for you outside,' he said with a chuckle.

'Have we reached Kythira?' she asked hopefully. She'd done her best to hide how miserable she was.

'Not yet, darling. Put on your dressing gown and come and see. There's no need to get dressed.'

'But I'll freeze,' she protested.

'No, you won't, I promise.'

They went upstairs into the lounge, out on to the deck, where the air sparkled brilliantly and the water was a lovely lucid blue and the long, smooth waves were trimmed with lacy white foam. The motion of the boat was a gentle sway. Through the thin material of her dressing gown, she could feel the warm, early morning sun caressing her shoulders. Hector Sutton, who took over Trefor's duties when he was otherwise engaged, waved to them from the wheelhouse. An exhilarated Queenie waved back. So far, she'd hardly exchanged a word with Hector, or the other members of the crew.

'What's happened?' she gasped. It would appear a miracle had occurred overnight.

'We sailed through the Straits of Gibraltar while you were asleep,' Theo said gleefully. 'We're in the Mediterranean. Oh, Queenie!' He took her in his arms. 'I know you've hated every minute so far, even though you didn't say a word. Next time we come, we'll fly halfway and you'll never have to make that terrible journey again. Now, do you feel like a hearty breakfast?'

'Yes!' she breathed. Afterwards, she'd put on her shorts and sunbathe.

That night in the lounge, she and Theo drank champagne and danced to Frank Sinatra records. It was turning out to be the holiday of a lifetime, after all.

Five days later, having stopped for twenty-four hours at the island of Majorca to take on more fuel and fresh supplies of food, they arrived at Kythira, by which time Queenie had acquired a rich, golden tan and couldn't recall ever having felt so relaxed and rested before. She thought frequently about her friends back home but, perhaps because she was so happy, was able to convince herself that everything was bound to turn out all right in the end.

At eleven o'clock one morning, *Queen of the Mersey* docked in the bustling little port of Kapsali, dwarfing the fishing vessels and tiny cargo boats delivering supplies from the mainland, which were being loaded on to horse-drawn carts. Beyond the port, the village of Chora, the capital, soared upwards in a cluster of pretty white houses. Hector Sutton carried the suitcases ashore and Queenie wished him and the crew a temporary goodbye. Trefor, Jim McCardle, the engineer, and Frankie Lucas, who did a bit of everything and was a wonderful cook, were about to sail to Athens for a little holiday of their own, returning in four days to take Theo and Queenie on a cruise around the Ionian Islands.

She was wondering how they would get to the villa in Potamos on the other side of the island, hoping it wouldn't be by horse and cart, when an ancient black taxi drove on to the quayside, the horn honking madly. A giant of a man with long black hair and a delightful smile leapt out and shouted, 'Theo! I've been watching for you from my window. I came as soon as I saw your monstrous boat dock.'

'Peter!'

The two men embraced warmly. Theo took Queenie's hand and drew her forward. 'Darling, this is Peter Vandos, my favourite cousin and best friend, whom I've told you about many times. Our fathers were brothers. We went to school together in Liverpool and he was best man at my wedding, but we haven't seen each other for a good ten years. Peter, this is Queenie Tate. I've mentioned her in my letters, now here she is in the flesh.'

'How do you do, Miss Queenie Tate.' Peter shook her hand politely.

'Your English is perfect,' she commented. 'I don't know a word of Greek.'

'Most of the books I read are in English, I didn't want to lose touch with the language,' Peter said as he stowed the cases in the boot of the cab. 'My father sent me to live in Liverpool with Theo because he wanted me to have a good education, be successful, and make pots of money, something he had never done himself and I was unlikely to do in Kythira. I stayed until I was twenty-one, then decided I'd had enough. I was missing my island too much. I came back and brought her with me.' He patted the roof of the cab affectionately with his big hand. 'She's called Helena. Thirty years ago, you would have seen Helena parked outside the Adelphi Hotel. She is the love of my life, the only taxi on the island, and has provided me with a reasonable living over the years. I am the only Vandos of my generation,' he said proudly, 'who hasn't made a fortune or married into one. I don't believe in having more than is necessary for my simple needs.'

'Peter is very clever, much cleverer than me. He is also

a communist,' Theo said with a smile. 'We used to argue all the time. He accuses me of being a capitalist.'

'Of course you are a capitalist.' Peter gave a good-natured snort. 'You use people, hire and fire them when it suits you. You are a leech on the bum of mankind, sucking the life out of us little people.'

'He's very good to the staff,' Queenie said mildly. She found Theo's cousin somewhat intimidating. She tried to think of other things Theo had said about him and remembered his wife had died in childbirth when they'd been married less than a year. He'd never married again.

'That's nice of him. What does he do? Give them half a crown bonus at Christmas?'

'Are we going to stand on this quay arguing for the rest of the day?' Theo enquired.

'Get in, man. Get in,' Peter boomed. 'What are you waiting for?'

'For you to stop accusing me of all sorts of dreadful misdeeds.' Theo helped Queenie on to Helena's back seat and got in beside her. 'And for your information, I give my staff an extra week's wages at Christmas.'

'Huh!'

To Queenie's relief, Peter forgot about politics and treated her to a running commentary on the various sights as Helena rattled her way through the lush, spectacular scenery, up and down hills, past tiny, white-washed cottages, bigger houses with intricately tiled fronts, a beautiful Venetian mansion with a coat of arms over the studded doors, abandoned houses, the windows empty, gardens overgrown. Now and then she glimpsed a white, deserted beach.

After a while, Helena turned off the road, and went down a steep path, coming to a halt inside a paved courtyard surrounded on three sides by a single-storey white stone building.

'This is it.' Theo opened the cab door and helped her out.

'It's very nice,' Queenie said dutifully.

'My darling girl, this is only the back. Wait until you see the front.'

The sun woke Queenie next morning; narrow stripes of brilliant light bursting through the slatted blinds. Theo was fast asleep beside her. She crept out of bed and went through the door that led to a terrace with a cream tiled floor that ran across the entire front of the house. There were three more doors leading to other rooms. An elaborate stone balustrade separated the terrace from the garden, sheering sharply away in a series of broad shelves, about six feet in depth, covered with lacy vines. Stone steps cut the garden into two halves and finished at a stretch of sand, pure white, looking more like ice the way it glittered in the light of the sun.

She held her breath, reminded a little of her first visit to the sands at Caerdovey, though the view hadn't been nearly so grand, the water not nearly so blue, nor the sand so pure and white. It was hard to credit that so much had happened between then and now.

The sun had only half-risen and looked unnaturally big. She watched it emerge, very slowly, knowing that somewhere else in the world other people were watching as it slipped away and disappeared behind a different horizon. She went down a few of the steps, despite feeling quite chilly in her thin nightie, and turned to look at the white building, but all she could see was the wide terrace and the black tiled roof. There was nothing to tell it was like a palace inside, with its Venetian tiled floors, arches leading from one room to another, little round stained glass windows in the most unexpected places, including the black marble bathroom. Theo said the fittings and the furniture had come from all over the world. His father had spared no expense with his villa in Kythira. He wanted the whole island to know he had become a very rich man.

Queenie ran up the steps, into the bedroom, where Theo was sitting up in bed, rubbing his eyes. He looked rather old, rather creased, rather more than his fifty-three years. She sat on the bed and kissed him. 'Thank you,' she said.

'For what, my darling,' he said sleepily.

'For being you, for loving me, for bringing me to this lovely place, for buying me a boat. For everything.' For some reason she wanted to cry because she loved him so much.

He patted the empty space beside him and she was about to get into bed, when there was a knock at the door and a harsh voice said something in Greek. It was Evadne the housekeeper. Theo shouted back in the same language, then said, 'Evadne saw you outside and has made coffee. Would you like some now?'

She looked reluctantly at the bed, but there'd be plenty of time to make love over the next two weeks. 'I'd love coffee. Could we have it on the terrace? I noticed tables and chairs out there, but I'll get dressed first. It's a bit cold outside.'

Evadne was eighty if a day, a tall, grey-haired woman with a severe, unsmiling face, dressed all in black, including thick black stockings. She looked as if she had been outstandingly beautiful in her day. She had lived in a room at the back of the villa since it had been built, cooking for the frequent guests – Theo let his cousins and their families use the villa whenever they wanted. Last night's meal had been out of this world; yoghurt with cucumber, stuffed vine leaves, and lamb kebabs, a strange combination to Queenie, used to a more conventional menu, but absolutely delicious. Evadne brought the coffee on to the terrace and wished Queenie a surly, 'Good morning.'

'Doesn't she ever smile?' Queenie asked when she'd gone.

'Only rarely. She's led a very unhappy life.'

'Why? What happened? Do you know?'

Theo shrugged. 'She was engaged to my father. He left Kythira to make his fortune and married my mother instead.'

'How awful!' Queenie gasped. 'Did Evadne marry someone else?'

'No. She became my father's mistress. Every time he came back to Kythira they slept together.'

'Did your mother know?'

'Yes. Often she was here, with him, as well as me and some of my aunts and uncles and cousins.'

'Didn't she mind?'

'She minded awfully. They had loads of rows. But my father didn't care what anyone thought. He also had a mistress in Liverpool. Remember Patricia James – Miss James – who interviewed you?'

'Miss James was your father's mistress!' Queenie's jaw dropped so far she heard it crack. 'It was strange,' she said, frowning, 'she was so nice at the interview, but horrible afterwards. Vera said she was jealous, because you were giving me special treatment by putting me on the book counter with Steven.' She laughed. 'She said it was so you could ask Steven questions about me. "Pump him" is how she put it.'

'Vera was right,' Theo said surprisingly. 'Steven is an inveterate gossip. He told me all about the young man you were about to get engaged to. That's why I suggested you become a buyer in the hope of putting you off marriage, at least for a while. You see, from the moment I saw you in Miss James's office, I wanted you for myself, though I had no idea how to go about it. I'm not like my father, who would have invited you into his bed immediately. As for Miss James, in her way, I expect she was only trying to protect you. Like Evadne, she wasted her life on a married man and she didn't want you to do the same.'

Queenie watched a yacht, far away and hardly moving, the white sails resting like a butterfly on the sparkling, sapphire water. 'But I love you,' she said. 'I love you with all my heart.'

'Evadne and Miss James both loved my father,' Theo said drily, 'but that didn't stop them from ending up bitter, lonely old women.' He reached across the table and laid his hand on her cheek. 'That's why I'd like you to have a child, my darling, so you can love each other when I'm gone.'

She took his hand and kissed the fingers, one by one. 'When you're gone, I won't feel the least bitter, just glad that I met you and we had such a wonderful time.' But she had come to the conclusion that, yes, she would very much like a child. She hadn't used her cap since the day of Daniel Monaghan's christening. Nothing had happened so far, but it was early days yet.

Peter was coming to collect them at midday. 'You don't mind, do you?' Theo asked anxiously. 'Helena is the only taxi on the island and buses are few and far between.'

'I don't mind a bit. I liked Peter very much.' She wished she knew more about politics so she could argue with him. 'Won't he lose money, taking us around? Or will you pay him?'

'Peter would never take money off me. I bring him presents instead – presents for Helena. There's a set of tyres on the boat, a magneto, and one or two other things. Spare parts aren't available on the island. I'll give them to him the day we leave.'

'Please don't talk about leaving when we've only just got here.'

'I shall never mention leaving again, not until the time comes.'

They lunched in Chora in a long, narrow restaurant, so dark at the back there were lighted candles on the tables. The meal consisted of *Kotosoupa avgolemono*, which turned out to be chicken soup with egg and lemon, followed by *Piperies sto fourno* – baked sweet peppers – then *Papoutsakia*, which translated as 'little shoes' and was in fact aubergines stuffed with something utterly delicious and covered with an equally delicious sauce – Peter said the dish had about seventeen ingredients and took ages to make. Queenie felt slightly ashamed when her plate was empty in less than five minutes. Delicious it might be, but it seemed an awful waste of somebody's time. She remarked as much to the men.

'There speaks someone who can't cook,' Peter said with a huge, booming laugh. 'For some people, men as well as women, cooking is an art, comparable to writing a poem or painting a picture.'

Queenie confessed she could just about boil an egg. 'Someone's always done the cooking for me and Theo has meals sent up from the restaurant. Sundays, when Freddy's is closed, we eat out.'

'You make a lovely sandwich, darling,' Theo remarked.

'And I can toast them, too,' she said proudly. She felt a little bit drunk, though it couldn't be the wine as she'd only had a single glass. Perhaps it was Kythira itself that was making her feel so strangely lightheaded, so pleasantly inebriated when in fact she was perfectly sober. The small island had an air of mystery about it, an otherworldliness, as if it were set in a different time, a different century. Peter said Kythira was known as the Island of Love and that it was here that Aphrodite had been born.

Later, as they chugged up and down the hills in Helena, she thought it incongruous that they should be sitting in a taxi, even one so ancient, as it seemed entirely at odds with the primitive landscape and the empty villages that hadn't been lived in for a hundred years.

Helena climbed a hill, painfully slowly, and they came to the ruins of another deserted town, Palio Chora, so old that the roofs had long gone, the windows just gaping holes. The town had been built on the edge of a deep abyss she refused to go near. She had no wish to look down, see how deep it was.

'It was here that frantic mothers flung their children, and then themselves, to avoid being captured by the Byzantine pirate, Barbarossa,' Theo said soberly.

Above the stillness, the complete and utter stillness, the smell of dust and decay, the eerie, moaning sound of the wind whistling through the empty windows, Queenie could hear the faint, desperate screams of mothers and the wailing of their babies as they dropped to their death down the abyss only yards away.

'Can we go somewhere else?' she asked in a shaky voice. Kythira was getting to her. She could feel its history, the bad as well as the good, sense the magic that held the island in its thrall. She wasn't herself any more.

Theo was still asleep next morning when she woke. At first, she found it hard to remember where she was because the room looked quite different from the one in which she'd fallen asleep. It took several seconds for her to realise that it was full of dense, white mist that had seeped through a partially open window.

She got up, forgetting she and Theo had made love during the night and she was naked, opened the door, entered the mist, and was aware of a tingling dampness all over her body. Through the door she went, on to the terrace, where all she could see was more mist.

Once again she was reminded of Caerdovey, when the town had been buried in a similar mist. It was the day Carl Merton had died, thrown to his death by two little girls, just as the babies had been thrown into the abyss. She shivered and wondered if she would ever forget that day, the memory of which returned frequently, haunting her with its horror, giving her nightmares. She shivered again, realised she had nothing on, and felt her way back into the bedroom where she cuddled against Theo's warm body, and didn't open her eyes for a long time. When she did, the sun was shining, and the mist had gone, along with her dark thoughts.

'I have to concede, my dear Theo,' Peter said with his huge grin, 'that you are a rather nice capitalist. A Father Christmassy sort of capitalist.'

'Don't talk nonsense, Peter,' Theo said mildly.

'I'm not talking nonsense, old fellow. It's true. You come down the chimney with a sack full of bonuses for your grateful staff.'

'Less of the old fellow, if you don't mind. I'm two months younger than you.'

That was hard to believe, Queenie thought, lazing in an armchair, a glass of after-dinner wine in her hand. She wore a black, crêpe, sleeveless frock, and a white silk stole with a silver fringe. The room was in semi-darkness, only the light of half a dozen candles casting a flickering, dancing pattern on the low ceiling. Outside, the waters of the Mediterranean rippled, a gentle, melodic sound.

In another armchair, Theo looked equally content. On this holiday, for the first time she'd known him, he hadn't worn a tie, though his linen suits were perfectly pressed, the trousers with sharp, knife-edge creases, his immaculate shirts showing too much cuff, as usual. His thick black hair, always a mite too long, was neatly combed and parted.

Peter was lying on a Turkish rug in front of the fireplace where the grate was full of golden leaves. His hair was just as black and thick as Theo's, but even longer, almost reaching his massive shoulders. His face, his brown eyes, were hugely expressive; bright and alive, always laughing, sometimes angry, rarely in repose. He never went to bed before midnight and was always up by five, even when it was dark, when he would read one of his large collection of books, tidy his house, play chess with the devil – the black squares were for the devil, the white for himself. 'I'm always far more cunning and devious on the black squares,' he said.

Since she'd met Peter, she sometimes wished, rather traitorously, that Theo were more like his cousin, that he too had a touch of the devil in him, wasn't quite so set in his ways, so predictable. She watched Peter now through lowered lids. He wore a navy-blue jumper, clumsily darned here and there, with the sleeves pushed up to his elbows, exposing his heavily muscled forearms. His trousers were dark blue made from heavy cotton he said was denim. In America, they were called 'jeans' or 'Levis'. A tourist had sent them to him after he had admired the man's own jeans. 'He's going to bring me another pair next time he comes.'

People loved him, men and women alike. No matter where they went on the island, everyone knew him, called him by his first name, seemed extraordinarily pleased to see him.

She sighed for no reason that she could think of and

Peter looked up. Their eyes met and something indefinable passed between them. She quickly looked away, and thanked God that Theo's eyes were closed and he hadn't noticed.

'I think I'll go to bed,' she said, stretching her arms, and wishing she hadn't when she saw Peter was still watching. 'It's about time you both turned in too,' she said lightly. 'Aren't you getting up at some unearthly hour to go fishing?'

Theo agreed lazily that they were. 'And *Queen of the Mersey*'s due back tomorrow. Trefor phoned to say they'd probably arrive early afternoon.' It was the only phone call he'd received so far and he was rather put out that Freddy's seemed to be managing all right without him.

Next morning, Evadne brought Queenie coffee in bed. 'Good morning,' she said gruffly. That, 'goodnight', 'goodbye' and 'thank you' were the only English words she knew.

'Good morning to you,' Queenie replied. She would have liked to make friends with Evadne, but conversation was impossible when neither spoke the other's language. She gave the woman her biggest smile. Evadne smiled back, said, 'Goodbye,' and left.

Later, when she could bring herself to get out of bed, she decided to sunbathe. There was a bikini in her suitcase, terribly daring, that she'd been too embarrassed to wear on the boat with the crew around. It was white, with a little matching frock to go over, a bit like the wraparound aprons Vera wore, but much shorter. She still felt embarrassed, now, when she looked at herself in the mirror with the bikini on. It showed far too much of her small breasts and the bottom half was hardly bigger than two hankies joined together.

She lay on a rug on the terrace, the frock within reach, so she could put it on the minute she heard the men come back. She preferred Peter not to see her in such a brief garment. What on earth had got into her last night? She hadn't considered it possible to be happier than she already was with Theo, yet she'd actually wished he were more like his cousin. With these rather disturbing thoughts in her mind, Queenie fell asleep.

A voice woke her. The voice had said, 'Well, you certainly fell on your feet.' She looked up, so quickly, that her head swam and the bikini straps fell off, exposing her breasts. She was too busy struggling to pull the straps on to her shoulders to look and see where the voice had come from.

When she did, she was astonished to see Trefor Jones had come on to the terrace. Evadne must have let him in. 'I beg your pardon?' she said stiffly, feeling her face turn red, hoping it wasn't noticeable beneath her tan.

'I said, you certainly fell on your feet.' He wore khaki shorts, a cotton shirt without a collar, and plaited sandals. Out of the smart, white uniform that invested him with an air of authority, he looked very different; just as handsome, but a bit of a rogue, rather rakish. He sat on the balustrade. 'You don't remember me from Caerdovey, do you?'

Queenie shook her head. She got up, still feeling dizzy, conscious of his eyes on her almost naked body. She put on the frock and sat on a chair, so they were more or less on the same level.

'My mother ran the Post Office. You often came in to buy stamps.'

She remembered that the garrulous Mrs Jones had a son who'd joined the Merchant Navy, but couldn't recall having seen him. 'Why didn't you mention it before?'

'Didn't think you'd be interested.' He shrugged and the shadow of a smile crossed his rather grim face. 'I understand you got rid of Carl Merton, did the world a favour.'

'I did no such thing,' she said hotly. 'He fell, on top of me, as it happens. My arm was broken.'

'Seems as if he did *you* a favour. Your arm looks much better than it did.' He reached in his breast pocket for a packet of cigarettes and held them up questioningly. 'Mind if I smoke?'

'No,' she murmured.

'You know, the girl Carl raped, she was in the same class as me at school. Her name was Myfanwy and she was never the same again.'

'I'm sorry,' she whispered.

'So am I. She was a sweet little thing, a bit like you.'

'Really?' Queenie felt uncomfortable. He was looking at her thoughtfully and she wondered what was going on in his mind.

'Nice place Theo's got here.' He turned to look at the garden. 'Still, money isn't everything, is it? Me, I'd hate to be rich if it meant knowing where I'd be this time next year, next month, come to that. Perhaps I'll feel differently when I'm old.'

'Theo's not old,' she said defensively.

'No, of course he isn't. I didn't mean it that way.' She'd like to bet he did, and that the remark was meant for her, not Theo. He thought she was too young to have settled down with a man of fifty-three.

'I think I'll go back to bed. I have an awful headache.'

'It's the sun,' Trefor said sympathetically. 'The terrace is a sun trap and you're not used to it.' He reached for her hand to pull her out of the chair, though there was no need to hold it for quite so long. She was super-conscious of how hard *his* hand felt, how strong, not soft and well-cared for like Theo's. 'Is there anything you want, Queenie?' There was another glimmer of a smile as his eyes fixed on hers. 'Just say the word and I'm at your service.'

'There's nothing, thank you.' Perhaps it was the sun,

the headache, the fact she still felt dizzy, but there seemed to be a double meaning to his words.

She was enormously relieved when she heard a voice bellow, 'Queenie! Where are you? Do you like fish? We caught a whale, especially for you.'

Peter came on to the terrace, followed by Theo, who looked surprised to see Trefor there. 'You're early!' he said. 'I wasn't expecting you till much later. Stay to lunch, why don't you? We caught some trout and a few crayfish. Peter's just given them to Evadne. We're having the crayfish. I don't know how long they take to cook.'

'Thanks, I'd like that.'

Queenie groaned inwardly. She would have preferred Trefor to leave – Peter too. Kythira, the Island of Love, had too many temptations to offer. For the briefest of seconds, while Trefor Jones had been holding her hand, she had wondered how it would feel to be made love to by a young, virile man.

She told Theo she wasn't hungry, that she had a headache and needed to lie down. Everyone had eaten and gone out again – Theo wanted to show Peter over the boat and Trefor went with them – when she got out of bed, found the Aspro, and took them into the sunny kitchen for a glass of water. Her head was thumping madly and she felt sick.

Evadne was there, sitting at the table, smoking a black cigarette, and finishing off the remains of the wine. The dirty dishes were piled on the draining board. Queenie showed her the tablets and turned on the tap, hoping the woman would understand she wanted a glass. Evadne nodded furiously and took a wineglass from the cupboard. She kicked the chair beside her, indicating Queenie should sit down. Queenie filled the glass and did so. She took two Aspro and smiled weakly at the older woman.

'It's hurting,' she said, tapping her head.

Evadne understood. She twisted her face grotesquely and extended her hands, as if to say, 'These hurt too.' Her fingers and wrists were badly swollen.

'You poor thing,' Queenie said sympathetically. 'They look very painful.' She took two more Aspro from the packet. 'These might help a bit.'

'Thank you.' The Aspro were washed down with the wine.

The two women sat companionably together, smiling at each other from time to time, until Evadne got up and made some strong coffee. After it had been drunk, Queenie helped with the dishes, and when Theo and Peter returned, without Trefor Jones she was relieved to see, her headache had completely gone and she felt fine.

After her encounter with Trefor Jones, Queenie had rather gone off the idea of cruising around the Ionian Islands, added to which, she would much sooner stay in the villa. It made her feel guilty, the preference for land over water when Theo had actually had a boat built especially for her.

Even worse, on Sunday morning, when they were due to leave, she was horribly glad when Theo woke up complaining of stomach pains. 'It must be that trout,' he groaned. 'Do you feel all right, darling?'

'I'm fine, but I didn't have trout, did I?' She hadn't liked the sad, frantic look in the dead trout's eyes. She put her hand on his forehead. It was boiling. 'You've got a temperature.'

'I should let Trefor know we're not going, but there's no way of contacting him.'

'He'll soon come looking for us if we don't turn up.'

Not long afterwards, Peter arrived. He wasn't feeling too hot himself, he confessed. It could only have been the fish. Perhaps his constitution was stronger than Theo's as he felt able to drive to Chora and give Trefor a message. 'Then I'll come back and keep Theo company – we can compare symptoms. By the way, Queenie, there's a big market in Potamos on Sundays. Why don't you go with Evadne? You seem to be getting on extraordinarily well. The Vandos women are an arrogant lot, you're the first to treat her like a human being. The market would be better than sitting around all day with a couple of sick old men.'

'Please don't say that.'

'What?' He looked puzzled.

'That you and Theo are old.' Back in Liverpool, she rarely thought about the difference between her age and Theo's, but in Kythira she was being reminded of it constantly.

'All right, two sick *young* men.' Peter gave a half-hearted smile. 'Young at heart, anyway.'

The vivid covers of the market stalls rippled in the slight wind that blew in from an equally vivid sea. Evadne was proudly linking her arm, introducing her to everyone she knew. She'd lost track of the number of hands she had shaken. Everyone seemed very friendly.

Lots of stalls were selling over-sized fruit and vegetables, a selection of which Evadne bought. Queenie was tempted to buy loads of flowers, but they would be awkward to carry with the other woman hanging on to her arm – not that she minded. She did however pause for ages at a stall selling silver jewellery set with semi-precious stones; turquoise, amber, jade, pink quartz. Everything was terribly cheap. It dawned on her she hadn't got a single present to take home.

Within minutes, she had purchased rings with adjustable bands for all the women she knew, including the five members of the War Widows' Club; a long amber bead necklace for Vera, bracelets for Hester and Mary, a tiepin for Roddy, another for Theo with a large milky stone she didn't recognise, but was suitably showy for his taste, and an amethyst pendant, earring and bracelet set for herself. Laura wasn't mad on jewellery and she'd get her something else, a handbag, for instance. As an afterthought, she bought a tiepin for Duncan too. It would be unkind to leave him out.

A few stalls along was one selling clothes, all hand-knitted in a complicated cable pattern, and she got an oatmeal-coloured jumper with a polo neck for Peter, and an extra-long, beautifully warm black cardigan for Evadne, with capacious pockets in which to keep her swollen hands. Both presents she would keep until the day she and Theo left.

'I love buying things for people,' she enthused. Evadne replied in the inevitable Greek.

A few days later, just when Theo was beginning to feel better, the weather changed. The temperature plummeted and it started to rain. Once again, Queenie felt horribly glad. A cruise in the pouring rain wasn't exactly an alluring proposition, Theo decided. They stayed in the villa and Evadne lit fires in the grates. Queenie had brought with her *Gone With the Wind*, which she had been meaning to read for ages. She felt luxuriously lazy, reading by firelight, a glass of wine in her hand, while Theo slept in the chair.

After a few days of this, she had a longing to return to Liverpool, for the holiday to be just a memory. She yearned for her office, the hustle and bustle of Freddy's, particularly at Christmas. In January, she would jet off to

Paris for Fashion Week. She couldn't wait for everything to be normal again.

Home at last, late on Thursday night, Freddy's closed, ghostly and silent, the apartment looking excessively gloomy, as well as feeling as cold as the North Pole. Someone had forgotten to turn on the central heating, which made Theo extremely cross. If such a simple task had not been done, what else, possibly far more important, had been neglected?

It was too late to go out for a meal. Queenie raided the fridge in the restaurant, returning with two meat pies and half a gateau. She heated up the pies in the hardly-used kitchen and made a pot of coffee, thinking Peter wouldn't have been enamoured with such a paltry meal.

They ate in front of the television, which she turned on so loud in an effort to relieve the gloom, that Theo complained his ears were in danger of bursting.

'I'm sorry, I'm missing Kythira,' she confessed. She was being very perverse. This time yesterday, she could hardly wait to get home. Still, the feeling would fade in a few days. There was something else, though, that would take longer than a few days to forget, and that was her betrayal of Theo, if only in her mind; wanting him to be more like Peter, wondering how it would be making love with Trefor Jones.

She looked at him now, Theo, hunched in the chair, his face grey with tiredness. He was the only man she'd made love with and she'd never wanted anyone else. But now she had a feeling she was missing out on something and it wasn't just Kythira.

But Queenie had thrown in her lot with Theo who had always been, always would be, the person closest to her heart – and with Theo she would stay.

Chapter 14

She spent the four-hour train journey in the lavvy, retching as loud as she could when the ticket inspector knocked on the door. 'There's someone sick in here,' she croaked, and the man went away. She only had a few coppers in her purse, not nearly enough to buy a ticket.

It was well after midnight when the train puffed into Lime Street station, too late to catch a tram to Bootle, so she sat the night out on a bench in the waiting room, hardly sleeping a wink. It didn't seem fair, Agnes Tate thought piteously, on a woman of fifty-five who'd led such a dead hard life.

At about six o'clock, the station started to come to life. She went to the ladies, badly needing to pee. A woman was just coming out of one of the lavvies and held the door open, so she didn't have to put one of her precious pennies in the slot. She emerged, feeling better, but a glance at her reflection in the mirror only made her feel worse.

God! She looked a sight. It was ages since she'd been able to afford a bottle of peroxide for her hair. The roots were grey at the front, brown at the back, the ends a horrible orange, brittle and as dry as dust. Her imitation leopard skin coat looked as old as the hills, the collar filthy, the pockets hanging off. As she renewed her lippy, she wondered if it was time to change the colour. Purple lips and orange hair didn't exactly go together. She rubbed off the smudge of mascara underneath her eyes, added more rouge to her sunken cheeks, patted her hair, and made her way out of the station. She passed the restaurant, just opening for the day, and was reminded that she'd kill for a cuppa.

Where the hell did you go to catch the tram to Bootle? She hadn't a clue, couldn't even remember the number, but knew they started from the Pier Head. She'd just have to walk that far, get on a tram there, easier said than done in her flimsy, too-tight shoes, quite unsuitable for wearing on such an icy December day. She needed wide-fitting shoes because her feet had spread, not surprising considering all the standing around she'd done.

It was all Derek Norris's fault. He'd turned out to be nothing but a bloody liar, no more fond of her than she was of him. All he'd wanted was a meal ticket. Agnes hadn't been in London five minutes before she'd found herself on the game.

It had happened quickly, but quite subtly. 'Show this chap a good time, and I'll be grateful for the rest of me life,' Derek had said. 'His name's Ozzie and he's a friend of mine who can throw a bit of business my way, like.' They'd only been there a few days. So far, she hadn't seen the Strand, like he'd promised, and there'd been no sign of the mink coat, a coat of any sort, come to that, though he'd bought her a smart white blouse to wear with her black skirt, and little imitation pearl earrings and necklace to match. They looked quite classy on. They were staying at a mean hotel in Islington, more like a lodging house than anything, sharing the same room, the same bed yet, somewhat surprisingly, he hadn't touched her. Well, not in the way she'd been expecting.

They'd been out a few times, always to the same pub, the Leather Bottle – off Liverpool Road, as it happened.

It was a funny place, not exactly top drawer, but the clientele, men and women alike, were quite well-dressed and she didn't feel out of place. It wasn't long before she realised the women were prostitutes and the men on the look-out for a shag.

She'd thought she was doing Derek a favour, sleeping with Ozzie – it wasn't as if she hadn't done the same thing before. Next day, Derek had given her twenty-five bob, as much as she'd earned in a whole week in the Black Horse, which had been much harder work.

That afternoon, in the same pub, he'd approached her with another 'friend'. Agnes had obliged a second time and had been in receipt of a further twenty-five bob. With it came the suspicion that Derek hadn't brought her to London to give her a good time, but to line his pockets at her expense. She wasn't even faintly disillusioned. It only confirmed her belief that men were all the same. He hadn't let her down because she hadn't trusted him in the first place. She contemplated leaving, finding a job as a barmaid, but after a quick calculation – two shags a day, seven days a week, equalled eight pounds, seventeen and sixpence, an unbelievable sum – it seemed madness to slog herself to death behind a bar for less than half as much. She didn't mind Derek creaming a bit off the top for himself. He saved her the trouble of flaunting herself around, trying to pick up customers on her own, and he usually made sure she had a few drinks down her first.

Before long, she had a nice room to herself in Theberton Street, quite close to the Leather Bottle. All she had to do was bring the customers round the corner. After she'd paid the rent, she spent most of her earnings on clothes, make-up, and loads of fags. It was then she'd bought the leopard skin coat, thinking it was real, if the truth be known.

As Derek had predicted – it was the only thing he'd promised that came true – there were rich pickings during the war, particularly when America joined in and London seemed to be full of Yanks. They weren't short of money and, afterwards, often gave her a quid or two for herself that she didn't mention to Derek, who still gave her her share next morning.

She and Derek were quite chummy and enjoyed sharing a joke. She didn't mind when he took on another girl, Bessie, then a third one called Olive. They'd all sit together in the Leather Bottle and have a good laugh, though none of them laughed when Derek was killed, stabbed in the chest by a member of some gang who ran a whole string of girls and wanted Agnes, Bessie and Olive for themselves, on their books, as it were. Derek, with his own little stable of girls, was regarded as competition and eliminated.

Suddenly, everything changed. By then, the war was over, and Agnes found herself working in the West End, though not in the way she'd always imagined, but standing outside a seedy little flat in Soho with her skirt almost up to her arse, not exactly on for a woman approaching fifty who didn't feel well most of the time. She was expected to service at least a dozen customers a day and they had to be out in half an hour. The men were a different breed altogether to the ones in the Leather Bottle; perverts, most of them, who expected her to do all sorts of horrible things, some of which she'd never even heard of. She was beaten up on more than one occasion, sometimes by Barry, her ponce, who believed in roughing up his girls from time to time. It kept them in line, he claimed. Agnes had never thought of Derek as a ponce, but supposed the description applied as much to him as it did to Barry, though he'd never found the need to lay a finger on his girls. Despite working ten times harder, she earned hardly more than she had done before.

Agnes had stuck it out for a year before running away to Wapping. Once again she'd thought of getting a different sort of job, but she'd been selling her body for so long it didn't bother her any more, and it still paid better than any other work she could think of.

As the years passed, the customers grew fewer as she grew older. She was forced to hang around in the darkest places where her worn, lined face wouldn't be seen. Twice, she went into hospital with pneumonia. A few months ago, she'd collapsed, struck down by a mixture of exhaustion, disillusionment and self-loathing. She was weary of life, of what she'd become. She didn't want to go on living any more.

Some geezer, one of those do-gooder types, had taken her to a convent where the nuns had cleaned her up, fed her, knelt beside her bed and prayed for her wicked soul.

'Do you have a relative who will take you in, care for you?' one of the nuns had asked gently.

'There's not a bugger in the world I can turn to,' Agnes said pathetically. 'Oh, I've got a daughter.' She'd forgotten about Queenie. It was a wonder she could remember her name. It was years since Queenie had crossed her mind.

'Perhaps it's time you threw yourself on your daughter's mercy,' the nun suggested.

'Oh, yeah!' Queenie had been less than useless since the day she was born. 'I don't think I'll bother,' Agnes said to the nun.

She'd left the convent, gone back on the game, sick to her bones with every damn thing. It was then she'd caught the clap and had to go in hospital again.

'If you don't stop smoking, stop drinking, and stop

fucking, you won't last another year,' the young doctor had said brutally. 'You're a complete physical wreck.'

'But how will I live?' Agnes cried.

'I've just said, you won't live, if you continue with what you're doing.' He shrugged. 'It's up to you.'

It was then Agnes decided to return to Liverpool and try to find Queenie, starting at Glover Street. It wouldn't hurt. Queenie might be married, though it could only be to a no-hoper like herself. She might have a room to spare in which she could put up her old mam who'd sacrificed much of her own life looking after her as a kid.

She'd reached the Pier Head, limping badly because her shoes were killing her. The small suitcase containing all her worldly possessions had seemed quite light when she started out, but now felt as if half a dozen bricks had been added on the way. One of the waiting trams had Bootle on the front. She limped towards it. When the conductor came round for the fare, it virtually cleaned her out. If Queenie no longer lived in Glover Street – and it would be amazing if she did – Agnes didn't know what she'd do.

Twenty minutes later, she was hammering on the door of the house to which she'd moved when she'd married George Tate. Looking back, the time she'd spent there hadn't been too bad, especially when compared to the last few years.

The door was opened by a young woman with a huge, swollen stomach, obviously about to drop a baby any minute. She looked extremely annoyed when she saw Agnes. 'It's only half past seven,' she snapped. 'What the hell do you want at this time of morning? I was in bed, and if I hadn't thought you might be the postman, I wouldn't have answered the door.'

'I'm looking for Queenie Tate. She used to live here.

I'm sorry I knocked you up, but it's urgent,' Agnes added. She had completely forgotten the time.

'Never heard of her,' the woman said shortly. She was about to close the door, but Agnes put her hand against it.

'Do you live upstairs or down?'

'Down, but what difference does that make?'

'Who lives upstairs?' If Queenie had married, she'd have a different name.

'The Monaghans; Iris and Dick and their kids.' The woman scowled. 'They make a helluva lot of noise.'

Vera Monaghan had lived somewhere in Glover Street. Dick must be her son, Iris his wife. There was just a chance they might know where Queenie had gone. 'Can I go up and ask them?' Agnes pleaded.

The woman looked her up and down and must have decided she didn't want her in the house. 'I'll ask them for you,' she said shortly, slamming the door.

A few minutes later, it opened again. 'She's at Freddy's in town.'

'Freddy's?' Agnes had never heard of the place.

'Frederick & Hughes. It's a shop in Hanover Street, far too posh for the likes of you and me. I've never been inside.'

'Is she a cleaner?'

'How the hell would I know? Now, if you wouldn't mind, I'd like to go back to bed. The baby's due at the end of the week and I feel like a bloody elephant.'

'I don't suppose,' Agnes said in a wheedling voice, 'that you could lend me a few coppers for me fare back into town? I'll pay you back.'

'You must be joking.' The door slammed shut for the second time.

Agnes looked down at her feet. The heels of her stockings were soaked with blood, the flesh having been rubbed red raw. She daren't remove the shoes to see the state of her toes, as she'd never get them on again. She sighed and hobbled towards the Dock Road. It seemed the quickest way back to town.

The walk was sheer torture. It didn't help that it was so cold, the wind lashing against her, making her ears turn numb. She had no feeling in her hands. Every now and again, she'd stop for a breather and to rest her feet. A foreign seaman approached when she was standing in a doorway. He winked and said something in a foreign language and a suggestive voice. Agnes told him to sod off, though if there'd been somewhere to take him, she wouldn't have hesitated. At least she'd earn a few quid and could catch a taxi straight to Frederick & Hughes' front door. At the rate she was going, the bloody place would be closed by the time she got there.

Eventually, she did get there, so tired that her body felt as if every ounce of strength had been drained out of it – it was almost twenty-four hours since she'd had anything to eat or drink. At times, she'd felt tempted to abandon the suitcase, but everything she possessed was inside.

She dragged herself inside the shop, where the warmth took her so much by surprise she could hardly breathe and the smell of scent threatened to make her puke up her guts. She gasped and grabbed a counter, but her freezing hands slid off the glass and Agnes dropped the suitcase and collapsed in an untidy heap on the floor.

When she came to, she was lying on a bed in what looked like a doctor's surgery, and a nurse was bending over her. Her shoes and stockings had been removed. 'Am I in the ozzie?' she asked.

'No, dear,' the nurse said briskly. 'You're in Freddy's First Aid room. But you'll be in hospital soon. I've rung for an ambulance. It should be here any minute. In the meantime, someone's making you a cup of tea.'

'But I don't want to go to hospital. I came to see Queenie, Queenie Tate. That's the only reason I'm here.'

'I'm afraid that's not possible. She's busy.'

'But I've *got* to see her!' She'd travelled all the way from London in a smelly lavatory, walked through Arctic winds for what felt like a hundred miles, all to see Queenie. Her feet were bleeding, her ears felt like two blobs of ice and ached so much she could hardly hear. Seeing the daughter she'd once so despised, and would probably still despise when they met again, had become something of a mission for Agnes.

'I told you, Miss Tate is very busy,' the nurse insisted.

'Does she know I'm here?'

'Of course not. Why should she?'

'Because I'm her mam, that's why. Tell Queenie her mam's here to see her. She'll come then.'

The tea arrived. The nurse cranked up the bed so she could sit up and lean against the back. Agnes was gratefully sipping the tea, conscious of a tingling sensation in her extremities as the feeling gradually returned, when the door opened and a girl came in. The first thing she noticed was the girl's hair; pale and blonde and as smooth as silk, surrounding her pretty heart-shaped face like a cap. Where on earth had she got such a lovely tan at this time of year? She wore a smart black frock with a white lace collar and cuffs that had obviously cost a bomb, fitting her trim body perfectly. Her shoes were black suede with cut-away sides and had the highest, thinnest heels Agnes had ever seen, hardly wider than a pencil. She was quite stunning, the sort of girl who could have made a mint on the game; twenty, thirty, possibly as much as fifty quid a night, operating from one of the top

London hotels; the Ritz, or the Savoy. She didn't close the door, but held it open, smiling at the nurse. 'Do you mind, Hilda?'

The nurse hurried out. It was obvious the girl was a boss of some sort.

'I'm waiting for Queenie Tate,' Agnes explained, in case the girl wanted to know what she was doing there.

'I'm Queenie Tate, and you, apparently, are my mother.' The girl folded her arms and looked at her with contempt. 'Why are you back, Mam? The best thing you ever did for me was go away.'

'What on earth am I going to do with her?' Queenie demanded of Theo some time later.

'Where is she now?'

'In hospital. She looked on the verge of kicking the bucket, if the truth be known. I hope she kicks it soon.'

'You don't mean that!' Theo sounded shocked.

'I do.' Queenie's usually soft voice was hard. 'She's not *your* mother. You don't know what she was like, the way she treated me when I was little, the things she made me do, the things she used to say. You never saw the place where I used to sleep. When I was four, she broke my arm and didn't bother to have it set. I only remembered that when I was in hospital in Caerdovey, after it was broken again. I hate her, Theo.' She began to weep. 'I hate her so much.'

'Then you shall have nothing to do with her, my darling,' Theo said. 'But nevertheless, she *is* your mother. Leave everything to me. I'll make sure she's looked after.'

When Agnes woke next morning, she was no longer in the ward in which she'd fallen asleep, but a little room on her own. 'What happened?' she asked the nurse who brought her a cup of tea.

'You've been transferred to a private room. And some things arrived for you last night. They're in that bag over there.' There was an expensive tan leather travelling bag on a chair by the window. She noticed her old suitcase on the floor.

'What's in it?'

'I've no idea. Do you want to have a look yourself?'

'Yes, please.'

The nurse put the bag on the bed. 'Don't let your tea get cold,' she said as she left the room.

Agnes unzipped the bag and took the contents out one by one, examining them with increasing wonder.

Nighties, three of them, warm but glamorous, the sort a duchess would wear; a dark green velvet dressing gown, slippers to match – Queenie must have got the size from her shoes, which had been left in the First Aid room. She didn't doubt that all these lovely things had been sent by her daughter. There were towels, two of them, blue, with an embroidered band at each end, a face flannel the same; a big quilted toilet bag containing soap that smelt of roses, a bottle of lavender water, shampoo, talcum powder, face cream, and a hairbrush. A smaller bag held cosmetics; a lovely enamelled compact, rouge, an eyebrow pencil, mascara and a lipstick. Agnes looked at the make – she usually used Rimmell – and gasped when she saw it was Helena Rubinstein.

'Well, Christmas has come early for someone,' the nurse said when she returned to take the patient's temperature. 'That lot looks expensive. You've obviously got some very rich friends.'

'They're from me daughter,' Agnes said proudly. 'She's got some dead posh job at Freddy's.'

'Me daughter!' She whispered the words under her

breath. 'Me daughter.' Queenie hadn't exactly looked pleased to see her but, secretly, she must be glad her mam was back to send all this lovely stuff. She imagined her, walking round Freddy's, picking things out. 'Mam'd love that, oh, and she's sure to like that.'

She wondered why Queenie wasn't married? That nurse had known who she meant when she'd asked for Queenie Tate. She was pretty enough to nab a millionaire, just like Rita Hayworth had captured that Aly Khan geezer.

Agnes felt as if she'd just glimpsed the eighth wonder of the world. She had a daughter, a rich, pretty, successful, *single* daughter who would look after her mam in her old age. Queenie was bound to ask if she'd move in with her, they'd go to the pictures together, perhaps on holiday – she hadn't got that tan in England in December. She rubbed her hands gleefully, more glad that she'd returned to Liverpool than she'd been about anything before. In fact, she'd have come back sooner if she'd known Queenie was going to turn into such a bobby dazzler. Or perhaps never left in the first place. Think of all the suffering she'd have missed if only she'd stayed.

Perhaps it was thinking about suffering that made her remember Queenie's arm. Fancy forgetting a thing like that! She must have had an operation and had it set proper, because now it looked so perfect no one would ever guess there'd been anything wrong.

'To tell the truth, I'm moidered to death,' Queenie complained. It was a few days after her mother's return and she'd gone to see Laura, who asked how she was. 'Mam's back, but you already know that, and Irene, Theo's wife, keeps phoning, threatening suicide. She knows about Kythira and is wildly jealous. To cap it all, this afternoon, the hospital rang; would I mind going in to see Mam? Apparently, she's pining for a visit.'

'Are you going to go?'

'Not likely!' Queenie felt on the verge of exploding. 'I'm not going anywhere near her. Theo's arranging for a place for her to live. He's got some Greek thing about children respecting their parents, no matter what they've done. It upsets him that his girls will have nothing to do with him. *He* can go and see my mother if he likes. If it had been up to me, I'd have sent her away with a few bob and a flea in her ear.'

'I've never seen you quite so mad,' Laura remarked.

'I've never *felt* quite so mad.' She shook her head impatiently. 'Oh, let's change the subject, talk about something else. Have you asked Hester if she'll come to Paris with me?'

'Yes, and she'd love to. She's sent you a letter to say as much. At Christmas, she intends to leave that job, find something new and more interesting, even go abroad.' Laura gave a tired smile. 'Things have turned out so differently than I expected. By now, I thought we'd be immersed in plans for the wedding, that Hester and Duncan would get a house nearby, have children, and that we'd all be together, one big happy family.' She looked very listless, as if it was her who'd been jilted, not her daughter.

'You're letting things get you down far too much. Anyroad,' Queenie said darkly, 'I don't think there's such a thing as a happy family. Have you seen Vera yet?'

'No. The trouble is, I blame Mary for the whole horrible situation, and Vera probably blames Duncan. After all, he was Hester's fiancé, and she'll think we should have kept him under control. If we meet, I'm sure we'll row.'

'Don't talk daft, Laura. I don't see how it's anyone's

fault except Mary and Duncan's. OK, she seduced him, but he didn't have to let himself be seduced. He's not an animal. If anyone should have kept Duncan under control, it was Duncan himself.'

Agnes was in hospital for five days. Her blood and urine were checked, her eyes, ears and throat examined, her chest X-rayed, and other tests carried out. It was fortunate that the antibiotics she'd been given in London had cleared up the clap, otherwise she'd have felt dead ashamed. She was pronounced malnourished, anaemic, but otherwise reasonably healthy, and advised to cut down on the ciggies, eat a more balanced diet, and take the iron tonic she'd been prescribed. By now, the rest had made her feel immeasurably better. Not a drop of alcohol had passed her lips, she'd had fewer fags than usual, and hadn't been in a position where she could ply her trade.

On Saturday morning, she sat on the bed, waiting to be discharged and wondering what would happen to her now. It had been a bit of a comedown, putting on the leopard skin coat and her other old stuff after the expensive things she'd been wearing all week, but they were the only outdoor clothes she had. Furthermore, she was wearing the velvet slippers – she assumed her shoes had been chucked away.

A nurse entered with two large carrier bags. 'These have come for you,' she said. 'The chap said to tell you he's coming back to collect you at twelve o'clock. The doctor will be along in a minute to sign you out.'

'Ta.'

The bags were black and white striped with a string handle and had 'Freddy's' on the side in big, gold letters. The first contained a coat wrapped in leaves of tissue; camel, double-breasted, with horn buttons and a big collar to turn up against the cold. It felt soft and rich when Agnes held it out. She looked at the label; cashmere. Lord Almighty! She felt herself trembling. She'd never worn cashmere in her life. In the other bag, she found a brown jumper and skirt, underwear, stockings, brown leather gloves and a handbag to match, a hat shaped like a turban that would cover her ears, and brown boots lined with fur. She'd have had to work years to pay for this lot.

She was sitting by the reception desk, wearing her finery – everything fitted perfectly – having left all her old stuff behind with instructions to the nurse to dump it in the bin, when a well-dressed, smooth-cheeked man in his forties came in, went over to the desk, and spoke to the receptionist.

The woman nodded in her direction, and the man approached and picked up her bag. 'Good afternoon, Mrs Tate,' he said courteously. 'I'm Roy Burrows, Mr Vandos's personal assistant. Would you like to come with me?'

Agnes got wordlessly to her feet and followed him outside. It was a cold, dull day, but not as cold as when she'd arrived, though perhaps it was the coat and boots keeping her warm. She climbed into the back seat of a long grey car, as big as a bus, and Mr Burrows put her bag in the boot, then slid behind the steering wheel. The car moved away, the engine hardly making a sound.

'Where are we going?' she asked nervously after a while.

'Freddy's.'

'Will Queenie be there?' She was disappointed Queenie hadn't come with Mr Burrows to pick her up.

'I'm afraid Miss Tate isn't in today. She's in London.'

'Who's Mr Vandos?'

'The owner of Freddy's.'

Agnes got the impression he didn't want to talk. 'I see,' she said, though she didn't see at all.

The car drew up in a little street that turned out to be the back of Freddy's. Mr Burrows jumped out and opened the door for her to alight.

'What about me bag?'

'It's all right to leave it in the car. I'll be back for you in a few hours' time.'

A dazed Agnes was taken through the staff entrance, along a narrow corridor, through a swing door, emerging in the sparkling brilliance and deafening chatter of Freddy's ground floor. She had hardly time to take it in when she was led through another door marked 'Lift'.

The ornate lift was operated by an ancient individual wearing a splendid green and black uniform trimmed with gold.

'Fifth, please, Eustace,' said Mr Burrows.

Eustace treated both to a beaming smile. 'Funny old day out there today,' he said, shaking his head in bafflement, as if it was the funniest day he'd ever encountered in his life.

'Am I going to see Mr Vandos?' Agnes whispered. It was all incredibly mysterious.

'No, Mrs Tate. You're going to the hairdresser's. Valerie, the manageress, will look after you.'

She hoped she wasn't expected to pay, as there was only tuppence left in her purse.

Valerie looked about the same age as Agnes, but there the similarity ended. Her blonde hair was beautifully coiffured, her make-up perfect, and she spoke dead posh. Like all the staff, she wore a cream nylon overall with a blue collar. Agnes had never been in a hairdresser's before, but would like to bet that few were as sumptuously fitted out as this one, with such plump, comfortable leather chairs, gleaming silver dryers, row upon row of sparkling mirrors with their own individual strips of light.

'Well, I think that orange frizz needs getting rid of,' Valerie said sternly when Agnes was tucked inside a blue gown, and seated in front of a mirror where the strip light showed up every one of her wrinkles and her ghastly piebald head.

'I've been so busy, I haven't been near a hairdresser's in ages,' Agnes lied.

'I suggest you stick to your original colour. It's quite a nice shade of brown at the back and I could dye the grey at the front to match. What do you think?'

'Yes, please,' Agnes said meekly.

Valerie attacked the orange frizz with gusto. 'You look better already,' she said when it had all gone. She ran her fingers through the remaining hair. 'You know, I'm not sure that you need a perm. This is nice and thick and it's got a bit of lift to it. An urchin cut would look nice. They're all the rage at the moment and very easy to look after.'

'Anything you say.' She was perfectly happy to leave everything to Valerie, to just sit there, completely relaxed, and listen to the hum of the dryers, savour the smells, smile at the girl who put a black towel around her neck and began to apply dye to the front of her head.

'Would you like coffee or tea?' the girl asked when she'd finished.

'I'd love a cup of tea.'

Jesus! This was the life. As well as tea, she was handed half a dozen glossy magazines. Flicking through them, she didn't feel as alienated from the smartly dressed models inside as once she would have. 'Far too posh for the likes of you and me,' the young woman in Glover Street had said about Freddy's. Agnes would have agreed with her then, but not now.

Another girl approached, pushing a little trolley and smiling. 'Would you like a manicure while you wait?'

'I wouldn't say no,' she gulped.

She'd heard people say they felt like a million dollars, but it was the first time it had happened to her. If the truth be known, the hairdresser's had done her more good than the ozzie.

'Where are we going now?' she asked when Mr Burrows arrived to collect her and they got in to the car parked behind the shop.

'Aigburth Drive.'

It must be where Queenie lived. Well, Queenie was certainly doing her old mam proud – though not so much of the old, Agnes chided herself, not now. The new hairstyle had taken off a good ten years; she could have sworn some of her wrinkles had disappeared along with the orange frizz.

It wasn't long before the car drew up outside a big, double-fronted, detached house with a neatly tended garden. Mr Burrows got out, opened her door, and collected the tan bag from the boot. She followed him down the drive. The front door opened when he turned the knob – she was surprised it wasn't locked. Inside was a square, carpeted lobby, the only furniture a fancy little table with a pile of letters on top. Four doors, all numbered, led off. Mr Burrows produced a key and opened the door marked '1', and they entered an enormous room with an equally enormous bay window framed by silky grey curtains and overlooking the front. The walls were covered in paper that matched the curtains, the furniture was elegant, the carpet expensive. A bowl of fresh flowers stood on the vast mantelpiece.

'Is this where Queenie lives?'

Mr Burrows shook his head. 'No, this is yours. It's a

flat. The bedroom is at the back, along with a kitchen-cum-dining room and a bathroom.'

'I could never afford the rent for a place like this!' she gasped.

'You won't have to. Mr Vandos will see to any expenses. He said to give you this.' He handed her an envelope. When Agnes looked, it was jammed with pound notes, at least a hundred. 'That's to buy clothes or any other odds and ends you might need. As from Monday, you will be in receipt of a weekly allowance. I suggest you start a bank account. It will make things easier.'

'But what about Queenie? When will I see her?' Agnes cried.

'I'm afraid I know nothing about Miss Tate's movements.' As ever, his voice was neither cold nor warm. He handed her a card. 'If you have any problems, get in touch.' He bowed slightly from the waist. 'Goodbye, Mrs Tate. I hope you'll be happy in your new home.'

Everything matched. In the bedroom, the blue eiderdown matched the quilted headboard, the pans matched the frying pan in the kitchen, and they in turn went with the kettle and the electric toaster. Virtually everything in the yellow bathroom was yellow.

Agnes didn't know why, but as she wandered round the lovely rooms, so tastefully and thoughtfully furnished, she began to feel less and less like a million dollars. Memories kept returning, tumbling into her mind. Memories of Queenie, the only ones she had, the only ones Queenie would have. They had started in the bedroom, when she'd given the eiderdown a tug as it wasn't quite straight. It was then something had clicked in her brain, moving it into a different gear. She looked up and saw her reflection in the dressing-table mirror, except it wasn't the right reflection. Her blood ran cold when she saw herself a good twenty years younger, possibly more, tugging at a different eiderdown, threadbare and full of lumps. There was a child lying in the middle, curled up in a ball, fast asleep.

'Lazy little bitch!' the reflection screamed. 'So this is what you do when I'm at work.' The eiderdown was pulled with such force that the little girl, startled out of her wits, had been thrown on to the floor. There were other things, endless other things; bruises and cuts, wallops around the head, bashings and beatings for no reason at all.

'I wish I'd given you away at birth; I wish you'd never been born. Get out, I can't stand the sight of you. You're useless, as thick as two short planks, as ugly as sin; I *hate* you.'

'I was the worst mam in the world,' she whispered, trembling ever more violently as the memories piled in. Of Queenie standing on a chair in front of the sink attempting to wring out the washing; keeping the girl up till all hours so she could make a cup of tea when she came home from the pub; leaving when she was barely fourteen and hadn't a job to go to. What had happened? she wondered, glancing around the expensively furnished room. How had Queenie been able to afford all this stuff?

'I never bought her a single toy. I never *talked* to her. I only shouted.'

And there was, of course, the broken arm. The fact that Queenie, so rich and smart, so lovely, shared precisely the same memories as her mother, made the shame ooze like treacle through Agnes's veins.

Her daughter had only provided all this stuff through the goodness of her heart. 'The best thing you ever did for me, Mam, was go away,' she'd said.

She would never see Queenie again, of that she was convinced. She would never get the chance to apologise. Agnes lit a cigarette and sank into the settee. Never had she envisaged ending up in such opulent surroundings. And never before had she felt so wretched and so alone.

'I suppose,' Queenie said later the same day, 'I should thank you for everything you've done for my mother. But I didn't ask you to do it, Theo. There are millions of women, far more deserving, that you could have spent your money on.'

'She kept asking for you. Roy Burrows said she thought the house with the flat was yours, that she was moving in with you.'

'Ugh!' Queenie shuddered delicately. 'Hell could freeze over before I'd live with *her*.'

Theo looked at her strangely. 'You certainly know how to bear a grudge, darling. Remind me never to get on your wrong side.'

Queenie lost her temper. She'd been losing her temper a lot since they got back from Kythira. The holiday had been very unsettling. 'Stop saying things like that,' she cried. 'Unlike you, I'm not a saint. I can't suddenly feel love for a woman who doesn't know the meaning of the word. She hated me, she told me so enough times.' Theo opened his mouth to speak and she stamped her foot. 'And please don't say, "But she's your *mother*, Queenie," as if that made an iota of difference. If it hadn't been for Laura, God knows how I would have ended up. In the poor house, begging on the streets, and if my mother had known, she wouldn't have given a damn.'

'Isn't Laura coming to dinner tonight?' He must have decided it was wise to change the subject.

'Yes, and Vera.'

'I thought they weren't speaking.'

'They will be by the time dinner's over,' Queenie said grimly.

Theo wouldn't be there for dinner. Tonight was the Freddy's Christmas party and he always put in an appearance. These days, he went alone, his unwilling family no longer forced to accompany him, and Queenie equally reluctant, but only because she would imagine everyone looking at her, nudging each other, telling the new staff, if they didn't already know, that she was his 'bit on the side'.

He left at seven, looking faintly like a Mafia Godfather in an evening suit and an over-large bow tie. When the door to the apartment opened, Queenie could hear music coming from the restaurant and thought wistfully how much she'd like to go with him, enter the room on his arm.

'Laura's here, darling,' he shouted before closing the door.

'I always feel as if I'm entering a time warp when I come here,' Laura remarked when she entered the big living room with its heavy, brooding furniture and darkly patterned walls. 'It feels very Victorian.' She threw herself into a stiff, leather armchair. 'What are we having to eat? I bet it's not something you made yourself.'

Queenie laughed. 'It's Christmas dinner, actually, from the restaurant; turkey, stuffing, roast potatoes, all the usual, followed by Christmas pud.'

'Yum, yum. I'm starving.'

'Would you like wine or sherry now?'

'Wine, please. White. I don't know if you're supposed to have white with Christmas dinner. If not, I don't care.'

Queenie went into the kitchen. She was pouring the

wine when she heard the doorbell ring. It must be Vera. 'Will you see who that is, please?' she called.

She poured a glass of sweet sherry, Vera's favourite. When she returned, the two women were weeping in each other's arms and she clucked with satisfaction. It was what she'd hoped would happen when they came face to face.

'I've missed you so much,' Vera sobbed.

'And I've missed you,' sniffed Laura.

'How's your Hester? Oh, I was so sorry about what happened.'

'Me too. As for Hester, she's better than she was, but I'm not sure if she'll ever get over it. What about Mary?'

'She's as miserable as sin, but as I said to her, "You made your bed, girl, so you'll just have to lie on it." As for Duncan, he seems the most miserable of all. At least the girls have got their families around. He hasn't got a friend in the world.'

'I brought him and Mary presents from Kythira. He seemed pathetically pleased,' Queenie remarked. She put the drinks down. 'Vera, I've brought you sherry and, Laura, here's your wine. I'll get dinner in a minute.' She sighed with pleasure, relieved her friends had made up in time for Christmas, and looking forward to a good old jangle over the meal.

Chapter 15

It was the worst Christmas of Mary's life. She only received two cards; one from Queenie, the other from Mam. Duncan got one signed by his mam and sisters, but not by his dad who didn't believe in such things. She'd no idea if he'd told them about her, about the baby, and that he wasn't going to marry Hester.

The mantelpiece looked dead miserable with just three cards, so she'd stuffed them in a drawer. Her brothers still weren't speaking to her and nor were the Olivers. It was the first time since they were little that she and Hester hadn't spent Christmas together. They'd always gone to loads of dances – she particularly missed the one on New Year's Eve in St George's Hall.

Mary crammed another chocolate in her mouth. It was Turkish Delight, one of her favourites, but she wouldn't have cared if it was a hated nut praline so long as it was covered in chocolate, preferably milk. Perhaps she should take up smoking instead. At least ciggies wouldn't make her fat and give her spots.

She wondered what to give Duncan for tea that night. Something nice, a casserole of some sort, or liver and bacon with mashed potatoes, which was his favourite. He hadn't *said* it was his favourite because they hardly spoke to each other, but he always ate it faster than anything else she made. The only good thing about Christmas had been the food – and the drink. Duncan had spent most of the time in a drunken haze while she stuffed herself with chocolates, thinking about the house in Glover Street, which would be bursting at the seams whatever the time of day. Mam hadn't managed to come and see them until New Year's Eve. 'Lord Almighty, girl,' she'd puffed, 'this last fortnight, it's been like living in the middle of Lime Street station. This is the first free minute I've had to get away. Where's Duncan?' She tried hard to be nice to Duncan, but the trying showed.

'At the pub.'

'You should've gone with him, luv. It'd've got you out the house for an hour or so.'

'I didn't want to, Mam. Anyroad, if I'd gone, I wouldn't have been in when you came, would I?' The truth was, Duncan hadn't asked. He went to the pub most nights, to escape from her and the tragedy their lives had become.

She decided to do liver and bacon for tea. It was Duncan's first day back at school after the holiday. He'd looked extra-miserable when he'd gone this morning.

Mary sighed, put on her hat and coat, and walked to the South Road shops. There was half an apple pie in the fridge, which she'd warm up for afters with custard. She'd discovered she quite liked cooking. It was said that the way to a man's heart was through his stomach, but she didn't think that would apply to Duncan whose heart already belonged to someone else.

Things had been bad enough before, but over Christmas, Duncan thought he could quite easily go mad. Months ago, he'd been invited to stay at the Olivers' over the holiday. The contrast between what could have been, and what was, struck him like a blow every time he thought about it.

Christmas morning, he honestly felt like killing himself

when he woke up on the settee and considered the day ahead. He lay there, imagining himself at the Olivers', kissing Hester under the mistletoe when he gave her her present. He'd intended getting presents for everyone, had even bought one – a leather-bound volume of Shakespeare's plays for Gus. It was around somewhere.

He tortured himself, thinking about dinner, wearing a paper hat, pulling crackers. It would have been his first *real* Christmas and, what's more, would have been spent with the woman he loved. Instead, he was spending it with Mary, for whom he felt nothing at all.

There were noises in the kitchen. Mary was up. A few minutes later, she came in with a cup of tea. They looked at each other. Neither felt inclined to wish the other Merry Christmas. Mary merely nodded. 'Breakfast will be ready in a minute.'

He'd say this much for her, she looked after him well. She washed his clothes, ironed them perfectly, kept the flat clean, prepared exceptionally tasty meals. His lips twisted bitterly. She was the perfect wife in every way but one; she wasn't Hester. He'd been expecting histrionics, rows, accusations of blame once they were living together, but there'd been nothing of the sort. He guessed she felt as responsible as he did for the position they were in.

'You're seriously overweight,' the woman doctor said at the end of January when Mary climbed on to the scales in the pre-natal clinic. 'You've put on more than a stone since December, two and a half stone since you first came.' She gave Mary a severe look. 'You're only twenty, you're not very tall. Do you want to lose your figure completely at your age? You'll find it hard, caring for a young baby, when you've got so much fat on you.'

'I've got a weakness for chocolate,' Mary confessed.

'Ah, and so that accounts for the awful skin. I suggest you get a weakness for apples or something equally healthy. Give the chocolate a miss from now on.'

Mary didn't answer. She wasn't all that bothered if she got fat. She'd always been a fraction plump, but it was an endearing, cuddly plump, or so she'd been told. What point was there in staying attractive for a husband who didn't love you and never would? She'd far sooner gorge on a box of Cadbury's Milk Tray than eat a single apple. The afternoons were the worst, when the housework and the shopping had been done and she was left to her own devices, to look out of the window at the flat, deserted sands, the grey, leaden waters of the Mersey, the occasional lonely ship sailing past, and to think about the fine old mess she'd made of her life.

It was Duncan who made her look at things in an entirely different way – she doubted if he'd noticed how fat she was, or that her face was full of spots – but he came home from school one day in January with a strange look on his face; thoughtful and determined.

'I've been thinking,' he said the minute he was in. 'After the baby's born, it'd probably be best for both of us if I went home, back to Scotland and my family. I'll send you a weekly allowance and you can either stay here, or live with your mother. In fact, Vera could look after the baby and you could go to work. If you like, we'll get divorced. It's up to you. I'll never get married again.'

'What about Hester?'

Duncan shrugged and said simply, 'Do you think she'd have me now?'

'Not really.' After a week spent in Paris with Queenie, Hester was now in California, Hollywood, to be precise, where Steven Vandos was making a film and had offered to find her accommodation and a job. When Mary heard, she'd felt green with envy. Trust Hester to emerge from the mess on top.

'What do you say?' Duncan asked.

'Would you stay if I wanted you to?' She just wondered.

'No, but I'd sooner leave knowing you agree that we'd both be better off without each other.'

'You're right,' she said with a sigh. 'We would.'

'Right then.' He nodded grimly. 'Tomorrow, I'll tell the headmaster I'll be leaving at the end of term. You're supposed to give a whole term's notice, but he'll probably be too glad to get rid of me to mind. I haven't been much of a teacher over the last few months. I'll hang around for a couple of weeks after the baby's born, make sure everything's all right. What date is it due?'

'The fifteenth of April.'

'Right then,' he said again. 'I'll leave on the first of May.' He smiled for the first time since they'd got married, but it wasn't a very happy smile. 'I'm glad that's sorted out.'

The more Mary thought about the idea, the more she liked it. The day they'd got married, a photographer from the *Bootle Times* had been hanging around the registry office and there'd been a picture in the paper with their names underneath for all the world to see. If she went back to Glover Street with a baby, no one would think there was anything funny about it. She'd tell people she and Duncan hadn't hit it off. She could go back to work at Freddy's, make new friends, go dancing. And if she and Duncan divorced, she could even get married again. All of a sudden, life seemed worth living. There was a reason to stay attractive. As from tomorrow, she'd cut out the chocolates, go for walks, do exercises, and eat apples by the dozen.

Now that they knew they weren't stuck with each other until the end of time, they found it easier to talk.

'What will you do with yourself in Scotland?' Mary asked after tea.

'Teach, I suppose.' He didn't look exactly pleased about it. She remembered Hester saying his father was very strict and bullied his mother terribly. His sisters couldn't wait to get married and leave home.

'Why don't you do something more exciting?'

He closed his eyes momentarily and his face wore an expression of utter weariness. 'I want peace, not excitement.'

'I can't wait to go dancing again.'

'You've been very good, Mary,' he said, looking at her directly. 'It's been hard for you, hasn't it? You must miss your old life badly, but you've never shown it. You'll make someone a fine wife one of these days.'

'And you'll make someone a fine husband. I'm just sorry it wasn't Hester.'

He didn't go out that night, but sat at the table correcting a pile of exercise books. When had he done them before? she wondered. It must have been when he got back from the pub when he wasn't exactly sober.

At ten o'clock, she made cocoa and a sandwich. Duncan stretched his arms and took them gratefully. 'I think I'll sleep well tonight for the first time in ages.'

'I'm hardly likely to sleep at all. The baby kicks like mad all night long.'

'Does it?' He looked astonished. 'I can't imagine it being *real*.'

'It's real all right.' Mary grimaced.

'I wonder if it will be a boy or a girl? You know, I hadn't thought of that before.'

'I don't think about it much either. Sometimes, all this,' she swept her eyes around the room, 'seems very unreal, and one day I'll wake up and find it hasn't happened.'

'You know,' Duncan said, 'I often feel the same.'

Late in February, she found herself unable to keep still, unable to settle to anything. She managed to snatch only a few hours' sleep a night. Duncan started getting up first and fetching her a cup of tea. 'Have you had a bad night?' he'd ask sympathetically.

'No worse than usual,' she would reply. She felt enormously heavy and badly in need of a crane to turn her over. She'd lost some weight, but not enough to make much difference. Her spots had completely gone.

'If you ever need anything in the middle of the night, just give us a shout,' he said one morning. 'A drink, a hand with turning over, or just to talk. It might help if you went for a walk before bedtime. We could stroll along the beach.'

From then on, every night after they'd eaten, they'd walk along the sands. She linked his arm, she had to as she needed his support. Sometimes, they came back via South Road, turning right into Crosby Road, then down Cambridge to the Esplanade and home, where Duncan would make cocoa for them both and a sandwich for himself.

One night, halfway along South Road, she paused in front of a shop with a display of tiny clothes in the window. 'I haven't got anything new for the baby,' she said. 'Mam's given me loads of things, but they're all second-hand. They might even be third- or fourth-hand, for all I know.'

'We can't have our baby wearing fourth-hand clothes,' Duncan said indignantly. 'Let's make a list of everything we need and we'll get them on Saturday. It'll need a bed too, and a pram.'

'Queenie's offered to buy us a pram.'

'Good for her.' He thought the world of Queenie who'd bought him a tie pin back from Greece. It was nice to know that there was one person left who didn't hate him.

It was almost April, the last day of term and Duncan's final day at school. He seemed almost cheerful when he left. Mary had asked the other night if he'd written to his family telling them to expect him home shortly.

'Not yet. I keep hoping another, more appealing idea will hit me. But it hasn't, yet.'

'Once you leave school, you won't have a job.'

'I've enough money to tide me over – tide *us* over. I was thinking about what you said the other week, about doing something exciting. I don't know why, but I don't feel quite as hopeless as I did. I might even stop teaching and do something different.'

Mary didn't feel even faintly hopeless. The future looked very bright, as did the view, she noticed when she looked out of the window and watched Duncan get into the little blue car he kept parked outside. The sun shone brilliantly, making the water glisten and turning the sands into a gleaming patch of gold. A woman pushed a pram, a toddler at her side – a little boy wearing Wellingtons and a duffle coat. Every now and then, he would desert his mother – she assumed it was his mother – to try to capture one of the gulls pecking at the sand in search of scraps.

She eased herself down on to the settee with a groan. She'd wash the dishes and tidy up later. After only a few minutes, she felt the urgent need to go to the lavatory, and uttered another groan as she struggled to get up. Halfway, she felt a wave of pain pass through her stomach.

A contraction! She'd had her first contraction! The baby must be coming early, though it might be a false alarm. She stumbled into the lavatory, then to the kitchen where, for some reason, she began to wash dishes like a mad woman, worried the baby might come before she'd had time to dry them. She made the bed and tidied up with the same, desperate panic. She was dusting the mantelpiece, only dusted the day before, when she had another contraction that made her double up in agony.

The baby was definitely on its way. By the end of the day, she would be a mother. She thought of another day, in this very room, when she'd pressed herself against Duncan, teasingly, thinking it was nothing more than a game, regretting it now with all her heart. 'This isn't what I want,' she whispered.

She took her suitcase from under the bed, not sure whether to go to the maternity hospital in Southport now, or wait until the contractions were becoming more frequent. She decided to go now, badly in need of company, not wanting to be alone with the pain, wishing Mam was on the telephone so she could call her. Perhaps she should phone Duncan. Since they'd decided to separate, they'd become friends. But did she want him there in the intimate hours before the birth? And afterwards, with the staff congratulating him on becoming the father of a child he didn't want and might never see again after he'd gone back to Scotland?

Oh, but she needed *someone*, and Duncan was the only friend she had. She picked up the telephone and dialled the number of the school.

Duncan Maguire was nowhere to be found. The classroom was empty when the school secretary went to say his wife urgently wanted to speak to him. Then she remembered; all the classes in year five had gone to the

Odeon in Waterloo to see *Richard III*, which was included in that year's English O-level syllabus. The cinema had arranged a special showing for schools in the area and the headmaster thought it would be a treat for the children on their last day at school before the Easter holiday. The secretary somehow doubted this.

She wondered if she should ring the Odeon and ask the manager to put a notice on the screen, but it seemed a bit extreme. It would be best to phone the wife and explain the situation, see what she thought. But when she rang the Maguires' number, there was no reply. 'Well, it can't have been all *that* urgent,' she said to herself, replacing the receiver in its rest.

By this time, Mary had also remembered about the film and was on the train on her way to Southport. The contractions were coming about every quarter of an hour and she was worried the baby might arrive any minute. She looked around the carriage to see if there was anyone who looked up to giving a hand with the birth, but there were only two very elderly men arguing over something that happened during the First World War, a young woman with her arm in a sling, an enormously fat man having a conversation with himself, and a middle-aged couple who seemed to be deliberately ignoring each other. The woman looked reasonably capable, but the pair got off at Formby.

She was relieved when the train drew into Southport and the baby was still in place. A porter leapt forward to take her suitcase.

'Shall I put you in a taxi, luv?' he asked anxiously.

'I think you'd better.' She hoped the driver would know what to do if she gave birth on the back seat.

It was almost midday when Duncan got back to school

and was told of Mary's message. Wordlessly, he rushed out to the car and drove home, half-expecting to find Mary prostrate on the floor and a baby crawling around the room. But the flat was empty, as well as being beautifully tidy, he noticed. He looked under the bed, saw the suitcase had gone, ran back to the car and set off for Southport. He had no idea why he was in such a hurry to get there. Perhaps it was because he knew the child about to be born would be his only child.

He found Mary on her own in a room adjacent to the delivery room. 'She's being very brave,' said the nurse who showed him in. 'The contractions are coming every minute, but there's not been a peep out of her. Sister Fitzgerald will be along soon. Any minute now, and your wife will be ready to deliver.'

Mary's face was wet with perspiration. She looked very young, hardly more than a child herself in the plain white hospital gown, damp curls sticking to her forehead.

'I'm sorry I'm so late,' Duncan said softly. 'I didn't get your message until about an hour ago. I came as fast as I could. I wish you hadn't been alone all this time.'

The eyes that turned on him were glazed with pain. 'Hold my hand, Duncan,' she whispered. 'I need someone to hold my hand, really hard.'

The hand was damp and slippery. He clutched it as hard as he could, but Mary clutched his even harder when another contraction came. Her body seemed to convulse, then relax. She uttered a sigh. 'What was the picture like?'

'Good, but I'd sooner have been here with you.'

'I wish you'd been here, too.' Two tears ran down her pale cheeks. 'I'm sorry about everything, Duncan. If only we could go back in time and do things differently.'

'I'm just as sorry, but don't think like that, Mary, not

now. We can't go back. What's done is done and we just have to live with it.'

Mary's lips twisted in an ironic smile. 'Yes – a baby neither of us want!'

Another nurse in a dark blue uniform, presumably Sister Fitzgerald, entered and said briskly, 'Out in the corridor, if you don't mind, Mr Maguire. It's time your wife went next door.'

Duncan paced the corridor for what seemed like hours; eleven steps one way, eleven the other. Afterwards, he discovered it had been little more than twenty minutes. He badly needed a drink, a cigarette, something to calm him. A different nurse appeared and fetched him a cup of tea that didn't help a bit, though he went in search of another when he'd drunk it. When he returned, noises were coming from the delivery room. Mary was shouting, Sister saying something in a loud voice. There was a slap, then the sound of a baby crying – no, not crying, more yelling its head off. It sounded extremely angry.

The door suddenly opened and Sister stuck out her head. 'You've got a little girl, Mr Maguire. She's a lively one, I must say. No, you can't come in yet,' she said sharply when Duncan made a move towards her, 'your wife needs tidying up first.'

Duncan stepped back, the tea in his hand forgotten. He was still in exactly the same position when the door opened again. 'You can go in now. Mother's very tired, but baby isn't. I think she'd quite like to go to a dance or something. Would you like me to take that cup and saucer off you, Mr Maguire? Or are they attached to your body permanently?'

Mary couldn't stop talking, but hardly a word entered Duncan's brain. All he could do was stare at the baby in her arms. She was the most beautiful thing he had ever seen. Her eyes were wide open. She was staring straight at him! She just knew he was her father. God, she must be intelligent. The eyes were very blue, very large, very wise. She was waving her arms, as if trying to escape from the tight confines of the blanket in which she was wrapped.

'Isn't her hair the most gorgeous colour?' Mary babbled. 'Have you noticed her nails? They're perfect. And she's got toes, ten altogether, the nails are just little pink dots. Would you like to hold her?'

'Yes.'

'Be careful with her neck, no her head. I mean, her neck's not very strong, so be really careful.'

He had a *baby*, a daughter. He gingerly picked up the tiny bundle, conscious of the fragile bones, the soft flesh, the waving arms, the blue eyes, the little feathery curls that were an unusual dark gold. The pink mouth was opening and closing, like a fish.

'She's saying something,' he murmured.

'Earlier, she smiled at me, but Sister Fitzgerald said it was just wind.'

'Sister Fitzgerald doesn't know what she's talking about.'

'That's what I told her.'

They smiled at each other, just as the door flew open and Vera sailed in. 'You've had a girl! The nurse told me. Oh, let me see her. Jaysus, Mary and Joseph, if she isn't the prettiest baby I've ever seen. If only your dad was here to see her.' Vera burst into tears. 'How much did she weigh? She looks a big 'un.'

'Eight pounds, two ounces.'

'What are you going to call her, luv?'

'I dunno, Mam. I hadn't given a thought to names. What do you think, Duncan?'

'I don't know either,' Duncan muttered as he handed over his precious baby to her eager grandma.

'What's your mam's name?' Mary enquired.

'Flora.'

'That's a lovely name. Shall we call her Flora? Your mam'll be pleased.'

'Flora would be just fine.' It was the name of the Roman goddess of flowers and spring. Duncan had written to his parents just before Christmas and told them he and Hester had decided not to get married, giving no reason. He hadn't mentioned Mary or the baby that was on its way, assuming, once he'd left Liverpool, that this part of his life would be over and he would do his best never to think of it again. But how could he forget he was the father of such a remarkable little girl?

I should have gone away before she was born, he thought bitterly, never set eyes on her, never known if it was a boy or a girl.

'How did you know to come, Mam?' Mary asked her mother.

'Laura came to Glover Street and told me. She'd heard you'd rung the school, so called the hospital and they said you were here. She brought me in the car. One of these days, I'll just have to get a telephone of me own.'

'Is Laura still here?'

'She's waiting outside to take me home.'

'I wonder if she'd like to see the baby?'

'Shall I ask her?' Duncan offered. He wanted to see Laura to say goodbye and how sorry he was for everything – that's if she was willing to speak to him. He'd let her and Roddy down badly.

Laura was reading a book propped against the steering wheel. She looked up, surprised, when he knocked on the window. The surprise turned to shock when she saw who it was. She rolled the window down. 'Yes?' she asked in a cold voice.

'Mary wants to know if you'd like to see the baby. It's a little girl, Flora.'

'That's a pretty name. Congratulations, Duncan,' she said in the same cold voice. 'I'll go and see her, yes, if only to please Vera.'

'And I'd like to say . . .' He paused.

'What?'

'Oh, nothing. Just goodbye.'

'Goodbye, Duncan.' She got out of the car, locked the door, and marched stiffly away.

Duncan watched until she disappeared into the hospital. Then he leant against the car, buried his head in his hands, and began to cry. Instead of being over, it seemed to him that the worst of his troubles had only just begun.

He was still weeping, when he became aware that his back was being subjected to a violent assault. He looked up and found Caradoc Monaghan standing over him, battering him with all his might. He'd long been expecting an attack from one of Mary's brothers and just stood there, taking it, like the coward he was. Why, though, was Caradoc grinning so inanely and regarding him in such a friendly way?

'Gets to you, doesn't it?' Caradoc boomed, bestowing another painful slap on his back. 'Meself, I cried worse than our Danny when he was born. I've just been to our mam's, and the woman next door told me about Mary. What did she have, a boy or a girl?'

'A girl,' Duncan sniffed. 'Flora.'

'Congratulations, mate.' His hand was pummelled furiously.

'Thank you.'

'I'm sorry we gave you the cold shoulder, Dunc, but it

comes as a shock to find some geezer's been at your little sister – and not just any old sister, but our Mary. But you stuck by her. Not every chap would've done that.' Caradoc chuckled. 'Anyroad, she's not the first Monaghan who's had to get hitched in a hurry, but don't tell that to our mam.'

'I won't.'

'Anyroad, Dunc, I'll just say hello to Mary, then perhaps we could go for a drink? Wet the baby's head, as they say. There's a pub not far away and we can down a few pints before it closes. I've rung our Charlie, he doesn't work far from here, and he'll be along soon. The others will come tonight.'

After they'd been thrown out of the pub, Duncan spent the rest of the afternoon wandering along Southport beach with Caradoc and Charlie Monaghan, taking turns to swig from a bottle of whisky. When it was time to visit Mary again, he was sloshed to the eyeballs. Her six other brothers were there and, afterwards, they insisted the baby's head be wet a second time.

One of the brothers, he couldn't remember which, brought him home in a lorry, as he completely forgot he had a car, and wasn't fit to drive it anyway. He arrived home, pleased to have been accepted into the bosom of the Monaghan family, but more confused than he'd ever been in his life before. Not only that, he vaguely recalled having promised to become a Catholic. On reflection, it didn't seem a bad idea except, any minute now, he would disappear out of the Monaghans' lives for ever and it wouldn't matter what religion he was.

Next day, he went to the hospital on the train, nursing his first hangover and resolving never to have another. Mary was her old self again and greeted him cheerfully.

'You look the worse for wear. Did you have a nice time last night?'

'I think so,' Duncan said gingerly because talking hurt his head.

Flora was in the nursery, wide awake. He was convinced she'd grown at least an inch and looked wiser and even more beautiful than the day before. How could he possibly go away and leave her behind, see her once or twice a year? That morning, he'd packed his books, ready to take with him when he left. When he got back, he unpacked them.

Ten days later, mother and baby were due to leave hospital. Vera had cleaned the flat thoroughly, though it hadn't needed it. As a mother-in-law, Vera was an entirely different cup of tea to Laura Oliver. Duncan couldn't help but like her. The awkwardness between them had disappeared with the birth of Flora and he enjoyed being fussed over in the way his own mother had fussed over him. Vera insisted on washing his clothes and making his meals. If he felt lonely on his own, he was invited to stay in Glover Street.

'You'll never feel lonely there, luv,' she said comfortably.

As soon as Mary arrived home, she announced that, after a cup of tea, she'd like to take Flora for a walk. 'I feel as if I've been in prison, not hospital. And I'd like to buy something, a new lipstick, or some scent, make meself feel human again.'

Flora was snugly wrapped up and placed in her new pram. They set off, Duncan pushing it, and he was amazed by the number of people who stopped to ask if they could see the baby. Some had seen them out on their evening walks and wanted to know if they'd had a boy or a girl. What was she called? How much had she weighed? Flora was showered with compliments and her parents warmly congratulated at least a dozen times.

Duncan was very quiet that night. Mary, cuddling a sleeping Flora in her arms, asked if he felt all right.

'Yes,' he said, not very convincingly.

'Are you sure?'

'Not really.' He sighed. 'To tell the truth, I feel a bit stunned.'

'Stunned? What do you mean, stunned?'

'I never dreamt I'd love Flora quite so much.' He tried to hide the break in his voice.

Mary looked at him with understanding in her eyes. 'You don't want to leave, do you?'

He shook his head. 'No,' he said in a small voice.

'Well, in that case, why not stay?' she said sensibly. 'Stay here, in the flat, and I'll move in with Mam. You can see Flora as much as you want. It'd be best for her if she grew up with both parents around.'

Duncan's heart leapt. Some of the confusion he'd been feeling began to ebb. 'Won't she think it funny, us living apart?'

'I'm sure we'll think up an explanation when we need to.'

'You could leave her with me at weekends when you go dancing,' he said eagerly.

'I don't think I want to go dancing any more. Something changed in me when I had Flora.' Her eyes glowed as she softly touched the baby's chin with her finger. 'It's made me feel far more grown up and mature. Dancing seems silly when compared to being a mother. Duncan?'

'Yes, Mary?'

'Would you like us to stay together? I don't love you, and I know you don't love me and would far sooner be with Hester, but perhaps we should try to make a go of it for Flora's sake. Think about it first. You don't have to tell me now, and I won't be the least bit hurt if you say no.'

Duncan couldn't think of what to say. Through the window, he could see a liner sailing past. Dusk was falling and the windows of the boat were bright pinpricks of light. He realised he hadn't thought about Hester since his daughter had come along. He also realised he couldn't possibly have loved Flora more had Hester, not Mary, been her mother. It struck him that he quite fancied being a member of the Monaghan clan, being Vera's only son-in-law. But what about having Mary permanently for a wife? Did she mean a *proper* wife? If so, he wasn't too sure about that.

She was watching him and, as if she could read his thoughts, she said, 'Of course, we'd need a bigger place, with three bedrooms; one for you, one for me, and the third can be a nursery. You can't go on sleeping for ever on that settee.'

'I'd like us to stay together,' he said simply. 'And we'll get somewhere bigger. I'll have to find another job too.' He wasn't sorry he'd given up teaching and it would be nice to do something different for a change.

It all seemed very practical, like a business arrangement. All they were doing was making the best of a bad job.

Duncan discovered he had enough money in the bank to pay for a deposit on a house. The mortgage repayments would actually be less than paying rent. Mary was thrilled at the idea of being the first Monaghan to become a property owner. They decided they'd live in Waterloo, within easy reach of the beach and the shops in South Road.

But before he could get get a mortgage, he had to find

a job. With a First Class Honours degree and two years' teaching under his belt, Duncan found it relatively easy. Within a month of Flora's birth, he was working for the North-West Examining Board, which had its office in Southport. It suited him to sit, alone, in a quiet office, preparing O-level and A-level papers, though it wasn't even faintly exciting.

The house they bought was in St John's Road, a solid semi with three bedrooms and gardens front and back, in urgent need of modernising throughout. Mary, who'd turned out to be such a brick, set about decorating while he was at work, Flora in her carry cot on wheels, making approving little noises as she watched her mother work.

Flora was an increasing joy. It was a delight to watch her examine her toes, or giggle with ecstasy when Duncan played peek-a-boo with one of her fluffy toys.

Weekends, a couple of the Monaghan lads would turn up and help with the major work, like fitting a new bathroom suite or units in the kitchen; Vera still referred to her sons as 'lads', though Dick had turned forty at Christmas.

Duncan wrote to his parents and told them he was now a married man with a Catholic wife and baby daughter. As expected, his father didn't reply, but his mother came to stay for a few days, very much against her husband's wishes. She and Mary liked each other immediately. 'I prefer her to Hester,' his mother confided privately. 'Hester was nice, but Mary's got more life in her, and Flora's a bonny little girl. I'm so pleased you called her after me, son.'

In another few weeks, Mary would be twenty-one, but the house wouldn't be finished in time for a party. Vera offered to hold it in Glover Street on the Saturday, two days after the actual birthday.

On the day itself, Vera came to babysit, and Duncan took his wife to the cinema in town, then to dinner. They saw *Singin' in the Rain* with Gene Kelly and Debbie Reynolds, and agreed it was probably the best, the happiest, picture ever made. Over dinner, they discussed what colour tiles to have in the bathroom, and whether or not to buy a television.

Home again, Duncan drove his mother-in-law to Glover Street. When he returned, Mary was in the living room breast-feeding Flora. There was nothing faintly sexual about a woman's breast when it had a baby attached. Duncan watched until the baby had had enough and Mary said, 'Would you like to burp her while I make a drink?'

He held out his arms and curled his daughter over his shoulder, tenderly rubbing her back, while a wide-awake Flora wriggled mutinously against him. He was convinced she held on to her burps for as long as she could out of sheer perversity, just as she lay awake half the night, cooing, making chirruping, bird-like noises, and kicking off her blankets, as if determined her parents wouldn't sleep until she slept herself.

Eventually, she made a gruff sound, like an old man, that always made Duncan laugh. He laid her on the settee so he could drink his cocoa. Mary changed her nappy, and said, 'I'll take her up and then I think I'll turn in myself.'

'I'll go up first and switch Daisy on.'

The baby's room had been the first to be decorated; white paper patterned with buttercups and daisies, white woodwork everywhere, white lace curtains, a white cot. It had a lamp shaped like a huge white and yellow flower on the dressing table that they'd christened Daisy, which Flora found quite fascinating. He switched on the lamp, glanced around the pretty white room with its creamy yellow carpet, wished he'd slept somewhere as charming when he'd been a child. But his father scorned anything that might lift the heart, which included pretty lamps and pretty wallpaper. If it wasn't in the Bible, he wasn't interested. Duncan was glad he was providing his own child with fond memories to look back on.

Mary came in and laid Flora in her cot. She looked quite sleepy for a change. The bedclothes were tucked firmly around her. Duncan kissed his finger and put it against her lips. 'Goodnight, sweetheart,' he whispered.

They went on to the landing, leaving the door slightly ajar. 'Thank you, Duncan, for tonight,' Mary said in a low voice. 'I had a marvellous time. The meal was lovely and I've never enjoyed a picture quite so much. And thank you for the present.' She touched the gold locket around her neck. 'It's the gear.'

'Well, you're only twenty-one once in your life. By the way, happy birthday.' He kissed her cheek and was never sure what happened afterwards. Perhaps it was her perfume, or the softness of her skin, or the fact she had given him the most beautiful daughter who'd ever existed, but next minute they were kissing, if not with passion, then with a certain amount of enthusiasm. Still kissing, they shuffled into her bedroom and fell on to the bed, where they made love with the same enthusiasm.

They fell asleep. When Duncan woke, it was pitch dark and Flora was having a long conversation with Daisy. He listened, his heart filled with love, and tried to keep his mind a blank, because if he allowed himself to think, he would only become confused again.

'Are you awake, Duncan?'

'Yes. Can you hear Flora?'

'I think it was her who woke me. Duncan, was it all right – before?'

'It was fine, Mary. What about you?'

'It was fine for me, too. Goodnight, Duncan.' She turned over.

'Goodnight, Mary.'

It hadn't been wonderful or magical or ecstatic, just fine for them both. Duncan allowed himself to think at last. He was a very lucky fellow. Things had turned out immeasurably better than he'd had a right to expect, yet he knew, Flora aside, there would always be a slight feeling of them being second-best. And he was pretty sure they'd always be second-best for Mary too.

The phone in Queenie's office rang early on Saturday morning. It was Laura, asking if she was free for lunch that day. 'I badly need someone to talk to.'

'Of course. Would you like to eat in the flat or go somewhere else? As you know, I never use Freddy's restaurant.'

'I really don't care, Queenie.' She sounded very fed up.

'Let's go somewhere else for a change. How about Owen Owen's? They serve excellent lunches.'

'Owen Owen's it is. Say about twelve-thirty?'

Queenie got to the restaurant first. When Laura came in, she was struck by how much she'd changed since they'd first met sixteen years ago. People were bound to change, but with Laura it seemed to have happened overnight, some time between Duncan marrying Mary, and Hester leaving home. Nowadays, she didn't seem to care how she looked. Those stern horn-rimmed glasses were probably useful in the classroom, but she only needed them to read. She didn't have to wear them all the time. Nor did she need to have her lovely hair cut quite so short, or wear such sensible costumes in such sensible colours; various shades of grey and brown. Her skin had lost its bloom, her cheeks were sallow, her lips pale. Queenie longed to suggest she use a bit of make-up and buy some smarter clothes.

They kissed. Laura didn't just sound fed up, she looked it.

'What's the matter?' Queenie asked.

'Is it that obvious?'

'Yes. Why do you need someone to talk to when you've got Roddy?' She could have bitten off her tongue the minute the question was out. Perhaps it was Roddy she wanted to talk about.

'I can't talk to Roddy, because he's hardly ever there, nor Gus. It's all Theo's fault,' Laura said sourly. 'Ever since he got you that boat, Roddy's been aching for one. He's bought a day boat, halfway between a dinghy and a yacht. He and Gus virtually live on the damn thing, even sleep there. They disappear every Saturday morning, come home exhausted on Sunday night, have something to eat, then go straight to bed. I'm fed up to the teeth with the pair of them.'

'Why don't you go with them?'

'Because I'd hate it. Wouldn't you? You were seasick on that great big thing of yours. Not only that, I can't swim, and I can't think of a more boring way of spending my time.'

'Poor Laura!' Queenie reached for her hand, just as the waitress came for their order.

After they'd ordered and the waitress had gone, Laura continued to complain. 'It wouldn't be so bad if Hester were here, but she's in California and, if her letters are anything to go by, having a wonderful time. The day after tomorrow, she'll be twenty-one. If everything had gone the way it should have, she would be marrying Duncan. Now she's not even coming home and there'll be no party, no wedding.' Her eyes narrowed. 'Do you know if she and Steven Vandos are having an affair?'

'I don't know, no. I've wondered meself.'

'Oh, you must think I'm a terrible old misery,' Laura cried. 'I'm just feeling unusually down, that's all. It didn't help when Vera told me about Mary's party last Saturday. It sounded a very lively affair. Did you go?'

'Yes, Theo went too. He loves Vera and the Monaghan lads because they're so down to earth and uncomplicated. His family are the very opposite.'

'And was it as lively as Vera said?'

'Have you ever known a party at the Monaghans' that wasn't?'

'No,' Laura said gloomily. 'She invited us, but I said no. I hope she wasn't hurt, but I couldn't stand the thought of seeing Mary and Duncan together, and I'd have to have bought the horrible girl a present. Is the baby still as gorgeous?'

Queenie sighed wistfully. 'She's absolutely beautiful.'

'How do Mary and Duncan get along? Oh, please tell me they can't stand each other. The thought that everything's worked out all right for them, while Hester, the innocent party, is living halfway across the world, just doesn't seem fair.'

'I didn't see much of them,' Queenie said evasively. Mary and Duncan had danced quite closely together at the party.

'Oh, come on, Queenie. You must have noticed something.'

'They seemed to be getting along OK. Perhaps they're doing their best for Flora's sake.'

'That makes sense – not that I can imagine Mary doing anything sensible.'

'She's changed, Laura.' She looked at the bitter eyes behind the severe glasses. 'Circumstances can change us all. When Hester and I were in Paris,' she said slowly, 'she told me she was determined to put everything behind her, get on with her life. She wasn't prepared to let Duncan spoil it. And that's what she's done. I doubt very much if she wants him and Mary to be unhappy. I reckon she'll be glad they're getting on.'

Laura shook her head impatiently. 'Is there a point to all this?'

'It seems to me that you've taken what happened much harder than Hester. She lost her fiancé, yet all you lost was a rather weak son-in-law.'

'I can't begin to explain how it made me feel,' Laura cried tragically. 'And it had an effect on Roddy and me. We've been very distant with each other since.'

'Are you sure it's not you being distant with him? Perhaps that's why he goes sailing every weekend.' She smiled, as if she were making a joke, though suspected this was the truth.

The soup arrived. During the meal, they talked about more mundane things. Queenie mentioned they were expecting some lovely clothes in for autumn. 'Soft jersey frocks and costumes in rich, muted colours. They'd look smashing on you.'

'Is that a hint? I know I look a frump, but I can't be bothered with clothes these days.'

'You used to love sewing.'

'I don't any more.'

'Shall we join something?' Queenie suggested over coffee. 'A tennis club, maybe? I've always wanted to learn to play tennis. We could go evenings and on Sunday afternoons.'

Laura laughed. 'Queenie, dear, I know darn well Sunday is the only day you and Theo have together. Don't pander to me. I'll sort this out my own way. All I wanted was a good moan.'

'Do you feel better for the moan?'

'I haven't finished yet. I've kept the worst till last. I'm

pregnant,' she said in a hard voice. 'Thirty-seven and pregnant. I've just missed my second period. Next year, I was due to be promoted to assistant head, but by then I'll have a baby. Except if I get rid of it. What do you think, Queenie?'

She can't have been all *that* distant with Roddy, Queenie thought as she stirred her coffee, hearing the spoon scrape against the bottom of the cup. She stirred it the other way and it made a slightly different sound. First Mary, now Laura. How could God be so unfair? Why had these women, who didn't want a baby, conceived, when she, who wanted one more than anything on earth, had failed after almost a year of trying? Theo had left it entirely up to her. He didn't know she'd stopped using her cap.

'I could never get rid of a baby,' she said slowly. 'It's a decision only you can take. Does Roddy know? What does he think?'

'Roddy doesn't know,' Laura said brusquely. 'I've no idea what he'd think if he did. Anyway, I only care about *me*. All I've got left is my career, school. My family have deserted me.'

'Aren't you exaggerating a bit?' For the first time since she'd known her, Laura was getting on her nerves. 'Hester won't stay away for ever, and Roddy and Gus can't go sailing in the winter – it might even be just a five-minute wonder and they'll get fed up with it soon.'

'No, they won't. When winter comes, they'll be out painting the damn thing, and Hester mightn't be home for years.' She finished the coffee with a flamboyant gesture, throwing back her head until the muscles showed in her neck, swallowing it in a single gulp. 'Actually, Queenie, you're beginning to irritate me. All you've done is criticise since we met. I was expecting sympathy, not a lecture.'

'I'm afraid I can't feel sympathy for someone who wants to get rid of a baby.'

'I was considering it. I hadn't made up my mind.'

'It amounts to the same thing.'

Laura picked up her bag and got to her feet. 'I'll pay on the way out. Thanks for the company, Queenie, though I can't say I've enjoyed it.'

Queenie felt sick as she watched her friend walk away. 'I'll ring in a few days, see how you are,' she called.

'I'd prefer it if you didn't bother,' Laura called back.

Chapter 16

People were starting to leave, much to Hester's relief. It hadn't been a very enjoyable party. The apartment was too small for so many guests, particularly on such a hot night. The noise was deafening. She'd pretended to be invisible, drifting from the edge of one crowd to another, hoping no one would notice and speak to her because she couldn't hear a word being said. She didn't even know whose party it was, or why it was being held – not that in Hollywood anyone needed a reason. Though she was glad she'd come. Anything was better than spending the night in her hotel room, alone. She was equally glad when Steven Vandos approached and asked if she'd like to go. It was nearly midnight and she could go to bed and hopefully sleep.

'Haven't you clicked with a girl?' she asked. Steven had loads of friends. He was asked to parties two or three times a week and nearly always took her with him, though she insisted on going as just another friend, not as a couple. 'I'd feel awful if I stopped you from meeting a woman,' she'd told him. Once they had arrived, she insisted he ignore her. On the times he did meet someone, Hester would go back to the hotel by herself, but Steven always made sure she was safely in a taxi before he left.

'Clicked?' He laughed. 'Is that a Liverpool expression?'

'I'm not sure. Mary used to say "copped off" – "copped off with some feller'." She could mention Mary's name now without feeling any emotion at all.

'Back home, I didn't mix with the common people like you. I've never heard of either expression.' He sighed and looked mournful. 'I didn't click with a soul, which means we can have coffee together in Dave's.'

They strolled arm in arm along La Cienego Boulevard, still brightly lit and full of people at such a late hour – Los Angeles was a city that never slept. She and Steven got on well, 'strangers in a strange land', as he'd said once. He'd been there over a year, having had a small part in a film, and then a slightly bigger one. Now he'd landed a part big enough to have his name on the screen. 'It'll probably be at the very bottom of the cast list, but I don't care. I'm gradually getting there.'

Hester wasn't surprised. He was thirty-one and terribly attractive, with a languorous charm and old-fashioned manners, rare in such a crazy, hectic place, where people were usually too busy or too rude to say 'please' or 'thank you'. Women loved him, enamoured by his courtesy, his lovely, deep voice, his perfect diction. He was the epitome of an English gentleman.

'Be careful with Steven,' Queenie had warned before she left England. 'When we first met, he flirted like mad, kept asking me out, but wasn't the least bothered when I turned him down. He makes women feel very special, as if they're the only one in the world for him, but inside he's very shallow. I hasten to say he's also very nice, incredibly nice, in fact. I like him very much.'

So did Hester. Steven hadn't said anything that could be remotely considered flirtatious. Instead, he'd looked after her, got her a room in his hotel, the Wellington, not far from the Dodgers' stadium. It was a nice hotel and a bit expensive, but she lived in one of the small rooms on the top floor that were let at a reduced rate, which she could just about afford out of her wages. He'd also found her a job as a typist with an agent, Elfreda Hicks, who was probably the most unscrupulous, untrustworthy and cynical person who'd ever lived. But Hester didn't mind. The job was fascinating. She mostly typed contracts for actors for whom Elfreda had found parts in films, taking a huge cut of the fee for herself.

For all its faults, and there were many, Hester loved Hollywood. There was so much to do, so many films to see, so many parties to go to, even if some were tedious, like tonight's. She'd been to Mann's Chinese Theatre where there were hand and footprints of famous stars, the Hollywood History Museum, Sunset Strip, which was a bit tawdry, and loads of other famous places. It left her with little time to think, to dwell on things like Duncan's betrayal. It was funny, but once the baby, Flora, had arrived, it seemed as if a final line had been drawn, and she could actually think of him and Mary without wanting to weep until there was no tomorrow. But the betrayal! She would never get over that. She would never trust a man again.

They had reached Dave's, a diner only a few doors along from the Wellington. Dave's never closed. When she first came, in the middle of the night, when she couldn't sleep, Hester had often gone there for a malted milk. The night waitress, Jo, was very friendly, as well as breathtakingly pretty. Jo wanted to become a film star, but had had no luck so far – there were an awful lot of breathtakingly pretty girls around who wanted the same thing. She worked nights, so she could be free during the day to attend auditions. Virtually every person Hester met wanted to be a film star, a screen writer, a director – anything to do with the movies. She wondered if she was the only person who had no ambition to be anything except happy. And, like Steven, she was gradually getting there.

'Coffee?' Steven asked when they went into the half-full diner. Jo waved to them from behind the counter and came to take their order.

'No, it keeps me awake. I'd like a malt, please.'

'Have you two been somewhere exciting?' Jo enquired.

'Some guy's just had a script accepted by Warner and his pals threw a party to celebrate.'

'Is that what it was for?' Hester exclaimed. 'If I'd known, I'd have congratulated him.'

'I didn't know until I was leaving, by which time the guy had left himself. Black coffee and a malt, please, Jo.'

'Coming up in just a minute.' She left.

'I had a phone call from Queenie today.' Steven lit his hundredth cigarette of the day. 'It was to tell me that next Monday you'll be twenty-one. Were you just going to let the most significant birthday of your life pass without telling a soul?'

'Yes,' Hester conceded. 'It was the day I was going to marry Duncan and I'd sooner not be reminded.'

'What tosh! Duncan sounds a prick. Why spoil your birthday on account of him? Thanks, Jo. Sit down, join us. I'm just giving Hester a severe telling off.'

'I don't like intruding on a private conversation,' Jo said, sitting down all the same.

'This young lady's twenty-one next week and she doesn't want a party.'

'Everyone has a party on their twenty-first.'

'Tell *her* that.'

'They do, you know, hon,' Jo said earnestly. 'In Hollywood, anyways. It'd be a sin not to.'

'A mortal sin,' Steven added. 'What were you going to do, sit in your room and sulk?'

'Why should she want to sulk?'

'Because she expected to be doing something else on her birthday, like getting married. Now she's not, and she's going to sulk instead.'

'I never said anything about sulking!'

'What were you going to do then?'

'I don't know,' Hester said sulkily. She'd had no intention of staying in, but hadn't made up her mind where to go; lose herself in a movie maybe, though not a romantic one.

'OK then, a party it is. But where?' Steven raised his perfect eyebrows. 'Not the Wellington, the manager would go crazy.'

'What about Harvey's across the road?' Jo suggested. 'It's a bar and a great place for parties. They don't close till two and Harvey gives a special price if you bring a crowd. Dave's can supply the food; bagels, cookies, donuts and stuff. I'd have to bring it over, so I could shut this place down and stay awhile. Excuse me, folks.' She got up when a woman came in carrying a tiny dog. 'I've got a customer.'

'I'm glad that's sorted.' Steven gave a satisfied smile.

'Who's going to pay for everything?' Hester demanded. 'I can't afford to.'

'Yours truly. It'll be my present. And Queenie said to give you fifty dollars for a new frock, she's sending a cheque to cover it.'

Hester felt as if she should resent Steven and Queenie – and Jo – for organising her life, but felt secretly pleased that people cared enough to arrange a party on her twenty-first.

The frock she bought was red. It was the first time she'd worn such a vivid colour. It was sleeveless with a deep, frilled V-neck that she sewed together a few inches so her breasts didn't show.

On the night, Harvey's was packed. The bar was in a basement, darkly lit, smelling richly of a mixture of tobacco and whisky. The well-worn leather seats and scratched tables looked a hundred years old, and one of the walls was covered with signed pictures of major movie stars whom Steven said had used the bar when they'd first come to Hollywood, young and hopeful.

Steven had invited most of the guests and Hester had no idea who they were. She'd asked a few of the actors, male and female, familiar faces by now, who hung around Elfreda's in the hope of finding work, and a couple of girls, Hope and Emma, more would-be actresses, whom she'd met at another party and sometimes went to the movies with. Also, Chas O'Reilly, a writer who lived on the same floor as her at the Wellington and kept asking her out. Sometimes, she felt tempted to accept, because he had an interesting face and she rather liked him. But she wasn't quite ready, not yet, to go out with other men.

She hadn't been expecting presents, but pretty soon a table in the corner was piled high with extravagantly wrapped parcels, which she intended to open later, touched and grateful for the generosity of people who didn't even know her.

The night flashed by in a daze. She'd never been hugged and kissed so many times, told how beautiful she was, a genuine English rose. Her voice was admired. 'It's so soft and gentle, honey. I could listen to it for hours,' a woman said stridently.

Music was coming from somewhere, dreamy and romantic. They were songs from the thirties, the decade in which she was born; 'Lovely To Look At', 'Smoke Gets In Your Eyes', 'Cheek To Cheek'. People started to dance and Chas asked Hester, holding her very close, but she didn't mind because everyone was doing it. Anyway, she was just a little bit drunk on champagne.

'You're a great-looking girl,' Chas whispered in her ear. 'Why don't you try to get into movies?'

'I can't act, I can't sing, I can't dance.' She giggled. 'They're just three reasons.'

'Yeah, but you look like an angel. That's reason enough.'

'I'll think about it,' she promised. Tonight, she felt as if she could do anything.

Later, she went to the Ladies – the Americans called it, 'the powder room' – and looked at herself in the mirror. Her eyes shone like stars, her cheeks were flushed, her blonde hair as smooth as satin. The red frock went well against the tan she had acquired sunbathing on Santa Monica beach with Steven and a crowd of friends – one of them had a sort of minibus that was big enough for a dozen passengers.

Did I ever look like this for Duncan? she wondered, and realised it was the first time she'd thought about him all night. Yet, if things had gone as expected, they'd be married by now. In England, it would be early morning, she and Duncan would be on their honeymoon, just waking up. They hadn't made up their minds where to go when Mary had revealed she was having his baby. Right now, Hester wasn't totally sure if she'd sooner be with Duncan or here, in Harvey's bar.

She looked at her face again. It hadn't changed. Her eyes were just as starry. Perhaps I'm over him, she thought exultantly. I'll think of him again, of course I will, but it won't make me cry, it won't make me feel sad. One of these days, I might even be glad we didn't get married. She wasn't sure if she didn't already feel that way.

Two weeks later, she slept with Chas O'Reilly and felt quite certain.

Chas was a slight, not very tall young man, with pale brown hair and green-brown eyes. His face was very thin and intense and he had a wonderful smile. He wrote screenplays, thrillers. He gave her some to read and she said she thought them very good.

'Yeah, but not good enough,' he said gloomily. 'They always come back straight away. I'm not even sure if they're read.'

'If they're not read, then how can you be sure they're not good enough?'

'Jeez, Hes,' he sighed. 'I dunno.'

He was a tender, thoughtful lover, more experienced than Duncan, though she tried not to compare them. This wasn't a romance, merely a relationship. She liked Chas, might grow fond of him, but was determined not to fall in love or let him change her life. Steven, she went out with as often as before. It would be horrid to drop him just because she had a boyfriend.

'I'm surprised,' Steven said, when she told him about Chas. 'I thought your heart had been permanently broken.'

'It's mended now, so it can't have been permanent.'

He grinned. 'If I'd known that, I'd have made a move myself.'

'You wouldn't!'

'I would,' he assured her, still grinning. 'You're a sweet girl, Hester. I fancied you from the start, but I've been treading on egg shells, trying not to show it in case you were upset.'

'Well, *you* certainly don't look upset that I'm going out with Chas.'

'Not much point, is there?' he said, shrugging.

'Well, one thing's certain, Steven Vandos, no woman's ever going to break *your* heart.'

Hester had loved Hollywood before, but after her party, she loved it even more. All of a sudden, she found herself very popular, and in receipt of loads of invitations to dinner, parties, the theatre, and a variety of other functions, including the occasional film premiere. She felt obliged to buy a couple of evening outfits, and wrote home, asking her mother to send the nicest of the frocks she'd left behind.

A few days later, early one morning, Steven brought a letter postmarked Liverpool up to her room while she was getting ready for work. It was too soon for her own letter to have arrived. 'I found this in your box downstairs when I was on my way out. Thought you'd like it straight away.' He sat on the bed. 'When you've read it, we can have breakfast together in Dave's.'

'It's from Daddy.' She opened it quickly. Daddy's letters were usually very amusing. She'd never noticed so many funny things happening in the house in Crosby when she'd lived there.

'Oh,' she gasped, after reading the first few lines. 'Crikey!'

'What's wrong?'

'Nothing's wrong.' She could hardly believe it. 'It's just that my mother's expecting a baby.'

'A bit old for that, isn't she?'

'Not really. She's only thirty-seven, but she was getting on so well at school. I told you she's a teacher, didn't I? It's due at Christmas. I wonder why I wasn't told before? I was going home then, anyway. I'll have been away nearly a year.'

'You're not going for good, are you?' Steven said quickly.

'Lord, no. Only a fortnight. I've been saving my holidays for exactly that. I don't think Elfreda approves of holidays, but she'll just have to like it or lump it.' She doubted if she could ever bring herself to leave Hollywood for good.

Laura had never known Roddy so angry as when she told him she was pregnant. It was the day she'd had lunch with Queenie. 'But I'm thinking of having an abortion,' she added.

'You're *what?*' He looked horrified.

'I'm pregnant.'

'I heard that much. It's the other part I'm not sure of.'

'I'm thinking of having the baby aborted,' she said nervously. 'It will play havoc with my career.'

His face was like thunder. 'That's murder, Lo.'

'Don't be ridiculous, Roddy. Women do it all the time. At least two girls at school have had abortions.'

'How, when it's against the law?'

'There's places that do it, quite respectable places. There's one in Southport, a nursing home. They don't even ask your name. You just pay your money, and it's done. You're out the next day.' The telephone number was in her bag and she intended calling tomorrow to arrange a date. She wouldn't have told Roddy, had she not had to stay the night.

'So, it's that easy to murder a child!' He got up and banged his fist on the sideboard. Inside, the bottles and glasses clinked furiously in protest.

'Since when have you cared about things like that?' she asked in an icy voice, no longer nervous, but annoyed. 'You're not exactly religious. It's not as if you go to church. You don't even believe in God.'

'Just because I don't believe in God, it doesn't mean

I'd go along with the killing of a child – *my* child, just as much as yours, I might remind you.'

'No, but you won't have to give up your job to look after the damn thing, will you?'

There was a long silence. Laura realised she'd gone too far. Roddy was watching her, such a strange, puzzled look on his face, that it made her go cold.

'What on earth's got into you lately, Lo? You've not been yourself for months. You're nervy, jumpy, short-tempered. Gus and I are scared to open our mouths in case we say something wrong. Have you taken on too much at school, darling?' he said gently. 'Evenings, weekends, all you seem to do is mark books. If you're not doing that, you're getting lessons ready for next week.'

'I love school, I like being busy. It takes my mind off things.'

'What things?'

'Things like my daughter's in America, and my husband and my son would prefer to spend their weekends on a stupid boat rather than with me!' Laura knew she was making things worse, but couldn't help it. She *wanted* to be awkward, get under his skin, even when she knew it wasn't fair.

'Did it not cross your mind, darling, that Gus and I felt in the way? Frankly, I thought you preferred us out of the house. You seemed too busy to notice us when we're here.'

'That's stupid and you know it,' she snapped, when really she should have said, 'I'm sorry, darling. I love you and Gus with all my heart.' What *had* got into her? She'd felt so much for Hester when she'd been jilted. It had brought back her own feelings of desolation and despair when Roddy had done, more or less, the same thing to her. What was to stop him doing the same thing again?

Life was so precarious, unsure. You couldn't be certain of anything. It was fatal to plan for the future, like tempting fate. She'd lost all her faith in human nature. No one could be trusted, *no one*. There was only school, where she would always be needed, where nothing would change, only small, unimportant things on the periphery. She couldn't give up school to have a baby, lose the only certainty she had.

Roddy ran his fingers through his hair. 'I don't know what to do,' he said. 'I don't know what to say. If you like, once you've had the baby, *I'll* give up work and look after it. You don't earn much less then I do. We could live quite easily on your wages.'

'Don't talk daft, Roddy,' she said contemptuously.

At that, he lost his temper. 'It's not daft. It's what I'd do to save the life of our child. I'll tell you this much, Laura, if you get rid of that baby, I'll . . .' He paused and shook his head in perplexity. 'I don't know what I'll do. All I know is things would never be the same between us again.'

They hardly spoke to each other for the rest of the week. He slept in Hester's bed, but Laura didn't care. She felt quite reckless, gaining a certain amount of satisfaction out of not caring. She'd rung the nursing home and they were expecting her on Monday. When she told Roddy, he just shrugged and turned away.

On Saturday morning, he came down in the old corduroy trousers he went sailing in. 'Where's Gus?' he asked shortly.

'Gone to the library. He'll be back soon.'

'Once Gus gets in the library, he loses all sense of time. I'll pick him up on the way past.'

'What time will you be back?'

'I've no idea. Anyway, what do you care?'

'Roddy?' She took a step towards him.

'What?' There was a glimmer of hope in his eyes.

But the words wouldn't come. 'Nothing,' she said.

He went out without saying goodbye and could be heard coupling the boat on to the hook at the back of his car. Laura stood at the front window, waiting for him to appear, she didn't know why. Only the car, a dark blue Morris A40, was visible; the boat was kept at the side of the house. Eventually, Roddy came and opened the car door. Laura gasped, overwhelmed by the same thrilling, heart-stopping sensation she'd had when she first saw him in the book shop in Tunbridge Wells. Men were rarely described as beautiful, but Roddy was. His features were perfect, his hair still fell in the same careless quiff, his eyes were the same cornflower blue.

As she watched the boyish figure climb into the car, she wondered what he saw in her. He looked so much younger than his age, yet she looked so much older. She'd never been much of a one for make-up, but she'd always dressed smartly, looked after herself. Now she was letting herself go. The other day, Queenie had dropped a rather heavy hint, telling her about the clothes Freddy's were getting in for autumn. She'd buy herself a couple of new outfits, a lipstick, let her hair grow – the last time she'd had it cut, Gus had said she looked like a Nazi.

Yes, she'd do all these things, but realised it would have no effect whatsoever, not where Roddy was concerned, not if she got rid of the baby. But she was determined to go ahead. If it wrecked their marriage, it was just too bad. She'd still have Hester and Gus, but not even her children could provide the certainty she so desperately needed. Only school.

Roddy had been gone about an hour, she was marking books, her head throbbing, when a gust of wind shook the house, making the windows rattle in their frames and the trees outside rustle angrily. She looked out at the garden; the trees were still swishing to and fro in the aftermath of the wind. When a second fierce gust caught them, the slender eucalyptus bent almost double. It had scarcely had time to straighten up when it was bent double again by another tremendous gust.

They wouldn't go sailing in such a gale. She wondered if there'd been time for them to launch the boat before the wind had risen. Would Roddy have had enough time to collect Gus, drive to Formby, where he always parked the car at the edge of the sands and drag the boat across to the water? She felt a moment of fear, listening to the wind lashing against the house and imagining the tiny boat being tossed to and fro in the middle of the Mersey, but dismissed it. Even if the boat had been launched, it couldn't have got far and Roddy would have returned to shore immediately. He wouldn't risk Gus's life. Any minute, they'd be home, having abandoned the idea of sailing.

Laura returned to the marking, expecting all the time to hear the car stop outside. Roddy would uncouple the boat, wheel it on its trailer into the drive, and reverse the car in front.

Another hour passed, the wind grew fiercer, but Roddy and Gus didn't come. She couldn't concentrate on marking, and stood at the window, peering down the road, expecting to see the car turn the corner. Several cars did, even a dark blue Morris, which made her heart lift, but it went past, being driven by a woman.

She was getting agitated now, couldn't sit still, kept making tea and forgetting to drink it. She thought about ringing the library to see if Gus was there, having turned down the idea of a day's sailing, but knew it would be a waste of time. Gus would never miss the opportunity of going out in the boat with his dad. And although he lost all track of time in the library, he'd never stayed this long; three, four hours. Hunger would have driven him home, if nothing else. She remembered Roddy hadn't taken a flask of tea, and she hadn't made sandwiches for them to take. All he'd wanted was to get out of the house as fast as he could, away from her. Perhaps that's why Gus had gone to the library so early, to escape from his bad-tempered mother.

At one o'clock, she rang Queenie, who always knew what to do, entirely forgetting they'd parted on such a sour note after lunch the other day.

'Ring the coastguard,' Queenie said crisply. 'Do it straight away, then ring back and tell me what happened. You poor thing, you must be out of your mind with worry.'

'Say if they drown!' Laura said hoarsely. 'They're both strong swimmers, but . . .' Her voice trailed away in horror as she visualised the churning water, the boat being shattered by the giant waves, her husband and son thrashing helplessly about, getting weaker all the time, desperately trying to save each other, one of them – it could be either – watching the other disappear for ever beneath the waves.

'Laura!' Queenie shouted. 'I said, *ring the coastguard*. We can talk about it later.'

The coastguard had received no reports of a boat in trouble. 'Perhaps that's because it's already sunk,' Laura said shrilly.

'Where did your husband set off from, and at about what time?'

'It must have been about ten o'clock. He usually sets off from Formby beach.'

'We'll alert other vessels in the area, madam. Please let

us know immediately should your husband return.' He asked for her name and telephone number.

She put down the phone, having forgotten she'd promised to call Queenie. The phone rang about ten minutes later, and she leapt upon it.

'What's happening?' Queenie asked.

'They're looking for them.'

'Roddy's such a sensible person. I doubt if he'd go sailing in this weather.'

'Then where *is* he?' Laura cried hysterically. 'Oh, Queenie, what am I to do if he dies, if Gus dies? Do you think this is a punishment for wanting to kill my child? God's taking his revenge. Roddy said it was murder.'

'You've told him?'

'Yes,' she whispered. 'He was so angry. This morning, he left without saying goodbye.' And he hadn't listened to the weather forecast on the radio, which he always did before setting off for a day's sailing. All he'd wanted was to get away from her. It was her fault, all her fault. 'I'm sorry, Queenie. I'll have to ring off now.'

She needed to think, quite seriously think. If she made a pact with God, promised not to get rid of the baby, then perhaps he'd save Roddy and Gus as His part of the bargain. She'd keep it, anyway, she vowed, whether they came back or not.

It was hours later, she'd no idea how many, when the Morris drew up outside. Roddy and Gus got out, laughing, and together they unhooked the boat. Laura had spent the hours going slowly out of her mind and no longer felt entirely sane. Her legs could hardly support her when she went to the front door and opened it.

'Where have you been?' The inside of her mouth was as dry as a bone.

'The weather didn't look so hot, so I parked by

Formby station, and we caught the train into town. Gus wanted to look up something in Picton Library. Afterwards, we had rather a nice meal in Freddy's, didn't we, Gus?'

Gus nodded. 'Super, Dad.'

'We roamed around Freddy's a bit, thought about dropping in on Queenie, but decided she'd be too busy for callers, then went to the pictures; *River of No Return* with Marilyn Monroe and Robert Mitchum. You'll be pleased to know Gus is madly in love with Miss Monroe.'

'She's a cracker,' Gus agreed with a stupid grin.

'You'd better get in touch with the coastguard, tell them you're safe.'

'The coastguard! Hell's bells, Laura, why on earth did you contact them?'

'I've no idea.' Laura turned on her heel and went upstairs to bed. She slept for twelve solid hours, and when she woke up she felt her old self again. Almost.

'I'm not leaving for ever,' Hester protested laughingly. 'I'll only be gone a fortnight.'

Steven got out a neatly ironed handkerchief and pretended to dry his eyes. 'How can I possibly live without you for a whole fortnight?'

'Idiot!' she said fondly.

'If you don't come back, I'll kill myself.'

'There'll be no need for such drastic action. I'm definitely coming back. I love Hollywood too much to even think of leaving.'

'But you don't love me?'

'I do not, and you don't love me. We're not making a movie here, Steven Vandos, so stop putting on an act.'

'I do, you know – love you.'

'Idiot!' she said again.

They were in Dave's diner, which was gaily decorated for Christmas. A tree smothered in tinsel stood by the door. It was midday, and they were having lunch, coffee and pizza, before Hester left for the airport in an hour's time. She mopped her brow. Outside, the sun beat mercilessly down and it was hard to believe it was December and that tomorrow she would be in England where the temperature would be about forty degrees lower. There were warm clothes at the top of her suitcase to change into as soon as she arrived.

Steven reached across the table and took her arm, holding it very tightly. 'I've loved you for almost a year,' he said urgently, 'ever since the moment I met you off the plane. I've watched you having affairs; Chas, Douglas Muck, the guy with the crewcut, I can't remember his name, Frankie Wahlbugger.'

'Wahlberger,' she said. 'Frankie Wahlberger. And it's Douglas Mack, not Muck. Do you mind letting go of my arm? You're stopping the blood from flowing. My fingers might drop off.'

He released her arm. 'How about me?'

'How about you?'

'When you come back, how about having an affair with me?'

'You're too old. It would be like having an affair with my father.'

'Thirty-one isn't exactly ancient.' He looked hurt.

'Nearly thirty-two,' she reminded him.

'Thirty-two isn't exactly ancient, either. Anyway, Douglas Muck looked at least eighty.'

'He was twenty-nine.' She regarded him, head on one side. 'I can't take you seriously,' she said.

'I'm deeply serious when I say I love you.'

'You don't *look* it.'

'I *feel* it.' He put his hand over his heart. 'In here. Now, about that affair . . .?'

'I'll think about it while I'm away.'

'I mean it, Hes. You know when you first came and you said you'd never trust another guy again, has it ever entered your pretty little head that I might not trust women?' This time, he *did* sound serious. His brown eyes, usually so bright and smiling, looked sad. He wasn't pretending.

'What happened?'

'During the war, when I was in France, I met this girl, name of Julia. She was in the WAAF and she was my first love, and the last – until I met you. We had this fantastic affair, swore our undying love for each other. Trouble was, she forgot to tell me she was married.' He shrugged and bit his lip. 'After that, I swore I'd never fall in love again – just like you, I should imagine. Whenever I'm attracted to a woman, I laugh it off, make a joke of it, determined not to be hurt again.'

'I'm sorry, Steven,' she said gently, both touched and surprised.

'And I'm sorry about you and that prick, Duncan. Mind you, your permanently broken heart mended much quicker than mine.'

'Is it mended now?'

'It must be if I'm in love with you.'

'I don't know – about an affair,' she said slowly. 'I do love you in a way, but as a friend. If we had an affair, everything would change, and I wouldn't want to lose your friendship. I wouldn't want to break your heart again either.'

'I'm prepared to take a chance on that. With you.' He took her hand and Hester was surprised when she felt a little thrill. 'Let's make a vow, that whatever happens between us, we'll always stay friends.'

'I'll go along with that, but let's not make any plans until I come back, see how we feel then.' She raised her coffee cup.

'Let's drink to us.'

'To us!'

The long flight to England was very pleasant, mainly because her mind was preoccupied with Steven. She'd never thought about him in a romantic way before, but the idea of having him as a lover, possibly a husband, was exciting. Although she was looking forward to spending Christmas and New Year with Gus, her parents, and the new baby, which could arrive any minute now, she was looking forward to going back to Hollywood, and Steven, even more.

It was snowing when she got off the plane at Heathrow at eleven o'clock next morning – she'd gained time on the way. The passengers hurried across the tarmac to the arrivals lounge. Once the formalities were over, she went into the Ladies to change her thin clothes for warmer ones; jumper, skirt, stout shoes, and a heavy coat.

The clothes felt strange and rather cumbersome. She went outside and indulged in the luxury of a taxi to Euston Station, where she discovered she had over an hour to wait for the Liverpool train. She rang home to tell them what time she'd be arriving. Gus answered.

'How's Mummy and Daddy?' she asked him.

'OK, sis.' There was something guarded in his tone.

'Are you sure?'

'Well, Mum went into hospital last night. Dad's with her. I'd be there too, but Dad said you might ring. He'll pick you up from Lime Street station.'

'Rightio, Gus. I'll be there about five o'clock.' She would have been quite happy to make her own way home, though a lift would be more than welcome. 'I can't wait to see you.'

The Liverpool train was uncomfortably hot. She wasn't sure if it would have been better uncomfortably cold, as the grid under the seat threw out so much heat it scorched the back of her legs.

Mountains of black clouds lumbered across the leaden sky, and the countryside looked deserted and lonely. She was glad when it became properly dark and all she could see were little specks of light shining here and there. The occasional town they sped through was brightly lit. She was even more glad when they passed over the Mersey, the black water gleaming like a satin ribbon.

Liverpool at last! She was looking forward to the warmth of the house in Crosby, her cosy bedroom, and hoped no one would mind if she went to bed early tonight, after going to see Mummy first, of course.

Daddy and Gus were waiting on the other side of the barrier. She saw them before they saw her, and she was surprised at how glum they looked. Gus noticed her first and nudged his father's arm. They both smiled and waved, though the smiles looked a bit forced. She was so pleased to see them, she forgot about Steven, who'd been at the forefront of her mind throughout the entire journey.

She hugged them both extravagantly, remarked that Gus must have grown a foot since she'd left, and asked, 'How's Mummy? Has she had the baby yet? Have I got a little brother or sister?'

A look of pain passed over her father's face. 'The baby arrived last night. It was a girl, but I'm afraid she was stillborn. We didn't think it right to tell you before you got here. As for your mother, as you can imagine, she's not very well.'

*

Laura had her own little room at the end of the ward. She didn't open her eyes when Hester crept in. Vera was sitting beside the bed; she and Queenie had been bricks, according to Daddy. He didn't know how he would have managed without them.

Vera put a finger to her lips. 'She's asleep, luv,' she whispered. 'Don't wake her. This is the first sleep she's had since it happened. Perhaps she'll feel better when she wakes up. She's been awful agitated.'

Hester could have wept when she looked down at her mother's pallid, waxen face, hardly recognisable from the rosy-cheeked woman, full of life, she'd left behind ten months ago – it felt more like ten years.

'Will she be all right?'

'It'll take a while, Hester, luv. Imagine what it must feel like, carrying a baby for nine whole months, then losing it at the last minute! C'mon, let's go outside, in case we disturb your mam.'

Daddy and Gus were in the corridor. Hester became aware of how wretchedly tired her father looked. He said, 'Go home, Vera. You've been here for hours. I'll sit with Laura tonight.'

'You sat with her all last night,' Vera protested, 'when she was at her worst. No, you go, and I'll stay, so you can have a nice, long rest.'

'I think you should both go home. *I'll* stay,' Gus said firmly.

'You're too young. *I'll* stay,' Hester insisted. He was only thirteen, Daddy was already worn out and Vera was seventy and needed to rest.

It was Sister Fitzgerald, the same nurse who had delivered Mary Maguire's baby, who settled the rather heated argument by telling them there was no need for anyone to stay.

'Your wife is unlikely to wake up during the night,

Mr Oliver, not after all she's been through. If she does, I promise I'll give you a ring and you can come straight away.'

There was a beef casserole being kept warm in the oven when they got home. Daddy said it was courtesy of Freddy's. 'Queenie brought it earlier. She reckoned you'd be starving, and Gus is starving all the time.'

'I'll see to everything, Daddy.' Hester gave her father a little push. Despite what had happened, she was quite hungry. 'Sit down and I'll make tea.'

'But, darling, you must be exhausted after that long journey.'

'I am, but not as exhausted as you. You'll give me a hand, won't you, Gus? Let's eat off our knees in front of the fire. I shan't bother setting the table.'

While they ate, she told them about Hollywood. There was a limit to what you could say in letters. She toned things down considerably. Under the circumstances, it didn't seem right to describe the marvellous time she'd had.

The meal over, Gus went to bed and she was left alone with her father, who stared silently into the fire for a long time before he began to speak.

'I think I should explain a bit about your mother, darling,' he said, sighing wearily. 'When she wakes up, she's going to say things that you'll find very strange.'

Hester frowned. 'What sort of things, Daddy?'

'That it's her fault the baby died,' he said dully. 'That she murdered it. You see, at first, when she found out she was pregnant, she didn't want the baby. She was going to have an abortion.'

'Mummy! An abortion! That's not like her.' She could hardly believe it.

'She hasn't exactly been herself in a long while.' He

went over to the sideboard. 'I need a drink, something stronger than tea.' He returned to the armchair with a bottle of whisky and a glass. 'I know it doesn't make sense, but that thing with Duncan affected her far more than it did you.'

'But I never noticed!'

'Probably because you were so upset yourself, that's why. When you went away, she became much worse, almost impossible to live with.'

'You should have told me,' she cried. 'I would have come home straight away.'

'What would I have told you?' he asked patiently. 'That Mummy was in a stinking bad temper all the time? Would you have come home for that? It didn't cross my mind there was a reason for it other than she'd taken on too much work at school. Perhaps that *was* the reason. I wouldn't know. It's only lately that I began to wonder if she should see a psychiatrist, but then I thought she'd be all right when the baby was born.'

'Why did she want an abortion in the first place?'

'She didn't want her teaching career disrupted. I insisted it was murder, but now I wish I'd just left her to it. Anything would have been better than the way things did turn out.'

'It *is* murder, Daddy. I'm all in favour of abortion, but no one can deny it's murder.'

'You're in favour!' He looked surprised. 'Strange, I never dreamt you'd think like that. I clearly don't know you very well, do I?' He smiled ironically. 'Would you have been in favour of your mother aborting your sister? She had to have a name, by the way, for the burial. Mummy wasn't in a fit position to pick one, so I chose Christine. I didn't want to use the name of anyone I knew, and can't remember ever having met a Christine in my life.'

'I knew some girls in Hollywood who'd had abortions. They didn't want a child disrupting their careers, either. I thought that very hard, but who am I to approve or disapprove? It was *their* bodies, *their* careers, nothing to do with me or anyone else.'

'Was Mummy being hard?'

'Of course she was, but please don't let's get into an argument, Daddy,' she pleaded. 'I'll tell you this much, when Mary became pregnant, I desperately wanted her to get rid of the baby. I had to stop myself from going to Glover Street and insisting that she did. If she'd agreed, I'd've been willing to forgive Duncan and take him back. I thought it more selfish of Mary to have the baby, than make love with my fiancé in the first place. Just think of all the misery that would have saved! Mary, Duncan, me, Vera, and now you say Mummy – we all would have been so much happier.'

Daddy smiled drily. 'Possibly, darling, except I'm not sure if Mary and Duncan would agree with that, not now. I understand Flora is a beautiful baby, absolutely delightful. And would you sooner have not gone to Hollywood?'

'What you don't know, you don't miss, Vera always says that. There's just one last thing, Daddy. What made Mummy change her mind and go ahead with the baby?'

'I'm not sure, Hester.' She thought he looked rather evasive. 'I'm just not sure.'

Chapter 17

After Hester had spent a week in Liverpool, she realised there was no chance of going back to Hollywood when she'd planned. Mummy had been discharged from hospital forty-eight hours after the baby's birth. The doctor said that, physically, she was quite fit, but it would do her mental state no good at all to remain in a place where other women's babies could be seen and heard. 'Perhaps a good rest in familiar surroundings will do the trick.'

The familiar surroundings didn't help a bit. Her mother was nothing like her old self. Daddy did his utmost to persuade Hester to return. 'I'll hire a day nurse,' he argued. 'I can take over when I come home from work. Gus will help.'

But Hester had no intention of allowing her brother's young life to be taken up helping to care for an invalid, at least not while she was around. Even less did she want a strange woman looking after her mother.

'I'm staying,' she told her father flatly. 'You can argue until the cows come home, but you'd be wasting your time. I'll go back, don't worry, once Mummy's better.' She wrote and asked Steven if he would cancel her room at the Wellington and put her possessions in store. 'I don't know when I'll be able to get away from here, but I will one day, I promise. And please tell Elfreda she'd better get someone else.'

Steven wrote back to say her things were now in the wardrobe in his room.

You had a pathetically small amount. I'll take them with me when I move into my new apartment, which means you'll have to live with me when you come back! You'll love the new place, Hes. It overlooks the Hollywood hills. I thought it about time I moved out of that crap hotel and found a place more fitting for a guy who'll be making his fourth movie in the New Year (with an even bigger part this time).

He finished by saying he'd told Elfreda and she sent her love, which Hester didn't believe for a minute.

But as the weeks turned into months and her mother showed no sign of getting better, Hester was forced to face the likelihood of it being a long, long time before she could get away.

According to the family doctor, Laura was suffering from something called Post-Natal Depression, which could have happened even if the baby hadn't been stillborn. 'Hopefully, she'll snap out of it soon. Until she does, I'd advise she went into a nursing home where she can be looked after properly.'

'I'm already looking after her properly,' Hester had snapped. 'She'll go into a home over my dead body.'

Roddy demanded a second opinion. The new doctor considered that the patient had been suffering from depression for a long while and the stillborn child was merely the catalyst that had tipped her over the edge. He also suggested a nursing home.

Roddy had no intention of letting his wife go into a home, but again suggested they engage a nurse so Hester could go away.

'No,' Hester said stubbornly. 'I'd never enjoy myself in Hollywood, not in a million years. I'd be thinking about Mummy all the time. I'd sooner stay here with you and Gus.'

She felt guilty for not noticing her mother hadn't been well before she went away, for seeing nothing odd about the fact that most of the letters she received were written by her father and her mother's had been very short and didn't say much at all. She felt guilty for not coming home when things had got really bad, even though she hadn't known. Roddy felt guilty and blamed himself for everything. Gus thought he should have been kinder and less impatient. 'I stayed out as much as I could. I thought she was just being bad-tempered.' Even Queenie wanted to kick herself for not being more understanding when Laura had told her she was pregnant. 'I was terribly short with her. It was the mention of abortion that did it.' Vera hadn't noticed anything other than her friend seemed a bit out of sorts, but felt guilty for not wondering why.

Everyone was looking at things with hindsight. *If only we'd known this. If only we'd done that.*

There were days when Laura seemed quite normal. 'Shall I make us something to eat?' she would ask, but when Hester went into the kitchen, she would find her mother in floods of tears, having forgotten all about food. 'I killed my baby,' she would sob. 'I *wished* it dead.' This was usually a signal for her to go into a sort of trance, hearing nothing, saying nothing, just staring into space for hours on end.

Other days, she refused to get out of bed. 'I feel so tired, sweetheart,' she would whimper and sleep for hours, often waking with a raging headache, sitting up in bed, rocking back and forth, holding her head because the pain was unbearable. Some nights she hardly slept, tossing and turning, keeping the whole house awake with her groans.

She seemed to have forgotten she'd been a teacher. When her friends from school came, she would stare at them in utter incomprehension. 'I don't like to be rude, but who are you?' Hester was glad when the friends stopped coming.

Once, she went looking for her mother in the bathroom where she seemed to have been an awfully long time, and found her with a razor blade pressed against her wrist. 'Stop!' she screamed, and cut her own hand badly when she wrested the razor out of her hand.

'What was I doing, sweetheart?' Mummy asked mildly.

'Don't you know? Can't you remember?'

'Didn't I just have a bath?'

'Yes, but . . . oh, it doesn't matter.' She put all the razor blades on top of the wardrobe and remembered the same thing had been done when Gus was little, though it hadn't been to prevent him from killing himself.

Her father was horrified when she told him. 'Christ Almighty.' He put his head in his hands. 'She'll have to be watched every damn minute.'

'This won't do,' Queenie said sternly when Hester had been back from America for six months. 'You've got to get out more. When was the last time you went out at night or shopping in town on your own?'

'Last week,' Hester replied. 'I went to the pictures with Gus, but I don't like leaving Daddy to cope on his own.'

'*You* cope on your own all week, and it won't do, Hester, love. Oh, I know how badly you want to look after Laura, but it's not right. In another few days, you'll be twenty-two. Will you still be doing the same thing when you're twenty-three? Or thirty-three, come to that?'

'I don't know,' Hester said miserably, thinking about the lovely time she'd had on her twenty-first.

'Why don't you get a part-time job?'

'I couldn't possibly! Who'd look after Mummy?'

'I know someone who would, someone you can rely on. And there's a part-time vacancy in Freddy's; two until half-five on the toy counter. It would suit you perfectly, get you out of the house so you can talk to people other than Laura and yourself.'

'Did you just make that job up?'

'Of course not,' Queenie said indignantly, though Hester suspected that she had.

'Who's the someone I can trust?'

'My mother.'

Theo had said, so many times, so reproachfully, 'I can't understand you, darling. I can't understand how anyone could not care about their mother. She's your only blood relative. She came to you when she was on her uppers because you were the only person she had in the world.'

Queenie had given up pointing out her mother hadn't bothered to contact her when she wasn't on her uppers. Theo thought loyalty to a parent should rise above such trifling matters as the parent beating you black and blue when you were a child and throwing you downstairs.

So, with great reluctance, she'd gone to see her mother, whose welcome had been so effusive, so obsequious, that Queenie had felt hugely embarrassed.

'I knew you'd come one day,' Agnes had said breathlessly. 'Thank you, luv, for everything; the flat, the clothes, the allowance. I never dreamt I'd end up in such a grand place.'

It seemed mean to say that her daughter hadn't paid for any of these things. 'That's all right,' Queenie muttered.

Her mother went on to say how much she was enjoying herself, playing cards on Monday afternoons with a woman upstairs and her friends, learning to play Bridge, regularly attending the Methodist church around the corner. She had also joined the Townswomen's Guild.

She was a fine-looking woman, Queenie had to give her that, what with the new hairstyle, the subdued make-up, the clothes, even the elegant apartment, which she kept spick and span, all had contributed to turning her into a vastly different woman from the one who'd arrived at Freddy's a few short months ago.

'The church is having a coffee morning a week on Saturday, luv. Perhaps you'd like to come?' she said eagerly.

'I work all day Saturdays.' She wouldn't have gone had Saturday been completely free.

'Oh, well, luv, never mind. Would you like a cup of tea?'

'Please.' It would help pass the time.

'Let us know beforehand when you come again, I'll get in some nice cakes,' Agnes said when she returned with a nicely set tray of tea things.

'I will,' Queenie said through gritted teeth.

The tray was put on the coffee table, Agnes leaned over, picked up the teapot, put it back, then collapsed on to the settee in a flurry of wild tears. 'Oh, luv,' she sobbed. 'Oh, Queenie. I'm dead sorry. I was an awful mam, dead cruel. You've no idea how bad I feel when I think back and remember all the horrible things I did. I don't know what got into me, I really don't. I must have been dead unhappy or something.'

'Well, you made me feel dead unhappy,' Queenie said coldly. If she'd been embarrassed before, she felt even more so now. She reached gingerly for her mother's arm and patted it. 'Don't cry,' she said stiffly.

‘I can’t help it. I think about it all the time. I cry meself to sleep every night. Will you ever forgive me, luv?’

‘Never!’ Queenie wanted to say. ‘Never, never, never.’ Instead, she said, ‘I don’t know.’

‘I wouldn’t blame you if you didn’t.’ Her mother sniffed pathetically. ‘I’d feel it hard to forgive someone who’d done to me what I did to you. That’s why I started going to church, to beg God for his forgiveness.’

‘Tell me something, Mother.’

‘What, luv?’

‘If you’d come back and found me living in Glover Street, my arm still twisted, maybe married with a couple of snotty-nosed kids, would you still be sorry for the way you treated me? Or would you feel the same contempt that you did before?’

‘Of course not, luv . . .’ Agnes paused and Queenie watched as her face gradually became confused. A flush of shame spread over her cheeks. ‘Yes, I would have, Queenie,’ she said in a small voice, ‘because I’m a wicked woman. It was seeing you, so pretty and smart, that brought me to me senses. I couldn’t stand the thought of someone like you remembering the things I’d done to a helpless little girl.’

Next time Queenie visited her mother, she was knitting a pair of uncomfortable looking booties for an African charity supported by the church. ‘Do these look all right to you?’ She held up a misshapen lump of knitting.

‘Not so bad.’

‘I’m trying to make up for me past sins, but I’m not so sure if I’m not committing another sin with these. Some poor baby might end up wearing them.’

‘Perhaps it would be best to buy some. Not Freddy’s, they’re too expensive. T. J. Hughes’s would be best.’

‘I think you’re right, luv.’ The knitting was discarded

with a sigh. 'I'll try something else. I'm reading a book to this old lady next door, *The Good Earth*. I go every night and read a chapter at a time. Last night, we finished off a whole box of Black Magic between us.'

'She seems to have gone through some sort of miraculous conversion,' Queenie told Theo that night. 'I'm pretty sure she's sincere.'

'It can happen,' Theo said serenely. 'Aren't you glad you went to see her now?'

'I suppose I am. I suppose it's best not to think about your mother with loathing. I'll never love her, because I'll never forget the things she's done, but I can't loathe her any more. She's become a different person from the one I used to know.'

Relations continued to improve and there came a time when Queenie was able to think of Agnes Tate as a perfectly normal, civilised human being. She invited her to lunch on Christmas Eve, booking a table well in advance in George Henry Lee's restaurant, but had to cancel when Laura went into hospital and the baby was stillborn.

'Of course, it doesn't matter, luv,' her mother said warmly when she rang to tell her that lunch was off. 'You look after your friend. What ward is she in? I'll send some flowers. Oh, and let me know if there's anything I can do to help.'

Six months were to pass before Queenie remembered the offer and thought of something her mother could do.

Agnes found the best way to keep Laura amused was to talk. She'd always liked talking, but the trouble was finding someone who'd listen. Laura provided a perfect audience, listening avidly to everything she said, giggling occasionally if it was funny. She seemed to have forgotten they'd once known each other slightly in Glover Street.

As Agnes's past life wasn't worth repeating, she invented an entirely new one. In London, she told Laura, she'd lived in a dead posh hotel and been waited on hand and foot. 'I must have had a hundred lovers,' she said nostalgically, as the new life took shape in her mind with such clarity that she began to believe it herself. 'One was a sheikh, another a jewel thief, one a famous film star.'

Sometimes, Laura's eyes would glaze, as if she was about to go into one of her trances, so Agnes would talk louder, raising her voice, gruff from the thousands of cigarettes she'd smoked over the years, snapping her thin fingers, even resorting to jumping up and down in order to catch Laura's attention. It usually worked.

Agnes took Laura for walks on Crosby Sands, firmly linking her arm in case she made a rush for the water. Queenie had pressed upon her the importance of keeping an eye on her charge at all times. 'If she goes to the lavatory and doesn't come out in a few minutes, knock on the door. If she doesn't answer, see what she's up to. Roddy's removed the lock because she's not safe in there on her own.'

She'd been entrusted with the care of Queenie's best friend and Agnes was determined to impress her daughter. Poor Laura had had a stillborn child and she felt sorry for her, but despite the new life she'd invented, she couldn't forget that there'd been a time when she'd wished Queenie had been born dead. She wasn't sure if it was possible to make up for that.

Mary parked the pram outside her mother's house in Glover Street. It wasn't quite ten o'clock and unusually warm for late September. Seagulls squawked angrily overhead, a sound she'd grown up with and missed now that she lived further inland. The front door was wide open. Flora, eighteen months old, was sitting up in the pram, beaming at everything and everybody. The straps undone, Mary picked up her daughter, not all that easy when you were eight months pregnant, and set her down. Flora ran into the house screaming, 'Nana, Nana, Nana.' Mary lumbered after her, and found a strange young woman in the living room, a strange baby crawling madly around the floor, and a familiar one – Vicky, their Caradoc's latest – fast asleep in Mam's arms.

'Hello, Mary,' the strange woman said.

'Hello,' Mary replied.

'You don't recognise me, do you? It's Tess Kennedy, used to be Nicholls. We went to Caerdovey together, along with our Jimmy and little Pete.'

'I thought you'd emigrated to Australia?' Tess had certainly improved over the years. Her once scraggy brown hair was now shoulder-length, thick and straight. She had on a fashionable linen costume in a dark lilac shade. Even her face looked different, probably because it wasn't set in the deep scowl that she'd always worn in the past.

'We did. It must be about ten years ago now. I'm only home because Frank's mam's ill and she hasn't long to go. Frank's me husband and he comes from Liverpool too. He wanted his mam to see me and the baby before she passes away.' She smiled fondly at the little bundle of energy racing furiously in circles around the floor, watched by a curious Flora. 'His name's Mark, and he's eleven months old. How old's yours?'

'One and a half. She's called Flora.'

'She's a lovely, bonny girl. What lovely coloured hair. Come and sit on me knee a minute, pet?' Tess held out her arms and Flora went willingly. She adored being petted. 'I'm expecting another in six months and I'd quite like a girl. That's another reason for coming now. I mightn't have felt up to it later. When's yours due?'

'The end of October.'

'She's hoping for a boy, aren't you, luv?'

'I don't really mind, Mam, so long as it's healthy. How's your Jimmy and little Pete?' She'd had her very first crush on Jimmy.

'Our Jimmy's doing marvellous,' Tess enthused. 'Remember how mad he was on cars?' The other women nodded. 'Well, he's got his own garage and is about to open another for our Pete to manage. Jimmy's married, by the way, and he's got two smashing kids, both boys. His wife, Joanna, is a nurse. Do you see much of Queenie Tate these days?'

Tess had only come to boast, Mary realised. Mind you, it was something she'd have done herself given the same circumstances. Queenie had turned her brother down, and Tess wanted her, more than anyone, to know how well he was doing in Australia.

'We see Queenie all the time,' Vera replied. 'She's done marvellous too. She's got a dead important job in Freddy's, that big posh shop in Hanover Street.'

'Did she ever get married?'

'Yes,' Mary lied. 'Her husband's awful well off.'

'If someone will take Vicky, I'll make us all a sarnie and a cup of tea,' Vera offered. Tess was still holding Flora, so Mary took Vicky out of Mam's arms.

'Your mam's not looking so well,' Tess remarked when Vera had gone into the kitchen.

'Isn't she?' Mary was startled. Like all Vera's children, she imagined her mother would go on for ever.

'She looks dead tired.'

'Maybe she didn't sleep so well last night.'

'You know,' Tess said thoughtfully, 'talking about Caerdovey, I was only thinking, the other day when

Frank's mam was on about the war, that we were dead lucky living there. I hated it at the time, but we always had enough to eat, not like the people back here. And it was a gear place to play. Remember Queenie giving us lessons in the room over your garage? We called it the den.'

Mary had darker memories of the den. 'It was OK,' she murmured.

'I've often wondered,' Tess continued, 'why you lot disappeared all of a sudden. One minute you were there, next you were gone. We didn't see you again until the war was over.'

'Queenie went into hospital and me mam and Laura thought it best if we stayed nearer home. We all went to Southport.'

'There were all sorts of rumours after you left.'

'Rumours?' Mary frowned. 'What sort of rumours?'

'Well, you know that chap, the son of the woman whose house you lived in? I'd never remember his name.'

'It was Carl, Carl Merton.'

Tess lowered her voice so Vera couldn't hear. 'Apparently, it was well-known in Caerdovey that he had a thing about young girls, that he'd actually raped a couple, but got away with it. Some people thought he'd been at Queenie and she went into hospital because she'd had a miscarriage when she fell out the den.'

'That's daft!' Mary said, annoyed. 'It was because she broke her arm.'

'Whatever.' She shrugged. 'Anyroad, everyone was glad that he died. He deserved it, they said.'

'Carl Merton's dead?'

'He died the same night Queenie went into hospital. Only landed on his head, didn't he, and was killed instantly? I'm surprised you didn't already know that, Mary.'

*

Mam and Tess must have thought she was mad, the way she suddenly remembered she'd made an appointment at the doctor's for Flora to have an injection.

'What's the injection for?' Tess wanted to know.

Mary made a wild guess. 'Typhoid fever.'

Tess also wanted to know if they could meet again. 'Give us a ring some time. Mam'll give you the number,' Mary shouted as she hurried down the hall as fast as an eight-month-pregnant woman could, clutching Flora's hand.

She hurried all the way to Marsh Lane station, slightly faster now that she had the pram to hold on to. Flora squealed with delight at this unexpected treat. When she got off at Crosby, she hurried again in the direction of the Olivers' house.

Hester opened the door and her jaw dropped in amazement when she saw who it was. She wore a smart black dress and her hair was smoothed back into a bun. Mary was shocked by how pale her face was, how dull her eyes. 'What do *you* want?' Hester asked shortly.

'To speak to you. It's important. I'll just get Flora out the pram first.'

'I'm not interested in anything you might have to say, no matter how important.' She didn't move aside to let Mary in and looked about to close the door.

'*Please*, Hes. I've got to talk to someone, and I can't possibly tell Du— I mean anyone else.'

'I know who you're married to, Mary. You can say his name.'

'Can I come in a minute? I need to sit down. I've been walking too fast for someone in my condition.'

'Only a minute,' Hester said grudgingly. 'I've got loads to do before I go to work.'

'Mam said you'd got a job on Freddy's toy counter. How's your mam, Hes?'

'She's asleep at the moment, but she's been a little

better since Agnes started coming. Agnes goads her into doing things. I think I'm too gentle with her.' A wistful smile touched Hester's lips when Mary carried Flora past and the little girl made a grab for her nose.

'What is it that's so important?' she asked when they were inside. 'To tell the truth, I never expected to see you in this house again.'

'I've just been to see me mam,' Mary said, sinking on to the settee and setting Flora on the floor with a rag doll. 'Tess Nicholls was there – Jimmy's sister, remember? She's married now, with a little boy.'

'I thought the Nicholls lived in Australia?'

'They do. Tess has come back for some reason. Oh, Hes, she said a terrible thing.' She repeated, word for word, what Tess had said, finishing with, 'We killed him, Hes. We killed Carl Merton.'

'Oh, my God!' It hadn't seemed possible for Hester's face to look any paler, but it did. 'You took one foot, and I took the other . . .'

'And we tipped him over the edge. According to Tess, he landed on his head. It means we're murderers, Hes.'

The two women were silent for a while, then Hester said angrily, 'Did you have to come and tell me? Couldn't you have kept it to yourself? As if I didn't have enough troubles at the moment, without something like this on top.'

'I just didn't think. I had to talk to someone and there was only you.'

'That's the trouble with you, Mary. You never think. You just go ahead and do exactly what you want without any regard for other people's feelings.'

Flora was fed up being ignored. She threw the doll at Hester and it landed on her lap. Hester picked it up and gravely gave it back. 'Here you are, darling.'

'Tank you,' Flora said politely, and proceeded to chew the doll.

'I'm sorry, Hes,' Mary said humbly. 'Sorry about everything. Anyroad, as regards Carl Merton, we did the world a favour. Tess said he'd already raped two other girls. Everyone in Caerdovey thought he deserved to die.'

'Yes, but it wasn't our job to act as judge and jury.'

'Say if we'd let him pull Queenie into the den. What d'you think he would have done to her?'

'We'll never know. Do you think he *raped* her?' Hester said slowly. 'Remember I told you about waking up, weeks before, and he was in our bedroom?'

'I remember. Do you think Queenie really had a miscarriage?'

'She could have.'

'We talked about it when we were in Southport,' Mary reminded her. 'We told her what we'd done.'

'And she told us Carl Merton was still alive.'

'So we wouldn't be frightened, knowing the truth. And she said he'd only come into the bedroom because he was drunk. Should we tell her we know he's been dead all along?'

'It would only upset her, bring everything back.'

Mary made a face. 'I'm not sure if I'll sleep tonight, knowing what we did.'

'I can't imagine ever sleeping again.' Hester shuddered. 'Would you like a drink, Mary?' She got to her feet. 'I think I need a very strong cup of tea.'

'I'd love one, Hes. No sugar.'

'You've stopped taking sugar? You used to take two spoons, heaped.'

'Well, I have to think of me figure. I put on loads of weight last time I was pregnant. I've tried to be more careful this time.' Mary rubbed her swollen stomach and dropped her eyes. 'I'm sorry, Hes, like I said before. I never think before I act, Mam always tells me that. The last thing I wanted was to spoil things between you and Duncan.'

'Then what were you doing in his flat?' Hester asked hotly. 'Why did you have sex if you didn't want to spoil things? Why, Mary? Why?' she demanded. 'He was *my* boyfriend.'

'I was jealous, that's why. I wanted to prove something to meself, I'm not even sure now what it was. It was all my fault, Hes. Duncan didn't want to do it, he just couldn't help himself.'

Hester laughed. 'Poor old Duncan, forced to have sex when he didn't want to. I bet he hated it.'

'I think he did.'

'I won't ask if he hates it still, it would be rude. I'd better go and make that tea before I tear your eyes out. Would Flora like something?'

'Have you any orange juice?'

'There's some in the fridge.'

Mary followed her into the kitchen, Flora holding on to her skirt. 'Hes, is there the faintest chance of us being friends again?'

'No chance at all,' Hester said bluntly.

'I'd love it if we were.'

'*I* wouldn't.'

'But you're over Duncan now, aren't you? Mam said you had a great time in America. Did you meet anyone there? A man, like?'

'Yes.' Hester put the kettle on the stove. Her lips were tightly pursed. 'Yes, I did.'

'What was he like?'

'Gorgeous. He loved me, but I wasn't sure if I loved him. I'm sure now, but I don't know what good that will do. I'm never likely to see him again, am I? I can't leave Liverpool until Mummy's better, and there's no way he'd leave

Hollywood. I wish I was hard, like you.' She turned to Mary, her blue eyes full of tears. 'Oh, Mary! I'm so unhappy. I'm never going to get married, have children. Every time I fall in love, it all goes horribly wrong.'

Mary took her old friend into her arms. 'There, there,' she whispered, gently patting her back. 'There, there.'

Christmas at the Olivers' was almost normal compared to the disastrous one the year before. At least, it started off normally.

On Christmas Eve, Agnes had taken Laura to have her hair set, Hester had bought her a new frock in soft, pale blue jersey. It was a long while since she'd worn anything so pretty and feminine. Roddy gave her a gold locket with pictures of her children inside; Gus had bought her a chiffon scarf, all the colours of the rainbow.

'You look like the girl I married,' Roddy said softly when Laura came downstairs in her new frock. Her black hair had grown and was a mass of curls and waves, and her cheeks were pink.

When they sat down to dinner, Hester held her breath. Was this the beginning of the end? Would Mummy soon be completely better? Perhaps it wasn't far off the time when she could go back to America, start living again. She recalled it was a long time since she'd heard from Steven. At first he'd written every week, then every month, but there'd been nothing at all since October, not even a Christmas card.

The meal went well until they reached the pudding stage, when her mother suddenly, and for no apparent reason, burst into tears. 'I'm so sad,' she sobbed. 'I feel so terribly, terribly sad.'

Roddy put his arms around her, Gus leapt to his feet and began to stroke her hair, Hester reached across the table and took her hands, but all the love in the world couldn't stop Laura from feeling so terribly, terribly sad.

Agnes Tate thoroughly enjoyed her Christmas. She went to church first thing, then to the church hall where dinner was being prepared for twenty or so old age pensioners who would otherwise have eaten alone. After the old people had finished, played a few games, and had been taken home, she went back to her flat, feeling virtuous, and had a late Christmas dinner with her card-playing friends upstairs, all widows like herself – Agnes took it for granted that by now she really was a widow. They drank a bit too much and swapped some rather risqué jokes. Agnes didn't contribute, the only jokes she knew were downright filthy.

On Boxing Day, she slept late, snacked on some cold turkey, then went to a sherry party thrown by a member of the Townswomen's Guild. She'd never realised you could enjoy yourself *and* behave yourself, both at the same time.

Queenie and Theo spent a quiet few days in the apartment on top of Freddy's. They'd spent a blissful two weeks in Kythira in November and *Queen of the Mersey* had been waiting for them in the port of Catania, Sicily. The boat was now under a new captain, William Porter. Trefor Jones had started his own business and couldn't spare the time. Whether this was true or not, Queenie didn't know.

Now they were both exhausted after the hectic run-up to Christmas. In a few days, the sales would begin, and things would be even more hectic.

On Christmas Day, they went to the Adelphi for dinner, where a jazz quartet offered foot-tapping renditions of 'White Christmas' and other seasonal numbers.

The meal was perfect, the wine potent, the atmosphere terrific. Looking around, Queenie wished they belonged with a crowd like most people there, that she had a father, a normal mother, sisters, brothers, that she could have got to know Theo's daughters, that she *belonged*. She had friends, good friends, but they had their own lives to lead. Most of all, she wished she had a child, but it seemed that was not to be.

'Enjoying yourself, darling?' Theo whispered in her ear.

'Oh, *yes*,' she said, turning to him. The love in his eyes made her want to weep. Nothing else in the world mattered when she had Theo.

The new baby was called Christopher; Chris for short. Duncan was dead pleased it was a boy, Mary too, though she wouldn't have minded another girl. 'Now we've got a perfect family,' Duncan crowed.

They did their best to make sure Flora's nose wasn't put out of joint by the new arrival, and made more of a fuss of her than usual, which suited Flora down to the ground. She seemed quite taken with her little brother, insisted on helping to change his nappies, push him in the pram, and demanding a turn on her mother's breast when Chris had finished. But Mary was having none of it. 'You've got teeth. You'd only bite.'

Chris was a handsome little chap with tufts of dark brown hair, like little bushes, on his otherwise bald head. Unlike his sister, he slept all night and was no trouble at all.

At twelve o'clock on Christmas Day, when Chris was just one month old, the Maguires set out for Glover Street. It was the custom for all the Monaghans to spend the day with their mother. Mary wore a lovely white lace blouse that Duncan had bought her for Christmas – she hoped her breasts wouldn't leak. Flora, conceited little madam that she was, had refused to wear a cardigan that would have hidden her new taffeta frock, pink with puffed sleeves and an enormous sash.

'If she's that fussy now, at twenty-one months, what on earth will she be like when she's older?' Duncan chuckled affectionately.

The house in Glover Street was packed to capacity. 'Next year, we'll take over Bootle Town Hall,' Dick gasped, as he struggled through the living room in an attempt to reach the kitchen. 'Our mam definitely needs another lavvy installing, even two.'

A perspiring Vera was sitting in a chair, hidden beneath layers of children, big and small. They all adored their nana. Although her daughters-in-law helped on these occasions, working out between them who would bring the cake, the pudding, the mince pies, the trifle, the turkeys, and other delicacies, it was Vera who did the real hard work. She'd been up since dawn, peeling spuds, nipping the tails off Brussels sprouts, buttering half a dozen loaves, and making the gravy well ahead, otherwise she'd forget and everyone would sit down, half in the living room, the other half in the parlour, their dinner going cold, and her in a desperate panic while she hurriedly prepared a lumpy mess.

After dinner, Mary went upstairs with Chris who was due for a feed. She took him into her old bedroom and found Diane, their Charlie's wife, who was also feeding her latest baby.

'It's like a madhouse down there,' Mary remarked, opening her blouse.

'I know, it always is, but I wouldn't miss it for worlds.'

'I wouldn't either.' Mary remembered the Christmas she *had* missed. It had been dead horrible. She shuddered, remembering, and comforted herself with the thought it would never happen again.

*

As soon as dinner was over, the men went to the pub, taking Duncan with them. They came back for a lively tea, everyone watched television or played games and, as soon as the pubs opened, the men disappeared again and didn't return until after closing time. More tea was made, the leftovers finished off, and sleeping children were collected off beds all over the house. Everyone kissed Vera and said what a lovely day they'd had, and all of a sudden, the house was dead quiet.

Vera was too exhausted to move out of the chair, even though she longed for her bed. Now that everyone had gone, she was aware how hard and fast her heart was pounding. Her arms were shaking and wouldn't keep still.

'Oh, Lord, I'm so tired,' she said aloud. Despite this, she wouldn't have changed the day one whit. She loved the feel of little bodies pressing against her, little hands stroking her hair, her face, her arms, pinching her elbows. She loved the way her lads placed big, sloppy kisses on her cheek when they came and went, or if they were just walking past and felt like it, saying, 'Love you, Mam.' Mary did the same.

She was glad their Mary seemed settled with that nice Duncan chap. The relationship hadn't exactly started off well, but they appeared happy enough with each other now, and their kids were little darlings; all her grandchildren were. If only Albert could see them, she thought tenderly. If he'd been there, the day would have been perfect. She'd been dead lucky, having such a wonderful husband and nine lovely kids.

The shaking in her arms was becoming quite painful. She twitched her shoulders, trying to shake the pain away, but it didn't work. And now she was having difficulty breathing and there was another pain in her chest, quite fierce.

Vera closed her eyes, little realising that she would never open them again.

It was Iris who found her. Dick and Iris still lived across the road in the flat once occupied by Agnes and Queenie Tate. She'd come to help give her mother-in-law a hand tidying up the house, which had looked a tip the night before when she'd left.

She found Vera in a chair by the fire that had burnt itself out. At first, Iris thought she'd fallen asleep and gave her hand a little shake. But the hand was as cold as ice.

Vera's big, kind heart had beaten its last during the night.

Six days later, on New Year's Eve, a Requiem Mass was held in St James's Church. Vera's children were finding it hard to accept that their mother was dead. They'd imagined Mam being there when they died themselves, holding their hands, trying to kiss them better, saying how much she loved them.

The church was packed. Vera had friends all over Bootle. Four of the Monaghan lads carried the coffin with its precious burden into the church, the other four carried it out to the hearse, which would take it to Ford cemetery, where their beloved mam would rest in peace in the same grave as her darling Albert.

A cruel, freezing wind carried little specks of snow across the desolate cemetery. The heap of soil beside the grave was a little mountain of ice and the mourners shivered inside their thick coats.

Laura Oliver had taken Vera's death badly. 'It's the end of everything,' she said to Roddy when Vera's body was lowered into the grave. Her children, Mary first, queued to throw in little lumps of earth that landed with a hollow bang on the coffin that had a brass crucifix fixed to the lid.

'Don't think like that, darling.' Roddy squeezed her arm.

'But it is!' Laura said dully. 'For years now, there's been Vera, Queenie and me. We went through so much together, but now Vera's gone and nothing will ever be the same again.'

'Darling, tomorrow's the start of a new year, nineteen fifty-seven. Let's look to the future, not the past.' God, it had been a lousy two years, Roddy thought. First that business with Hester, then Laura virtually losing her mind, and now Vera. He comforted himself with the thought that the years before had been good ones. He and Laura had been happy most of the time. And there'd be good years again. After all, if a person didn't think that way, they may as well be dead.

'Steven rang on Christmas Day,' Queenie told Hester, when everyone was walking back to the cars. 'He said the weather was lovely in Hollywood. The complex he lives in has its own pool. He'd actually been swimming! It's hard to believe, isn't it, when it's so cold here.'

'Did he ask about me?' Queenie had warned her Steven wasn't to be trusted, so she hadn't mentioned they'd been about to become romantically involved.

'I can't remember, dear,' she said vaguely, which Hester took to mean he hadn't. 'He's got a new girlfriend. She was in that film he made earlier in the year. She sounds a beauty; half Spanish and half Irish. He's sending us a photo. I'll show it you when it arrives.'

The wake was held in Glover Street, starting off quietly; sherry was sipped, sandwiches handed around. The atmosphere was sombre, everyone dressed in black, wondering if they'd ever smile again. No one sat in Vera's chair. Iris and another daughter-in-law had looked after the smaller children, those too young to attend a funeral. They too seemed aware of the seriousness of the occasion and were subdued.

Later in the afternoon, things began subtly to change. The men removed their black ties and jackets, the women their funereal hats. The barrel of beer in the kitchen, hardly touched so far, became enormously popular. Dick went to the off-licence for half a dozen more bottles of sherry for the women, and Caradoc began to sing an Irish ballad, his mam's favourite, 'The Wild Colonial Boy'. Everyone joined in and very soon the noise was loud enough to burst the walls of number seventeen, Glover Street.

Jigs were danced, Victor did the fandango with a flower between his teeth, more songs were sung, screaming children raced up and down the stairs. The barrel of beer was emptied and another acquired.

'I've never been to a funeral like this before,' a mystified Theo bellowed in Queenie's ear.

'I wish Laura had stayed. It might have cheered her up a bit,' Queenie murmured. 'Hester too.' Hester had looked a bit crestfallen when she'd mentioned Steven had a new girlfriend, and she hoped the girl hadn't allowed herself to be taken in by his hollow charm.

'I can't hear a word you're saying,' Theo shouted. 'I thought everyone was upset Vera was dead.'

'Oh, they are, of course they are, but this is exactly the sort of funeral Vera would have wanted.'

March, 1973

Chapter 18

Mary supposed it wasn't possible to *un*spoil a child after almost eighteen years of spoiling the same child rotten. 'But Flora, luv,' she said despairingly, knowing she was wasting her time, knowing, also, that she wouldn't have wanted Flora any different, 'hot pants are dead common. Just look at this!' She held up a pretty peasant dress in ethnic-patterned voile, ankle-length, with a square neck, and long bishop sleeves gathered tightly at the cuffs. 'I would have loved a dress like this when I was eighteen.'

'Yuck!' The dress was accorded a withering look. 'It's dead old-fashioned.'

'Freddy's don't stock old-fashioned clothes, luv.'

'Maybe they stock them for old-fashioned women. No, Mam. I want hot pants. They've got them in C and A, made out of shiny plasticky stuff.'

'Have they got a skirt with them?' Some hot pants had a long skirt over, split from the midriff. Mary was slightly relieved when Flora said that they had. Duncan would blow his top when he saw the outfit, but Flora would soon put a stop to that. All she had to do was pout her pretty pink lips and her father was lost – and her mother was just as easily pacified, Mary thought fondly, when they left Freddy's and made for C and A.

There could have been another argument when Flora chose the hot pants in fluorescent pink, but Mary forced herself to keep her mouth shut when she emerged from the cubicle looking for all the world like a teenage prostitute. The top and pants were all-in-one and the skirt was see-through gauzy stuff. 'What do you think, Mam?'

'Fine,' Mary said faintly. 'What sort of shoes would you wear with that?'

'Boots, Mam. Black, knee-length boots, skin tight.'

'We have them in the shoe department in the corner,' the assistant said helpfully.

'Thank you.' Mary sighed. Flora disappeared into the cubicle to change. At least the outfit wasn't going to cost an arm and a leg. She and Duncan had thought it would be nice to splash out on a dress for the forthcoming party, which was why they'd started off at Freddy's, a shop Mary couldn't have afforded for herself. Thinking back, she supposed that, at the same age, she herself would have turned up her nose at the voile dress and wanted hot pants – mini skirts even more so, really wowing the chaps at dances. But in her day, young and old wore the same sort of clothes. Now, there were fashions a woman of thirty-eight – herself, for instance – would look ridiculous in, hot pants being a prime example.

Perhaps Freddy's *was* becoming a bit old-fashioned. It was about time they had a teenage section, where young people wouldn't pretend to vomit when faced with a selection of party clothes. She'd suggest it to Queenie next time they met.

Flora came out and they went over to look at boots. Mary sat down and left her to it. Her opinion wasn't required. She transferred her thoughts to the party next Friday. How on earth would they cope with so many guests? Flora had invited at least half the class at school, her friends from the youth club, the dramatic society, loads of Monaghans about her own age. Everyone had accepted. Her daughter was a very popular girl, particularly with boys – not surprising considering her looks. Only today, Mary noticed the way male heads had turned when they saw the little heart-shaped face, huge brown eyes, and perfect mouth, framed in a cascade of golden brown waves and curls. The combination of Duncan's ginger and Mary's black had produced a truly spectacular colour. Poor Chris had ended up with *un*spectacular brown.

She watched her daughter stretch out a slim leg and pull on a high-heeled black boot, also made of shiny, plasticky stuff, as thin as paper. She'd look even more like a prostitute in them *and* the hot pants.

The boots purchased, Mary suggested lunch. 'But not in one of them fast food places. I'd like to go back to Freddy's. The meals don't cost an arm and a leg, unlike the clothes.'

Flora seemed about to demur, but must have reckoned it wouldn't hurt to do what her mother wanted for a change. On the way out of C and A, she bought a pair of bright pink hoop earrings and black, fishnet tights. Her party outfit was complete.

'Jaysus, Mam!' Flora snorted when they sat down in the half-full restaurant. 'We're the only ones here under a hundred. It's like being in an old people's home.'

'Shush, Flora! Someone might hear.'

'I bet they're all stone deaf. Can I have a hamburger?'

'They don't do hamburgers. Read the menu, it's full of healthy, nourishing food. I think I'll have cottage pie. It's ages since I made it at home.' The thought of food was making Mary drool. It was five hours since breakfast, and then she'd only had half a grapefruit. She wished she didn't care so much about being slim – well, not getting any plumper. What heaven it must be to eat anything you wanted.

'I'll have a mushroom omelette. Can I have a glass of wine? *Please*, Mam,' Flora said in her most cajoling voice. 'In another five days, I'll be old enough to go in pubs.'

'Oh, all right.' She was impossible to resist. 'We'll both have one.'

'By the way, Mam, I've invited someone else to me party.'

'Flora!' Mary gasped, dismayed. 'There's already about fifty coming. We'll never fit them in.'

'No one'll want to sit down,' Flora said, shrugging carelessly, 'so it doesn't matter.'

'Who have you asked now?'

'Chap by the name of Edward Cunningham. Everyone calls him Ned. He's a writer and last week he came to school to talk to the A-level English students about twentieth-century literature. He actually made it sound interesting.'

'It probably is. And you asked him to the party there and then?'

'No. I waited until he'd finished talking. Actually, Mam, he's dead gorgeous.' Flora's cheeks had gone slightly pink, which happened very rarely. She must fancy this Ned Cunningham character. Mary quite liked the idea of her daughter marrying a writer. It would certainly be something to boast about.

'I hope our Chris hasn't invited that twit Roger Jefferies,' Flora said sulkily.

'It's Chris's house just as much as yours. He's entitled to bring anyone he wants.'

'Yes, but it's not his party. He never has parties 'cos he hasn't got any friends, only Roger, and he's dead peculiar, Mam.'

Mary worried about Chris, who'd spent his life living

in the shadow of his exuberant sister. He was so quiet and well-behaved, half the time she and Duncan forgot he was there. 'Flora's got as much personality in her little finger as Chris has in his whole body,' Duncan was fond of saying.

The food arrived. Flora picked at the omelette, ate the mushrooms, but left most of the egg. She sighed, bored, tipped back her chair, and stared at the ceiling, while her mother plodded through the cottage pie.

'There's all sorts of bits missing off the chandeliers,' she announced after a while.

'What sort of bits?'

'Glass bits. I'm glad we're not sitting underneath one, because the ceiling's all cracked and one could come crashing down on us any minute. The ceiling could do with a fresh coat of paint an' all. It's filthy.'

Mary looked up. Flora was right. In fact, not just the ceiling, but the whole restaurant was looking rather shabby. The carpet was threadbare in places, the chairs and tables chipped. Perhaps it was time Theo Vandos retired and someone younger took over.

'Why is no one playing the piano?' Flora demanded, as if her mother could do something about it. 'This place could do with a juke box.'

'Tell Queenie that on Friday at the party.'

'She's not coming, is she?' The front legs of the chair crashed on to the floor. 'She's *old*, Mam. You shouldn't have asked her.'

'Queenie's only forty-seven, luv, and she's helping with the refreshments, Hester too. We can have a nice natter. If you prefer, we'll go to the pictures and you and your friends can see to the food yourselves.'

'There's no need for that, Mam,' Flora said hastily, 'but Queenie's not bringing her feller, is she? I mean, the guy's truly ancient.'

'She's not bringing Theo, no, but he's one of the nicest men I've ever known, so don't be rude,' Mary said crossly. Flora had gone too far. 'Always remember, either we die young or we grow old. One or the other will happen to us all, you included.'

Flora made a grotesque face. 'Me, I'd sooner die young any day. If I'm not dead by thirty, I'll seriously consider killing meself.'

'If you're still as horrid when you're thirty as you are now, then I'll tell you this much, Flora Maguire, *I'll* seriously consider doing it for you.'

'Nowadays, they don't have parties like we used to,' Mary complained the following Friday when her daughter's party was in full swing. 'They don't *sing* any more, not like we did. I used to love a good sing-song.' She groaned. 'It's a good job Flora didn't hear me say that. She'd say I was showing me age.'

'It's gone suspiciously quiet in the parlour,' Hester commented.

'We never did *that* sort of thing, either,' Mary said primly. 'We were too busy having a good time.'

Hester smiled. 'Perhaps they're having an even better time. Don't worry, Mary. They can't get up to much. There isn't the room for it. Anyway, I think we still made as much noise.' Having gone through all Flora's Status Quo LPs, whoever was operating the gramophone had now started on T-Rex.

Queenie came in with two empty plates. 'More sandwiches,' she cried. 'I was hardly in the room a minute, when it seemed as if a million hands shot out and there wasn't a sarnie left.'

'Will sardine and tomato do? There's no more ham and hardly any cheese.' Hester set about buttering another loaf.

'There's some crab paste in the larder. At the rate they're going, they'll have no room left for afters. They've already eaten a hundred sausage rolls between them.'

'Gobbled, you mean,' said Queenie. 'Is there much left to drink?'

'Not enough, I bet. I'll send Duncan out in a minute for more.' Mary sat down at the table looking moidered. 'I don't know where I am or what I'm up to! I wish Laura were here. She'd soon sort me out. Lord Almighty!' She looked even more moidered. 'I'm sorry, Hes. It just came out. Every time I open me mouth, I put me foot in it.'

'That's all right,' Hester said in a level voice. She put three tins of sardines on the table in front of her friend. 'Open these and mash them up with mayonnaise. Queenie, will you slice the tomatoes, please? I seem to be the only person here doing a job of work.'

'I don't know what I'd've done without you both. Has anyone seen Duncan, by the way?'

'He's on the stairs with a pile of kids discussing rock 'n' roll,' Queenie said. 'He took *two* sarnies.'

'Greedy bugger, he's getting a paunch.'

Hester had noticed Duncan's paunch. When they'd gone out together, she'd considered him very good-looking. She wondered if she'd still think the same if she'd married him? Had Mary also noticed her husband's receding hair, his white, pasty face, the sagging jowls? Duncan Maguire, not quite forty, was doing nothing to stave off middle age. These days, she found him most unappealing.

The women worked industriously until there were two more plates of sandwiches for Queenie to take around. Mary went to look for Duncan to tell him more drink was required. Left alone, Hester examined her face in the mirror over the sink. Perhaps she too had deteriorated with the years. Perhaps Duncan found *her* unappealing. She stroked the skin under her eyes. No wrinkles and no bags. No wrinkles around her mouth, either. Raising her head, she turned sideways to check if there was any sign of a double chin and was pleased to note there was none.

'Don't worry, you're dead beautiful,' said an amused voice.

She turned quickly. A man had entered the kitchen; not very tall, not very handsome – his nose was too big, his mouth too wide for that – but his face was quirky and good-natured, and his brown eyes were friendly and warm. He had brown hair tied in a ponytail, and wore an earring in his left ear, a green cotton Indian shirt without a collar, and rather grubby jeans. He looked in his mid-twenties, slightly older than the other guests.

'Can I help you?' she asked, slightly embarrassed.

'I'm after a cheese sarnie.'

'There's hardly any cheese left, just crumbs. There's sardines and crab paste.'

'I don't eat fish or meat. I'm a vegetarian,' the man said with an engaging grin.

'Are you now!' She'd met a few vegetarians in Hollywood, but never in Liverpool. 'Would crumbly cheese and tomato do?'

'It'd do nicely, thanks very much. I'm Ned Cunningham, by the way. And who are you?'

'Hester Oliver. You must be the writer. Mary said Flora had invited you.' Mary had also said Flora had raved about him all week. She was dead keen. 'Have you had much published?'

'Only a couple of poems in the local paper – for which I wasn't paid. It did, however, provide me with a certain amount of prestige, which, in a roundabout way, is how I managed to get invited to Flora's party.'

'Then how do you live if not by writing?' she asked curiously.

'I'm a postman. Where do you live? I might deliver post your way.'

'Crosby.'

'I cover Seaforth, well part of it.' His brown eyes twinkled. 'If you want your letters delivered by a writer, you'll just have to move house.'

'You could always change your route.'

'I might well do that.' He sat at the table. 'I'm starving,' he announced, sniffing pathetically.

'I won't be a minute.' She hurriedly buttered four rounds of bread and sliced a couple of tomatoes. 'Would you like salt and pepper?'

'Both, ta. Is there any tea going?'

'I'll make some. Is there anything else you want while you're here?' she asked sarcastically. 'Shoes cleaning? Shirt washing? A five-course dinner making?'

'Not just now, Miss Oliver. But if you'd like to come round our house tomorrow, you can do all of them things.' He gave her a leery wink while taking a huge bite of sandwich. 'I can think of one or two other things you can do while you're there,' he said through a mouthful of bread.

'I was always taught not to speak with my mouth full.' Hester couldn't help it, she burst out laughing.

'You were obviously brought up better than me. Where do you work, Hes?' he asked chattily.

She put the kettle on and sat opposite him at the table, rather enjoying herself. 'I work for a detective agency; Quigley Investigations. I'm Sam Quigley's secretary.'

'Honest! I bet that's interesting.'

Hester was about to tell him how interesting it was,

when Queenie and Mary came into the kitchen together. 'Our Flora's looking for you everywhere, Ned,' Mary said. 'I never dreamt you'd be out here with the old folk.'

Queenie choked. '*Old* folk! Do you mind!'

'Well, none of us are exactly young.'

'None of us are exactly old, either, Mary.'

'Whatever your ages, you are three enchanting and most desirable ladies.' Ned Cunningham stuffed the final sandwich in his mouth, got to his feet and gave a little bow. 'Particularly you,' he said in a low voice when he went past Hester.

Quigley Investigations operated from a drab, entirely featureless building above a travel agency in Exchange Street East. The name was painted on the door of the second-floor office, along with, in smaller letters, 'Surveillance, Matrimonial Enquiries, Process Serving, Insurance Claims, Missing Persons Traced, Confidential and Caring Service, Store Detectives Supplied'.

Once, Hester had spent the afternoon as a store detective, but hadn't so much as glimpsed a thief, and a member of staff had reported her for 'lurking suspiciously'. It was when Sally, Sam Quigley's wife, who usually did that sort of thing, had been indisposed.

Sam Quigley, sixty-one, and a retired police sergeant, was the type of private detective seen in films, an impression gained because he modelled himself on Humphrey Bogart. Sam was too old, too small and too stout to look much like his hero, but he wore the same heavily studded, tightly belted mack, the same dark trilby hat with the snap-brim tipped over one eye.

Business was good. As well as Hester and Sally, Sam employed two investigators to deal with dodgy insurance claims, keep a watch on individuals whose spouses suspected they were having affairs, and track down missing persons. If a case involved travelling far, Sam usually went himself.

When Hester had started eight years ago, Sam had said, 'I don't care how well you type, luv, or how fast, as long as you're sympathetic to me clients when they come in. For some, a private detective's their last resort. What they really need is a shoulder to cry on. Can you do that, luv?'

'Yes,' Hester had promised. So, if Sam was out or had a client in his office, she would often spend ages on the phone listening to a desperate voice explaining that someone close to them had disappeared and the police couldn't do anything about it, or they were worried their husband or wife was cheating on them. Sometimes, people came without an appointment and she would treat them gently, make them a cup of tea.

The job was interesting, as Ned Cunningham had surmised. It could also be very sad and occasionally very funny.

Five days after Flora's party, Hester was in the office alone with nothing to do except read the novel lying open on her desk. Instead, she stared wistfully out of the window at the crisp, sunny April day and the cloudless blue sky. Working in a shabby little room lined with metal filing cabinets full of yellowing paper wasn't so bad in winter, it felt warm and cosy. But the sun always made her discontented, wanting to be somewhere else; Hollywood, for instance, where the sun seemed to shine all the time.

I've never *lived*, she thought miserably. There was just that one, single year when I had a good time. She told herself she was being ridiculous. She'd had a perfectly good time before she'd gone to America, not counting that business with Duncan, of course, and she'd had a reasonable time since. She enjoyed her job and had a boyfriend – well, a boyfriend of sorts. Andy Michaels was more a companion, someone to go to the pictures with, the theatre, accompany her to parties or if she was asked to dinner. Hester did the same for him. Andy was a nice-looking man in his early forties, divorced. It had all been rather unpleasant and he had no intention of having a serious relationship with another woman. They'd met four years ago and all he'd done so far was kiss her cheek, which suited Hester down to the ground as she had no wish for him to go further.

'The trouble with you, darling,' her father had said loads of times, 'is you have too kind a heart. There's no need for you to stay home any longer. I can manage all right on my own. Go back to America – go anywhere – before it's too late.'

'I'm quite happy here, Daddy,' Hester always replied. There was no way she'd leave him on his own after what had happened.

She remembered the day as clearly as if it were only yesterday. She was still working part-time at Freddy's, but had taken a few days off because Agnes had gone to Brighton with some friends and there was no one else to look after Mummy.

During the five years since Vera's funeral, Laura had hardly set foot outside the house, leaving when only absolutely necessary; to see the dentist or an optician. Some of the time, she seemed perfectly content, spending ages in the kitchen preparing that night's meal, or sitting in her chair, a needle in her hand, bent over some exquisite embroidery. She never read a newspaper, refused to watch the television news, had no idea that Harold Macmillan was the British Prime Minister, that Britain had just exploded its first hydrogen bomb, or Russia had sent a satellite into space. If there was a knock on the door, she would go up to her room and refuse to come down until the person had gone, even if it was someone like Queenie or Mary. Inevitably, they stopped coming. Queenie was terribly upset, feeling she was letting her friend down and being no help at all to Roddy and Hester. Agnes was the only outsider Laura would tolerate.

She had switched herself off, created her own secure, private little world where nothing, no one, could touch her. She had bad times, when she would weep that she wanted to kill herself, that life wasn't worth living. These times often occurred in the middle of the night and Roddy would help soothe away the tears and the horrible thoughts, give her a tablet, sit with her until she slept.

Hester had more or less got used to the way things were. She was twenty-seven, and had long ago given up all thoughts of Hollywood or of leading even a faintly interesting life. She couldn't imagine things ever being any different. Her main concern had been for Gus. It wasn't a very healthy environment for him to grow up in, but by then Gus had happily settled at Durham University, much to Hester's relief.

The day it happened, Laura had woken up in one of her worst moods, groaning, wailing that she wanted to die. Hester could hear Roddy speaking to her when she went downstairs to make breakfast. Not long afterwards, he had gone to work, refusing anything to eat, his face dark with grief or possibly some sort of impotent rage at what their lives had become. Hester took her mother a cup of tea, her heart heavy at the thought of the day ahead. Laura was sitting up in bed. She looked shocked, as if she'd just seen a ghost.

'Are you all right, Mummy?' Hester asked.

'I don't know,' Laura said vaguely. 'Oh, is that the post?' The letterbox had just rattled and there was a thud of letters on the mat. 'I wonder if there are any Christmas cards?' She leapt out of bed, suddenly as happy as a lark, went downstairs in her nightdress, and opened the cards, oohing and aahing over each one, saying how pretty it was before putting it on the sideboard with the ones that had already come.

It could happen in a flash, the change between wanting to die and running excitedly downstairs to collect the post.

'What shall we have for Christmas dinner, sweetheart?' she asked. 'Do you fancy duck for a change? Oh, I do love Christmas,' she said with a breathy sigh. 'I think I'll make the mince pies today, save a last-minute rush.'

Hester hadn't yet bought a jar of mincemeat, but Mummy had seemed so well that, after lunch, she didn't think it would do any harm to go to the shops and buy it now.

But, despite the evidence of the morning, she had actually forgotten how quickly things could change. When she got back, her mother was dead. She was lying in the bath, wrists slashed, the blood pumping into the water, so that it looked as if she was lying in a bath of blood. Her clothes were neatly folded on the cork-covered stool.

How could Hester possibly leave Daddy after that?

The front door of the office opened and Sam shouted, 'It's only me, luv.' He came along the corridor into her room, bundled in his Humphrey Bogart mac, the hat perched on the back of his head for a change. 'You're looking a bit under the weather, girl. What's up?'

Hester sighed. 'I was just thinking how nice it looked outside.'

'Off you go, then,' Sam said brusquely. 'It's nearly dinner time. Take an extra hour. There's not much to do, and I'll be here till three.'

'You're a lovely man, Sam Quigley. I'll take you up on that.'

'You'd better get going quick before I change me mind.'

She wandered down to the Pier Head where the air smelt salty and a fresh, sharp breeze blew. The Seacombe ferry had not long docked and a small queue of passengers was waiting to get on. On impulse, Hester ran down the pontoon and bought a return ticket. The short journey would only take about half an hour both ways. She had plenty of time to get back for one o'clock when she was meeting her father for lunch.

The water was a greeny-grey, quite smooth, with scarcely a ripple. A few minutes after she'd boarded, the boat gave a series of creaks and groans and started to move. She leaned over the rail and watched the curls and waves of creamy foam spurt from the stern. Flora's party had unsettled her, made her feel terribly old and past it. The music hadn't helped. She loved rock 'n' roll, but had never seen the Beatles and had only managed to get to the Cavern twice, both times with Gus. That wonderful, crazy time when Liverpool had seemed to be the centre of the universe, had passed her by – or perhaps *she* had passed *it* by, one or the other.

Never before had she met anyone like Ned Cunningham. If only she was ten years younger or he ten years older! They'd sort of 'hit it off', as people said nowadays. She'd liked him, but was unlikely ever to see him again, unless things got serious between him and Flora. If Flora had set her sights on him, he was unlikely to escape. She usually got anything she wanted.

Back in Liverpool and on dry land again, feeling better for the little voyage across the Mersey, Hester walked up Water Street, turned into North John Street, and came to the pub where she had arranged to meet her father. They rather clung to each other these days and often met for lunch. They were the only Olivers left. Gus had stayed in Durham and married Isobel whom he'd met at university. Perhaps it was the bad memories he had of the house in Crosby that stopped him from coming home to see them more than once a year. Isobel was expecting their third child in June.

Daddy was already there. He jumped to his feet, smiling, though the smile hadn't reached his eyes in a long while. He was only fifty-seven and still devastatingly attractive, at least so Hester thought. It seemed such a shame that he hadn't remarried.

'Darling!' He kissed her cheek. 'You look incredibly healthy. Your cheeks are glowing.'

'I've been for a ride on the ferry, all the way to Seacombe and back. Sam let me have an extra hour off.'

'Sam is an angel in disguise.' Since Hester had gone to work for him, Roddy's firm Glyn & Michaelson had engaged Sam a few times on some rather delicate matters. 'What shall I get you?'

'Just a sandwich, any sort, and an orange juice, please.'

'Coming up.' He went over to the bar.

Hester glanced around the crowded pub. There were few women there, the rest were businessmen, dressed like her father, in dark suits, dark ties, highly polished shoes. They all looked quite happy, quite normal, as they loudly discussed their work, their families, the headlines in that morning's papers. She supposed she looked happy and normal too. No one would have guessed the tragedy that lay behind her. But who knew what other tragedies might be hidden behind some of these happy, normal faces?

'Here you are, darling.' Daddy had returned. He'd bought a whisky for himself. He drank an awful lot of whisky, usually picking up two bottles off the supermarket shelves when they went shopping on Saturday morning. 'I got you a cheese sandwich. Is that OK?'

'Fine.' The mention of cheese sandwiches reminded her of Ned Cunningham. Hester smiled, but at the same time felt just a little bit sad.

Two days later, on Friday afternoon, Hester was typing away on the ancient, clanky typewriter that Sam kept promising to replace with a more modern machine, but always forgot. She was too busy to look out of the window. Sam had just dictated about a dozen letters that she wanted to finish before she went home. Sam came out of his office and shouted, 'I'm off now, luv. See you Monday. Have a nice weekend.'

''Bye, Sam,' she shouted. 'Same to you.' The front door opened and she thought it was Sam going out, but it must have been someone coming in, because Sam said, 'Good afternoon, son. Can I help you?' and a vaguely familiar voice replied, 'I'm looking for a missing person. Girl by the name of Hester Oliver. I met her at a party and I haven't been able to find her since.'

Sam laughed heartily. 'Well, son, you're in luck. You'll find the person you're looking for behind the door to your right. Be careful with her now. She's me fave person next to me wife.'

The front door closed, her own door opened, and Ned Cunningham came in. 'Hi, Hes,' he said, grinning his lovely grin.

'What do you want?' she stammered. She couldn't quite believe he was there. He wore the same jeans, and a different shirt under an incredibly hairy sweater.

'You, obviously. I thought we could have dinner together, nothing posh, just this veggy restaurant I know.'

'I don't finish until half-five.'

'That's OK. I'll wait.' He sat in a chair.

'But it's only half past four!'

'That gives us an hour to talk.'

'I haven't got time to talk,' she cried. 'I've got work to do.'

'Then I'll sit here and keep me mouth shut.'

Hester returned to the letters, but it was impossible to concentrate with Ned Cunningham watching her from the other side of the desk. She couldn't think, her shorthand had become incomprehensible squiggles, her hands were shaking and her fingers kept hitting the wrong keys. Worst of all, she kept wanting to laugh. She stopped typing and looked at him. 'Why are you here?' she asked.

'I've already told you, Hes.'

'Yes, but why on earth do you want to go to dinner with *me*?'

'Because I like you,' he said simply. 'And I got the impression the other night that you liked me.'

'But I'm thirty-eight, old enough to be your mother!'

'Strewth, girl! You must have been sexually active at an awful early age. I'm thirty-one.'

She did laugh then. And for some reason, she also wanted to cry. She looked across the desk into his dark brown eyes. They were very gentle and held an expression that caused a strange sensation to flutter through her body, as exquisite as it was unexpected.

And this was only the beginning!

'Please don't hurt me, Ned,' she whispered.

He knew exactly what she meant. 'I'll never hurt you, Hes.' He leaned over the desk and softly kissed her forehead. 'You'll always be safe with me.'

On Sunday, she went to see Mary and told her she was

going out with Ned Cunningham. If Flora's heart was to be broken, then the quicker, the better.

Mary looked cross. 'But our Flora really fancies him, even more so since the party.'

'He's a bit too old for her.'

'Pardon me, but aren't you a bit too old for him?'

'I'm seven years older, but that doesn't matter.'

'Anyroad,' Mary said nastily, 'I went right off him when I discovered he was only a postman. He's not even a proper writer. All he's had is a couple of poems published. Me, I couldn't stand poetry when I was at school.'

'Thanks, Mary.'

'What for?'

'Being so nice about my new boyfriend.'

'Oh, I'm sorry, Hes.' Mary's face crumpled. 'The truth is, I'm jealous. I don't know why, I've always been jealous of you. Just look at you! All starry-eyed and your smile's a mile wide, as if you've just won a million quid on the pools. I've never looked like that in me life. And your hair's all loose. You hardly ever wear it like that. It looks dead pretty.' She gave Hester's arm a warm squeeze. 'I wish you and Ned all the luck in the world.'

Ned Cunningham lived in a tiny terraced house in Townsend Street, Seaforth. The front door opened on to the pavement and there was a small yard at the back. The youngest of six children, his brothers and sisters had all married and now lived in different parts of the country. Both parents were dead. They had lived in the house for almost sixty years, and Ned's dad, the last to go, had left his son the rent book.

'It's all he had to leave,' Ned said angrily. 'He worked like a navvy all his life, and all he had to show for it was a bloody rent book and a few odds and ends of crappy furniture.'

Hester wondered what his dad would have thought if he could see his house and furniture now, everything painted in such an extraordinary array of colours; a bright red sideboard with blue drawers and white knobs, green chairs, a purple bed, pink wardrobe. There wasn't an inch of the house that wasn't painted; not a ceiling, not a wall, not a door, not even a floor.

Entering Ned's house was like entering a fantasy world. It was a fairy-tale house, with spangly cushions on the chairs, gaudy hangings on the wall, silvery shades on the lights.

'It's not very restful,' Hester said when she first went. 'I mean to write in.'

Ned replied that he found colours restful. 'The brighter, the better.' He showed her the back bedroom where he wrote at an old kitchen table – painted, of course, a vivid emerald green. It held a typewriter, even older than the one in Quigley Investigations. Beside it was a heap of loose paper, two or three inches deep.

'What's that?' she asked.

'That's me novel,' he answered, very seriously. 'I've been working on it for years.'

'I didn't know you were writing a novel. What's it called? What's it about?'

'I haven't got a title yet, but it's about me mam and dad, *their* mam and dad, me brothers, me sisters, their husbands and their wives, their kids. It's about me, and any minute now, it'll be about you too.'

'It means a lot to you, doesn't it, the novel?' She could tell by the way he spoke.

'Next to you, Hes, it means everything. I was the only Cunningham to go to university. Me mam and dad were dead proud. The others had left home by then and they could have done with the money. I suppose I just want to prove meself worthy of what they did for me. That's them there, Mam and Dad. It was taken about the time of their Golden Wedding.' He pointed to a photograph on the table of an elderly couple, unsmiling, staring grimly at the camera. 'They weren't used to having their photeys taken. I think they were a bit scared.'

'They look like another couple I used to know; Vera and Albert,' Hester said softly. 'They were wonderful, kindness itself, and so . . . *selfless*. They'd have given you their last penny. I loved them very much, but they're both dead too.'

'So, it's not true that only the good die young!' Ned took her in his arms. 'I love you, Hes. Shall we go to bed again and I'll show you how much?'

'You've already shown me,' Hester breathed. 'But, yes, I'd like you to show me again.'

She gave herself to him completely, told him everything, could be herself. She knew, just knew, that Ned would never let her down. At first, he and Roddy didn't get on. Roddy had been a staunch Conservative all his life and Ned was a Socialist. Even the Labour Party wasn't left enough for him. They met in the lunch hour and argued the whole time. It got quite heated.

'Is it serious?' her father asked that night.

'Yes,' Hester assured him.

'I rather hoped you'd do better than a postman,' he said stiffly.

'A postman is a quite respectable job, and responsible too. We'd be lost without them. Anyway, Ned's a writer. That's what drives him. He's in the middle of writing a marvellous novel.'

'Have you read it?'

'No,' she conceded. 'But I'm sure it's wonderful.'

Her father smiled. 'I'm glad you have faith in him, darling. Anyway, what does my opinion matter? You're the one who's going to marry the chap.'

'We might not get married, Daddy. We might just live together.' There'd been a great upheaval in moral values in the sixties. Nowadays, people quite openly lived together, had babies out of wedlock, without too many people turning a hair. Hester was surprised when her father's face froze in a frown.

'I'd be very much opposed to that idea, Hester.' He leaned back in the chair and briefly closed his eyes. 'I'm not being moralistic, I'd be a hypocrite if I were, but darling, I don't think I could stand it if something bad happened to you again. I feel . . .' He paused. 'I think "fragile" is the word. I feel fragile, as if the least thing could knock the legs from under me.'

'Daddy!' She ran across the room and knelt on the floor beside him. 'Oh, Daddy! You've had a horrible time. I hate the thought of leaving you.'

He looked at her anxiously. 'But you will leave, won't you, darling? I'll be happy, knowing you're happy, although I'll miss you more than words can say.'

'There'll be no need for you to miss me. I'll only be five minutes away in Seaforth.'

'I wish you were getting married though,' he said. 'On reflection, I'd quite like Ned for a son-in-law. I admire people with convictions. I remember Duncan used to agree with every word I said. It got on my nerves rather. Ned doesn't pretend. What you see is what you get.'

Just to please her father, who'd been through so much, in June, on her thirty-ninth birthday, Hester married Ned Cunningham in a simple, registry office ceremony. It was eighteen years to the day that she would have married Duncan Maguire. She was already two months pregnant.

'I've never seen Hester look so lovely,' Queenie whispered to Roddy after he'd given his daughter away.

Hester wore a blue crinkly cotton frock with a drawstring neck, loose flowing sleeves, and an ankle-length, three-tiered skirt. There was a wreath of forget-me-nots on her blonde hair that streamed like satin ribbon down her back. Her face was radiant when she kissed her new husband, who was wearing jeans and an embroidered shirt, and whose own face was just as radiant when he kissed his new wife back.

'Neither have I,' Roddy muttered.

Queenie took his hand and squeezed it. He looked really wretched. She recalled the dashing Roddy of old, the man who'd wanted to be an architect, but had been stuck in an office selling stocks and shares instead. He'd miss Hester terribly. Together, they'd kept each other sane. Later, she'd suggest he come to Freddy's from time to time and they could have lunch.

Mary Maguire remembered her own registry office wedding. It had been a dead miserable affair. Queenie and Mam had been the only guests, whereas today there were a good forty, mostly friends of Ned and a few of his brothers and sisters. The friends were an untidy lot, dressed like Beatniks. There weren't many people on Hester's side, just herself and Queenie, and Roddy, of course, and that detective Hester worked for and his wife. Gus couldn't come, his wife was expecting another baby any minute.

She was glad Duncan wasn't there. It was exam time and he couldn't take the day off. She'd sooner he didn't see Hester as she was today, so beautiful, looking only half her age. He might start wishing things had gone differently. Very occasionally, Mary wished the same, but then she wouldn't have had Flora. Flora was the glue that kept them together.

The wedding over, everyone went to the Blundellsands Hotel for a sit-down meal, strictly vegetarian. Roddy had pleaded to pay for *something* when it seemed as if his daughter's wedding wasn't going to cost him a penny.

Queenie and Mary agreed the food was surprisingly nice. 'And so are the guests,' Queenie remarked. 'Nice, that is. There's none of the backbiting or catty remarks there are at some weddings.'

After the food, came dancing. A rock 'n 'roll group – more friends of Ned – let rip with '*I Wanna Hold Your Hand*'. Roddy came over and asked Queenie to dance.

'I'm not sure if this is a quickstep or a foxtrot,' he said. 'Shall we experiment with a few steps and find out?'

'I think it'd be best if we just jigged around on the spot, otherwise we'd look daft, trying to do a proper dance.'

'I'll feel daft jigging around on the spot. I already stick out like a sore thumb in this formal suit. Hester said to wear something casual, but I couldn't bring myself to go to a wedding in jeans and sweatshirt. You fit in perfectly in that frock.'

Queenie was hatless. Her straw-coloured silk frock was plain except for the fluttery cape collar. She didn't say it was a Nina Ricci and had cost £250. 'I remember talking Theo into buying a consignment of jeans, it was years and years ago now. His cousin in Kythira was wearing them. I'd never seen jeans before.' She giggled. 'Not a single pair sold, they ended up in the stock room. Now they're all the rage. I must ask someone to see if they're still there. Oh, come on, Roddy!' she coaxed. 'Take your jacket off and give jigging around a try.'

Roddy laughed. He was looking much more relaxed, no doubt because he'd drunk an awful lot of wine with the meal. 'Why didn't Theo come with you?' he asked when they were on the floor.

'He doesn't feel well. Oh, Roddy. I'm so worried about him,' she said with a catch in her voice. 'He's tired all the time and feels nauseous and has raging headaches. I'm scared there's something badly wrong.'

He stopped dancing. 'I'm no good at this. Let's go downstairs and have a drink at the bar. I'm in need of something stronger than wine.'

'How long has Theo been like this?' he asked when they were seated, a glass of whisky in his hand. Queenie had preferred a pot of tea. The bar was empty apart from themselves.

'A few weeks, a month.' Queenie shook her head helplessly. 'He refuses to see a doctor. I think it's because he's scared of what they'll say. He hasn't been in his office for over a fortnight. People don't know what to do. Theo insisted on taking all the major decisions himself. The shop's been going downhill for ages, anyroad. We have fewer and fewer customers every year.'

'I'm sorry, Queenie.'

'I don't know how I'll live without him,' she said in a low voice. 'I shouldn't have come here and left him, but I couldn't bear to miss Hester's wedding.'

'It's no use me sitting here assuring you Theo's bound to get better, because what the hell do I know? But if he doesn't, Queenie, you'll be all right.' It was Roddy's turn to take *her* hand and squeeze it. 'You're a survivor. Is someone with Theo now?'

'My mother. She's seventy-three, a year older than him, but as fit as a fiddle. They get on really well. I think she tells him dirty jokes when I'm not there.'

'Perhaps I could pop in and see him from time to time,' Roddy suggested. 'I've always liked Theo.'

'That's a lovely idea, Roddy. He likes you too.' She sighed. 'As soon as I've finished this tea, I'll say goodbye to Hester and Ned and go home.'

'I'll always be there for you, Queenie,' Roddy said warmly. 'You were a wonderful friend to Laura. I've never forgotten that.'

'And you can count on me, Roddy.' She'd been a pathetic little creature when they first met and he'd seemed the handsomest man on earth. She'd fallen head over heels in love with him. Despite everything that had happened since, it still felt odd to be talking to Roddy Oliver as if they were equals.

Chapter 19

Theo was asleep when Queenie got home. Her mother crept out of the bedroom, her finger to her lips. 'You'll be pleased to know I've persuaded him to see the doctor,' she whispered. 'He's coming first thing in the morning.'

'Thank goodness for that.' Queenie breathed a sigh of relief.

'Was it a nice wedding?'

Agnes Tate was unrecognisable as the woman who used to live in Glover Street. Her hair was a pretty silvery grey, and she wore a smart, black and white striped shirtwaister frock. An expert Bridge player, her presence was eagerly sought in card-playing circles.

'It was lovely, one of the nicest weddings I've ever been to.' She couldn't have been more pleased that Hester had found happiness at last.

Later in the evening, after her mother had gone, and Theo was still in bed, she heard a sound in the bedroom and immediately went in. She'd been checking every few minutes, watching him sleep; twitching restlessly, muttering things that didn't make sense.

This time, she found him wide awake, getting out of bed. She fussed around, shoving slippers on his feet, urging him into his Paisley silk dressing gown.

'My head hurts,' he complained. He didn't ask about the wedding and must have forgotten she'd been.

She stroked his face. 'Would you like some tea and aspirin, darling?'

'Yes, please.' He frowned. 'Are Lila and Stephanie here?'

'The girls haven't been here for years, Theo.' Not since she'd come to live with their father. She felt alarmed. 'They live in Calderstones.'

'Of course!' His face saddened. 'I feel a bit muddled. I had a dream about my children. It's a long time since we've seen Steven.'

'It was last Christmas,' she reminded him. 'We met up in New York, remember? He was doing that television thing.'

His face creased. 'Did we?'

'Yes. It'll come back to you soon. Now sit down and I'll make the tea.' She thanked God that the doctor was coming tomorrow.

Theo insisted on taking three aspirin with the tea, as two had no effect on his headaches, not that three helped much either. They sat in silence for quite a long time, his face working furiously, as if he was having an argument with himself. Queenie watched, frightened. What was going on in his mind?

'You know, Queenie,' he said suddenly, and much to her astonishment. 'I think Freddy's has had its day.'

'What a thing to say! Of course it hasn't.' She recognised something had to be done about the shop. Some of the departments looked as if they were stuck in a time warp, and the entire place was beginning to look rather shabby. But it was Theo himself who'd turned down her suggestions, and those of other senior members of staff, that modernisation was necessary to attract new, younger customers, as their old patrons gradually died off.

'We haven't kept up with the times,' Theo said seriously, as if he'd only just realised. 'We're half a century out of date. It's my fault for resisting any sort of change. I thought Freddy's would go on for ever exactly the way it always has. But now,' he continued, shaking his head sadly, 'it's too late to do anything about it. It would cost a fortune to modernise, we'd have to close for months. We'd lose all the staff.' He spoke as if he'd already formulated the words in his mind and knew them off by heart.

'There'd be no need to close,' Queenie said forcefully. 'One floor could be done up at a time. We'd just have to move departments for a while until it was all finished.'

'But it's not worth it, Queenie, my love,' he said with a sigh. 'We're in the wrong place. Bold Street's no longer what it was. It doesn't draw the people with money like it used to.'

That was true. Bold Street had changed character over the years. The expensive shops had closed and been replaced with cheaper ones. Meanwhile, George Henry Lee's, Freddy's main rival, had taken over its neighbour, Bon Marché, and was now twice as big. St John's Market had been developed and was full of little boutiques. Owen Owen's, C & A Modes, Marks & Spencer, these too were part of a dense shopping circle, while Freddy's was tucked out of the way in Hanover Street, around the corner from Bold Street where the rich no longer came.

'Let's talk about it in the morning, after the doctor's been,' she suggested.

Theo nodded and yawned. 'I think I'll go back to bed.'

'I'll be with you in a minute.'

He was asleep when she got in beside him. At least this

time his breathing was regular. She lay, listening to the soft, in-and-out breath, wondering how she would feel if Theo were genuinely ill, if he died, if she had to sleep in this big bed for the rest of her life on her own. She would go to pieces, she knew she would. He had been the sweetest, most precious of lovers and she would never cease to miss him grievously. She edged across the bed until their bodies were touching, only slightly so as not to disturb him and, after a while, she also fell asleep.

When she woke, it was still dark, and the place beside her was empty, but warm to the touch. 'Theo?' she called, sitting up.

There was no reply. She got out of bed, checked the living room, the kitchen, the bathroom, even the two spare bedrooms, rarely used. He wasn't in the flat, but the front door was slightly ajar. She went out, looked in his office and all the other offices, but there was no sign of Theo.

Queenie went down the brightly lit stairs, her bare feet making no sound in the still, silent building. In the restaurant, she called his name, and again on the fourth floor as she wandered through the ghostly furniture department, half expecting to find him fast asleep on a bed or in one of the armchairs, although she could think of no reason for him to do such a thing.

'Theo? Theo?' she called when she reached Gentlemen's Clothing and Footwear on the floor below, jumping nervously whenever she came face to face with a mannequin, or glimpsed a dark form silhouetted against the window. 'Theo, where are you?'

By now, she was beginning to panic. She kept feeling as if she'd just missed him, that he'd not long left as she'd gone in. There was always the faintest scent of the musky aftershave he used hanging in the air. She reached Ladies' Exclusive Fashions and he wasn't there, nor in Ladies'

First Floor Fashions. He was nowhere to be seen on ground level either. If he wasn't in the basement, she'd alert the night watchman, ask him to turn on all the lights.

He *was* in the basement, wandering up and down the aisles, a strange, shambling, shuffling figure, just visible in the light from the stairwell, picking up the occasional item; a book, a toy, a dish from the china section.

Queenie watched for a long time as he peered intently at the thing in his hand, before putting it back and choosing something else to examine, just as closely. 'Theo,' she said softly, not wanting to frighten him, 'what are you doing?'

He turned and came towards her, shoulders bent like an old, old man. 'Queenie! I was taking a look around. I'm sorry, were you worried about me?'

'Of course. You used to tell me off for taking midnight excursions.' It was an odd thing to do in the early hours of the morning. His voice sounded odd too, as if he were having difficulty forming the words with his mouth.

'You were sleeping so peacefully. It seemed a shame to wake you,' he said in the strange voice.

He had reached her by now and she took him in her arms. 'Come along, darling, let's go upstairs. You feel cold. You should have put your dressing gown on,' she chided, shivering herself, just in her nightie and with nothing on her feet. She led him over to the lift, pressed the button and heard it spring to life on another floor, like a monster from the deep, clicking and clanking its way towards them, accompanied by a whirring noise. It fell into place in front of them, the doors opened.

Once inside, she could see Theo properly and felt shocked. His face was paper white, incredibly shrivelled. His mouth had fallen open and he seemed unable to close it. He was shaking and all of a sudden could hardly stand. She supported him until they reached the top floor, through the door, into the flat, into the bedroom, where she helped him into bed, then got in beside him, tucking her arm around his waist, nestling her head against his shoulder.

'Could we go to Kythira, do you think?' he asked.

'If you want, darling.' The summer Sales were starting soon, but other people could see to them.

'I'll ring Trefor Jones tomorrow, tell him to get the boat ready and bring it to Liverpool.'

Trefor Jones hadn't captained *Queen of the Mersey* for almost twenty years, but she didn't bother to tell him that now. Anyroad, it would be quicker to fly and sail back, the sea would be calm in summer. All of a sudden, she ached to be in Kythira, convinced that Theo would quickly get better living in his father's villa, with the blue sea visible from the windows, the vines and the trees, the warm, invigorating air.

'I'd love that, Theo,' she said softly.

He raised his head, it was an effort, and kissed her. 'Goodnight, my darling girl.'

'Goodnight, Theo. I love you.'

Queenie had no idea what time it was he died, but when she woke his body was cold beside her. She held him for a long time, her brain too numb to register anything other than the fact that Theo had gone and this was the last time he would lie in her arms. A few days later, after the post-mortem, she was told it was a brain tumour that had killed him.

Roddy Oliver kept true to his word. During the days that followed, he proved himself the very best of friends. Remembering his words, said only a matter of hours before at Hester's wedding, he was the first person Queenie phoned after the doctor and he came immediately. The next person was her mother.

'He was such a *kind* man,' Agnes sobbed.

It was Roddy who went to the Vandos house in Calderstones and told Irene that her husband was dead, Roddy who took Queenie to the undertakers and helped choose a coffin, the best that money could buy, Roddy who telephoned the *Liverpool Echo* to inform them of Theo's death. The staff in the shop were wonderful, but they weren't close friends, not like Roddy. She asked him not to tell Hester about Theo. She and Ned were on their honeymoon in the Lake District, but would be back in time for the funeral. 'It would only cast a shadow over their holiday.'

Two days later, a message came from Irene Vandos in the form of a hand-delivered note. In her heavy, black scrawl, like a row of crazy blackbirds perched on a wall, she requested that the funeral service be held in St Nicholas Greek Orthodox Church in Princes Road.

> *It's where Theo and I were married, where our children were baptised. I feel you should pay regard to my wishes. After all,* I *am Theo's widow, not you. Also, the children and I would like to see him before he is buried. There is room for him in the grave with his mother and father.*

'Buried!' Queenie groaned. 'He never went near church. He wasn't the slightest bit religious. I wanted him cremated with just a simple service and people getting up to say how much he meant to them. I know it's what he would have wanted.' She shrugged. 'Still, it wouldn't hurt to let Irene have her way. She lost Theo a long time ago. I've had him all these years.'

'You're right,' Roddy murmured. 'It wouldn't hurt.'

She looked at her watch and asked what he was doing there at seven o'clock at night? 'You've been here all day for two days in a row. Aren't you expected at work?'

'I've told them I'm taking a week off. They won't mind, I'm owed it. I haven't taken a proper holiday in years. There didn't seem much point.'

Queenie wrote back to Irene and told her Theo's body was in hospital awaiting the post-mortem and she was free to go ahead with arrangements for a service in the church of her choice. 'I have already arranged for a coffin and as soon as the post-mortem has been carried out, Theo will be moved to Austin's Funeral Parlour in Brownlow Hill. Your family are welcome to see him there.' She sealed the envelope and stamped it with her fist. 'I just hope they don't turn up when I'm there – or the other way around.'

She felt that she was coping extremely well. There hadn't been time to succumb to the tears that were never far away, or think about the future without Theo. She had taken over his office and sat behind the desk with the twelve apostles carved on the front. The door was always open to anyone who wished to come in. Judy Channon and Gladys Hewitt came together to offer their sympathies. They were the only ones left at Freddy's of the War Widows' Club; Mona was dead and the others had retired a long time ago. Gladys had risen to head of Accounts and Judy was still with Ladies' Exclusive Fashions.

Queenie embraced them both. 'Thank you for coming.'

'We know how you must be feeling, luv,' Gladys said tearfully. 'And we loved Mr Theo, everybody did.'

Letters of condolence poured in, the phone never ceased to ring. Her mother answered the phone in the apartment and kept appearing with cups of tea or coffee and little snacks.

On Friday morning, Theo's doctor rang with the result of the post-mortem. 'If it's any comfort to you, at least he died a relatively peaceful death.'

Just then, Queenie couldn't judge whether it was a comfort or not. Theo hadn't suffered, as some people did, for months, even years. Perhaps, in the course of time, she would come to see it as a comfort.

She conveyed the news to Roddy. 'Shall I ring Austin's and ask them to collect him from the hospital?' he asked.

'Please. And ask when he'll be ready. I'm longing to see him.' She would only go once, say goodbye to her beloved Theo for the final time.

The phone continued to ring all morning. Sometimes Queenie answered, sometimes Roddy. It went about midday, and this time it was Roddy who picked up the receiver.

'*What*!' he said in a stunned voice. He listened, nodding grimly. 'I see. Well, thanks for telling us. I understand there was nothing you could do. Goodbye.'

'What's wrong?' Queenie asked, alarmed by the expression on his face. 'Has something happened to Hester or Gus?'

'No, that was Austin's. Their men went to the hospital, only to be told Theo's body had already been taken away.'

'Who by?' She knew the answer before the words were out of her mouth.

'His family; his wife and daughters.'

Queenie rested her head in her hands and stared at the wall, though saw nothing. If Irene thought she was wreaking revenge for past hurts, she was badly mistaken.

Theo was dead, and she didn't begrudge his family weeping and wailing over his stolen corpse.

'They sound an unpleasant lot,' Roddy said quietly. 'Did Austin's know where Theo had been taken?'

'They've no idea.'

The telephone rang again. 'It's Steven Vandos,' Roddy said, handing her the receiver.

'Queenie!' Steven said breathlessly. 'I've only just got up. I didn't arrive until late last night. You'll never guess—'

Queenie cut him short. 'I know what's happened, Steven. All I want to know now is where Theo is?'

'Here, in the house. It's a bloody nightmare. Can I come and stay in the flat?'

'Any time, Steven. You're always welcome, you know that.'

When Queenie entered the church, the front pews were already packed and Irene Vandos, sitting at the end of the first row turned, lifted her black veil, and gave her a look of such hatred that she flinched. Irene must have been waiting for her, waiting to give her the look, storing it up for days, perhaps years.

Queenie pretended not to notice. Theo's open coffin stood in front of the altar. She walked towards it, an expectant smile on her face. She hadn't seen him since he'd been taken from the flat ten days ago. Dressed in a white satin robe, his hands bent around the brass crucifix that lay on his chest, he looked peaceful, young again, his face unlined. It would be easy to believe he'd merely gone asleep, that any minute he would open his eyes, smile, say, 'Hello, Queenie, my love.'

'Goodbye, my dearest Theo,' she whispered. She kissed her fingers and pressed them lightly against his icy cheek. 'Sleep well.' Taking one, last look, she walked away, head held high, to the rear of the church, where Roddy was waiting with her mother and about a dozen Freddy's staff; Roy Burrows, who'd been Theo's loyal second-in-command for over twenty years, two senior managers, the youngest employee, the oldest, the longest-serving, and a representative, chosen by lot, from each floor.

That afternoon, Freddy's was closing. The staff would gather in the restaurant in honour of Theo. Hester and Mary were coming and a few other people she would have invited to the funeral had she organised it herself. Out of courtesy, Steven was going back to his mother's house where a feast had been laid on for the mourners. He was coming to Freddy's later.

The church service was dignified and moving, conducted by a tall priest with a black beard dressed in a magnificently embroidered robe. The church reeked with the pungent smell of incense. But these people, the ones at the front, had never loved Theo as she had. Most she didn't recognise. She was glad when it was over, and left quickly, before Irene could waylay her and come out with a mouthful of bile.

Back at Freddy's, the shop seemed rather forlorn, closed on a weekday, not a soul going in or coming out. She took the lift to the top floor, went into the flat and took off her hat and black lace gloves. She stood in front of the wardrobe mirror and combed her hair. The mirror revealed a still pretty woman, even though she'd turned forty-eight only the other day. If there was grey in her hair, she couldn't see it, and her figure was as slim as it had always been, possibly slimmer as she hadn't eaten much lately. Would Theo have remembered it was her birthday? she wondered. He'd been terribly vague over the last few weeks. Sighing, she dabbed a hint of rouge on her pale cheeks, and renewed her lipstick.

Then she took a deep breath and went down to the restaurant where the staff were waiting.

She gasped when she entered the room and saw that every table was covered with flowers. There were more on the piano and the window sills, even some lying on the floor. The air was heavy with their strong, heady perfume.

A gradual silence had fallen as people began to notice she was there. Then, out of the silence, someone started to clap and soon the entire room were applauding, clapping *her*, Queenie Tate.

She was too stunned to speak, just stood there while people came up and shook her hand, hugged her, kissed her, said how sorry they were that Mr Theo was dead. There'd never be another boss like him. 'You made him very happy, luv.'

Her voice returned. 'Thank you,' she murmured. 'Thank you, very much. And thank you for the flowers. They're beautiful.'

'We thought they'd be better here, where everyone can see 'em, rather than in some foreign church.'

The kitchen staff came in with trays of wine and cups of tea. Queenie felt badly in need of both. She gulped down the tea, took a glass of wine, and began to circulate, shaking more hands, assuring people over and over that, no, Freddy's wasn't going to close because Theo was dead.

'But I think we need to make some improvements,' she said. 'I'm not sure which floor to start on. Theo and I were discussing it not long before he died.'

She was inundated with suggestions, too many to remember, so asked for them to be written down and submitted to her office.

Steven arrived with a woman Queenie had never seen

before; not very tall, painfully thin, her plain face devoid of make-up.

'You don't remember me, do you?' the woman said. 'I'm Stephanie Vandos. Perhaps we can talk later. It's a bit hectic now.'

Hester and Mary came and gave her a hug and a kiss. Ned and Duncan sent their condolences. 'And you know, Queenie, you can always rely on me and Hes,' Mary said warmly. 'No one could have looked after us in Caerdovey better than you. Now it's our turn to look after you.'

Queenie rather hoped she wouldn't need looking after, but thanked them all the same.

After an hour or so, people began to drift away, much to her relief, as she was feeling very emotional and yearned for a good cry. On top of everything else, she had been deeply touched to discover the staff thought so well of her. 'He's lucky to have had you, dear,' Mr Harper from Gentlemen's Toiletries had said.

Stephanie Vandos approached. 'Could I have a word?'

'Let's sit in the corner.' She pointed to a table covered with red roses. 'Everyone will have gone soon.'

She hoped the woman hadn't come with a nasty message from her mother, but the first words Stephanie said were, 'I'm sorry about everything that's happened, particularly this last thing with Father's body. I was wholly against it, but once Mother gets something into her head there's no stopping her.'

'It's a pity you didn't come when Theo was alive,' Queenie said coolly. 'He often spoke about you and your sister. He missed you both terribly.'

'The trouble is,' Stephanie said in her dry, flat voice, 'my mother is the sort of person who never forgives and never forgets. When she and father split, we were told never to contact him, to have nothing whatsoever to do with him again. If we had, she would never have forgiven us.'

'What about Steven? It seems she forgave him.'

'That's because Steven's Steven. He can charm the birds off the trees. She never expected loyalty from him. But you see, although I loved my father,' Stephanie explained, 'I loved Mother more. *She* was the unhappy one, the loser in the situation, not him. That's how Lila and I saw it.'

Queenie felt her cheeks flush. 'I'm not in the mood for a row. If you're going to be unpleasant, I'd sooner you left.'

'I was just telling you how Lila and I saw things. I know full well Mother's no saint, but she needed our support. In order to give it, she lay down conditions. We complied, we had no choice, because we loved her. To tell the truth, I would have quite liked to get to know you.' She plucked a petal off a rose and began to stroke the velvety surface. 'I remember seeing you at Lila's twenty-first. Father kept looking at you and I thought you seemed very nice. If things had gone differently, I think you would make a great friend. Steven was always on about you.' She looked at Queenie shyly. 'I've been in need of a friend since my parents split up. Lila was married, Steven away most of the time, and Mother – well, she was busy being herself.' Her gaunt face wore an expression of utter weariness. 'It's been hard,' she sighed.

'You never married?' Queenie said softly.

'I nearly did, but mother refused to have him in the house. His name was John. In the end, I just gave up. I didn't have the energy to fight any more.'

'It's not too late for us to become friends. Your mother need never know. Come round some time and we'll have dinner. Oh,' she cried, 'I wish Theo had known you were so unhappy. He would have done something about it – he had a thing about blood relatives sticking together, no matter what they'd done. He bullied me into getting to know my own horrible mother when she turned up out of the blue. I've never regretted it.'

'Strange,' Stephanie muttered, tearing the petal into two pieces.

'What's strange about it?' Queenie asked curiously. Someone shouted, 'Tara, Miss Tate,' and she waved. Roddy came towards her, but she shook her head slightly. He nodded and went to talk to Hester.

'The "blood relative" bit,' Stephanie said hesitantly. 'I shouldn't really tell you this, but I've always wanted to get it off my chest.' She took a deep breath. 'One day, Mother was particularly mad. I think it was when she learnt about the boat. She used to have you followed in those days, did you know?' Queenie nodded. 'Anyway, she was in a terrible state. She told me Theo wasn't our father, that it was someone else, a man called Peter Vandos, a cousin, who'd lived in Liverpool when she was young. They'd had an affair. I asked why she hadn't married him, and she said that love wasn't nearly as important as money, which is why she'd married Theo Vandos instead.'

Queenie could feel a pulse beating madly in her throat. 'That can't be true,' she said. 'I've met Peter Vandos. He left Liverpool about a year after your mother and Theo married.'

'Well, that could account for Steven and Lila, wouldn't it? They're only twelve months apart. Perhaps Mother conceived me on Kythira. She used to go every year to stay in grandfather's villa. Peter was living there by then, and Father – Theo,' she shrugged, 'whatever, only came for the last week.'

'I see,' Queenie said faintly. If this were true, if Theo had known, he could have divorced Irene for adultery.

'Please don't tell Steven and Lila what I've told you. Mother was terrified when she realised what she'd done. She made me promise not to breathe a word to a soul.'

'I think I know why.'

'Anyway,' Stephanie was looking slightly more cheeerful, 'about the invitation to dinner, I'd love to come. When are you moving out of the flat?'

'I've no intention of moving anywhere.'

'Oh! Mother has a copy of father's Will. It says everything has been left to her. There's no mention of you.'

'I think you'll find it's a bit out of date. Theo's last Will leaves everything to me, apart from a few bequests to his children and some of the staff.'

Stephanie laughed. 'I think I'll find a reason to go away for the next few days. I'd sooner not be there when Mother finds out; she'll blow her top. Love does have its limits, you know. Anyway, she'll still be comfortably off.'

Sleep was impossible. She tossed and turned, beat the pillow with her fist, thinking about Steven, six inches taller than Theo, broader, and so similar to Peter Vandos she wondered why she hadn't seen it before. Had Theo noticed their similarity? She doubted it, convinced he would have mentioned it if he had.

She turned over again, shook the pillow again, willed herself to sleep, when there was an unearthly crash from down below that sent all thoughts of sleep out of her mind. She sat up, trembling, wondering what on earth it could be.

There was a knock on the door. 'Queenie. Did you hear that?' It was Steven.

'Yes. It sounded like a bomb.'

'I'll go and investigate.'

'I'll come with you.' She slid out of bed and put on dressing gown and slippers and they crept downstairs together. The source of the noise was found, almost immediately. In the restaurant, one of the chandeliers, the centre one, had fallen to the ground, leaving a gaping hole in the ceiling. The mess on the floor resembled a modern work of art; half a dozen smashed tables, a huge mound of twinkling crystal, mixed with hundreds and hundreds of flowers.

'Well, at least I know which floor to start on,' Queenie said later when she and Steven were calming their nerves with alcohol; whisky, which she hated, but Steven said it would do her good.

'I was thinking Freddy's was looking a bit dilapidated,' he said, lighting a cigarette.

'Now it's falling to pieces. The restaurant will have to close and the other chandeliers be taken down.' She shuddered. 'Thank God it didn't happen while anyone was there.'

'Father always wanted me to take over Freddy's. I'm glad things went the way they did and it's your responsibility.'

'Do you fancy sharing the responsibility with me? Theo would have liked that. I'm nervous at having to do it on my own.'

'Not on your life!' He grimaced. 'I'm sorry you're nervous, but I can't wait to get back to New York.'

'Not Hollywood?'

'I've still got my apartment there, but the soap I'm in is being shot in a studio in New York.'

Queenie grinned. 'The hospital one? They've started showing it over here. You make a wonderful doctor, Steven. You suit a white coat and stethoscope.'

He looked a little bit hurt. 'You may smile, Queenie Tate, but it brings in an awful lot of money. And you should see my fan mail. Doctor Morrison is deluged with admiring letters every week – and offers of marriage, I might add.'

She didn't say that this wasn't what he'd wanted when he'd first gone to Hollywood. He'd hoped to become a highly regarded actor, but instead had been cast as the same charming, upper-class Englishman, playing an identical part in every film, until producers assumed he had no range.

'Hester looked well,' he said. 'I didn't realise she'd only just got married.'

'Ned's a lovely person. He's a writer as well as a postman. They're very much in love.'

'I was in love with Hester once.'

'For how long?'

'Ah, Queenie!' He laughed out loud, reminding her of Peter. 'How well you know me. For about three months, I reckon.'

'Did you feed her that sob story about falling in love during the war and the woman being married?'

'I'm afraid so,' he said, not the least abashed.

'You fed me the same story, but when I mentioned it a few days later, feeling sorry for you like, the woman had a different name. I realised then what a good actor you'd make, because I'd really believed you the first time.'

'I'm a fickle guy.'

'You're that all right.' He was about to divorce his third wife, or she was about to divorce him, she wasn't sure.

'I honestly was in love with you though, Queenie.'

'Oh, yeah!' He was flirting with her when Theo was still warm in his grave. 'Goodnight, Steven.' He was going back to the States tomorrow. He might be fickle, an outrageous flirt, and have other not very admirable traits, but she would be sorry to see him go.

Two days later, the builders were in, taking down the other chandeliers and repairing the ceiling, and Queenie was reading the dozens of ideas the staff had submitted for modernising Freddy's. Installing escalators seemed the most popular idea. Others included providing a coffee bar on the ground floor, lowering the ceilings throughout, and getting rid of Ladies' Exclusive Fashions, which was very sensible, because these days, many of the very expensive clothes ended up being sold for half-price in the sales. Someone thought they should stop selling furs, because it was *cruel*, the writer added indignantly. Another person proposed franchises, definitely worth looking into. Various colours were suggested for the walls and, finally, 'I hate the idea of anyone losing their job, but do we really need a doorman and a lift operator these days? None of the other big shops have them.'

She put the assorted bits of paper in a file, ate a sandwich at her desk, and told Roy Burrows in the next office that she was going out and wouldn't be back for a couple of hours. 'When you've got a minute, could you look into the idea of franchises? I don't know much about them.'

'They're a shop within a shop. A famous name, like Weatherall's, for instance, takes over their own section, supplies their own staff and sells their own clothes. It can be done with cosmetics too. It's not a bad idea,' he mused. 'I'll try to find out more.'

'Good. I'll see you around three-ish.'

The gynaecologist was situated in an elegant, four-storey house in Rodney Street. Queenie was shown into a tastefully furnished waiting room with pale green walls, where a nurse presented her a form to fill in. 'Doctor Wickford will see you in ten minutes.'

Queenie completed the form accurately except for the question asking if she was married. She put that she was.

Dr Susan Wickford was a pleasant, middle-aged woman with a friendly demeanour that immediately put Queenie at her ease.

After the formalities of shaking hands and remarking on the weather were over, she seated herself behind the desk and asked, 'How can I help you?'

'I've just got married again and I wanted to know if there's any chance of me having a baby,' Queenie said bluntly.

The doctor looked at the form. 'At forty-eight! That's most unlikely, but not impossible. You haven't had a child, but I see you had a miscarriage in your teens. What caused it?'

'An accident. I fell.'

'And you never conceived with your first husband. Did he ever try to find out why?'

'No.'

'And the second one – have you been married long, by the way?'

'Only a few weeks.'

'Well, congratulations.' She smiled. 'I take it he's about your age. Has he been married before?'

'Yes, he's a widower. He has two children.'

'And are you still menstruating?'

Queenie nodded. 'Regularly.'

'All I can say is it's worth a try,' Dr Wickford said encouragingly. 'The older the woman, the less healthy are her eggs, which makes them much harder to fertilise and harder to carry to term, though I must warn you that, if you're successful, an unhealthy egg can produce a damaged child. On the other hand, when I was in general practice, I came across quite a few expectant mothers in their late forties, even one who was fifty. As I recall, their babies were perfect.'

'I'd still like to try, whatever the risk,' Queenie said evenly. Vera had had Mary when she was forty-seven.

'Well, trying with a new husband isn't exactly a chore, is it?' She smiled. 'Would you like me to give you an internal examination, see if everything's in order, as it were?'

'Please.'

Her insides were 'in perfect running order', as the doctor put it fifteen minutes later. Queenie returned to Freddy's. The easy part was over, the more difficult part lay ahead. Now she had to ask Roddy if he was prepared to give her a child. Or at least try.

She invited him to dinner. As Freddy's restaurant was closed and she didn't trust herself to turn out a decently cooked three-course meal, she suggested that on Monday they went to a new Italian place, Nero's, which had just opened in Tithebarn Street. 'Shall we meet about half six, save you going all the way home to Crosby and back?'

'You're very thoughtful, Queenie. What's this in aid of? The dinner, I mean?'

'Just a thank you for all you've done for me lately.'

'There's no need to thank me, but I never say no to a free meal – and I love Italian food. See you Monday.'

She felt terrible on Monday, getting ready to go out with another man, determined to look her smartest, making up her face with extra care, having her hair set that afternoon in the hairdresser's downstairs, yet it was less than three weeks since Theo had died. She had been expecting to wallow in the past, but after what Stephanie had told her, all she could think about was the future and the vague possibility of having a child.

Roddy was there before her. He looked very dashing – he was the only man she'd ever known who suited the word – in a dark grey suit and sparkling white shirt. He jumped to his feet and held the chair for her to sit down.

'Who washes your shirts?' she asked.

'The laundry. I send them every week.'

'I thought as much. Will you order the wine, please?'

'White or red, medium or dry?'

'Medium white, but get a bottle of red as well if that's what you prefer.' She might well drink an entire bottle herself in order to pluck up the courage to ask the delicate question she had in mind.

'I'll do that. I think red would go better with spaghetti.'

Queenie licked her lips. Her mouth was dry. Never before had she been so looking forward to a glass of wine.

She ordered pâté for starters and ravioli to follow – much easier to eat than spaghetti. 'It's nice here,' she said, looking around at the murals of Italian scenes on the walls. She recognised the leaning tower of Pisa and the Trevi fountain, but that was all.

'Very nice.' He seemed very jovial tonight and she remarked on the fact.

'Well, it's the first time in my life that a beautiful woman has invited me to dinner. I feel quite chuffed.'

'You think I'm beautiful?'

'Extremely so. I thought as much the night I came back to Glover Street during the war. I was quite astounded. You'd changed out of all recognition since I went away. Oh, Lord!' The joviality vanished in an instant. 'That was the night I told Laura I didn't love her any more, that I'd met Katherine. She was devastated, but I didn't care.'

'That was an awful long time ago, Roddy. I should forget about it if I were you.'

'I can't!' he said wretchedly. 'Ever since she killed herself, I torture myself, going over all the terrible things I did. I shouldn't have been so cruel when she said she wanted to get rid of that baby.'

'It was only natural. Getting rid of a baby is the cruellest thing of all. I wasn't very nice to her, either, when she told me she was thinking about an abortion.'

'But that's not all, Queenie,' he went on, his voice bitter with regret. 'There was the time Gus and I were supposed to go sailing, but the weather was so bad we gave up on the idea and came into town instead. I knew Laura would be worried, about Gus, if not me, but I deliberately didn't let her know. I wanted to punish her for being such a bitch. From then on, she never mentioned the word abortion again.'

'I remember that day. She rang me in a state and I told her to get in touch with the coastguard.'

'Did she? Did you?' He looked at her piteously.

'She *was* being a bitch, Roddy,' she reminded him.

'Yes, but she was *ill*.'

'We didn't know that, did we? We're not doctors.'

'I should have got a doctor for her.'

'How could you, when you didn't know she needed one, not then? Oh, let's stop this at once. Any minute now, I'll think of all the horrid things I did to Theo. We'll both collapse in buckets of tears and they'll throw us out. Finish your wine, have more. You're not driving, are you?' she demanded, suddenly concerned.

'No.' He sniffed. 'I use the train. I usually have a couple of drinks in town before I go home. I'd just like to say one thing, I bet you didn't do a single horrid thing to Theo.'

'If I try hard enough, I'll probably think of some.' She'd already remembered the first holiday in Kythira when she'd wished Theo had been more like his cousin, Peter, and had wondered what it would be like to make love with Trefor Jones.

Her pâté came and Roddy's shrimp salad. They ate in silence. It wasn't until the waiter had removed their plates that Roddy spoke again. 'I'm sorry about my outburst, but the least little thing reminds me.'

'There's nothing to be sorry for. How's Hester coping with married life?' It was only a few days since she'd seen Hester, but at least she provided a more pleasant topic of conversation.

'Wonderfully. Have you seen Ned's house? It's the sort of place where the three bears might have lived.'

'Mary told me about it.'

'I thought about letting them have mine. Hester's hoping to have four kids, though she's left it a bit late. They'll be packed like sardines in Ned's.'

'Will you live in his instead?'

He smiled at last. 'Not likely. I'll buy myself a little flat, in town somewhere, close to work.'

'Four kids, eh!' Queenie sighed. 'Lucky old Hester.'

'I didn't know you wanted children!' He looked surprised.

'Just one would have been enough.'

'Wasn't Theo keen?'

'He was dead keen. I wasn't at first, but after a while, I began to desperately want a baby.' She nearly said it was why she'd been so cross with Laura, but that might have set him off again. 'Can I tell why I didn't have one, why I *think* I didn't have one?'

'Does it include any gory details?'

She laughed. 'No.'

'Then tell me.'

While they ate the main course, she told him what Stephanie Vandos had said on the day of Theo's funeral. 'I always wondered why I never got pregnant. Theo had three children, I knew there was nothing wrong with me, so I thought it was just bad luck. But now!' She waved her knife. 'Perhaps there was something wrong with Theo. I'll never know.'

'And now it's too late. Strewth, Queenie. That *was* bad luck,' he said sympathetically.

'I went to see a gynaecologist the other day. She said there's still a slight chance I could conceive.'

'Yes, but it's still too late.'

'Why?'

He looked at her, nonplussed. 'Isn't it obvious?'

She felt herself go cold, then hot, then dizzy. She poured the rest of the wine, drank half in a single gulp and immediately felt more dizzy, even hotter. 'I'm asking you a favour, Roddy.'

His face was a picture of puzzlement, which slowly faded as it dawned on him what the favour was. He put his fork on the plate with a bang. 'Christ Almighty, Queenie! Do you actually mean what I think you mean?'

'Would you mind?' she asked timidly.

'Jesus!' He almost shouted the word. The restaurant was gradually filling up and a few people turned to look. 'Jesus!' he said in a normal voice. 'Excuse me.'

She thought he was going to the Gents, but instead he made for the door and went outside. Five minutes later, she wondered if he'd gone for good and if she should go after him, apologise. Now she felt nauseous on top of everything else, and very odd. The things on the table had grown to twice their usual size. She couldn't feel the chair she was sitting on. What a dreadful thing to ask of a man. She'd plummet in his estimation. He'd probably never speak to her again.

By the time she got the bill, it would be too late to look for him. He might be on the train by now. She wouldn't phone him when she got home, she felt too ashamed.

It was then she remembered he'd brought a briefcase with him, which he hadn't taken when he walked out. She looked under the table and it was on the floor beside his chair. He'd *have* to come back.

About a quarter of an hour later he did, bursting into the restaurant, raising more eyebrows, sitting heavily in the chair opposite, his face showing nothing. 'I've just experienced half a dozen different emotions,' he said.

'I'm sorry, Roddy,' she began, but he held up an imperious hand. 'Be quiet, Queenie.' He cleared his throat. 'First of all, I felt very angry that you'd asked me to do such a thing. You, of all people, Laura's best friend. It seemed a terrible betrayal of friendship. But how can you betray someone who's been dead such a long time? I have to keep reminding myself of that. Then I was sad, remembering the baby Laura had lost. After that, I felt amazement. I must be one of the few men in the world to have been asked such a thing. It made me feel rather proud, extremely flattered, plus a bit uncomfortable.' He smiled at last and reached for her hand. 'I would be happy to father your baby, Queenie. Or at least try.'

They decided to start straight away, on neutral territory – a place that wouldn't remind her of Theo or him of Laura.

'What about Mangold's?' he said. 'It's a quiet little hotel behind the Liver Buildings. The firm use it when they have to put people up.'

'It sounds fine,' she said in a voice that even she could hardly hear. She had never felt so embarrassed in her life.

'You can always back out, you know.' He must have guessed at her embarrassment.

'I want a child, Roddy,' she said doggedly. 'It's worth one last try.'

'Then I shall do my darnedest to give you one.'

She left the rest of the ravioli and said she couldn't face afters. Roddy felt the same, but thought a brandy would do them both a world of good.

They sat together on the foot of the double bed. Roddy had removed his jacket, but that was all. Queenie clutched her handbag tightly to her chest, as if determined never to let go. The light wasn't on, she'd closed the curtains, but they weren't thick enough to prevent the late evening sunlight showing through. They could see each other quite distinctly.

'This isn't getting us anywhere,' Roddy said after a while. 'Shall I get undressed and into bed?'

Queenie nodded nervously. 'I won't look.'

'I've done it,' he said a few minutes later. The bed shook as he got in.

Now it was her turn. 'Don't look,' she said.

Roddy pulled the bedclothes over his head. 'Will that do?' He sounded rather amused.

She nodded again, though he couldn't see her, and took off all her clothes, wondering if it was really necessary to be completely naked? She contemplated putting her petticoat and bra back on, but it seemed a bit daft. She slid into bed and lay, as far away from Roddy as she could, staring stiffly at the ceiling, the bedclothes tucked under her neck.

'Can I open my eyes?' Roddy asked.

'Yes.'

'I can't do this by remote control, Queenie. You'll have to move a bit nearer.'

She burst into tears. 'I can't! I can't do it!'

He sat up, bent over her, and rubbed the tears away with his thumb. 'Then we won't,' he said gently, kissing her cheek. She moved her head and his lips came into contact with her own. He kissed her again, harder this time, and with a feeling of horror mixed with excitement, Queenie found herself responding. Somehow, without even realising she had done it, her arms were around his neck and his hand was caressing her breasts and in between kisses, he was murmuring, 'Darling! My darling, darling Queenie,' and she was saying things herself, though afterwards couldn't remember what they were. She could feel him pressing against her, as hard as steel. Then his hand slid between her legs and she wanted to scream because the pleasure was so rapturous.

Then Roddy entered her and she was soaring up to heaven, flying through the stars, which suddenly exploded, showering them with golden dust.

'Ah!' she groaned blissfully as an exhausted Roddy collapsed on top of her. He buried his head in the pillow.

'What's the matter?' she whispered when a good minute passed and he didn't speak.

He turned his head towards her, his blue eyes dark with passion. 'Nothing. It was rather better than I expected, that's all. How was it for you?'

'Much better than expected.' She hoped Theo hadn't been watching. Their love-making had been good, but she'd never realised it could be *this* good. 'I think I'm going to cry again,' she sniffed.

Roddy smiled. 'Remember what happened when you cried before?'

'I don't mind if it happens again.'

Chapter 20

In the middle of December, Hester Cunningham gave birth to a robust baby boy weighing 8 pounds 12 ounces.

'We're calling him Evan,' Hester announced delightedly when Queenie went to see her in hospital the next day. The walls of the ward were decorated with garlands of glittering tinsel and there was a sprig of mistletoe over the swing doors. 'It's an unusual name, but not poncy.'

'It's a lovely name for a lovely baby,' Queenie said warmly. 'I took a look at him in the nursery on the way in. He's gorgeous.'

Hester winced. 'It didn't half hurt, but I don't care. We're trying for another baby straight away. I always wanted a big family.'

'I hope you manage it, love. Oh, I've brought you a glamorous bedjacket. I thought it would make a change from fruit or flowers.'

'Oh, Queenie! It's gorgeous.' Hester put the white lace jacket on straight away. 'How do I look?'

'Very pretty. Having babies suits you.' Hester's usually pale face was flushed and her blue eyes, exactly the same shade as Roddy's, glowed. 'I'm glad you're so happy.'

'I couldn't be happier, Queenie, except if Mummy were here, which she's not and never will be. I know it's silly to think like that, but I can't help it.'

'Of course you can't. By the way, Mary will be in any

minute. She's just taking a peek at Evan, and is looking terribly broody, I must say.'

'Did you know Flora has left home? She's moved into a flat in Upper Parliament Street with a pile of other girls. Mary and Duncan are gutted.'

'I know. Mary came to see me the other day. She didn't seem very pleased about it.' She looked at Hester searchingly, wondering how it must feel, having just had a baby, knowing you had produced your own little human being, holding him or her for the first time.

Mary arrived. 'One look at Evan, and I feel like starting a family all over again. That's a pretty jacket. Where's Ned?' She glanced around the ward. 'He must be the only father not here,' she said tactlessly.

'He'll be along later.' Hester didn't look at all upset. 'Evan's arrival has inspired him to work on his novel. It's almost finished. Daddy's coming straight from work – we're moving into the Crosby house in the New Year. I tried to persuade him to stay with Ned and me, there's loads of room, but he insisted on buying this horrible little flat in the centre of town.'

'I thought it quite nice,' Queenie said.

'You've seen it?'

'He wanted my opinion before he bought it.'

'You should have told him it was too small, that he should stay with us.'

'Maybe he thinks you and Ned would be better off on your own, particularly if you have a big family. And it's quite a nice flat, Hester,' Queenie argued. 'The sitting room's a good size and looks out over the river. I know the rest is rather small, but the kitchen and bathroom are super-modern and quite adequate for someone on their own.'

Hester wrinkled her nose and didn't look convinced. 'I hate to think of Daddy on his own.'

'*I'm* on my own, but I manage.'

There was a pause, then Mary said in a funny voice, 'I wonder what happened to Mrs Merton when she was left on her own?'

'Who?' Queenie frowned. The name didn't ring a bell.

'Mrs Merton, Carl's mother. Remember, from Caerdovey? She thought the sun shone out of his behind. I just wondered how she coped on her own when Carl died in such a horrible way.'

'Mary!' Hester hissed, irritation showing. 'We swore we wouldn't say anything.'

Queenie froze. 'How did you know Carl was dead? As far as I know, he was perfectly well when we came away, apart from a few cuts and bruises.'

'No, Queenie,' Mary shook her head. 'He was dead. You must have known. Tess Nicholls told us, ages ago. It's haunted me and Hes ever since, knowing that we killed him. We often talk about it. And Tess said everyone in Caerdovey thought you'd had a miscarriage, that Carl had made you pregnant.'

Hester no longer looked irritated, more relieved that the matter was being discussed openly. 'I remember one night he came into our room and got into bed with you. You said he'd made a mistake. I believed you then, but not now.' There were tears in her eyes. 'Did he hurt you, Queenie?'

'Do we have to discuss something like this when you've just had a baby?' Queenie said crossly, though inwardly, she felt shattered. 'This isn't the right time.'

'Yes, it is.' Hester folded her arms stubbornly. 'We've been dying to talk to you about it for ages, but didn't want to upset you.'

Queenie stared at them, seeing not the flushed, new mother and the rather matronly woman that Mary had become, but the two pretty little five-year-olds she'd taken to Caerdovey. 'I remember,' she said slowly, 'I think it was at Theo's funeral, you remarked how well I'd looked after you, but I didn't do a very good job of it, did I?' Her voice was bitter. 'There could hardly have been a worse thing to happen to you both.'

'Don't be silly, Queenie.'

'Shush, Queenie, don't talk daft,' Mary said loudly.

It could almost have been the same childish voices she was listening to. 'Gwen told me Carl Merton had already raped two girls before he did the same to me,' she said crisply, trying not to show how shaken she was, 'Each time he got away with it. If he hadn't died, he could have got away with it again – and again. And you didn't *kill* him,' she reached for both their hands and gave them a squeeze, 'not deliberately. You were protecting me. It was an accident.' The girls were watching her, hanging on to her every word, seeking reassurance. 'And yes, I *was* pregnant, though I didn't know it. I was very ignorant in those days and it wasn't until I was in hospital that Gwen told me I'd had a miscarriage. Oh!' she said plaintively. 'I wish we'd talked about this before. I hate to think it's been bothering you all this time.'

'It does more than bother me.' Mary shivered. 'Sometimes, I wake up in the middle of the night in a sweat. I hear the sound his head made when it hit the floor.'

'One day, when Evan is bigger, I'd like to go back to Caerdovey and get it out of my system. Could we do that, d'you think, Queenie?'

'If you like.' Queenie didn't think it possible to ever get that terrible day out of her system, not completely. Months could pass and she never gave it a thought, then the horror would return, quite out of the blue. She would feel the wet mist on her face, feel Carl Merton's hand on her arm, dragging her into the den. 'Gwen wrote and told me that Mrs Merton just disappeared one day, I doubt if anyone in Caerdovey knows what happened to her.'

To her relief, Roddy came in with a bunch of red roses and the conversation stopped. He kissed his daughter, said he thought his new grandson was, without a doubt, the biggest, handsomest baby in the nursery, and that he was terribly proud. 'Hello, Queenie, Mary.' He nodded at them both.

Queenie nodded back. 'Hello, Roddy.' No one would have guessed they'd spent last night, and almost every night since that first time in Mangold's, in each other's arms. Six months had passed and there was no sign of the baby she longed for, but neither she nor Roddy had ever considered giving up.

In the first week of the New Year, Roy Burrows and Maurice Gleason announced they were leaving Freddy's. Maurice, who had started at fourteen and now, thirty years later, was part of management, said he had a job with Lewis's in Manchester. Roy had decided to retire early.

'If you want the honest truth, Queenie,' Roy said. 'I feel like a rat deserting the sinking ship. I want out now to make sure I get my pension – and I'd like it in a lump sum, not monthly payments.'

'I don't understand, Roy,' she said, puzzled.

'It's my opinion that if Freddy's goes on as it is, in another few years the shop will be bankrupt. There'll be nothing left, not even for the pension I paid into.' He shrugged and looked bleak. 'All these improvements you intend to make, in my opinion, it's throwing good money after bad. Escalators are a fine idea, but will they increase our customer base? We can't put a big advert in the *Echo*, announcing "Freddy's Now Has Escalators". Everyone would laugh – and the cost would be prohibitive. A ground-floor coffee bar will only take people away from the restaurant. There's some new Health and Safety rules in the offing for buildings like ours. They'll cost the earth to have done.'

Queenie listened with sinking heart. 'You sound awfully gloomy, Roy.'

'I *feel* gloomy. I don't *want* to leave. If I could think of a way of getting Freddy's back on its feet, I'd contribute towards the cost myself. Queenie,' he said urgently, leaning forward, 'get rid of Freddy's before it's too late. Once it gets around that Maurice and I are leaving, others will leave too, and not just those in management. It's nothing to do with being disloyal. They've got families to feed, mortgages to pay. They can't afford to risk not having a job.'

'Did we get nowhere with the franchises?'

'No one's interested. They can sense a loser, and that's what Freddy's has become.'

'I'll give it another year,' Queenie said resolutely. 'I'll advertise more, sell goods at a discount, have fashion shows and . . . and other things,' she added vaguely. 'But I'll still keep on with the basic modernisation. I'm not going to give up without a fight.'

'Then good luck, Queenie. You deserve it.'

More staff did leave, mainly the younger ones. Adverts in the *Echo* for replacements brought little response. For the first time in more than twenty-five years, Queenie didn't go to Paris Fashion Week; it seemed an extravagance and she wasn't confident the clothes would sell. Meanwhile, the shop itself was in a state of utter turmoil. Each floor was being completely renovated in turn; walls painted in more subtle colours, the antiquated wooden counters replaced with glass and steel, strip-lighting and carpets fitted, new cash registers had been bought in 1971 when the country converted to decimal currency. So far only the fourth and fifth floors had been completed. Work would shortly start on the third. The furniture department would move back upstairs, Gentlemen's Clothing and Footwear transferred elsewhere for the time being, and room found for Sporting Goods, Luggage, Textiles, Bedding . . .

'I'd get rid of most of that furniture if I were you,' Roddy said when Queenie complained that night that the shop was in chaos. They were having dinner in Nero's, which had become a favourite place. 'I told you, when I looked in Freddy's for stuff for the flat, everything was much too big. Who wants such massive wardrobes these days? How many people need tables that seat twelve? Most big houses have been turned into flats or bedsits. Cut the department down to half its size, a quarter. As it is, it's just a waste of space. By the way, it might be a good idea to refer to the men's departments as just that, "Men's". It sounds rather more twentieth century than "Gentlemen's".'

'I wish you'd come and work for Freddy's. You seem much better at running things than me.'

'I'm not running anything, just offering advice. I'm not *there*, am I? I couldn't cope with an entire shop.'

'*I'm* not coping with an entire shop,' Queenie said wanly. 'I didn't realise so many decisions would be left to me. It's Theo's fault. No one thinks to do things on their own initiative.'

'Can't you promote someone, put them in overall charge?' Roddy suggested.

'I've tried, but they're not interested. I think they're scared. I advertised not long after Theo died. A few people came for interview, but as soon as they saw the shop, they declined. It's strange,' she mused, 'one minute we were jogging along quite comfortably, next everything began to fall apart, as if the shop became shabby and the customers stopped coming overnight. One of the last things Theo said was, "I think Freddy's has had its day."'

'How are you off for money?'

Queenie laughed. 'If you're offering, half a million wouldn't go amiss. I've sold Theo's share in Fleur – that's a well-known fashion house,' she explained when Roddy looked perplexed. 'It's already been spent. Freddy's isn't making enough to cover the running costs. And I'm selling my boat.'

'*Queen of the Mersey*! Are you *that* hard up?'

'I'm *that* hard up. But that's not the only reason. I'll never use it now that Theo's gone. I think he only bought it for himself. Me, I hated sailing, though I never told him. The boat only had to sway an inch and I'd be as sick as a dog.' She sniffed. 'I feel very sad about it. It was the most wonderful present, but I didn't really appreciate it.'

'Do you think about Theo often?' Roddy asked curiously as he stirred his coffee.

'Not as much as I expected. That's *your* fault,' she said. 'I think about you instead. It keeps me sane, during the day, when everything's so chaotic, and I remember I'm meeting you that night.'

'I don't think all that often about Laura – no, that's not true. I think about her every day, but I don't brood like I used to. In fact,' he said lightly, 'I was wondering, Queenie, once a decent period has passed, say another six months, if we shouldn't get married?'

Queenie didn't answer straight away. *Roddy Oliver had just asked to marry her*! When they'd met, she had considered him a god. Never, in her wildest dreams, had she imagined the day would come when he would propose marriage.

'Do we love each other?' she asked.

'I don't know,' he said truthfully. 'What I do know is you're on my mind an awful lot, and I can't wait for us to be together.'

'We might be using each other to get over our grief, make us forget about other things.'

'Does that matter? We're good for each other, Queenie. We make each other happy.' He gave her a sly smile. 'Please don't blush, but the sex is bloody marvellous. Put those things together, and they seem a good basis for marriage.'

'I don't want to be a substitute for Laura.'

'I'd sooner not be a substitute for Theo, but they're both dead,' he said bluntly. 'Between us, we've got a lot of years still to go. Why not spend them together?'

Roddy was right, Queenie thought the next morning as she walked around the furniture crammed on to the third floor. This stuff was for mansions, not normal houses. Theo had been living in the past. He'd seen no need to change until it was too late. An elderly assistant followed her, gasping with horror every time she drew a chalk cross on a giant bedroom suite, sets of baronial chairs and tables, sideboards that wouldn't have fitted through the average front door.

'What's to happen to it, Miss Tate?' he asked nervously.

'I don't know. What normally happens to furniture when no one buys it? As long as it doesn't go back upstairs, I don't care.'

'It can go in the store room for now.'

'Only for now. I want rid of it as soon as possible. The store room's already bursting at the seams.'

She went back to her office and summoned Roy Burrows who was working his month's notice. 'Who is our furniture buyer?' she asked.

'We never had one. It was something Theo did himself.'

'Did he now! I never knew that. Could you please find out the names of a few modern designers and ask them to send reps? I've got rid of all that antique stuff.'

'Are you sure you know what you're doing, Queenie?'

'Yes,' she said, slapping the desk, 'I'm reorganising the furniture department, bringing it up to date.'

'Have you seen the figures for the January Sales? They're the lowest for ten years, yet inflation has soared over that time.'

'The Sales have still got a week to go. Get on to advertising, tell them to put an advert in the *Echo* to say we're cutting the sales price by half. Let everything go at quarter price.'

'We've already done that, Queenie.'

'In that case,' she growled, 'cut the quarter price by half. I'll get customers in this shop if we have to give the damn stuff away.'

By the end of March, Hester was pregnant again. She rang Queenie to ask if they could go to Caerdovey. 'If we wait much longer, I'll be as big as a house. Longer still, and I'll have two babies to cart around. Mary said she'll take us in the car if we go on a Saturday when Duncan doesn't need it.'

'Wouldn't you prefer to go with a chauffeur? Theo's Mercedes is in the garage and I can get someone to drive us.' She hadn't much faith in Mary's driving of the

Maguires' rackety old Anglia. She was inclined to go too fast and often forgot to signal.

'Has it got a glass screen?' When Queenie admitted that it hadn't, Hester said, 'I'd sooner go with Mary, otherwise we wouldn't be able to talk.'

'All right,' Queenie sighed. Caerdovey was the last place on earth she wished to visit, but felt obliged to go for the sake of the girls.

They set off on 1 April. The day began inauspiciously in pouring rain, which didn't stop until they had crossed the border into Wales. She recalled how much she'd disliked the scenery then and found she still felt the same. The big hills covered with dark trees, the deep valleys crammed with even darker ones, made her stomach turn. She was sitting beside Mary, trying to ignore the scenery and concentrate on the map. Not surprisingly, Mary didn't know the way and needed directions. Queenie had never studied a road map before and couldn't understand it.

'Oh, give it here,' an impatient Hester demanded from the back. 'I bet I can read a map better than you, *and* breastfeed a baby at the same time.'

'Sorry,' Queenie said meekly.

'Go right at the next turning on the right, Mary.'

'I'm not likely to go right on the next turning on the left, am I?'

'Just shut up and do it.'

'Yes, ma'am.'

A weak sun appeared in the insipid blue sky as they entered Caerdovey and the mood in the car improved. Mary stopped by the Town Hall. 'Nothing's changed,' she remarked. 'Everywhere's exactly the same. I wonder if that woman, the one who never shut up, still runs the Post Office?'

'Her name was Mrs Jones,' Queenie said. 'She had a son called Trefor.'

'And there's the Councillor Wilfred Jones hall,' Hester squealed. 'They gave us drinks and a cake when we arrived. Gosh, that was a miserable day.'

'I quite enjoyed meself. I thought it was exciting.'

'Not at bedtime, you didn't, Mary,' Queenie reminded her. 'You bawled your head off.'

'Did I? Is that tea shop new? Shall we have a drink before we make our way to The Old School House?'

'I'd sooner have a drink after we've been. Let's get it over and done with first.' Queenie couldn't wait to get back to Liverpool. The gears squeaked and scraped when Mary started the car, setting her teeth on edge. She caught a glimpse of the Irish Sea, the water placid and grey, as they travelled down the High Street and eventually drew up outside The Old School House. There was silence for quite a while, apart from little chirruping noises from Evan, while they took in the building in which they'd once lived.

Quite a lot had changed. Pretty lace curtains were draped across the windows, the front door was buttercup yellow, the name, 'The Old School House' was now on a hanging board with the words 'Bed & Breakfast' underneath. The small front garden had been turned into a rockery full of heathers and ferns. But the biggest change of all was the fact there was no longer a garage. Instead, the place where it had stood, and the ground around it, had been concreted over and was now big enough to hold four cars.

'What do we do now?' Mary asked.

'I don't know,' Queenie said. 'It was your idea to come.'

'Before we do anything, I'd like to change Evan's nappy. He stinks.'

'I'm getting out while you do it,' Mary said quickly. 'Oh, look. The front door's opened.'

A pretty woman of about forty emerged from the house. She wore a flowered apron and rubber gloves. 'I was just dusting the lounge when I saw you stop outside. We've plenty of room, if that's what you're looking for. We're only full at the height of the season.'

Queenie had followed Mary out of the car. 'We don't want to stay. It's just that we were evacuated here during the war. We were just wondering what the place looked like now. I see you've wallpapered the hall. That's a great improvement.'

'Do you think so?' The woman looked pleased. 'Everyone thought we were mad, papering over wood, but I thought it looked awfully miserable. Every room has been papered or painted. As it was, it was like living inside a giant tree.'

'I remember thinking exactly the same when we first came to live here.'

'Were you here long?' She seemed very friendly.

'Only about eighteen months, but thinking back it feels much longer.'

'Why don't you come in and look around? I'm here by myself. My husband's taken the children out for the day, but I stayed because we're expecting guests at tea-time and they might arrive early. I'll make some tea. I don't like being on my own. I'm Rhona Jackson, by the way.'

'That's very kind of you. This is Mary Maguire, that's Hester Cunningham in the car. She's just changing Evan's nappy. I'm Queenie Tate.'

'You've got a baby with you! Oh, do let me see him! How old is he?' she asked as Hester climbed out of the car.

'Three months and eleven days.'

'He's beautiful. Hello, Evan.' She chucked the baby under his fat chin and he gave her a look of disdain.

They went into the house, down the hall, Rhona opening doors on the way to reveal bright, airy rooms.

'This was still fitted out as a classroom when we were here,' Queenie remarked. She recalled the rows of dingy desks, the ghostly atmosphere. Now the walls were painted eggshell blue and the flowered curtains matched the covers on the bed. 'Though it's smaller than I thought.'

'That's because it's been split into two. The separating wall is just plasterboard.'

'Was it you who got rid of the garage?' Hester asked.

'No, it was the people before us, an elderly couple. They bought the place just after the war – it had been empty for years – and turned it into a Bed and Breakfast. We bought it as a going concern. We were rather glad the garage had gone when somebody told us a man had died there in a rather horrible way. Here's the kitchen, though you'll know that, won't you?'

Everyone gasped when they went into a barely recognisable kitchen lined with dusky brown units with white Formica tops. The stainless steel sink glistened in the weak sunshine, the taps shone. A fridge, almost six feet tall, hummed briskly in the corner. There were brown and white gingham curtains on the windows, bowls of tulips on the sill.

'You've got an automatic washing machine!' Mary said in awe. 'I've always wanted one. You could do with one too, Hes, for Evan's nappies. It'd get them lovely and white.'

'I don't care if they're white, so long as they're clean.'

Rhona had put the kettle on. 'Sit down, everyone. Would you like a sandwich? And I've just made a fruit cake.'

'I'd love both.' Queenie sat on a white Formica chair. 'I'm starving. I'm sure Hester and Mary must be too.'

Hester said, 'Remember Gwen's fruit cakes? She'd made one the day we arrived.'

'And those lovely stews!' Mary sighed. 'Even Mam couldn't make a stew as good as Gwen's.'

All of a sudden, the memories came pouring out, as if they'd been locked away for years because all thoughts of Caerdovey had been centred on that one, last, horrible day.

Remember Jimmy Nicholls wearing those funny clothes he'd found in the den? Remember the little school Queenie used to run there? Remember this? Remember that?

Rhona had made the sandwiches and put them on the table along with the fruit cake. 'There's more tea if you want some. Can I hold Evan while you eat?' she asked Hester.

'Of course.'

'I miss having babies.' She cuddled Evan on her knee.

'Where do you come from?' Queenie asked. She clearly wasn't Welsh.

'Birmingham,' she said wistfully. 'I miss it badly. All my family are there, but we had to move away from the smoke and grime because one of our sons has asthma, quite badly. He's been much better since we came here, so there's no chance of us going back. My husband has to work in winter because this place doesn't make enough to live on. It can get terribly lonely when everyone's out and there's no guests. I've really enjoyed you being here.'

'I'm afraid we'll have to be going in a minute,' Queenie told her.

'Perhaps you'd like to come back one day and stay?'

Surprisingly, Mary said she'd love to. 'Me and me

husband will come one weekend in the summer. And if you're ever in Liverpool, you must come and see us.'

'I'll do that,' Rhona Jackson promised. 'Don't forget to give me your addresses before you go.'

On the drive home, they all agreed the visit to Caerdovey had done them the world of good, even Queenie who hadn't wanted to go. Hester said it had changed the way she'd always thought of The Old School House.

'From now on, I'll be able to see it in my mind without the garage. I half expected to walk in and find bloodstains on the floor.'

'I really will go back,' Mary vowed. 'I'd forgotten what a great time we used to have on the sands. Remember how lovely it was early in the morning?'

'The good memories have taken over the bad,' Queenie murmured. 'I'm really glad we went.'

An advert was inserted in the *Echo* introducing Freddy's' new furniture department. It included pictures of a Stag bedroom suite and a streamlined G-Plan three-piece. A ten per cent discount was offered to customers who bought within the first week, though a few pointed out that other shops were offering the same furniture at less than Freddy's, even when taking into account the ten per cent reduction. Queenie sent a spy to George Henry Lee's, who reported it was true. 'And they have a policy of refunding the difference if the same goods are found cheaper elsewhere.'

'Then we'll adopt the same policy.'

In the restaurant, two cream teas were offered for the price of one on Saturdays. Different types of coffee were now on the menu, as well as herbal teas, doughnuts, Coca-Cola, Pepsi, milkshakes and – Theo would have turned in his grave had he known – beefburger in a bap with chips.

Sales figures increased, but not enough to guarantee the shop's survival in a more and more competitive world. It wasn't easy to change people's perception of Freddy's being a place where only the rich and elderly came to shop. Queenie considered going downmarket, but Theo wouldn't just turn in his grave, he'd swivel.

News of Freddy's possible demise must have filtered through to the business fraternity as an offer was received from a firm of developers who wanted to demolish the building and erect a multi-storey car park in its place, subject to planning permission, of course. Queenie hadn't yet answered.

Now it was June. If things didn't improve soon, she'd close the shop at the end of the year with the biggest, most spectacular sale of all time. Freddy's wasn't going to go out with a whimper, but with an extra-loud bang.

June was the birthday month. It ended with Queenie, Hester and Mary one year older. It was also twelve months since Theo had died.

I haven't mourned him, Queenie thought sadly. It's been such a strange, emotional year, what with Hester's baby, the visit to Caerdovey, the worry over Freddy's and, most importantly of all, Roddy. I've hardly thought about Theo at all. And now she was forty-nine and having a baby seemed an impossible dream.

'It's time we got married,' Roddy reminded her. They were sitting on the tiny settee in his flat watching the sun slowly disappear into the black horizon while the river changed from silvery grey to dull pewter. A dark shadow swept over the buildings in front, as if they'd been covered with a layer of black lace.

'Could we leave it until the New Year, till Freddy's has closed?'

He raised his eyebrows. 'Freddy's is closing?'

'It's become a case of when, rather than if.'

'Are you sure you're not just putting it off? I'm talking about getting married, not closing the shop.'

She dug him in the ribs with her elbow. 'Of course not. I'll enjoy our wedding much more with Freddy's and all its problems behind me.' She wasn't putting it off, though there remained a thread of doubt that she was doing the right thing. They had agreed they weren't in love, that the sex was bloody marvellous, that they were the very best of friends, yet still Queenie had hesitated before agreeing to get married. She couldn't quite put her finger on why. Perhaps, she thought with a wry smile, her mind was unable to accept the fact she would become Mrs Roddy Oliver.

'Can we at least go public?' Roddy asked. 'I feel stupid, sneaking about the way we do. I want everyone to know we're a couple.'

'What will Hester think?' she asked.

'Knowing Hester, she'll be as pleased as punch.'

But Hester already knew. 'Mary and I guessed ages ago,' she said with a laugh. 'All of a sudden, you started to treat one another very coolly. You hardly spoke. At first, we thought you'd had a major row. Then we realised what had actually happened and were really glad.'

'See, I told you she wouldn't mind.' Roddy smiled fondly at his daughter.

'As if I'd mind! I'm thrilled to bits. If there's one woman in the world I'd like you to marry, it's Queenie.' She gave Queenie a hug. 'You've always been part of our family, anyway.'

*

Duncan came home from work, ate his tea, picked up the *Radio Times*, and planted himself in front of the telly. This was the pattern his life had taken since Flora had left home. He opened the magazine and began to peruse that night's programmes.

Duncan wasn't a complicated person. He couldn't 'put on a face', as Mam used to say. When he was unhappy, it showed. Mary remembered when they'd first got married, the way he'd mooched around the flat in Waterloo looking as if he was about to be executed.

He'd been happy when Flora had come along and had stayed that way until she left. She was his favourite person, his favourite topic of conversation, and now she had gone and he was as miserable as sin. Mary couldn't think of a way of making him happy again, apart from producing another Flora, something unlikely to happen, as they hadn't made love since his daughter's exit from the house.

'Shall we go to the pictures?' she asked brightly.

'No,' he grunted.

'What about going out for a drink? It's ages since we last went to a pub.'

'Don't feel like it.'

She regarded him impatiently. She was upset herself that Flora had moved out. She adored her daughter, but there was no denying she was a selfish, thoughtless girl – Mary couldn't bring herself to even *think* the word bitch. She hardly ever came home, she was enjoying herself too much to waste her precious time with her parents. When they went to visit, she made no secret of the fact they were in the way. 'It's dead embarrassing, Mam,' she hissed on the last occasion. 'None of the other girls' mams and dads come round.'

'Then we won't come again,' Mary had said huffily,

and Duncan had complained all the way home that it was no way to speak to his beloved Flora.

What made things worse was that he'd suddenly remembered he had a son. Chris had been dead amused when his father had started to ask his opinion on this and that, inviting him to football matches and the like.

'Why don't you ask Flora?' he'd said pointedly the other Saturday when Duncan suggested they go to Manchester to see the cricket. 'Me, I'm not interested in any sort of sport. Actually, Dad, I never have been.'

The sarcasm was lost on Duncan. He complained to Mary about Chris's attitude. 'I don't think Chris likes me very much,' he said, looking hurt.

'Have you only just noticed?' Mary said acidly. 'For most of Chris's life, you've ignored his existence. You didn't even know he doesn't like games. Now you want to be a father with a capital F, but it's too late. He's an intelligent boy, Duncan, he can see right through you.'

'I don't know what you mean.'

'He knows you're only interested in him because your darling daughter's no longer around. Anyone with half a brain would understand that.' Perhaps she should be trying to buck him up, rather than take him down, but he was getting on her nerves too much for that.

Chris was turning out to be remarkably clever. He reminded her of Gus Oliver, his head always buried in a book on some obscure subject like philosophy or astronomy. Duncan and Gus had got on like a house on fire. She just hoped one of these days Duncan and Chris might do the same.

He was changing channels on the telly. You'd never think he was an educated man from his choice of programmes. He went for the loudest and the brashest, usually games shows. If it wasn't hosted by Bruce

Forsyth, then it was Bob Monkhouse or Nicholas Parsons.

Mary felt bored. She'd go and see Hester if she hadn't already been twice that week. It seemed pathetic when she had a family of her own. The house in Crosby was always full of Ned's weird friends, and if they weren't spouting poetry, they were singing revolutionary songs, discussing the next march to go on, and smoking pot. Despite Hester being five months pregnant, she and Ned had taken Evan to a Campaign for Nuclear Disarmament demonstration the week before.

It all seemed terribly irresponsible, but she wouldn't have minded swapping Hester's life for her own.

It was September and time Queenie broke the news about Freddy's to the staff. They had noticed that only half the usual amount of winter stock had been ordered and were asking questions. She should have told them before. She had a letter duplicated, and addressed and signed each one personally. It took ages; she kept pausing, visualising the faces as she wrote down the names, some bringing back their own particular memory.

'Dear Judy', 'Dear Gladys', Dear Joe', . . . Joe Parker had been the doorman when she first came to Freddy's, only a young man then. Henry Quinn had taken over the main lift when Eustace had left. Dear Eustace was long dead, and so was old Rollinson who'd stayed in his beloved book department until he was nearly seventy.

'Dear Bob', 'Dear Alf', Dear Marie'. She was surprised by how many staff were already there when she'd started. Quite a few of the women had come as young girls, left to get married, then returned after their families had grown up. Freddy's closure would make a big hole in an awful lot of lives, as it would have done her own, but not now that she was getting married to Roddy and starting a completely new life.

She paused again. The wedding was on 5 January and they were spending their honeymoon in the villa in Kythira. Roddy didn't mind that it was the place she'd always gone with Theo. He was longing to see it, she'd talked about it so much over the years. Queenie couldn't wait.

Her letter was met with a mixture of resignation and anger. Most people understood that Freddy's had no future, but a minority thought she should fight on. Keith Hull who worked in Carpets came storming into her office. 'Why don't you become a limited company, float on the stock exchange, get people to invest?' he demanded.

'I went into that,' she told him. 'I was advised Freddy's would be a most unattractive investment and too much money would have to be spent to make that change. The bottom line is that we're too out of the way to make it a worthwhile proposition.'

And Theo had always been dead set against Freddy's becoming a limited company. The shop was *his*. He didn't want to risk it being taken out of his control, as had happened with Harrods, when Hugh Fraser had ousted the Burbridge family who had run the shop for seventy years.

'In that case I'm leaving.'

'I'll be sorry to see you go, Keith.'

'I won't be the only one,' he said threateningly, slamming the door behind him.

So long as too many didn't leave before the end of December, it didn't matter. Over the remaining twelve weeks, departments would shrink as the goods were sold. She wanted to disguise the shrinkage by moving sections closer to each other so the shop didn't look bare. As a start, half the fourth floor was about to be closed off. They wouldn't need so many staff. Keith wouldn't be missed.

Hester was making the bed when she felt the pain. It wasn't a contraction, but as if someone wearing heavy boots had landed a kick on her stomach. She gasped, clutched her stomach, and sat heavily on the bed. The baby wasn't due until the end of November, four weeks away. Evan gurgled at her from his little bouncy chair that she carried from room to room while she did the housework so they could talk to each other. At ten months he could crawl and wasn't safe to be left alone.

'What on earth was that?' she asked him.

He gurgled an answer and she told him he was being no help. 'I think your little brother or sister might be arriving early.'

Evan grabbed his feet and shrieked with laughter.

She didn't feel like laughing back when the heavy boots landed another kick, even fiercer than the first. A few minutes later, she felt a rush of warmth between her legs, thought her waters had broken, but when she stood up noticed the bed was stained with blood. She'd had a haemorrhage! She began to panic. Ned was in the middle of his round and could be anywhere. She should call for an ambulance, but first had to find someone to mind Evan. Next door would all be at work, and the old lady on the other side was very old, in poor health, and not up to it, and she herself wasn't up to running up and down the road, knocking on doors asking people if they'd look after her precious baby. She remembered Mary only lived five minutes away. Picking up the phone beside the bed, she dialled her number, but it rang out for ages and there was no reply.

'What do I do now?'

Hester picked up the phone again and dialled Freddy's. When the operator answered, she asked to speak to the woman who'd been like a second mother to her virtually all her life.

Queenie listened intently to Hester's hysterical voice. 'Call an ambulance immediately,' she said. 'Where is Evan now? Right, well, put him in his cot if you can manage it. If not, leave him where he is. He'll be quite safe in his chair until I arrive. I'll get a taxi and tell the driver to hurry. Good luck, Hester, love.'

She slammed down the phone, grabbed her coat, and told the woman in the next office to ring for a taxi. 'Tell them it's an emergency and I'll be outside Freddy's main door.'

The taxi driver took her at her word and drove like a maniac all the way to Crosby. She gave him double the fare, and saw she was just in time; an ambulance was parked outside the house and Hester was being carried out on a stretcher, her face pale and tight with pain.

'Thank God you're here.' She grabbed Queenie's hand. 'Evan's upstairs, crying. I nearly brought him with me, but I knew you'd come.'

'I'll see to him, darling. Don't worry. Will she be all right?' she asked the stretcher bearers, both men.

'Let's say the sooner she gets to hospital the better,' one of the men said grimly.

The ambulance drove away. Barely a minute later, Queenie was in the bedroom where Evan was bawling his eyes out. He stopped as soon as he saw her and began to chuckle and wave his arms about.

'You little rascal! You had your poor mummy dead worried. Would you like a clean nappy? Let's find out where they're kept. and don't you dare start crying again while I look,' she said sternly.

She found the nappies in the airing cupboard. Evan fought her all the way while she changed him. She took him downstairs, made tea, gave him some in his own special cup half-filled with milk, then sank on to the settee, pleased to see a fire burning brightly behind the old-fashioned fire guard. Her hands were shaking. As soon as she'd finished the tea and felt calmer, she'd try to get in touch with Ned, then ring Roddy.

The sorting office in Southport promised to send someone to look for Ned and tell him to go straight to the hospital. 'And let him know Queenie's looking after his little boy.' Roddy's secretary said he wasn't in his office. He'd gone to a meeting. 'As soon as he comes back, please tell him to ring his daughter's house. Have you got the number?'

'Is it the same number as his old one?'

'Of course it is. I'd forgotten he used to live here.'

Although Roddy had left the furniture behind, the room had changed drastically since he'd gone. The chintz covers and pastel curtains had been replaced with material of a more lurid design; a mishmash of dark, jewel colours. Even more lurid paintings hung on the walls. Queenie had tried to make sense of them, but failed. A massive fish, about four feet long, made from driftwood, so she'd been informed, adorned the wall over the mantelpiece, itself containing three small items of sculpture that made even less sense than the paintings.

'Am I getting old?' she asked Evan, but didn't get a reply; he was fast asleep, his little fat chin buried in his chest. His cup had fallen on the floor and tea had leaked on to the carpet. She took it into the kitchen, washed it, and returned with a paper towel to mop up the stain, feeling it was important to keep busy. The stain gone, she went upstairs, removed the bloodstained bedding, put it in the washing machine, then laid fresh sheets on the bed.

Hester would have reached the hospital in Southport by now. She phoned to ask how she was. 'It's too early to say,' she was told.

'Has her husband arrived yet?'

'Not yet, no.'

'Will you tell her he's on his way?'

It suddenly struck her that there might be something seriously wrong with Hester, but comforted herself with the thought that it was most unlikely. Women didn't die in childbirth these days, though she might lose the baby.

Her own baby had been lost before it had time properly to form. She sat down and stared at Evan, snoring slightly in his bouncy chair. It was impossible to visualise having once had a much tinier version of Evan in her womb.

The phone went and she jumped. It was Ned. He'd just got to the hospital, but hadn't been allowed to see Hester. 'It's something to do with the placenta. I'm dead worried, Queenie.'

'I know it's difficult, but try not to worry.'

'Is Evan all right?'

'He's fine, Ned, fast asleep. You just concentrate on Hester. Let us know when there's any news.'

Five minutes later, the phone rang again. This time it was Roddy, surprised to hear her voice when he'd been expecting Hester to answer.

She told him what had happened and he said he'd leave there and then. 'But should I come there or go to the hospital?' He sounded as worried as Ned.

Queenie wasn't sure. 'I don't know if Ned would want an anxious father-in-law for company. You might make each other worse.'

'Then I'll come to Crosby.'

He arrived much quicker than expected. She was nursing Evan who'd woken up in a funny mood. Perhaps he was expecting to find his mummy or daddy there. 'I drove like the wind,' Roddy explained. His face was haggard with worry. 'Has there been any word from Ned?'

'Not yet.'

'Lord, I'm glad you're here.' He took her and the baby in his arms. 'I don't know if I could cope if anything happened to Hester.'

'I don't think there's much chance of that,' she said soothingly. 'Here, hold your grandson. I'm about to make him something to eat. I hope the directions are on the tin. I've never done this before.' If the circumstances had been different, she would have enjoyed herself today.

Ned rang while she was in the kitchen. Glancing at her watch, she was surprised to find it was five o'clock. 'Hester's about to have a Caesarean section,' Ned said. 'Apparently, the placenta was blocking her vagina and she couldn't give birth naturally. As the baby was due in four weeks, the doctor said it would be safer to remove it now.' His voice was very wobbly. 'I hope that all makes sense, Queenie.'

'Perfect sense. Roddy's here. Would you like him to come and wait with you?'

'I'd sooner pace the corridors by meself, thanks all the same. I've got some hash with me. Every now and then I go outside and have a spliff. I doubt if Roddy would approve.'

'I doubt if the hospital would, either,' she said with a smile. 'There's just one thing, Ned, before you ring off. How much of the tin does Evan have to eat?'

'All of a main meal and half a tin of vegetables. Lamb

stew is his favourite. Hester won't let him be a vegetarian until he can make the choice himself.'

'Is that good or bad?' Roddy asked anxiously when she told him the news about Hester.

'Good. They've found out what's wrong and they're going to put it right. I don't know how long it will take. The operation hasn't started yet.'

Between them, it took half an hour to feed Evan. Roddy held him on his knee, while Queenie tried to spoon lamb stew and grated carrot into his mouth, watching despairingly as he let it dribble out. She scraped the food off his chin and spooned it back again. The baby's eyes danced. This seemed to be a game; he was willing to swallow it the second time.

'He needs to be force fed,' Roddy groaned. 'I've got stew all over my trousers.'

'You should have put a towel over them, though that's easily said with hindsight. Should we bath him?'

'I suppose we'd better, but let the little bugger's food go down first.'

An hour later, Roddy laid a sleepy, shiningly clean Evan in his cot. They both watched as the baby's eyes began to close and soon he was sleeping peacefully.

'He looks deceptively angelic,' Roddy whispered. The sleeves of his shirt were rolled up and the front was soaked after their ordeal in the bathroom. 'No one would guess what a little horror he is when he's awake. I wonder what Gus was like at this age? I never saw him until he was four.'

'Gus was a little horror too, into everything. We had to keep things on top of the wardrobe out of his way.' She took a last look at Evan and said, 'I'll clean the bathroom. You'd think we'd just bathed a herd of elephants in there.'

'I'll make some tea. I wonder if there's anything stronger on the premises? I could do with a stiff drink.'

When Queenie went down, Roddy was prowling the room. He stopped to examine the books on the shelf beside the fireplace. His own books and clothes were the only things he'd taken with him to his flat. Now the shelves were crammed with paperback novels, books on a wide variety of subjects, including many on politics. They all looked tatty and well-used. The curtains were drawn and the wall lights had been switched on. The old glass globes had been replaced with more colourful shades shaped like Chinese lanterns. More coal had been put on the fire.

'I've brought you one of Ned's shirts,' she said. 'It's not exactly your usual style.' She held up a pink cheesecloth shirt without a collar. 'You'd better put it on and I'll hang the wet one in the airing cupboard, otherwise, you'll get a cold.'

Roddy grinned. 'It's nice, being fussed over for a change.'

'What's that you're drinking?'

'Coconut rum. It's rather sickly, but it's all I could find. Tea's made in the kitchen. What have Hester and Ned done to my house, Queenie?' he asked plaintively. 'It looks like a bordello.'

'I've never been in a bordello, so wouldn't know.' She shrugged. 'I like it. I suppose they're just expressing their personality.'

'Ned's, more like. Remember how it was before Ned got his hands on it? What does that say about *my* personality? I must be very insipid.'

'Don't be daft. Most men aren't interested in decoration. Ned's rather unusual.'

'You can say that again.' He returned to examining the books and Queenie went into the kitchen to get the tea. She opened the fridge and looked at the contents. The last meal she'd had was breakfast and she was hungry now that she felt that Hester was going to be all right; loads of women had Caesareans. There were two rissole things – nut cutlets? – that had no doubt been for that night's tea. She was about to hunt for a frying pan, but thought she'd better check first that Roddy was hungry too.

'Do you fancy a nut rissole? What on earth's the matter?'

Roddy had taken a book from the shelf and was staring at it fixedly, his eyes unnaturally bright. 'Years ago,' he said hoarsely, 'when I first met Laura, we used to exchange messages in this book – not *this* one, another edition. I bought this when I came back after the war. Laura must have had it in her room and Hester or Ned found it and put it on the shelf. It's still got a note from me in the front. I daren't read it.'

'It doesn't matter what the note says, Roddy,' she said softly. 'It's a long time since it was written.'

'But I *want* to know,' he said stubbornly, 'Yet I daren't read it.'

'Give it here.'

He meekly handed her the book. It was bound in green leather and the title was *The Rise and Fall of the Roman Empire*. The author was Edward Gibbons.

'Laura told me about this book,' she said. 'She said you'd bought a copy.' She flicked through the pages and at the very front found a piece of folded notepaper, yellow with age. The paper was thin and through it she could recognise Roddy's bold handwriting. 'Can I read it? I won't read aloud.'

He nodded jerkily, like a puppet. 'Please.'

My darling, darling Lo, she read, *I love you totally,*

endlessly, eternally, for ever and ever and ever. Your totally, endlessly, eternally devoted husband, Roddy

'It's a love letter,' she said calmly. 'It's the sort of thing I might have written to Theo, or he to me. It's what thousands, millions, of husbands, wives and lovers could write to each other. You loved Laura, I loved Theo, but now they're dead and we have each other. I remember you saying more or less the same thing to me.' She crumpled the note into a ball and threw it on the fire.

'Why did you do that?' He looked at her, horrified.

'Because you wrote it twenty, thirty years ago. What it says doesn't matter any more.'

'It's easy for you, your conscience is clear.' His face was sullen, and his voice, too.

'We all look back and are sorry we didn't behave better, were kinder and more considerate.'

'You don't know what I did.'

'You've told me what you did, and it didn't sound all that terrible to me.'

'I didn't tell you everything.' He sat in the corner of the settee, all hunched up, as if trying to make himself smaller. 'The day Laura killed herself, she was following my instructions. I *told* her to do it.'

'But you didn't *mean* it!'

'Oh, but I did,' he said passionately, suddenly coming to life. 'I meant every word. She'd been making our lives hell for years. She bore no relationship to the woman I'd fallen in love with, married. She'd become a stranger. Hester had wanted to go back to America, but was still here, years later, looking after her mother. Agnes was a great help, but she was only here a few hours a day. Laura and I slept in separate rooms, hardly spoke to each other, except when she was depressed and would threaten to kill herself. It would take hours to calm her.' He was talking faster, almost gabbling. 'Some days she wasn't so bad. She sewed things, cooked a lot, but even on the good days, we could never leave her alone in the house, her mood swings were too unpredictable, and she refused to set a foot outside. We were like prisoners.' His face was clouded with bad memories. 'Sometimes, I'd hear her sobbing in the middle of the night. After a while, I stopped going in. I pulled the clothes over my head to shut out the sound. Then one morning she said she wanted to die, life wasn't worth living. It was the same old stuff I'd heard dozens, hundreds, of times before. She was in bed. I'd just popped my head around the door to say I was off to work, Hester was downstairs. At that moment, I think I wanted to die myself. I just couldn't take any more. I said, "So die! Kill yourself, then we'll all be happy." Then I slammed the door and went to the office. That afternoon, Hester phoned to say she was dead.' He began to cry. 'It was all my fault, Queenie. I may as well have cut her wrists myself.'

'Darling!' She sat beside him on the settee. 'You were at the end of your tether. Loads of people would have done the same.'

'Would you?' He looked at her tearfully.

'I've no idea how I would have acted in a similar situation. None of us do until we're faced with it.'

'I don't deserve to be happy.'

'You deserve it more than most,' she soothed. 'You put up with so much.'

'I should have let her go into a home, but this was Laura, Queenie. *Laura*!' His eyes were two holes of despair. 'Remember how she was in Glover Street? I kept thinking of her in that bookshop where we met; so young and bright and innocent, so *pretty*. How could I have let my darling Laura go away? I thought keeping her with us was the right thing to do. Anyway, Hester wouldn't have stood for it.'

'Oh, Roddy!' She went to take him in her arms, but he pushed her away.

'Don't!'

'Why not?' she asked, shocked.

'Just don't. I can't bear you to touch me, not now. I can't stand you making excuses for what I did. The words mean nothing. *I* know what I did.' He was shouting now and his face was ugly with misery and rage.

Queenie wanted to say, 'Don't shout. You'll wake Evan,' but didn't dare interrupt.

'*I* know I said the cruellest possible thing to a woman who was sick, to the woman who was my *wife*, goddammit. I *don't* deserve to be happy. I don't deserve you. What right do I have to spend the rest of my life in married bliss when Laura's dead and it's all my fault?'

His words hung in the air for a long time. They sat in silence, together, on the settee, while Queenie tried to digest their meaning. Was Roddy saying they wouldn't get married, not ever?

The telephone rang. He jumped to his feet to answer.

'That's marvellous news, Ned. Congratulations.' He listened for a while, then said, 'Give Hester my love. Oh, and Queenie's too. Don't worry, you stay as long as you like. Yes, Evan's fast asleep. He's been no trouble. Good night, Ned.'

He replaced the receiver and came back into the living room. 'Hester's had the operation. She and the baby are fine. It's a girl, she's only little and a bit fragile. You know what they're going to call her?'

How could she? 'No,' she said.

Roddy smiled bitterly. 'Laura.'

Chapter 21

NEW YEAR'S EVE

It was the last day of Freddy's' last sale and the shop had never been so crowded in its one hundred and one years. Full page adverts in the *Echo* every day, offering all sorts of enticing bargains, had brought in thousands of shoppers. There was hardly room to move between the counters, some of which were almost bare and had been for days. One of the most popular was Haberdashery in the basement, where women, mainly elderly, had been eagerly stocking up on embroidery silk and tapestry wool that were going for coppers. The last remaining skeins were now in a near impenetrable ravel that a couple of grey-haired customers were patiently trying to undo.

On the glittering, lavishly decorated ground floor, scarves were piled high in a vivid mountain of silk and wool, taffeta and filmy chiffon, like something out of an Arabian bazaar. Every now and then, someone would tug an end and find someone tugging the other. There'd been a few fights, not just over scarves – the shoe department had seen some heated arguments when one customer had found the right shoe, another the left, and neither was willing to give up *their* shoe. The matter was usually settled by the toss of a coin. A strong scent of expensive perfume hung in the air as passers-by liberally sprayed themselves with the demonstration bottles. No one noticed a yellow kid glove that had lost its mate being kicked around the floor.

The stock room on the fifth floor had been cleared and the staff were amazed at what had been found in the dusty corners; cardboard boxes, forty, fifty, years old, containing flesh-pink lace-up corsets, thick flannel nightdresses, lisle stockings, knee-length, lock-knit knickers, long velvet evening gloves without fingers. There were clothes with a Utility sign, acquired during the war, a long time out of fashion, but perfectly wearable nowadays when hems could be any length. Indeed, Queenie had found a brown tweed coat that was almost identical to a Jean Patou model that had come out only a year ago. It had fitted Hester perfectly.

Ladies' clothes had sold the fastest of all. Now the racks were almost empty and there was nothing left to put on them.

The bulk of the customers on the final day were women, on the prowl for cheap buys, or come for a last, nostalgic look around Freddy's, the shop where they had bought their wedding dress and trousseau and from where the bridegroom had hired his morning suit and top hat. Later, they'd come for their children's school uniforms and sports equipment; hockey sticks, cricket bats, tennis rackets, balls for every conceivable sort of game. The shop had played an important part in their lives.

A few people were collectors, interested in cards of pretty pearl buttons, stockings with flocked patterns on the heel, forties' evening bags, all unearthed from the stockroom and still showing their original prices; 9d, 1/11½d, 10/6d.

The younger customers were there for the first time, to take a look around the place that had once been a local landmark and was now about to close. They'd never been before; it was too old-fashioned and way beyond their means. Not today, though. They found themselves snapping up all sorts of unusual bargains.

Only a few men were present, dragged there by their wives, and taken to the Men's Department, where lambswool pullovers and comfortable baggy underpants were being sold for next to nothing. The loose-fitting overcoats and check suits that had looked distinctly pre-war had already gone, snapped up by younger men who considered them trendy. The floor now had a deserted air.

'See what I've got!' Hester opened the familiar black and white striped bag with 'Freddy's' in gold and showed Mary the contents. 'Loads of stuff for Annie, really cute baby clothes we'd never have been able to afford at the full price, three pairs of overalls and some T-shirts for Evan. I've got stuff for Ned and some nighties for myself. They're in Queenie's office, where I'm about to dump this lot, they're ever so heavy. It's an advantage, being able to leave your shopping with the owner.'

'It won't be an advantage for long. Excuse me a minute, Hes.' Mary went to attend to a customer who wanted to buy a bright red handbag in soft, squashy leather – extra staff had been taken on for the Sales and Mary had jumped at the chance.

'You can't get coloured handbags for love nor money these days,' the customer gushed. 'They're nearly always black. I haven't seen a red one in ages. Same with shoes.' She paid and rushed off to the shoe department to see if she could find shoes to match.

'Me legs aren't half aching,' Mary complained when she returned. 'We've been worked off our feet for days. We even came in Sunday to give the place a good tidy up. Today's the busiest yet. Still, there's not long left to go. How's Annie?'

'Coming along, putting on weight, but only slowly.

Ned's looking after her and Evan. He managed to get home from work a bit early.'

'Well, she was a whole month premature, wasn't she? In reality, she's only five weeks old, not nine. Why didn't you call her Laura, like you said?' she asked curiously. 'I didn't like to ask in front of Ned in case there'd been an argument.'

'Oh, no, there was no argument, just that Queenie said Daddy was a bit upset when he heard, so we called her Annie instead. It was second on our list of favourite names.'

'It's not suprising your dad was upset. Half a mo.' Mary went to attend to another customer. She was looking far more cheerful today, Hester thought. The month at Freddy's had done her good. Things had been tough at home between her and Duncan since Flora had moved out. She ducked when a woman passed behind, half a dozen bulging bags held aloft, and she was nearly decapitated. She still felt a bit tired, what with the Caesarean and worry over Annie. Pushing her way through the crowded shop didn't help, but she wouldn't have missed this historic day for anything. She had to be home by four. Annie was on the bottle and the breast and, as Ned had pointed out, he could manage one, but wasn't equipped to manage the other.

Mary came back. 'Was it your dad who called the wedding off, or Queenie? I've been dying to know.'

'I don't know either. They won't talk about it. Dad's been dead miserable for weeks, so I suspect it was Queenie.'

Queenie had already been for half a dozen excursions around the shop, giving a hand in places where the staff looked overwhelmed. Now she was back in her office, alone, with absolutely nothing to do; no letters to write, phone calls to make, catalogues to look at, buyers to see, no one to talk to – most of the office staff were helping behind the counters. The only people busy were in the cash office; tills were being emptied every hour and the contents counted and taken to the bank. After the banks had closed, the money would go in the night safe. Business had been brisker than anyone had expected and she felt guilty, sitting behind the desk that used to be Theo's, and finding nothing she could do.

As from midnight, Freddy's would no longer belong to her, but to the developers who'd made the first offer, which had turned out to be the highest. By this time next year, the building might have been demolished for a multi-storey car park or, if the Council insisted the original façade remain, it could be on its way to becoming flats.

She had vaguely thought of buying one of the flats, but had dismissed the idea straight away. It would be a sad place to live, full of too many memories, even if they were mainly happy ones. She had no idea exactly where she would live in Liverpool, but intended to spend a few months in Kythira before making up her mind. Eventually, she would return, because Liverpool was in her blood. And it was where her friends were; friends like Hester and Mary who had become more like family over the years.

Hester entered the room at that very moment. She looked weary. 'I've come to leave this bag with the others. I've had a marvellous time buying all this stuff, but I think I'd better stop and have a coffee before I drop.'

'I'll come with you,' Queenie said with alacrity. 'If the truth be known, I don't know what to do with myself.'

'Ned sent his novel to a publisher this morning,'

Hester said shyly. 'He finished it on Boxing Day. It took him nearly five years.'

'Wish him the best luck in the world from me. I hope it becomes a bestseller. Had things gone differently, we'd have stocked them in Freddy's and he could have come and signed them.'

The restaurant was crowded – cream teas seemed very popular. They managed to find a table by the window. It was a miserable day outside. A dirty mist hung in the air and the sky was the colour of mud. Down below, on Hanover Street, people were hurrying by, laden with carrier bags, quite a few of them Freddy's.

'You're practically giving things away,' Hester remarked.

'We had an offer for the goods left over, but it was so miserly, I decided I'd sooner let everything go for next to nothing. At four o'clock, prices will go down even more. We're closing at five.'

Hester wrinkled her nose. 'I'm afraid I can't wait till then. Four is when Annie's due for a feed.'

'I'll wander around later,' Queenie offered, 'pick you up some things, on the house, as it were. I'll enjoy that and I'll get some stuff for Mary too. This week, she's been a brick, like all the staff. They've worked like Trojans.'

'I understand you're giving them all a bonus.'

'They deserve it,' Queenie said warmly. 'Everyone's getting a basic hundred pounds on top of their wages, with an extra ten for each year they've been here.'

'You're being awfully generous, Queenie.'

Queenie's smile was a touch bitter. 'Who better to be generous with than the staff of Freddy's? I've no one of my own, have I?'

A waitress arrived, she looked ninety if a day. 'Oh,

hello, Miss Tate. I didn't realise you were here. Sorry about the wait, but we're dead busy.'

'So I can see, Lily. Can we have two coffees, please? Would you like anything to eat, Hester?'

'Actually, I think I'd prefer a cream tea, they look delicious. It'll be my last opportunity, won't it?'

'Coffee and a cream tea then, Lily. She's been here since the year dot,' Queenie said when Lily had departed. 'I wouldn't have minded a cream tea myself, but I've had terrible indigestion lately.' She patted her stomach. 'My tummy feels like a balloon and I apologise in advance if I burp. I've kept meaning to see the doctor, but we've been so busy.'

'Actually, your tummy does look a bit swollen. But you'll have time to see the doctor now, won't you?'

'Not that much time. I'm flying to Kythira on Saturday.'

'But you *will* see a doctor before you go?' Hester urged anxiously. 'I couldn't stand it if you were ill.'

'I will, I promise.'

'I wish you and Daddy were still getting married,' Hester said sadly. 'That would have been Saturday too. I was looking forward to having you as my stepmother.' She smiled wryly. 'Mary was terribly jealous. We used to fight over you like mad when we were little.'

'I remember – I was very flattered.'

'Is there absolutely no chance of you and Daddy getting back together?'

Queenie shrugged. 'You'll have to ask your dad that, not me.'

'But I thought it was you who jilted him!' Hester gasped. 'He's looked so unhappy since it happened.'

Lily had returned. 'One cream tea, one coffee,' she said. 'And good luck for the future, Miss Tate. We're not likely to speak to each other again.'

'Good luck to you, Lily.' Queenie got to her feet and gave the elderly woman a kiss. 'It's been lovely knowing you. I'm not sure if I can get through today without dissolving into buckets of tears,' she said when she sat down again. 'I've lost count of the number of people I've kissed so far.'

'About Daddy,' Hester began.

'If you have any questions, love, I told you, ask him.'

Fifteen minutes later, after Hester had gone to see if there were any clothes left in her size, Queenie sipped the coffee, cold by now, and remembered the night Annie had been born. 'I can't go through with it, Queenie,' Roddy had said wildly. 'I can't marry you, not after what I did to Laura. It would always be on my conscience and it wouldn't be fair on you.'

'I'm the one who should be the judge of that, and I think you're being unreasonable – with yourself as well as me. To put it bluntly, I also think you're being stupid, *dead* stupid,' she emphasised. 'It's about time you pulled yourself together. If you hadn't found that damned book, none of this would have happened.' She couldn't even remember its name.

He sighed tragically. 'It's nothing to do with the book. I'll never forget the cruel thing I said until my dying day.'

'We all do and say things we don't mean from time to time,' she said, trying to keep the impatience out of her voice. 'Look at me! I slept with you less than a month after Theo died. Not only that, I enjoyed it no end. How do you think that makes me feel?' she asked indignantly. 'Awful! But I'm sure Theo wouldn't have wanted me to mope for the rest of my life, and I'm equally sure Laura, the *old* Laura, wouldn't have wanted you to do the same.'

'It's no good, darling. It's no good.'

She stopped trying to reason with him. She had no

intention of talking any man, not even Roddy Oliver, into getting married, and most definitely not a man still deeply involved with another woman – a woman who was dead. If this was the decision he'd come to, then the matter was closed – unless one day he changed his mind, saw sense. She suspected he was having a long-delayed breakdown and it was best to leave him until he snapped out of it, something he could only do himself, without help from anyone.

That was two months ago and she still hadn't heard from him. Oh, but she missed him! She had visualised blissful years ahead with Roddy at her side. Her body ached for him at night, in bed, alone. During the day, every now and then, she would be overcome with a mixture of longing and rage; wanting him one minute, angry the next that he wasn't prepared to let her share his private torment, talk it through.

The restaurant was still crowded and she was taking up a table. She went downstairs to look for clothes for Evan and Annie. There were a few pretty frocks left, too big for Annie now, but would do for when she was older. She chose three, all different, some little frilly pants, a duffel coat for Evan, also too big, two Fair Isle jumpers, and an assortment of grey and white socks. The woman on the till she hardly knew. She'd only been with the shop about six months. 'Congratulations on the baby, Miss Tate,' she said as she put the goods in a bag.

'They're not for me.' Queenie laughed. 'They're for the children of a friend.'

'I assumed you were stocking up for when the baby got older.'

'I am in a way, but not my baby.'

'I'm sorry, I thought you were . . .' The woman's face turned crimson and she didn't finish.

'Thought I was what?'

'Pregnant,' she whispered.

'Because I'm buying baby clothes?'

'No. Oh, now I feel dead uncomfortable.' She looked distressed. 'We thought you had a very pregnant bulge. Quite a few women had noticed. And you've started wearing looser clothes.'

'Have I?'

'Yes, Miss Tate,' she said nervously.

Queenie looked down at her brown jersey suit. It had a long jacket and a wrapover skirt. A lot of her clothes had felt tight around the waist because her stomach was puffed up with wind. It was becoming more and more difficult not to belch in public.

Taking the bag without a word, she caught the lift to the top floor and went into the flat. Her mother was in the kitchen putting the last of the crockery in a wooden crate, wrapping each piece carefully in a sheet of newspaper. The crate was going into storage until she came back from Kythira, along with another containing cutlery, bedding, a few ornaments, and the clothes she wasn't taking with her. Her suitcase was in the hall, already packed. Theo's furniture had been sold. When it would be collected, she didn't know and didn't care.

'Some chap's going to take this lot to the storage place in about half an hour, so I thought I'd better get a move on,' Agnes said. 'Would you like him to take your luggage to the Adelphi at the same time?'

'Please.'

'I've packed your jewellery separate, luv. I'll keep it in me own place until you're back.' Agnes looked at her keenly. 'Will you be all right in that hotel on your own? You could have stayed with me, you know, until you were ready to go abroad.'

'I'll only be there a few days, until Saturday. I'll probably sleep the whole time.' Hester and Mary had also invited her to stay, but she'd sooner be by herself and get some rest after the last few hectic weeks.

'Well, if you feel lonely, just give us a call.'

Queenie smiled. 'I will, don't worry.' She turned to go into the bedroom, but her mother spoke again.

'Thanks, luv,' she said huskily, 'for all you've done for me, like. I know I didn't deserve it. I was a lousy mam, and I reckon I'd be a dead'un by now if you hadn't taken me in hand.'

'That's all right.' It was Theo she should be thanking.

Her mother held out her arms, hesitantly at first. Queenie hesitated too, before stepping forward, and mother and daughter embraced for the first time in their lives.

At last she achieved the privacy of the bedroom where she clumsily – her fingers had turned into thumbs – removed her jacket and examined herself sideways in the wardrobe mirror.

It wasn't much of a bulge, starting underneath her breasts and sloping gently outwards, but the soft, clinging skirt made it look quite prominent. *Could* she be pregnant? Was it remotely possible?

She sat on the bed, trembling, and thought what an utter fool she was. It was eighteen months since she'd first made love with Roddy but, a year later, she'd more or less given up on the idea of conceiving, convinced in her heart it would never happen. So convinced, that she'd thought the scanty periods she'd been having lately – there'd been none at all in December – had meant the onset of the menopause and her swollen stomach was caused by indigestion. The fact she might be pregnant hadn't entered her head.

Her mother shouted, 'The chap's come for the crates, luv, and I'm off to have a last look around the shop. See you later.'

'See you,' Queenie called. She longed to talk to someone. Looking at her watch, she saw it was almost four. Hester would have gone by now, Mary was busy. The gynaecologist! Her name was Susan Wickford. She got up and went to look for the telephone directory – her legs were shaking, all of her was shaking – found the directory, found the number, but there was no reply, not surprising so late on New Year's Eve. There was the same result when she rang her doctor's surgery. She remembered Theo had had a private doctor, and her heart leapt when she dialled his number and a woman answered. 'I'm afraid Dr Milton is away for a few days,' she said.

She collapsed in a chair, hugged her stomach, wondered if there really was a baby inside, closed her eyes, felt a movement, but it was accompanied by a gurgling sound that made her squirm. Did women get wind when they were having a baby? And if she was, how advanced was she? If there was a bulge, she could be in her fourth month, her fifth. How could she find out these things? Oh, if only it was a normal day!

Her watch told her it was half an hour since she'd last looked at it. In another half hour, Freddy's would close its doors for the very last time. There was no point sitting here asking herself questions she couldn't answer. She left the flat. The offices were still empty except for the one where the money was being counted. She looked inside and found five young clerks sorting through a vast pile of coins, putting them into their various piles. Gladys Hewitt was separating the notes and cheques. She looked up and gave Queenie a quick smile. Queenie saw, rather than heard, her lips form the words, 'Are you all right?'

Queenie nodded. 'OK.'

The accountant, Jerome Peters, was making entries in a ledger. A cold, reserved man, she had never liked him much, though he and Theo had been great friends. Rumour had it that he and Gladys were having an affair. Jerome would still work for Freddy's from his office at home, tying up loose ends, preparing the final books for the auditors. The money taken today would go towards settling numerous bills.

'Hello, Queenie,' Jerome said. 'Everyone's been looking for you. Apparently, they've run out of carrier bags downstairs and there's riots on the ground floor and in the basement. Whether it's because of the bags, I wouldn't know.'

'There's some bags in the stock room; old ones with a different design. I'll get them.'

'You'll do no such thing. You look shattered. Sit yourself down and I'll get someone else to do it.' She had never known him quite so friendly. He picked up the phone on his desk.

'Thanks, Jerome.' She had no intention of staying in the cash office. They might think she'd come to spy. She went down to the fifth floor. The restaurant had closed and gales of laughter were coming from the kitchen. Glancing through the door to the hairdresser's, she saw there was just one customer left, sitting under the dryer, and two of the young assistants were painting their nails.

The fourth floor was in darkness, having been shut off for weeks. The same with half the floor below which was relatively quiet, only a few customers left. The racks of men's suits, pants, shirts, overcoats were almost empty. A few pairs of bedraggled underpants lay on the floor, a heap of shoes, some odd socks. She wandered around. There were quite a few suitcases left, but most of the sports equipment had gone. A little boy was trying to persuade a man, presumably his father, to buy a cricket bat almost as big as himself. A few rolls of ghastly curtain material remained unsold, but the bedding department was completely bare.

As she walked, she heard voices, sounding very far away, as if all this was just a dream.

'We're nearly there, Miss Tate.'

'Only another twenty minutes to go, Miss Tate.'

'This must be a sad day for you, Miss Tate.'

She smiled in the direction of the voices, but didn't speak.

Ladies' Exclusive Fashions hadn't a single garment left. 'They sold like hot cakes,' Judy Channon said. She was still pretty, still blonde, just thirty years older than when they'd first met. 'I hope you don't mind, Queenie, but we bought quite a lot of things ourselves, the assistants, that is.'

'Of course I don't mind,' Queenie said dreamily.

'You must be feeling gutted, luv. What are you going to do with yourself now?'

'I don't know. I really don't know. What about you?'

'I'm due for me pension soon. I might give up work altogether, I don't know. There isn't a job on earth that could compare with Freddy's. Are you all right, Queenie? You look dead strange.'

'I'm fine, just fine. This floor looks almost completely empty.'

'The children's clothes went like wildfire, and there's hardly any shoes left and only a couple of hats. There's a few wreaths left in the Bridal Department, but only because they've been trodden on. It's the same downstairs. I got meself a couple of Jaeger jumpers there and a lovely Weatherall mac.'

'I'm so pleased, Judy. Well, goodbye and good luck for the future.' She kissed the woman on both cheeks, remembering it was Judy who'd taken her under her wing at Lila's twenty-first birthday party when she'd only been at Freddy's a few weeks.

'Are you *sure* you're all right, luv?' Judy was looking at her, blue eyes full of concern. Perhaps she wanted to mention the pregnancy, but didn't like to.

'I couldn't possibly be finer,' Queenie sang.

It was bedlam on the ground floor. She stood on the stairs, looking down. The crowd could well have been taking part in an exceptionally violent rugby match, pushing and shoving, using their elbows, even their fists. The clock said ten to five.

She was frightened to move, feeling too frail and delicate to thrust her way through the mob. From now on, she'd have to look after herself and the baby that might possibly be in her womb. And if there was, the trip to Kythira would have to be cancelled. She had no intention of flying in her condition.

There were queues at every till and she noticed the old black carrier bags from the store room were being used, with 'Frederick & Hughes' in white on both sides, rather than just 'Freddy's'.

People were snatching up anything they could get their hands on; jewellery, cosmetics, handbags, gloves, things off the Christmas gift counters that came in their own brightly coloured boxes. They must be stocking up on presents for the next ten years. A man smoking a pipe was struck sharply in the back by the elbow of the woman behind. The pipe flew out of his mouth. He bent to look for it and disappeared from sight.

A voice bellowed, 'This shop is closing in five minutes.' It was Joe Parker, the doorman, looking harassed and very angry.

The crowd paused momentarily and began to make for the tills with the smallest queues. Everyone would be served and encouraged to leave quickly.

Queenie watched the clock and held her breath. *Four minutes to five, three . . .*

Customers were pouring up from the basement, weighed down by bags. The few from upstairs came drifting down, aghast to find they had to tackle a rugby scrum to get out.

Two minutes to five, one minute . . . Her hands went to her face as she stood and watched the minute hand tick away the final sixty seconds. She had no idea what she felt, or if she felt anything at all.

Five o'clock.

'Ladies and gentlemen, this shop is now closed,' Joe yelled. 'Please pay for your purchases and make your way to the exit with all possible speed. And may I wish everyone a Happy New Year.'

'Happy New Year to you,' the customers shouted. Someone began to sing '*Auld Lang Syne*'.

Freddy's had closed for ever and in the nicest possible way.

She stayed in her office while the staff collected their wages, listening to the squeals and shouts of surprise when the envelopes were opened. It would have been embarrassing to have been there, having her hand shaken over and over, be kissed, hugged, thanked, wished Happy New Year.

People were asking, 'Where's Miss Tate?' but she didn't hear the excuse being given for her absence.

The squeals and shouts were becoming fewer and gradually stopped, as did the footsteps down the stairs and the noise of the lift. All she could hear now were a few distant voices.

There was a knock on the door and she shouted, 'Come in.'

It was Mary. 'How do you feel, Queenie?'

'Weird. Weird altogether.'

'Will you be at Hester's party later?'

'I wouldn't miss it for worlds.'

'I'll see you there.' Mary gave a steely grin. 'I'm off to give Duncan a good ear-bashing. If he won't come to the party, I'm going to threaten him with divorce. He's the sort of chap who needs his bum kicking every now'n again. I've had enough of him moping over Flora. It's time to remind him he's got a wife and son.'

'Good luck.'

'You're not going to stay here on your own, are you?'

Queenie shuddered. 'Not likely. I'll leave when the others do.' The cash office would still be hard at work counting the last of the money from the bursting tills.

'Tara then, Queenie.'

'Tara, Mary.'

The door closed. Queenie sighed and got to her feet. Outside, the corridor was deserted, and the shop was already beginning to feel chilly. She visualised the dark, empty floors, the empty racks, empty shelves. When she'd left the ground floor, it had looked as if a hurricane had swept through it; goods, bags, papers, strewn everywhere. Some of the Christmas decorations had fallen down.

She saw the door to the personnel office was open, and felt a sudden longing for human company. Today, she was being very contrary.

'Queenie!' Roger Appleby, the Personnel Officer, jumped to his feet. 'Would you like some champagne? We knew you were in your office, but thought you mightn't want to be disturbed. Here, sit in my chair. I'm afraid it'll be in a paper cup.'

'Can I have just a sip?' More than that and she'd be sick. There were four other people there; two men and two women. Their faces were familiar, but she'd forgotten who they were although they'd worked for Freddy's for years. She remembered Roger, though. He'd inherited Patricia James's job in Personnel. It seemed odd that she could remember a name from thirty years ago, but not those that she used every day.

They began to talk about the parties they were going to that night, the new jobs they were starting on Monday, the holidays they intended to go on next year. No one spoke to her, but they weren't being rude, just sparing her the ordeal of having to answer back. Perhaps there was something about her face that showed how she was feeling, not that Queenie could have described how she was feeling had anyone asked.

Jerome Peters and Gladys Hewitt appeared in the doorway. Jerome waved a leather bag. 'For the night-safe,' he said tiredly. 'We're all done in there. I've sent the girls home.'

'I think it's time we all went.' Roger put the paper cup on the desk. 'You coming, Queenie?'

'I'll just get my handbag and coat.'

She would never unlock this door again, she thought as she entered the flat and went into the bedroom. This is the last time I will see this room. Throwing a final glance at the bed where she'd slept with Theo, she put on her coat, picked up her bag, and closed the door,

Gladys, Jerome and Roger were outside. The others had gone ahead, Roger said. 'We're all meeting up for a drink. Would you like to come with us, Queenie?'

Queenie didn't answer. Her head was cocked to one side and she was frowning. 'I can smell burning.'

Everyone sniffed and agreed they could too, but didn't look too alarmed. 'It's probably just a stove been left on in the kitchen,' Gladys said.

'I'll go and have a look,' Queenie said. Until

midnight, Freddy's was still her responsibility. 'You three stay here and wait for me.'

'We'll do no such thing,' Jerome said curtly. 'We'll all look. Come on.'

But Roger was already at the top of the stairs. 'No one's going anywhere except out the back. There's smoke coming up the lift shaft. It looks to me as if the ground floor is on fire.'

Queenie remembered the man who'd lost his pipe. She wondered if he'd found it? Or had it been left to smoulder amongst the rubbish on the floor; the torn carrier bags, discarded boxes, a dropped scarf, the Christmas decorations?

They arrived at the front of Freddy's at the same time as the first fire engine. A good portion of the ground floor was alight and the fire was spreading rapidly, swallowing up whole sections in a matter of seconds. The glass had already started to crack, making sharp, snapping sounds, as if a gun was being fired. A passer-by must have noticed the flames and called the fire brigade. A small crowd had gathered and were watching, open-mouthed.

Queenie felt extraordinarily calm as she watched the flames race like wildfire through the shop. She'd been in a dream for most of the day and this was merely a continuation of the same dream. She even wondered why she felt so warm.

The windows on the first floor were already glowing a sinister orange, and the firemen's hoses seemed to be having no effect at all. Two more fire engines arrived, sirens screaming, followed by a police car. The onlookers were ordered to stand well back, out of danger.

'Is everyone out of the building?' a police sergeant shouted.

'There was only the night watchman left,' Roger told him. 'He's over there.'

She wondered what Roger was doing there, and who it was linking her arm? When she looked, it was Gladys Hewitt. Gladys noticed the look. 'You really shouldn't be here,' she said, giving the arm a shake. 'All this excitement won't do you or the baby any good, will it?'

'No, it won't,' said Queenie.

'Come on, luv, let's go and have a cup of tea. There'll be a few places open in Bold Street. I'll just tell Jerome.'

Gladys led her away and she went obediently. The coffee shop they entered was dimly lit and had candles on the table. There were only two other people there. A waitress came for their order, she looked no more than sixteen. 'Do you know what the fire engines were for?' she asked. 'Listen, there's more! It must be somewhere close.'

'Freddy's is on fire,' Gladys said.

'That big shop around the corner?'

'Yes. Can we have a large pot of tea, please?'

'I might go and have a look in a minute. The tea won't be long.'

'When's the baby due, Queenie?' Gladys asked.

'I'm not sure. I've been having periods, only little ones, and the doctor couldn't give an exact date.' She wasn't about to admit to Gladys what a fool she'd been.

'You could have knocked me down with a feather when someone told me. It wasn't until I saw you with me own eyes that I realised it was true. You look about four or five months' gone to me, that'll make it around April or May when it arrives.'

'I suppose it will,' Queenie said faintly.

'Are you glad? I mean, not every woman'd be pleased to find themselves pregnant at your age.'

'I couldn't possibly be more pleased, Gladys.'

'I hope your feller is too. Is it that tall, blond chap who helped out when Mr Theo died?'

'Yes. His name's Roddy and he's thrilled.'

'We thought that's who it must be. He's very handsome.'

The tea came and the waitress shouted, 'I'm going to look at the fire. Won't be a mo.'

'You'd better not be,' a voice from the kitchen shouted back, too late. The waitress had already gone.

She returned in about ten minutes, out of breath, eyes shining. 'It's dead spectacular,' she said excitedly. 'Like a film. I've never seen a fire before. The flames are coming out of the windows. There's at least six fire engines and more on the way, and a whole crowd of people have stopped to watch. The traffic's held up and there's bobbies everywhere.'

It wasn't long afterwards that Jerome and Roger came in. Jerome had deposited the money in the night safe and Roger's eyes were as bright with excitement as the waitress's. 'I've given my wife some pretty dodgy excuses for being late, but this one takes the biscuit. She'll never believe me until she sees it on the news. By the way, is Freddy's still insured?'

'Until midnight.' Jerome looked very down. 'I hope I never see such a terrible sight again. It was dreadful, watching a building being destroyed in front of your eyes and not just any old building, but Freddy's, where I worked for nearly forty years.' He sighed tragically. 'You'd think there'd been an air raid, the sky's turned blood red.'

'Come on, luv.' Gladys linked his arm. 'Let's go home.'

'I think we'd all better,' Roger agreed. 'We've got people coming to dinner. They'll be there by now and cursing me rotten. I'll walk you round to the Adelphi, Queenie.'

'There's no need. I can go by myself.'

'I'd sooner see you safe and sound before I leave. We'll go through Newington, avoid the fire. The crowd's so thick, we'd have a job getting through.'

More goodbyes, more kisses, more hugs, more Happy New Years. And a promise that they would all meet again in six months' time to see how they were getting on.

Roger left her outside the Adelphi. Another kiss, another hug. 'And congratulations,' he said warmly. It would seem everyone in Freddy's had known she was pregnant except herself.

She stood on the steps of the hotel and watched Roger walk away. The familar figure eventually turned a corner and she was overwhelmed with a feeling of loneliness, so acute that she wanted to shout aloud how lonely she was. Like Roger, she wanted someone to go home to, to open a door and be met with a cry of welcome. She wished now she'd agreed to stay with Hester or Mary, even her mother, not an anonymous hotel where she didn't know a soul.

From here, she could smell Freddy's burning, hear the faint roar of the flames, see the sky over her shop turning redder and redder. A man came up the steps towards her. 'Pity it wasn't the fifth of November,' he said. 'That'd be a bonfire to end all bonfires.' Queenie just nodded.

A young couple were running down Ranelagh Street, hand in hand. They didn't want to miss anything. 'We were there, we *saw* it,' they would tell people later.

She went down the steps and began to walk in the same direction. The nearer she got, the denser the crowds became, until she encountered a wall of people. But there was no need to go any further. She could see Freddy's quite clearly, see the flames spurting from the roof, showering sparks. Every window was ablaze. Two firemen were bravely perched on ladders, higher then the building itself, directing their hoses downwards, though it seemed a hopeless thing to do.

Everything would have gone by now, eaten by fire, or left twisted in its wake. She could have sworn she saw a figure in one of the windows on the top floor, a dark figure, standing completely still against a background of flickering flames. It might have been a ghost, disturbed by the fire. Freddy's had been full of ghosts and now they'd have nowhere to go.

Someone was shouting her name. It sounded very far away, another ghost perhaps. All of a sudden, there were arms around her, pulling her away.

'Darling,' Roddy cried. 'This is no place for you to be. Come home.'

'I haven't got a home,' she said simply.

'Then come to mine.' He tucked her arm in his. 'Your hands are cold. I saw the flames from my window, but never dreamt they were coming from Freddy's. Then Hester rang. She'd heard the news on the wireless and tried to contact you at the Adelphi. They said you hadn't registered, so I came to look for you. Christ, I was worried. I thought I'd lost you.'

'I'm fine,' she said. She must have told people that a dozen times today.

'You don't look it. Your eyes are all red and you seem completely exhausted.'

She remembered the baby and the need to look after herself. 'I'd like to sit down,' she said.

'Let's go to the hotel, sit down there. Come along, darling. I was expecting to see you at Hester's tonight. I wanted to apologise and ask if you'd have me back.'

Right then, Queenie wasn't quite sure. 'Not if I have to share you with another woman,' she said.

'That's all over, I promise,' he said quickly. 'It took a while, but I remembered the things you'd said and realised I was being a fool. The past is the past. I did some pretty awful things that I'll never forget, but I'm not a saint and never have been. Once I'd accepted that fact, I found myself able to face the future – with you, Queenie, if you'll have me. We could still get married on Saturday, it's not too late to get a licence.'

They had reached the hotel. She took a last look at the red sky over Freddy's, turned to Roddy and said, 'I'd like that, Roddy, but first of all, I've got something to tell you.'